THE
WITNESS

THE WITNESS

JAMES JAUNCEY

YOUNG PICADOR

First published 2007 by Young Picador
an imprint of Pan Macmillan Limited
20 New Wharf Road, London N1 9RR
Basingstoke and Oxford
www.panmacmillan.com

Associated companies throughout the world

ISBN: 978-0-330-44713-3

1 3 5 7 9 8 6 4 2

A CIP catalogue record for this book is available from
the British Library.

Typeset by IntypeLibra Limited
Printed and bound in Great Britain
by Mackays of Chatham plc, Kent

For my father

'Treat the earth well: it was not given to you by your parents, it was loaned to you by your children. We do not inherit the earth from our ancestors, we borrow it from our children.'

Native American Proverb

'If you approach silence with love, music may result.'

Arvo Pärt

HILL

ONE

B y the time John MacNeil was eighteen he had grown used to silence. The hours he had spent on the hill, often alone, in all weathers, had taken care of that. But there was something about the silence this morning that unsettled him. Made him feel as if the world was slowing, would soon stop spinning altogether.

Unfamiliar snow drifted among the pines, piling up along the top of the tumbledown dyke, draping the bushes and dead bracken. The cart rumbled and swayed, its cargo of snow-coated logs shifting this way and that.

But it was not the snowfall that was troubling him, rare though it was these days. There was something else in the air. Hector, plodding between the traces of the cart, could feel it too. He snorted and steam issued from his nostrils.

As they approached the top of the brae the old grey garron halted and shook his head. John could feel Hector's weight settle, his hooves rooting stubbornly to earth.

He gave the reins a flick, muttered a few words of encouragement. But Hector would not budge. With a sigh, John dismounted and walked forward to grasp the bridle, to turn pony and cart for home. But Hector stiffened, ears

3

suddenly pricked. John stood still. At first he could hear nothing but Hector's breathing. Then came a distant thud-thudding, faint but insistent.

He waited, blinking snowflakes from his eyelashes, listening intently. He knew how to listen; the silence had taught him that. Now the sound was coming closer. He turned Hector towards the trees, the cart creaking and shuddering as it left the track. But the ground was firm here, in among the spacious pines. In a short while they were sheltered by the tall trees, their outlines blurred by the snow, as good as invisible. He rested his hand on Hector's steaming, muscular neck, feeling the coarse damp coat beneath his palm.

'OK, mon. We'll just wait up here a minute. See what's what.'

A tremor ran down Hector's flanks. He snorted again, flaring his nostrils. John stroked him and murmured reassurance.

The thudding reached a crescendo and something huge sidled overhead, almost clipping the treetops. John pulled Hector's head close to his chest and blew on his quivering muzzle. The helicopter slipped down the brae to land in the field at the bottom, whipping up a maelstrom of snow around it.

He waited till Hector was calm again, then made his way forward to the top of the slope, where he paused in the shelter of a tree. He reached into his coat pocket for a pair of small binoculars. Pulling his coat around him, he lay down in the snow at the foot of the tree and brought them up to his eyes.

At the far edge of the field a number of grey stone buildings clustered by the roadside. Beyond ran the river. This was Blackriggs, a hamlet that had grown up around what was once a farm of that name. Today the farmhouse was a hotel that had done brisk business until the troubles started and the tourists stopped coming. Now only the public bar remained open, for the locals. Across the yard from the hotel, the main farm-steading had been converted into a small general store with a forecourt where coupons could be exchanged for fuel, when there was any to be had. Several of the outlying buildings had been turned into apartments and on the opposite side of the road was a row of four farm cottages that backed on to the river bank. Beyond and slightly apart, as if tolerated but not welcomed by the older buildings, a pair of modern single-storey houses stood on their own small plots. The whole place was cradled by woodland. In the snowy dimness, the trees seemed dark and oppressive.

He kept the binoculars trained on the helicopter as it began to disgorge soldiers. Its fuselage was dented and shabby, and one skid was bent. Something had leaked a rust-coloured smear across its insignia, the diagonal white cross and blue background of the Saltire. The soldiers loitered just out of range of the downdraught, clouds of fine snow swirling around their legs. They wore their green battle fatigues casually, handled their weapons with a certain nonchalance. John squinted, frowned and adjusted the binoculars. In closer focus some of the men looked swarthy and foreign.

A large sergeant was the last to emerge, barking orders as his feet hit the ground. With his solid build and florid complexion, there was nothing foreign-seeming about him. The men straightened up and started towards the buildings at a saunter. A figure appeared in the doorway of one of the cottages, looked out, then withdrew. The snow was easing now. Two soldiers moved ahead to position themselves where the trees met the road beyond the farm buildings. Two more made their way in the opposite direction and stationed themselves on the far side of the bungalows. Both exits were sealed now.

It was a house-to-house search, that much was soon clear. He could not hear a great deal because the helicopter had its engines still running, the idling rotors now spinning a thin drift of snow across the open ground. But he could see soldiers starting to bang on doors, being met by anxious faces, shouldering their way inside. The sergeant stood in the centre of the road, rifle under arm, directing operations, it seemed.

Whatever they were looking for, they didn't seem to be finding it. The casualness was starting to turn to frustration. Front doors were slammed, garden gates kicked open. One man stopped to piss behind a hedge in full view of the cottage he had just left. The sergeant shouted at him and eventually he moved on, zipping himself up as he went. Another lingered in the doorway of the general store. Eyeing up the checkout lass with the big tits, no doubt. An elderly man with a small dog walked out of one of the apartments. At once a soldier ran towards him, weapon levelled. The old fellow dropped the dog-lead, fluttering his hands in alarm as he was prodded back indoors at rifle-point. The dog scampered off.

Now two soldiers were walking up the road from the bungalows, a tall older man and a burly younger man with corporal's stripes and a swagger. They had a woman between them, half dragging her. The sergeant strolled over and appeared to start questioning her. She shook her head vehemently. The burly young corporal struck her in the face. Her head dropped. The sergeant repeated his question. The corporal raised his fist to strike her again, and for

6

a moment John sensed something familiar about the movement, the threatening posture. But before he could focus on the young man's face, the hotel door was flung open and a grey-haired woman emerged. The hotel-keeper's wife. She strode towards them, her indignation plain to see. She stopped in front of the group and started to remonstrate with the sergeant.

He listened for a while, then raised his hand and spoke. Whatever he said to her, it made her throw her fingertips to her mouth in dismay. The sergeant summoned two more soldiers and indicated that they should remove her. But the hotel-keeper's wife turned with dignity and started to walk away. The soldiers followed her and grabbed her by the arms. She struggled to turn, to voice her outrage to the sergeant. But then something caused all eyes to be raised to the top floor of the hotel. The sergeant barked a command and one of the soldiers raised his weapon and fired a burst. Glass exploded from an upper window. Splinters of wood and masonry flew in all directions. Twisted half round between her escorts, the hotel-keeper's wife stopped struggling and stared. Following her gaze, John realised that it was Gordon's room the soldier had fired into. Gordon, her half-witted son, John's former schoolmate. Now bottle-washer, occasional porter, sometimes even, God help the customers, relief barman.

At a further command from the sergeant three more soldiers sprinted across the yard and burst into the hotel.

For several moments all went quiet. John chafed his frozen fingers, stiff and cramped from gripping the binoculars. The blood flowed back and his hands began to tremble. He steadied himself and raised the glasses again as two of the soldiers reappeared from the hotel, dragging with them a struggling figure. They pushed him to the ground in front of the sergeant. He raised himself to his knees and looked up in confusion.

Now the third soldier emerged from the hotel and joined the group. Half a head shorter than the sergeant, he wore a thick moustache and his dark hair escaped untidily from beneath his beret. He began speaking to the sergeant, who listened then shook his head. The man with the moustache persisted, waving his hands. Again the sergeant shook his head, more emphatically. The man with the moustache turned on his heel with a furious gesture. Started to walk away. Then spun round, raised his weapon and fired a single shot into Gordon's stomach. He fell forward, mouth gaping in agony. Restrained by their guards, the two women looked on in horror.

For a moment the sergeant stood in stunned silence. Then another door opened at the far end of the steading. A figure appeared, glanced at the soldiers and began to run towards them, waving his arms and shouting. The hotel-keeper. His wife came out of her trance, shook her head and opened her mouth to warn him. But he paid no heed. The soldier with the moustache swung round and trained his rifle on the running figure. The sergeant also recovered himself. He turned, gesturing to the man with the moustache to hold his fire, and shouted at the hotel-keeper, who ran on. The sergeant started to shout again. The man with the moustache jerked his head in contempt and fired. The rifle kicked twice in his hands.

The running man staggered and pitched headlong down.

Released by her guards, his wife sank to her knees in the snow.

TWO

Not until long after the firing had stopped was John able to move, frozen hands shuddering as he lowered the binoculars. He could have been lying there for minutes or hours. He wouldn't have known. He climbed to his feet and looked around. No sign of Hector or the cart. He walked back on to the track, numbly following the trail of spilt logs homewards. Wishing his father would be there. Wishing anyone would be there so he wouldn't have to be alone with what he had seen. It felt as if he had swallowed something huge and poisonous.

The sky had cleared now. Late afternoon sunlight slanted through the pines, glinting palely on the snow, so unfamiliar in this warming world that its whiteness seemed almost miraculous.

Hector was waiting at the cabin, still attached to the empty cart, scraping away at the snow with his front hoof to get at the mossy grass. He looked up and gave a low whinny. John unhitched him, led him into the lean-to stable at the back of the cabin and fetched an armful of hay. Then, as Hector munched, he buried his head in the dusty mane and let the tears of shock and outrage come.

Some time later he went inside. He took off his coat and boots and wandered from room to room in his socks, unable to settle, picking things up and putting them down again. *Fifteen minutes later and he would have been down there in Blackriggs himself.* Panic surged inside him. The walls and furniture seemed suddenly strange, as if his inner compass had seized and he'd lost his bearings. He cursed his dad for having chosen this weekend to go visiting in Aberdeen. Picked up the phone in the vain hope that it might be back on again, and fingered the keypad with a sudden longing for the comfort of his mother's voice, two hundred and fifty miles away in Newcastle. Tears welled up again as he wondered what on earth he should do, tried to imagine what his father would do, racked his brains till they ached and the same answer came again and again: there's nothing you can do except stay put and keep your head down till he gets back.

He flung himself down on the settee, switched on the television and selected the news preset button. There was only one news channel these days. Channel One. The government had closed down all the others once the rebel Northern Land Alliance had stepped up their campaign and the fighting had begun in earnest under the leadership of the shadowy figure known only as the Tod, Scots for the Fox. Not that lack of reliable information had done anything to dampen people's support for the NLA, as they were commonly called, in their struggle to win back the Highlands from the hated Department of Land. Not round here anyway.

He watched for thirty minutes to be sure he caught a full bulletin. Reports were starting to come in that linked the identity of the Tod with that of the billionaire Swiss-based financier, Struan Fraser. The army was interviewing sus-

10

pected rebel sympathisers in Inverness, following a second consecutive night's disturbances on the Springfield housing estate. Another electricity substation had been sabotaged, this time in Dingwall. The authorities were in discussion with the oil companies about providing armed escort for northbound fuel tankers. A mass protest against the One Acre Act had been broken up by police outside the Parliament building at Holyrood. And just a few minutes ago the NLA had issued an apology for the downing three days ago of an army helicopter full of journalists over the eastern Grampians.

John drummed his fingers on the arm of the settee and closed his eyes as the voice droned on. He could clearly picture the moment when the twin insects had suddenly floated up above the heathery flank of a hill, crabbing across a pale November sky not three miles from here, the ground beneath them suddenly alive with panicking deer. His dad and he, the deerstalker and his apprentice, were lying up in an old peat hag, cursing the spoiled shot, when out of the corner of one eye John saw something streak across the blue. The leading helicopter erupted with a roar, in a ball of orange flame. For a heartbeat it hung there in the air. Then greasy black smoke plumed upwards and twisted metal rained down on the earth. There were dark doll shapes among the tumbling debris, the spits and gobbets of fire. The other helicopter swung around and hovered above the wreckage, then settled alongside it . . . There was an elbow in his ribs and his father's urgent whisper: 'Time tae shoot the craw, son.' Before uniformed figures had begun to jump out of the helicopter, the two of them had slipped away down the peat hag and were gone.

Investigations into the incident were ongoing, concluded the bulletin. Special forces continued to conduct a

11

thorough search of the surrounding area and a number of suspected terrorists had been taken in for questioning.

John felt sickened by the lie. *Suspected terrorists . . . taken in for questioning.* This wasn't one of those Third World countries where innocent people simply disappeared, swept up by brutal security forces never to be seen again. This, as Mrs Farquharson had constantly reminded them, was a sovereign, independent nation, proud and forward-looking in the early years of the twenty-first century. This was Scotland, cradle of the Enlightenment – whatever that meant – the home of Rabbie Burns, who believed all men to be equal, 'a man's a man for a' that', and the host of other civilised qualities that Mrs Farquharson had done her best to drum into them during the weekly nationhood classes in sixth year. And yet . . . something had gone wrong. He could see it quite clearly now, everything that had been wearing his father down for so long. Until today, of course, it hadn't really touched him. Annoying and inconvenient, yes, but mostly for the disruption it caused to the band. It was impossible to organise gigs when the phones worked only half the time, you couldn't rely on getting fuel and even if you managed to get yourself to the venue the event was quite likely to be brought to a halt by a power cut. Still, every other band in the Highlands was in the same boat, and as a result the live sessions in the pubs were enjoying a short-lived boom, people turning up on pushbikes with fiddles and guitars, accordions and mandolins and bodhrans strapped to their backs and even, in the case of Charlie Coulter, a double bass fitted with wheels. Short-lived, though, because now there was a rumour that the sessions were going to be banned. People were starting to sing rebel songs, getting stirred up, and the authorities didn't like it . . .

But none of that was life-threatening. And even when the Department of Land pay cheques had finally stopped coming and John and his father had started having to fend for themselves, selling logs and illegal haunches of venison to their neighbours, John had found something almost exciting about it, the idea of living off the land, living by their wits. There had been days out on the hill with the rifle, or back at the cabin splitting logs, when he could have imagined himself one of the old American frontiersmen.

But not any longer. Not now . . .

He got up from the settee and went into the kitchen area, opened the cupboard where his dad kept the whisky and poured himself a large shot. The first gulp burned his throat and made him cough, but he forced himself to down the fiery liquid in two more gulps and immediately poured himself some more. It made his legs feel weak and sent a glowing heat through his stomach. He ought to try to eat something, he thought.

He turned on the cooker and put the pot of venison stew on the ring to heat. Then, still holding the glass, he wandered unsteadily from the living room into the passage and leaned against the doorway of the cabin's back room, with its familiar smells of glue and wood shavings. He took another mouthful of whisky and as it seared its way to his belly gazed blindly at the shapes on the workbench.

He stood there for a long time. When he eventually turned away, as if on cue, the electricity died. He stood still, immobilised in the darkness, listening to his own breathing. Then, as he moved towards the shelf where the candles were kept, the faintest flicker intruded. He glanced towards the window. There was electricity of a different kind at play out there. He went to the door and stepped outside, feeling the cold air shrivel his scalp as he turned to face the north, where a diaphanous curtain hung low in the night sky. Aurora Borealis. Ghostly and billowing, a shifting veil of greens and purples and blues that seemed to be saying that what happened this afternoon was merely a prelude.

He shivered and turned to the cabin again, pausing for a moment on the threshold as a skein of late-homing geese went creaking overhead in the frosty, flickering darkness.

THREE

Next morning John swam to wakefulness and broke surface in a pool of light. He blinked and glanced around the sunlit cabin. Sat up and rubbed the back of his pounding head, felt the oily queasiness in his stomach. He climbed from the bed and wandered naked into the bathroom, glimpsing himself in the mirror as he approached the basin. He was long and lean as a fencepost these days, all traces of adolescent softness gone. The skin now strained at his cheeks and ribs and shanks. A thatch of dark hair crowned the tanned face with its raw-boned features and pale wind-scoured eyes.

He started to shave and the trembling began in his hands. The razor skittered on his jaw and nicked his flesh, then dropped into the basin with a clatter and splash. He held the sides of the basin to steady himself, watching the water pinken below him as droplets of blood fell from his chin. He thought he might pass out or throw up.

In time the trembling left him. He stuck a corner of toilet paper to the cut, swallowed a couple of painkillers from the bathroom cabinet, then returned naked to the bedroom and sat down on the bed, head in hands. But the electricity was still off and he soon started to shiver. He pulled on clothes and went into the workroom, where he opened the valve on the gas cylinder, removed the glue pot from the ring and lit it. He boiled enough water for one cup of tea and took it through into the kitchen area. He sat down at the table and drank in silence.

The tea finished, he went to his room and returned with tobacco and papers. He had only ever smoked occasionally and some time ago now, under pressure from his dad, had decided to stop for good. It had been easy enough, but he'd never got round to throwing away the remains of his tobacco. Now he rolled himself a thin cigarette with unsteady fingers. He placed the untidy white cylinder to his lips and lit the strands of tobacco that straggled from its tip. They glowed as he inhaled. He held in the smoke and let it out slowly, then shook his head and stubbed out the cigarette in the tea mug.

Outside it was a bright, frosty morning. Low shafts of morning sunlight cast long pine shadows on the snow.

Hector looked up as he came into the stable. John reached out and laid a hand on the broad back.

'So will we go back down there, mon?' The sound of his own voice grounded him, stopped his head feeling like a helium balloon that might take off and sail up over the tree-tops.

Hector snorted.

'Maybe we should see what happened, eh? Maybe there's folk needing help.'

It made no sense, this urge to return to the scene of all that horror. It had been with him from the moment he woke up and he didn't understand it. In truth it terrified him. But it was growing on him with every minute that passed.

'Tell you what, we'll just go to the end of the wood, have a wee look, OK? Take the cart in case we meet anyone.'

Hector stamped and grunted and refused to cooperate until John produced a bucket of treacle mash. Then he stepped outside and backed himself into position between the traces of the cart. He lowered his whiskery muzzle to the bucket and stood placidly eating while John harnessed him up.

'You're a thrawn old bugger, so you are,' said John as they set off through the wood. The only sounds were the creak of the cart and the muffled plod of hooves.

Half a mile from the cabin there was a fork in the track. John glanced to the left, the way they had gone yesterday. There the spilt logs lay waiting to be collected, worth a week's provisions. He'd go for them later. Straight on, a mile ahead, was the road.

Once on the tarred surface Hector's steady hoof-beats rang among the silent snow-dusted trees. The road was empty, as if nothing had yet broken the morning stillness. After twenty minutes they rounded a bend and Blackriggs came into view, enfolded in woodland. They reached the edge of the trees and paused. The village seemed still and silent.

'We'll go on a bit, will we?' John asked.

Hector fidgeted and snorted and refused to budge. John dismounted and grasped the bridle. Hector raised his head and rolled his eyes.

'Don't blame you.'

Leaving Hector at the roadside, John went on alone, past the front of the hotel and into the yard. It was sunny and peaceful here, the ground still lightly covered with snow. There was broken glass by the side door of the hotel, some earth spilt from a shattered pot outside the apartments.

17

Here and there a dark stain that could have been engine oil. And a faint but cloying smell of burning hanging on the air.

Sunlight streamed through the silent hotel hallway. John made his way upstairs, found Gordon's room, went in. Freezing air poured in through the shattered window. Opposite, the wall was pocked with bullet marks, high up near the ceiling, the floor littered with fragments of plaster. A chair was overturned, some clothes strewn about the place. He glanced around and went downstairs again.

Here doors were open. In the office a couple of silent screens, open files, papers, an upended cashbox on the floor. The lounge and dining room were orderly and empty. The bar seemed untouched, apart from an empty shelf where the malt whiskies usually stood. But there was blood in one of the staff bedrooms, the bed drenched with it. And blood in the kitchen too.

He left hurriedly and crossed the road to the first of the row of cottages. Connie, he didn't know her other name, a single mother, lived here with her young son, Calum, five or six years old. Yesterday John had watched the soldiers burst in, but he hadn't seen them come out again. Whatever they did here they did behind closed doors, then left by the back way. He pushed at the front door. It swung open and he stepped into a small open-plan living room. A cheery space, cheaply but colourfully decorated to please a child. Now it was a shambles of upturned furniture and possessions, as if it had been the scene of an energetic game of tag. John went upstairs to where there were two bedrooms and a bathroom. Nothing had been disturbed here.

He left by the back door and stood for a moment in the garden. The burning smell was stronger here. He glanced

18

down to the river, sparkling in the sunlight. Between the end of the cottage gardens and the river bank there was a snowy strip of vegetation, mostly bramble creepers and small bushes. He walked down and climbed over the garden wall, then followed the line of cottages, pushing his way though the undergrowth. After fifty yards he started to gag. But the trench was well concealed and he almost stumbled into it before he saw it. It was the bed of an old burn, three or four feet deep and heavily overgrown. He followed it for a few paces and the dead winter vegetation started to fall away, shrivelled and burnt. The sweet cloying stench filled his nostrils, coated his palate. He fumbled for a handkerchief, stuffed it into his mouth. Took a couple more steps and stopped. The blackened bodies were piled two or three deep. He knew many of them, though most were now thankfully beyond identification. He made a feeble attempt at counting. Somewhere around twenty, including at least three children. He turned away, vomiting into the undergrowth.

After a while he stumbled out of the rough ground and back to the buildings, where he started to search methodically. First the other cottages, then the apartments. In some there was evidence of slaughter, in others merely of struggle. Some were untouched. He wrenched open cupboards, peered under beds. Flung back the doors to garden sheds with increasing urgency. And found nothing. Though he understood now, knew why he'd come. One living thing, that was all he needed. One living thing would somehow make it easier to bear, would mean that he wouldn't have to face the terrible loneliness of being the only witness, the only one to escape.

Leaving the farm, he walked along the road towards the two bungalows. A bloody scrap lay on the verge. The old man's little dog. He paused, glancing back down the road to where Hector was shifting uneasily in the sunlight.

He was leaving the first bungalow when a sound made him jump. A voice in the living room. He paused in the doorway, listening. It was the television. The electricity had come back on again. A male and a female voice now, in cheerful conversation. He went into the living room and stood watching for a moment. Then leaned down and punched at the off switch. He made his way to the last bungalow, where there was nothing to be seen. He walked through to the back and out into the snow-covered garden. It was still and quiet. No birds sang. Nothing moved among the trees beyond the fence. He was about to turn back when a muffled sound came from the wood. A low, echoing moan, beyond the range of any human voice he had ever heard. A moment later it came again, turning his skin to gooseflesh.

At the end of the garden the wooded bank rose steeply. Some distance along there was a rounded mossy outcrop among the trees, like a large hummock. This was the direction from which the sound seemed to come. He climbed the garden fence and scrambled towards it. The sound came again, a strange booming cry like a long groan. Reaching the mound, he noticed the outline of an entrance-way, almost covered by dead bracken. He squatted down beside it, steadied his breathing and teased aside the dense lattice of fronds.

The mound was hollow and lined with slabs of stone. It had a vaulted ceiling and a concave, sump-like floor. An ice house, where in times long gone, when the winters were colder and refrigeration had yet to be invented, they would store blocks of ice cut from the river. Sometimes they would pack it with bracken or grass for extra insulation, so food would stay fresh in the cool and the darkness.

It was also an acoustic chamber of curious properties, as the boy crouching opposite in the gloom now demonstrated.

FOUR

The boy was hunkered down on the cold damp stone, chin resting on his knees, shivering. Deep shadow filled the vaulted space. He didn't know he was being watched. He lifted his head, cupped his hands in front of his mouth and hooted like an owl. A thin, mournful sound. But somehow the chamber snatched it up like a whisper in a conch shell. Rolled it around and around and expelled it, weirdly amplified, past John's ear. He flinched and the boy sensed the intrusion. Turned his whole body and stiffened as if to ward off a blow.

John hesitated on the threshold. There was something about the small hunched figure that reminded him of Davie. Not the looks or the build, not that he could see much in here anyway, though he was about eight, the same age Davie had been when . . . No, it was something else, more a feeling than anything, a sense of vulnerability. Enough, anyway, to bring with it the familiar clenching inside.

Minutes passed. The boy made no move, but John could feel his need sending tremors through the chill, dank air. Then he was ducking through the entrance, losing his footing on the slippery stone and slithering down to land on his arse in the well of the floor.

He sat there in a heap. The boy did not look up.

He picked himself up and crouched so that he was level with the figure in the gloom. He was not one of the Blackriggs children. There was something strange about him. Something fearful and uncontained, like an injured animal. John remained there, still and silent, for a long time. Still the boy made no move.

'I'll not hurt you,' he said softly.

No response.

'You'll be cold in here. Hungry too, I expect.'

The shoulders tightened.

'Come and we'll find you something to eat.'

Motionless and silent.

'Can't come with me, eh?'

Eyes firmly on the ground.

'Then we've a problem.'

Quietly John stood up.

'I've no food with me, see.'

He took a gentle step forward.

'And you won't come out.'

The boy tensed but didn't move.

'What'll we do about this, then?'

He stood still a while. Then reached out and laid his hand on the boy's shoulder. The muscles quivered but the boy didn't pull away.

'A good feed and a nice hot soak.' He lowered his voice, filled it with warmth. As if he were soothing Hector after a fright. Or Davie . . . 'Aye, that'll do you fine.'

As gently as he could he started to turn the boy around. The body moved but the eyes remained locked on the ground. Then the boy stiffened again, his features went rigid. He flapped his hands, stuffed them into his mouth. John crouched down again so he could see the boy's face, reached out to tilt his chin. With a yell, the boy spun away and bolted for the entrance. For an instant John hesitated. Then he was lunging forward, suddenly fearful for their safety. One hand closed around a retreating leg. The boy let out a high animal shriek. John held tight. The shriek went on and on and on. John gave a tug. A fist caught him across the bridge of the nose. He toppled backwards, sparks shooting behind his eyes. The boy slithered down on top of him, squirming and flailing. John took another blow, in the eye this time. Tears ran down his cheek. He wrapped his arms round the thrashing body, drew it towards him in a bear hug. Which stifled the noise, but brought him within biting range of determined teeth and a fiery feeling in his right breast. He grunted in pain. But still he held tight as the body squirmed and wriggled and the muffled voice howled. John tried rocking from side to side, mumbling nonsense. And at long last the fury started to abate, cries of rage yielding to long shuddering sobs of distress and exhaustion. Until the storm passed, the tension left him.

He sagged in John's arms. They sat there, bound together in the gloom of the ice house, for a long time.

Later John set the boy on his feet again, took his hand and led him outside. They walked together through the deserted hamlet, the boy's eyes fixed once more on the ground. He said nothing as they reached Hector, still wait-ing where John left him. Showed no expression as John lifted him and set him on the cart. But as they moved off along the road he watched the swing of Hector's tail, the sway of his broad back, with what might almost have passed for interest.

As they turned off the road and on to the forest track

John heard the rumble of a heavy vehicle. He stopped the cart in the shelter of the trees and dismounted.

'Can you bide here a minute?' he asked.

The boy said nothing. Showed no sign of moving.

John crept back to the roadside and glanced along at the hamlet. A large mechanical digger was trundling towards the cottages. It stopped just short of the furthest one and turned towards the river.

Heart pounding, he returned to the cart where the boy waited just as he had left him, staring into the trees.

John climbed up beside him and flicked the reins.

The deer stink hit him as he pushed open the cabin door. He kicked snow off his boots and entered. The boy followed, wrinkle-nosed. On a glowing cooker ring sat the pot, the remains of the venison stew now welded to the bottom. The room was thick with the rank, overcooked stench. John cursed the electricity, went to turn the cooker off.

The boy stood in the middle of the room, eyes averted.

'Want something to eat, then?'

No reply.

John shrugged and went to the kitchen cupboard. He took out a multipack of crisps. Opened one for himself and tossed another to the boy.

'These'll mebbe keep you going.'

The boy tore open the packet and stuffed a handful of crisps into his mouth. Glanced around the room and saw the television. He walked over, selected the cartoon channel and sat down on the floor in front of it. The crisps were gone within thirty seconds.

'Be my guest,' John muttered.

At one end of the living room was the small kitchen area

25

with the cooker, a sink and cupboards, and a wooden table. The rest of the space was taken up with a worn-out three-piece suite, a large wood-burning stove and the television. The pine-log walls were undecorated apart from one long bookcase, whose shelves were crammed with books, many of them old and cloth-covered. On top of it stood a cheap music drive and speakers. The place was strewn with clothes and tools.

'We'll get some heat going, eh?'

The boy might be OK, but John himself was starting to shiver again.

He walked over and fed kindling into the stove. As he prepared to light it he studied the boy out of the corner of his eye. He'd been right in the ice house, despite the gloom. About eight years old, nine at a push. Wearing dark blue cargo-type trousers, walking boots and an expensive-looking red all-weather jacket. Unlike delicate wee Davie, he was sturdy, a little thickset even. With his brown eyes and dense black curls there could have been something foreign about him. There was also a slightly elongated face which, along with jug-handle ears, gave him an almost comic look. Though there was nothing clownish about him right now, staring at the screen, a trickle of crisp crumbs stuck to the corner of his mouth, his expression blank as the moon.

'I'm John,' he said, raising his voice over. 'What are you called?'

The boy ignored him.

'Suit yourself then.'

The stove began to roar. A sweet resiny scent of pine crept into the room. Strathdon Smiddy, read the maker's stamp on the door. Locally cast and draws like a dream, Ferg MacNeil, his dad, was fond of saying. Get the dampers working properly and it'll stay in all night. Peats or sticks, doesn't matter which. Ferg had gone out and found it himself when the fancy autonomous heating system had packed up and the pressed bracken insulation began to rot inside the walls. He'd pestered the Department of Land, his employers, until they'd agreed to install it. Though it was six months now since they'd ceased to be Ferg's employers, six months since he'd handed in his notice and they'd stopped his pay. And although, on his dad's advice, John had hung on to his job – 'Ach son, you're young enough yet, you should keep takin' their money!' – three months later his cheques had stopped coming too. But whether it was because the fighting had since flared up, or because, technically at least, John still remained in their employment and lived at the same address, some kind of bureaucratic paralysis seemed to have set in and the Department had never got round to turfing them out of the cabin. In fact, they'd heard not a squeak from them since . . .

Better try and get him to eat something decent, John thought. He opened the fridge, where, for convenience, his dad kept everything they needed for their daily piece – a side of venison, several jars of gherkins and a dozen packets of thick, triangular oatcakes.

'Do you like meat?'

The boy made no reply.

John scratched his head. Then he set the table with cold meat, oatcakes, butter, more crisps, gherkins, a pale slab of processed cheese, a tin of sardines and a bar of chocolate. Finally he fetched a big bottle of Irn-Bru.

'Dinner's ready.'

The boy seemed absorbed by the antics of a crudely drawn cartoon family with spiky hair and bulging eyes.

They'd made John laugh when he was a kid. But the boy wasn't laughing, merely watching slack-jawed.

'I said, dinner's ready.'

The boy gave no sign of having heard.

'Up to you, then . . . but I need to eat.' John sat down and cut a slice of venison. He speared it with the tip of the knife and chewed.

The cartoon finished. The boy got up, came over to the table and sat down. John pushed the plate of meat towards him but he ignored it. He reached out with both hands and took the crisps in one, chocolate in the other. Tore the wrappings open and built himself a flaking sandwich, which shed much of its covering on the short journey from fist to mouth. He'd hardly finished the first mouthful before he was busy assembling another. As he chewed he examined the rest of the picnic.

John poured him a tumbler of Irn-Bru and watched as he slurped it down along with a mouthful of half-chewed crisps, then grabbed more chocolate. Gobbling at them as if he hadn't been fed for days.

He still hadn't looked John in the eye. But now something else had caught his attention. He was staring in fascination at John's left hand and the vestigial thumb that sprouted alongside the four fingers like a little claw.

Much as he tried not to mind, John had never got used to the attention it attracted. A curious glance was all it took to bring the blood to his cheeks, to remind him of the cruelty this small, almost insignificant deformity had brought down upon him at school.

But now, he thought, looking at the boy, it might serve some purpose.

'Stumpie,' he said, giving it a waggle. The word tasted bitter on his tongue. 'That's what they called me at school.'

The boy shifted uncomfortably but he couldn't tear his eyes away. John waggled it again. 'Stumpie John. That was my name when I was a kid.' He looked across the table. 'What's yours, then?'

A gherkin followed the crisps into his mouth. The boy took another slug from the tumbler. His jaws worked briefly, then he inserted thumb and forefinger. Half the gherkin reappeared, glistening with Irn-Bru, and dropped to the plate.

John sighed and shook his head.

'Won't speak. Won't tell me your name. What the hell are we going to do with you, eh?'

F I V E

During the afternoon the wind changed, swinging round to the south-west again, damp and mild as normal. John threw up the last log and turned Hector for home. The snow had almost gone now, the track starting to turn soggy.

The boy perched beside him, swinging his legs over the front of the cart. He still hadn't said a word or met John's eye. The food seemed to have quietened him down though. The jumpiness had gone. But John frowned and flicked the reins impatiently as Hector plodded through the woods, casting the occasional glance over his shoulder.

So long as the buses were running, Ferg would be back by mid-morning tomorrow. All he had to do was keep it together with the boy till then. Only a few more hours . . .

Back at the cabin he settled him in front of the television with a silent prayer that the electricity wouldn't go off again. Then he set about tidying the house, washing up from dinner, clearing junk off the settee, straightening his dad's bed, putting clothes away, anything to keep busy. Glued to the screen, the boy seemed content in a vacant kind of way. John felt almost envious. All day his thermostat had been going berserk. One minute he was sweating, the next minute freezing. Then waves of dizziness would break over him and he'd have to hold on to the furniture. His hands trembled and he felt constantly on the verge of tears as he pushed away the images that kept trying to crowd into his mind, inviting him to latch on to them and linger over them. God, he needed so badly to speak to someone. Hear someone tell him it was OK, he hadn't seen it all really. But that wasn't going to happen, not for the moment anyway, not ever in the latter case. It was just him and the boy. What had *he* seen down there? What had got his tongue?

Tea was a repeat of dinner, but this time he managed to get the boy to take half a baked potato smeared with butter. He still wouldn't look at the meat though. John shook his head.

'Tatties and chocolate. You'll never grow strong on that.'

He heard himself. It sounded just like his mother. He wondered for a moment whether he might be going mad. The boy ignored him.

After the meal he left the boy watching cartoons again while he washed up, standing thoughtfully at the sink. Then he went through to the bathroom and turned on the bath. It had been his mum's way of calming Davie down when he got overexcited, as if he'd been a fish in a previous life . . .

He waited for a break between cartoons.

'How about a hot soak? Get you warmed up for bed, eh?'

To his surprise the boy got up at once. Switched off the TV and followed him into the bathroom, where John hovered uncertainly. But the boy continued to ignore him, started to undress. Clothes dropped to the floor. John picked them up and stood holding them as the boy climbed into the tub and sank down till the peat-stained water was up to his chin.

The boy lay there, still and expressionless, as if pickled in whisky. Beneath the layer of puppy fat there was good strong muscle and solid bone, despite the diet. The skin was very pale and soft-looking. And there was something else about the body, he couldn't quite put his finger on it, that seemed – out of the ordinary . . . John realised he was star-ing and looked hastily away. He reached across to the basin for the soap and handed it to the boy.

The boy washed, got out and dried himself. Then let the towel drop and stood by the bath. Eyes on the floor. Naked and expectant.

John glanced down at the clothes he was still holding.

'I'll fetch you something to sleep in.'

He returned with an old work-shirt. It reached almost to the boy's ankles but he didn't seem to mind. The boy gave his teeth a vigorous scrubbing with John's toothbrush, then followed him through into John's father's bedroom and climbed into bed.

Again John hovered.

'Are you . . . will you be all right?'

The boy turned towards the wall and closed his eyes.

'Sleep well, then.'

He turned to leave the room.

'We'll start getting things sorted for you the morn, eh?'

Outside the bathroom the boy's clothes lay in a heap on the floor. Now John picked them up and carried them through to the living room. He sat on the settee and started with the jacket. He didn't know the make, but it was definitely expensive; he could tell from the lining, the fasteners, the feel of it. Apart from a half-eaten packet of wine gums its pockets were empty. The plaid shirt, of the same make as the jacket, had no pockets, and beneath that the boy had worn a plain white T-shirt. It was as if he'd been dressed from a magazine, thought John. Finally the trousers, a different label, foreign-sounding. There was a handkerchief in one pocket and a plastic cartoon figure from a cereal packet in the other. He held the trousers up. There was something stiff in one of the patch pockets on the left leg. He tugged at the Velcro and pulled out a postcard. The statue of the Little Mermaid on the rocks in Copenhagen harbour. He turned it over. It must have been sent in an envelope because the message, in large and characterless block handwriting, filled the whole of the empty space. HOW IS MY BOY? I HOPE YOU ARE WELL. I WILL BE ARRIVING ON 25 NOVEMBER. I WILL BRING YOU A PRESENT. LOOKING FORWARD TO SEEING YOU. MARIE ROSE SENDS HER GOOD WISHES AND SO DO I. UNCLE PETER. There was something about the message that seemed rather odd, John thought, though he couldn't quite put his finger on it. Maybe it was just the stiffness of a foreigner writing in English. He read it a couple of times, then shrugged and put it back in the pocket, none the wiser. The boy might have an uncle in Denmark who was planning to visit in ten days' time and who was now going to be disappointed, to say the least. But the boy himself still had no name, no identity.

For a long while John sat staring at the stove. Then he rose and walked through to the workroom, where he stood again in the doorway, breathing in the familiar glue smell. It combined momentarily with the clean, contrasting scent of wood shavings to take the edge off the other smell that stuck to his clothes, lingered in his sinuses, clung to the back of his throat. His hands started to tremble again.

He forced himself to focus on the pale womanly carcass, clamped to its block on the workbench. Sat down at the stool and ran a finger into the tuck of the waist, imagining how it would look when it was stained and varnished, tricked out with a nice piece of purfling. Oh aye. It would be the best one he'd made yet. The right pieces of timber had turned up just when he needed them, the way things did sometimes. A braw piece of sycamore for the ribs and neck and back. Came across that rummaging about in the stoke-house down at the old castle. And a real cracker for the belly. Bonnie yellow pine. His dad had found it for him, three hundred years old, a beam from an old kirk. Cost him a month's wages. But it would sound mellow with that on it, right enough. Mellow as a Strad. Or a MacNeil. Is that what they'd talk about in years to come, a MacNeil . . . ?

He picked up the neck, its half-finished scrollwork straining to break free from the rough rectangular block of maple. This was the bit he liked best. Teasing out the spiral on one side like the interior of an ear or maybe some delicate shell or fossil. Repeating the pattern on the other side. Striving for the impossible, perfect symmetry. He hefted it in his hand. Then set it down and picked up the gouge chisel. He turned the grinding wheel, laid the blade against it, a dozen revolutions, whirring and sparking. Then oiled the blue-black stone and worked the blade back and forth, back and forth. Something deeply familiar and soothing about the movement. Of course there was. Men had been at the sharpening since the very first flint. Testing the blade with a finger as they went. 'Ye'll niver mak a thing till ye've learnt tae put an edge on a tool,' as old Alec MacNab used to say.

34

And all at once John was back in old Alec's front garden. Crouching down behind the low hedge, arm around Davie's trembling shoulders, as their tormentors raged up and down the village street. 'Da-vie, Gay-vie, come oot and fecht wherever ye are.' Catcalls, hoots of laughter. 'Da-vie, Gay-vie, yer jist a wee poof, so ye are.' Then a louder, deeper voice. 'Ach, ah wouldnae bother, he'll be awa' shaggin' his brother.' And the chorus again. 'Gay-vie, Stum-pie, aff tae get a whum-pie!'

Davie was shivering and fighting back sobs, his small body racked with the effort. John felt the familiar rage in his heart, longed to go leaping into the street, fists flying, and teach the bastards a lesson for once and for all. But he knew there was no point. He wouldn't stand a chance. There were too many of them. And anyway the arch-bastard, tormentor-in-chief, Kel Foulis, had it all too well under control. It would just make things worse for them both . . .

There was a hand on his shoulder and a kindly voice in his ear.

'Ach, they're just hooligans, son. Dinnae you bother wi' the likes o' them.'

He turned round. An elderly, white-haired woman was looking down on them.

'Come away in. I'll put the kettle on.'

He hesitated.

'Well. Come on then. Nice cuppae tea. Set you right.'

With a protective arm around his brother's shoulders, John followed her inside, closed the front door behind them. Its stained-glass window washed the hallway with a dim, watery light. Davie blinked, wiped his eyes with the back of his hand. The MacNeils' house went with Ferg's job, sprawling on the site of an old gamekeeper's cottage on the castle estate, a mile out of the village. It was a modern bungalow, shoddy construction, cheap furnishings, overflowing with family chaos. But this was like another time, another world. A tidy little village house, built more than a century past with glistening blocks of dressed granite. There was dark polished furniture, plants and ornaments, books and pictures, wee lacy mat-things everywhere. And music. From a room next door to the kitchen came the strains of a fiddle. A slow, haunting air that halted John in mid-step, put up the hairs along his arms. The door was ajar. John felt the music reeling him into the room like a brown trout in a burn. The woman had paused in the kitchen doorway and was watching them. She smiled and nodded encouragement. Steering Davie ahead of him, John put his head around the door. It was a small room with an upright piano crammed into the space behind the door, shelves of old discs and books, two fiddles hanging on the wall. And a third tucked under the chin of the short stout man who sat on a stool by the window. He had thinning sandy hair and the broad warty face of an old puddock. He glanced up and nodded. The two boys stood uncertainly in the doorway. The old toad didn't seem to mind. He kept playing.

The woman came out of the kitchen with two mugs of tea and a plate of biscuits. She seemed quite happy for them to be there too. She smiled and stood beside them, nodding appreciatively. Waited till her husband had finished.

'So you like a tune, do you?' she asked.

Davie sniffed and nodded. John didn't know what to say.

'Play them another, Alec. While they have their tea.'

He cleared his throat. 'Aye, Bella, I will that.' He pointed John to an easy chair. 'Take a seat, laddie. And you,' to Davie, 'on the floor there.'

The boys did as he told them. Bella handed them the tea, set the biscuits on a little table and perched beside John on the arm of the chair.

Alec thought for a moment, then a twinkle came into his eye. He launched into a reel, fast and insistent, the theme repeating itself, round and round like waves crashing in on a shore. John's foot started to tap. His pulse quickened, he felt the blood fizzing in his veins. He knew this kind of music, of course. It was around them all the time, it was what people played. But now, all of a sudden, it was as if he was hearing it differently. There was something ancient and familiar and thrilling about it. He felt like he'd stepped into some old coat that had just been waiting there for him all this time and fitted him perfectly.

Alec ended with a flourish. Looked John straight in the eye as if he could read his feelings.

'D'ye ken the name o' that tune?'

John shook his head.

'Well, you should.' He nodded. 'It's John MacNeil.'

John's mouth hung open. 'But . . . that's my name. John MacNeil.'

'Aye.' The puddock eyes were twinkling again. 'It's an old tune. And he was a great Highland dancer in his day, big John MacNeil. Threw a fine leg, so he did.' He paused. 'And you . . . You're Fergus the stalker's lads. So . . . you like the fiddle tunes, do you?'

'Davie's good with a tune,' said John. 'On the piano. He's right quick, so you are, eh Davie?'

Davie gave a little shrug.

'And what about you?' asked Alec, looking directly at John. 'Can you play a tune?'

John shook his head.

'Would you like to?'

He thought. Then nodded.

'Well then, we could aye gie 'em somethin' to think about.'

'Who?'

'Those ruffians out there.'

'But – but how . . . ?'

Alec smiled thoughtfully. 'Show you somethin' not a one o' 'em can do.' He tapped the instrument with his bow.

John looked at him blankly.

'Learn you the fiddle, laddie. Learn you the fiddle!'

Bella was nodding her head like a wee bird at his side.

John blushed to his roots. Shook his head. 'I-I-'

'Give it a try, eh?'

'But-but-' He flapped his left hand. Stuck up the claw.

Alec glanced at it. Shook his head. 'Ach, that wee thing. That'll no gie you any bother. Here.'

He handed over the fiddle. Showed John how to hold it. The neck sitting fine between thumb and forefinger.

'That's all it needs do,' he said. 'Just rest there.'

Davie looked up at his brother and smiled.

SIX

Burrowed down beneath the blankets, John sweated and tossed in his sleep. He was at Blackriggs, trying to play the fiddle with gloves on while a dreadful sound rang through his head. An anguished wail that grew louder and louder. He sat bolt upright in the darkness. It was the boy.

He clambered out of bed and stumbled across the room to the light switch. Cursed as he stubbed his toe on the way. Cursed again as no light came on. Fumbled his way into the kitchen area. Found candles, lit one.

'I'm coming, I'm coming.'

The boy was sitting up in bed, hands over his face. Howling and gibbering and hooting. Snot and tears and dribble streaming down his chin.

'Wheesht there. Wheesht.'

John went to sit by him. The boy turned to the wall. John reached out and an arm came flailing backwards. He dodged the blow. Remembering what had happened in the ice house he leaned forward and, as gently as he could, pinioned the boy to the bed. The wailing grew louder, more piercing, but the struggle didn't last so long this time. Soon the sturdy body yielded to racking sobs as John spooned in behind it, clasping it to him as he'd done so often in the past with Davie and his nightmares. Feeling the warmth, the breathing, the closeness. Wondering if it was right to be doing this, this thing that seemed like yet more strangeness . . . and yet wasn't. He lay still for a while, trying to imagine what must be going on beneath those dark curls. Then, as the breathing softened and steadied, he began to hum faltering notes in the darkness. The John MacNeil tune.

Just before dawn something woke him again. An anxious whinny. He sat up. Squashed against the boy, one arm had gone to sleep. It dangled uselessly as he got up, started to tingle. The boy slept on. There was another whinny.

The first greyness was starting to seep into the sky. He pulled on clothes and boots, opened the door, felt a spit of rain on his face. He walked round the back of the cabin, past the shadowy bulk of the Department 4x4, which for more than six months now had stood fuel-less and abandoned beneath a tree.

In the lean-to stable Hector shifted and stamped at his approach.

'What's up then? What is it, mon?'

He turned his head to nuzzle at John's pocket.

'I've nothing for you.' He patted his neck, gave him a scratch behind the ears. But the old garron continued to snort and shuffle. John quietened him, then stood stock still, listening, straining. Nothing but a whisper of wind in the pines and a soft patter of cold dawn rain on the lean-to roof. He left the stable and walked across the clearing towards the hay-store. Hector snickered. He halted again, straining his eyes into the darkness. Then turned back to the lean-to and ran his hand along the tack shelf until his fingers closed on the night-sight. He took it down, went outside again and focused it, eyes adjusting to the dim green light, the wavering cross-hairs. Trees swam into view. He lengthened the focus, found a gap in the trees, scanned the open ground beyond. There. Oh God. A tiny distant figure, barely visible in the green gloom. There, another. And another. Six, seven, eight. Coming this way. Moving steadily, line abreast across the hillside.

John glanced at the lightening sky, then turned and sprinted for the cabin. He burst through the door and made for the bedroom, where the boy was dead to the world. He tore back the bedclothes, grasped him by the shoulders and shook. The boy squirmed and blinked, screwed up his face as if he was about to start wailing again. John clamped a hand over his mouth, from which came muffled squeaks, but no wailing. 'Listen if you can. They saw us yesterday. Hector. Or me. Or maybe just our tracks in the snow. I'm sorry but we've got to get out of here. Now. You get dressed quick as you can.' The boy shook his head, flopped back on the bed, reached for the covers. John cursed, then lifted him and heaved him over his shoulder. Grabbed a blanket. Marched through to the living room and dumped him on the settee, where his face crumpled and he started to whine. John threw the blanket round him, dashed back to the bed-room and collected his clothes. Then hurried round the living room scooping up food, woolly hat, ammunition, matches, pocket knife, flashlight, spyglass case, whatever caught his eye. Stuffed the whole lot in an old fertiliser sack along with the boy's clothes. Retrieved his rifle from its usual place under the settee and slung it over one shoulder. Heaved the sniffling blanket-wrapped boy over the other, grabbed the sack and went out to the stable. Unhitched Hector. Flung the halter over his head and towed him out

41

backwards. Shoved the startled boy up on to his back. 'Get your hands in his mane, then you won't fall off. Good lad.' He whacked Hector on the rump and the old garron set off at a trot towards the spur of trees that followed the burn out towards the hill. Dim grey light, rain pattering down. Hector swaying from side to side. Sobbing boy clinging on for dear life. John panting alongside, halter in one hand, sack in the other, rifle clattering against his shoulder. They reached the trees, stumbled down the bank, splashed through the burn. John's boots filled with freezing water. Up the other side and on to the path. Tears streaming down the boy's face, though he was still hanging on, blanket flapping out like a Batcape.

Hector steadied his pace, knew where he was going now. He'd trodden this path a thousand times. It followed the burn upstream for a couple of miles through wild woodland and out on to the open hillside. Spruce and larch jostled shoulder to shoulder here, knee deep in fox-cover thickets of brushwood. Darkness closed in again as the path began to narrow, forcing its way through the dense overgrowth of trees.

The boy's teeth were starting to chatter. His cheeks were blue, a drip hung from the end of his nose.

'Good lad. You're doing grand.' John laid his hand on one clammy, shivering leg. 'Just a while longer. Find us somewhere safe to wait up, get you warm agai—'

A distant *whumph* stopped him in his tracks. The sound an exploding gas cylinder might make. He sniffed the air. Frowned. Sniffed again.

'Oh no . . .'

It burst from him as if from a blow to the solar plexus.

It couldn't be, surely. But the smell of smoke on the air was unmistakeable. He stood for a long moment with his eyes closed and fists clenched, fighting back the tears. Trying not to think of the half-made fiddle, his bedroom, his possessions, the little shrine to Davie, the tune he'd never got round to writing for him. Trying not to think what his dad would do when he came home to a smouldering ruin. Trying not to think of anything except the need to keep going. But he was trembling all over now, and his brain didn't want to work. What should they do? Where could they hide? God, why wasn't his old man here with him . . .

The sound of voices drifted up from behind and all at once he remembered the cottage.

'C'mon!' He tugged at Hector's halter.

A couple of hundred yards up the path they stopped in front of a dense wall of undergrowth. Hector took one look at it and his hindquarters settled, his hooves splayed. John reached up for the boy, hauled him down into his arms and forced his way through a gap in the undergrowth to emerge into a small clearing. Mired in weeds and brambles, a tumbledown shepherd's cottage struggled to shrug off the encroaching woodland. A fallen tree had smashed most of the roof, a rowan sapling sprouted from the top of the wall, dog-roses crawled about the gaping windows. He put the boy down in the shelter by the old hearth, then turned back to the path for Hector, who made it plain he wasn't playing. Head down, eyes half closed, forelegs braced. John grabbed the halter, swung him round and tugged him on up the path as the voices drew closer. He dragged Hector into a trot, the voices becoming clearer now. He spotted a gap between two trees. Something had fallen behind them, crushing down the undergrowth. Running feet were approaching. 'C'moan, mon,' he urged. 'C'moan there!' And Hector paused. Then stepped towards the darkness,

43

over a big log and round behind a dense tangle of branches. Where John halted him.

'Wheesht now, mon.' He laid his palm against Hector's long jaw. Glanced in the direction of the unseen cottage. *Please, none of your hooting, not now.*

Boots went pounding up the path. John glanced up, saw the retreating back of the big corporal bringing up the rear.

He waited a little, then led Hector back to the clearing and stopped in panic. The boy wasn't there. The sack had been upended, the contents strewn about the ground. He walked into the open, peering this way and that. Then heard a sound from behind the bushes that sprouted where the dividing wall had once been. He looked through. The boy was down on his hands and knees in the furthest corner of the ruin. Under John's work-shirt he was wearing his jeans and socks now, but no shoes. He had pulled aside a big stone and disturbed a colony of slaters, which he was poking at with a stick. Chuckling to himself as they scuttled about in panic like tiny grey armadillos, feelers waving, legs paddling. In his other hand he was clutching an open packet of crisps. There was something strangely repetitive about his actions. Lean forward, poke with the stick, chuckle, rock back on the heels, stuff in a fistful of crisps, lean forward, poke with the stick . . .

It was broad daylight now and the rain was easing. John left him to it and went to tether Hector, who had got his head down the other side of the wall, munching old nettle stalks. He gathered up the scattered possessions and provisions and stuffed them back in the sack. Then glanced around the clearing for suitable firewood. Dead birch was what he needed for a fire that wouldn't betray them with its smoke.

'I'm going to find some wood. You just bide here now.'

44

The boy didn't even look up as he left the clearing and made his way back to the path, where he paused and listened. All was silent. He slipped across and fought his way up the overgrown burn-side towards an umber spray of birches. He gathered up an armful of fallen branches, the wood soft and rotten beneath the papery bark, and made his way back to the clearing.

The boy had more stones overturned when he got back, and more empty crisp packets on the ground beside him. John stood watching him. He didn't seem to want to hurt the slaters. It just amused him to make them run about. But it also seemed as if he was losing interest. His eyes were starting to dance around as if he was worried he wouldn't find something else to occupy them. He was cold too, shivering again. The work-shirt looked damp.

'We'll get the fire going. Warm you up.'

John returned to the hearth, peeled silver bark from the logs, made a little pile of papery curlings and built a pyramid of twigs over it. Prepared to light it, then paused, match in hand, at Hector's whinny. Moments later caught the faint thud-thud, thud-thud, thud-thud.

He ran for the boy, grabbed his hand. The boy didn't like it, the sudden contact. Turned his head away, screwed up his face, flapped his free hand. But John tightened his grip and dragged him round the end of the tumbledown wall and into the dead nettle patch. Hector's ears were pricked, his eyes wide. He stepped after them into the shelter of the trees.

The helicopter was almost overhead now. 'It's OK, it'll be over in a minute, gone. Just keep a hold of my hand. Don't want them to see us, do we?' He was stroking Hector's flank with the other hand. Speaking in the same tone for boy and horse. 'There now, there now. It'll all be fine.'

The helicopter had now stopped, dead above them. Hovering like some great mechanical raptor, ready to drop on whatever moved. The sack caught John's eye. Lying out there among the ruins. Brilliant white, bulging.

'Oh Jesus,' he muttered.

But after a few moments the helicopter moved on again. John breathed out, his heart doing an eightsome. The boy was shivering and chewing at the fingers of one hand. 'Good lad, well done.' John let go his other hand. 'We'll stay here a bittie longer though, in case it comes back again.'

Huddled close together under the trees, the boy's face was level with the scar on Hector's side, a livid puckering of the skin just below his ribs. He stared at it. Then reached out and touched it. Hector had found something else to eat in the undergrowth. He paid no attention.

'Want to know how he got it?'

The boy sniffed his finger. Kept sniffing. Then touched the scar again.

'I'll tell you. It was a few years back now. I was still at school. My dad killed a big stag, a real monster. Twenty-five stone if he was an ounce. We were way out on the furthest part of the hill. A steep place, narrow too. We'd not've got the 4x4 out there. Not in a month of Sundays.' The boy was showing no sign of listening. But John went on. 'It was my fault, see. Didn't have the beast roped on to him tight enough. Hector lost his footing. Just stumbled. That was enough. The beast slipped, all twenty-five stone of it. Pulled Hector over with it. And a horn went straight into him. God, you should've heard the noise. Poor old Hector. Lying there squealing and bellowing. Thrashing his hooves. Blood pouring out. Trying to get up. And the more he moved the further in the horn went. Man, it was bad.'

His breath was coming fast now. But the boy remained unmoved, sniffing at his fingers again, while Hector chomped away at whatever he had found among the dead branches.

'So . . .' he went on, 'we had to get in under him, downhill of him, and not get squashed, see. Or brained by the old hooves flying about. We tried breaking off the horn. But it was that strong and it just ended up jiggling about inside, hurting him even more. Finally my dad had to cut it off. The beast's head. With this . . .' He fished in his pocket, brought out the old bone-handled gralloching knife his father had given him on his fifteenth birthday. Opened its four-inch blade, honed to a thin sliver of razor-sharp steel. But the boy was unimpressed. 'Took forever. Thought he'd never get through the vertebrae. But he did. I had to hold the head steady while my dad helped Hector back on to his feet. Which hurt him more than anything. Finally yanked the horn out. Poor Hector. Gave a great roar and took off like his arse was on fire. Didn't see him for three days. But he was lucky, right enough. It missed his vital organs. So it could have been worse. Aye, could have been much worse . . .'

The boy was staring up at him. Full eye contact.

'You're crying,' he said.

John touched his own cheek.

'So I am.' He laughed to hide his embarrassment. 'So I am.'

'I want to watch cartoons,' said the boy.

SEVEN

'I want to watch cartoons.'

He said it again as if to make sure John had heard.

'But there's no cartoons here.'

'I want to go to your house.'

John shook his head. 'We can't go to my house. I don't think it's there . . . any long –'

A sob caught his throat.

'Don't cry. You shouldn't cry.'

'No.' He fished for his handkerchief. Blew his nose too loudly. 'You're right. Try not to think about it.'

'I want to go to your house and watch cartoons.'

John squatted down and took the boy's hand in his. The boy looked at him from under his thick lashes, as if he might bolt again at any minute.

'Listen, I don't know what happened to you back there. But if you saw things you shouldn't have, that's you and me both. Things that shouldn't have been done. And now there's folk don't want us to tell what we saw.' The boy was staring at him now. 'So I'm going to take you somewhere safe, eh? Where they'll not find us. An old house. By a loch. Where we can wait up till my dad comes for us. He'll know to look for us there.' He stood up. Blew his nose again. Forced a smile. 'OK? Good. So now you're talking to me, there's things I need to know. Like what's your—'

'Can we go swimming? At the loch?'

'Swimming . . . ?' John stared. The boy's eyes were suddenly wide and hopeful. 'Swimming? Don't be daft. It's November. Freeze the tits off you, it would . . .'

'I want to go swimming now.' The voice was rising, starting to whine.

'Look . . .' John softened his tone, 'I know it's hard, but right now there's no cartoons. No swimming. Not much of anything except me and Hector and this wood here. So you'll just have to . . .'

The small face clouded with anxiety. Anger. Incomprehension.

John looked at him, frowning. Then let out a long breath and shook his head in slow understanding.

'Oh man, it's nothing to do with . . . with Blackriggs, I mean – what happened back there, is it . . . ?' He was muttering, more to himself than to the boy. 'Oh, I'm sorry . . . awful sorry . . . I didn't realise . . .'

A word swam up from the deep well of his memory. *Windae-licker.* That was what they used to yell out when the minibus from the centre went past the school playground. Taking the dafties on outings or wherever they went, poor wee souls. With their faces pressed up against the steamy windows. Tongues out, blank looks in the eyes. *There go the windae-lickers.* Another tribe. Another race.

And now he'd got one all of his very own. He shook his head in desperation.

The helicopter was returning. John looked up and glimpsed it through the trees, travelling high and fast this time like a late-season grouse.

'Come on, then.' He took a deep breath and forced another smile. 'We'll not be seeing that again today, I doubt. Let's get this fire going.'

'I want to go swimming.' The boy sounded tearful now.

Oh God, it was all starting to sink in. How was he going to cope with this?

'See if there's any more crisps, will we?'

The boy nodded and followed him back to the hearth. John fished in the sack, pulled out the last packet and handed it over. The boy tore it open and crammed a fistful of crisps into his mouth.

'You're a wee gannet, so you are.'

The boy seemed to find this funny. He chuckled to him-self, sending out a spray of crisp crumbs, as John crouched down and struck a match. The bark sent up little tongues of flame, licking at the twigs. Soon the fire was burning merrily and smokelessly. The boy knelt in front of it, crisp packet between his knees, hands out to the warmth. John sat back on his heels and looked at his young companion.

'So, wee gannet . . . what am I going to do with you, eh?'

The boy grinned.

'How about telling us your real name. Can you do that?'

The boy nodded.

'Well . . . ?'

'Ninian,' he answered proudly.

His accent wasn't local. It had an odd edge to it.

'Ninian what?'

The boy looked at him.

'What's your other name?'

'Ninian.'

'Ninian Ninian?'

He shook his head. 'No, no, no! Ninian.'

'Just Ninian?'

He nodded.

'What about your dad, then? What's his name?'

'Dad.'

'What do other people call him?'

The boy leaned forward and poked at the fire with a stick.

'When can I watch cartoons?'

By late afternoon John had lost count of how many games he'd invented with stones. How many times he'd played hide-and-seek with the hider peering out from around a tree, hands over his eyes, thinking he couldn't be seen. How many swordfights he'd had with sticks, lunging and ducking, thrashing the air, leaping about, shouting *hiyaagh, hiyaagh*. For Ninian Ninian liked doing doing. The same things over and over. Even seemed to find it hard to stop sometimes. At which point, as John soon discovered, the tightrope loomed. Suggest an alternative that didn't appeal and the game went on. Admit to being beat and at once the brow furrowed, the voice became whiny and anxious. The more John watched him the less he understood, starting with his appearance. Apart from the sticking-out ears there was nothing the least bit daft-looking about him. He didn't roll his eyes or drool. His arms and legs worked fine together. His complexion was sallow, but not pale. And he was physically strong, if a bit overweight, which was hardly surprising since he seemed to want to eat all the time. He'd got over his choosiness now too. A piece of chocolate, oatcake, even a slice of cold venison. He seemed to be happy as long as he was munching. A bit like Hector. Perhaps it helped him slow down, allowed him to change what was

51

going on in his head so he didn't get stuck. Because however normal he might look, he didn't think normally.

Around midday they went down to the burn together to fetch more wood. When they got back John suggested that he make a nice tidy pile of it. It was all short lengths of dead birch, nothing more than a couple of feet long, easy to stack. But after several minutes of intense concentration the boy had built what looked more like a stork's nest than a log-pile. And later, when John suggested he put some of it on the fire, he ignored the nest but disappeared into the trees and came back dragging a large branch. John looked on in disbelief.

By the time dusk had begun to fall the boy was at last showing signs of weariness. A stillness had settled on the wood. The only sound was of Hector's occasional movements as he grazed the other side of the tumbledown wall. For a while they sat together with the blanket around their shoulders against the evening chill, gazing into the embers of the fire.

John took out the tobacco and papers. There was just enough tobacco for a final cigarette. He rolled it tightly.

'You shouldn't smoke,' said the boy.

'I don't. Not really.'

'You shouldn't smoke.' There was no conviction in his voice. It was as if he was parroting something he'd learned.

Somewhere high in the darkening sky, geese called to one another on their evening flight to roost. John lit the cigarette, drew deeply and coughed. Then smoked in silence until the calls of the geese faded away.

'Shall I tell you a story?' he asked.

The boy didn't respond. He was staring again in sleepy fascination at John's thumb, as if the abnormality of it struck some sort of chord with him.

During all the years he and Davie had shared a bed-room, John had lost count of the number of times he'd had to tell him stories to help him get off to sleep. They weren't particularly good. He made them up as he went along, old stuff usually, about Highland warriors and bogles and kelpies. But Davie loved them, maybe just loved the sound of his brother's voice. And John had grown to realise that the telling of them was soothing for him too.

'It was November,' he began, 'like now, and there was a bad fog one night. Could hardly see your hand in front of your face.

'We'd just finished our tea and we heard all this noise outside. Like geese it was. But they didn't seem to be going anywhere. Just circling overhead in the dark, round and round. So we went out. And sure enough, that was what it was. Geese, hundreds of them, lost in the fog. Round and round and round. Making this incredible racket. Honk, honk, honk.'

There was a glimmer of interest in the boy's eye.

'So my dad gets the spotlight we used for the foxes. Then he points it up in the sky. Few moments later there's an almighty thud as a goose hits the roof of the house and lands in the garden. Then another. And another. Well, my dad goes crazy with the spotlight. For ten minutes it's rain-ing geese. And we're running about the garden in the dark, dodging them as they come thumping down. Catching them and taking them to him to wring their necks. Till my mum stops him. Says it's cruel. Says we've got enough. She was right too. It was roast goose, goose pie, goose stew, goose every-bloody-thing-you-can-think-of for weeks after.' He tossed the end of the cigarette into the embers. 'But we never did discover what was going on. Why they flew down the lamp beam. Perhaps they thought it was the sun, poor things . . .'

'Honk, honk,' echoed a small voice.

'Aye. Honk, honk it was. Lost in the fog. Disorientated. Like everything they were used to suddenly wasn't there any longer . . .'

John stood up. Scuffed at the embers with his boot.

'We'll need to put this out in a minute. Just to be on the safe side, eh? Get going as soon as it's properly dark. It's three hours walking to the lodge.'

He picked up the sack and emptied it again. Separated out the provisions from the rest of the contents and inspected them. A big bar of chocolate, two tins of sardines, four packets of oatcakes and a large cut of cold venison.

'We'll maybe catch a trout in the loch. Gannets like fish, eh?'

But Ninian's eye had been caught by the worn leather cylinder of the spyglass case. An antique, given to John's grandfather by a grateful employer. Ninian reached out a tentative hand.

'Go on then,' said John. 'Open it if you want. There's no telescope in it though. Moisture got into it. Knackered it.'

Ninian removed the lid and let it hang on the thin leather strap that attached it to the body of the case. He plunged his hand into the cylinder and pulled out a quarter bottle of whisky.

'Central heating,' said John. 'That's what my dad calls it. Handy on your shoulder, see. When you're out on the hill. Never know when you might need some . . .'

But Ninian hadn't finished. He held up the case and shook it as if inspecting a wrapped gift. It rattled.

John gave a puzzled glance.

Ninian upended it and out tumbled a rectangular plastic object, along with three small black cartridges and a set of miniature earphones.

'Well . . . we've been looking everywhere for that!'

Ninian's eyes were bright and wide. He picked up the object without a moment's hesitation and fed a cartridge into the slot at one end of it. Then held it in front of him with each thumb hovering over one of two small pads. With practised forefinger he flipped a switch on the side, then pressed down on one of the pads. A faint light appeared in the small screen that occupied the top half of the rectangle. Thin, robotic music issued from a speaker hidden somewhere in the casing.

'Got one of these, have you?' asked John.

Ninian nodded without taking his eyes off the screen. His thumbs had begun to dance about on the pads. The tinny music went marching on.

'Mine originally,' John explained, 'but my dad got hooked on it a while back. Still plays it in the evenings sometimes when there's nothing on TV. But mostly he has it out the hill with him. Something to do when there's a long wait for beasts to show up.'

He moved across and peered over Ninian's shoulder.

'Ah, that's the easy one.'

Coloured squares and rectangles floated endlessly down from the top of the screen, ready to be grabbed and dragged into place in the wall that rose from the bottom as fast as the player could build it. Jumping up and down behind the wall, as he became gradually imprisoned by it, was a comical alien with an antenna sprouting from his head. From time to time he tried to punch out a brick before he could be immobilised by a laser blast.

'My dad likes to build that wall,' John went on. 'Keep

55

out that wee Martian or whoever he is. Bit weird, if you ask me – for a fifty-year-old.'

Practised though Ninian appeared to be, the wall wasn't rising very fast. In fact, it wasn't rising at all. But he seemed engrossed. John left him to it. Refilled the sack and put out the fire, then sat quietly in the dusk.

Telling Ninian the story had calmed him for a little while, but now everything was starting to spin round in his head again. The killing at Blackriggs, the ice house, the soldiers in the dark, the burning of the cabin, and now this . . . this daftie he was stuck with, who reminded him so strongly of Davie. It was like some kind of nightmare where everything he touched and smelt and heard and, most of all, felt was more real than real. Those tears just now, for example. He hadn't cried for . . . well, not since Davie died. Thinking about it all made him want to cry again now, made him feel like a wee boy himself, who just wanted to be scooped up by his mum or dad and told he was safe. But he wasn't. That was about the only thing he could be certain of. He needed to get real. Get to grips with the idea that he and Ninian weren't just taking part in their own movie. That if they were found by the soldiers they would be killed without compunction. That it was possible, though he hardly dared voice the thought to himself, that his dad might not show up like the US cavalry and save the day. If the bus had run on time Ferg would've been home a good few hours ago, and he would know at once that so long as John hadn't been taken by the soldiers, or died in the blaze, he would be making for the lodge. For a start, Ferg would see that Hector wasn't there, even if the stable was burned to the ground. Could something have happened to him . . . ?

Darkness had fallen now. Ninian was still bent over the games console.

'Time we got going,' said John.

The boy shook his head.

'We can't stay here all night. And you'll run the batteries down.' He put out a hand.

Ninian turned away, hunched over his new-found treasure.

'OK, OK. You can hang on to it. Keep it in your pocket. But if the batteries run out, you won't be able to play. And I've no more with me. So best stop now, eh?'

'No, no, no.'

'Don't you want to be able to use it again? On our . . . adventure?'

He looked up. 'Adventure . . .' Rolled the word around in his mouth like a gherkin. Not sure whether to swallow it or spit it out.

'Sure you do. So turn it off and put it away now, there's a good lad. Tell you what, you can ride Hector if you want.'

'Hector the horse.' He lifted one hand and sniffed his fingers. 'Are we going swimming? I can do the crawl.'

'That's grand. You'll need to show me.'

'When will we go swimming?'

'When we've been to the old house.'

'But when?'

'When we find somewhere we can. Not now anyway. It's dark. And cold. Look, you don't swim in the dark, do you?'

The boy shook his head.

'So. Are you going to ride Hector?'

He nodded.

'Fine. Let's get going.'

A wind had got up now, rattling the trees, threatening more rain. They set off up the path. Soon they left the shelter of the wood. The wind scoured the darkened hillside with a thin sleet. Hector hated weather like this; it made him nervous. But John walked at his head, halter hanging from the claw thumb, talking to him as they went.

In his warm jacket, the hood drawn tight around his face, the boy seemed quite happy jolting along. He ran his fingers repeatedly through the coarse mane, lifted them to his nostrils and sniffed. He sat comfortably, reached forward from time to time to pat Hector's neck, as if he'd done this kind of thing before. After a while he stopped sniffing and started singing to himself. He was surprisingly tuneful. John reproached himself. There was no reason why being daft should mean you couldn't carry a tune. Anyway, there was something catchy and familiar about what he was singing. John realised with a start what it was. The banned NLA anthem, 'Ours Is the Land'.

'Where d'you learn that tune?'

Pause. 'My auntie.'

'Where's your auntie live?'

'In her house. Auntie's house.'

John paused. 'In Blackriggs? That where you were staying, then? Auntie's house, eh?'

The boy nodded and started singing again.

EIGHT

Eyes watering from the night wind, sleet running down his neck, John was in a trance, plodding in the darkness up the hill road, though river bed would be a better description after so many years of neglect.

Ninian had stopped singing now. His fingers were still buried in Hector's mane, but his head had begun to loll forward.

John reached up and laid a hand on his thigh. The head jerked. The eyes opened, trying to focus.

'No sleeping now,' said John. 'You'll fall off. Then I'll have to carry you . . .'

'I'm cold.'

'Well . . . you could walk. Warm you up.'

He shook his head.

John halted Hector. Retrieved the blanket from the sack and helped Ninian wrap it round his shoulders.

'There. That'll do the trick.'

They moved on. Within a few minutes the blanket was sodden with sleet, but the boy didn't seem to notice. John kept a raised hand on his thigh, rubbing as they walked.

It wasn't just the vulnerability that reminded him of

Davie. It was this willingness to put up with things, a kind of bravery, he supposed. That was what John had loved most about his brother, his bravery. His will to go on and on and on when everything was against him, the eager spark burning bright in his wee monkey face. He'd never properly belonged in this world, Davie. At least that was how John had seen it. Not that Davie was handicapped in any way, not in the normal sense of the word, not like Ninian. Three years younger than John, he was just one of those unusually fragile souls, so physically slight and awkward he looked as if a breath could have knocked him over. And so emotional, so sensitive, so quick to get upset by things. A right pest too at times, like all younger brothers. But such a trier. Running, climbing, riding a bike, all the outdoor things, he was hopeless at them, but he wouldn't give up. He'd go at it, whatever it was, all arms and legs, till he was purple in the face and almost crying with frustration, and John would have to take him aside and explain that it didn't matter if he couldn't do it, you didn't have to be able to do everything in life, and anyway, there were some things he did way better than anyone else. The music, for example. He could hear a tune just once and go to the horrible old piano in the back room and play it straight off, note perfect. The extraordinary memory too, for the obscure and useless things he'd come across in the books he was always reading. The weird thing with the colours – synny-something, the word had never stuck in John's mind – that meant he saw letters and words and numbers, days of the week and months of the year in colour – though John had never been sure whether that made Davie better than other people or simply different. And then there was the kindness. When other people got upset, he'd get equally upset for them, and the strange thing was

60

that it always seemed to make them feel better. But there was so much that was hard for him, so much in life that hurt him, however determined he was not to show it. And in the end, after eight short years in this world he'd never really fitted into, he'd found a way to leave it. At least that's how John had come to see it, though he'd never dared say so to anyone else. It was seven years ago now and it had rocked the family. Things had never been the same again between his parents. His dad still refused to talk about it. His mum had hung on until John was ready to leave school and start working with Ferg at the deerstalking, then she'd gone back to her family in Newcastle, while John and his dad had left the gamekeeper's cottage on the castle estate and moved into the Department cabin at Blackriggs, five miles across the hill in the next glen. And John himself . . . he'd made a little shrine in his room with photographs, a poem Davie had written and oddments he'd collected – a shell, a jay's feather, some rabbit bones and a candle John would light from time to time. On his last visit to Newcastle his mum had asked if he still had it and suggested gently that maybe seven years was long enough, maybe it was time to move on. They'd ended up having a row about it. In the train on the way back John had found himself wondering whether the reason he'd chosen the deerstalking was so that he didn't get crowded out by people, so that he had the peace and quiet he needed to keep that sacred Davie place alive inside him. He felt a sharp pain at the thought that the shrine was gone now . . .

Hector snorted in the darkness, slowed his step. John came alert to the sound of running water. On the bend ahead a deep gulley had eaten its way across the road. A small burn rushed down it. John led him off to the side and into the heather. Hector gave a little grunt of satisfaction to be off the road, to feel the softer ground under his hooves, the grass and heather of the open hill, where he knew the real work always began.

John halted, shaking his head as the realisation suddenly hit him. Come daylight, Hector would be a positive danger to them.

'Whoa, mon.'

Ninian grunted sleepily.

'Come on, laddie. You'll have to get down.' He reached up.

The boy's eyes were half closed. He flopped against John as he set him down on the ground. Mumbled something about swimming. Found his legs and stood there in the darkness. Hector lowered his head, sniffed at the heather. John stepped close and scratched him behind the ears.

'Oh, Hector. What've I been thinking of? I'm sorry, mon. Truly sorry. There's no way you can come with us. Not on the open hill. They'd spot us a mile off.' He stroked the broad neck. 'Ninian and me, see, we can hide. Get behind a boulder, burrow down in the heather. It's deep enough these days, after all. But we can't hide you, can we, mon? Not from a helicopter, eh? Or soldiers with spying gear . . .'

He took the halter and turned the old garron's head for home. Rubbed the velvety muzzle with his open palm and muttered into one hairy ear, 'Don't know what you'll find there, old pal. But someone'll look after you somewhere. So off you go now.'

He stepped back, lifted his hand and delivered an almighty whack to the rump.

Hector let out a shout of indignation and cantered off into the darkness.

John stood there with his eyes prickling as the snorts faded, hoof-beats receded into the wind.

'Bye bye, horse.'

'Aye.'

He reached down and took a small cold hand in his palm. Cupped it with his other hand and rubbed.

'We'll need to walk now, eh?'

'Yes. Walk in the dark.' Ninian turned and peered back down the road. 'The horse has gone home.'

'He has.'

Hand in hand they trudged on up the hill.

'D'you have a brother? Or a sister?'

Ninian shook his head.

'Just you?'

'Just me. And Dad. And Auntie.'

'Where's Mum?'

'In heaven.'

'Is she now?'

'Yes.'

'So's my wee brother. What about your dad? Where's he?'

'At work.'

'Where's that?'

'The office.'

'Where's the office?'

He shrugged.

'And Auntie?'

'Shopping. Auntie's gone shopping.'

'Shopping, eh?'

'Yes. She'll be back soon.'

The dried-up burn behind the cottages stole back into John's mind. He lengthened his stride. Hand clasped in his, Ninian kept up without complaint.

People had always fought over land, he guessed. Bad though it was, what they were caught up in here was something as old as the ground beneath his feet. Yet surely no one could have suspected it would come to this. He'd been ten at the time the One Acre Act came into force, a year before Davie died. He hadn't understood what it was, but he'd sensed the excitement in the village on the day the colonel, former laird of all these darkened hills, his dad's employer for seventeen years, had handed over the deeds of the castle and the estate to the men from the Department. It was the only time anyone had ever seen the old man cry. Though he was in good company, with all the other folk the length and breadth of the country, lairds and farmers and smallholders alike, who owned more than one acre, and whose land was from that day on to be taken from them by the government on behalf of the people of Scotland. But for most people in the village who didn't own their homes, or whose houses had just a wee patch of garden, it was an excuse to join in the celebration in the pub. Which turned into an all-nighter, and John later heard that Ferg had got well and truly stottered and had stood up and made a speech and said that although the colonel had been a kind man and a good boss and he felt sorry for him, this change was long overdue because too few people had owned too much land here for far too long. So now anyone could rent a parcel of land for farming, or to make a village football pitch, or plant a bit of a wood, or anything else they wanted, but no one could actually own it, or would ever be able to again, and that was a very good thing. Then there'd been a lot of applause and Ferg had missed his chair and sat down in old Janet Fordyce's lap and spilt his drink into her handbag.

But all along there had been one big catch, as Ferg himself eventually admitted. John could remember him sitting at the kitchen table with a mug of tea in his hand and a downcast look on his face. The trouble had started, he explained, with the fact that no one was interested in renting land they couldn't make money from, which was most of the Highlands. Owning it was a different matter, of course, because as the years went by there were fewer and fewer wild places left in the world where wealthy folk could buy privacy for themselves, and so the value of the land itself continued to go up. But paying rent for thousands of acres of heather and hill with nothing on them but worthless sheep and deer was like throwing money down a well, Ferg said. So the Department, as expected, was left to manage much of the land itself. Which was how first Ferg, and then John, had come to work for them as deer-stalkers, since someone still needed to keep the deer under control. And which was all well and good, were it not for the real problem, and here Ferg's face clouded with anger and he clenched the mug in his fist as he went on, which was that a bunch of soft-arsed city boys in a glass-and-steel office in Edinburgh knew bugger-all about looking after the land. So people like him, whose livelihoods depended on it, were starting to get mighty fed up. Not only people like him, in fact, but also the old land-owning families and wealthy newcomers who hadn't wanted to give up their land in the first place and who now felt sad and angry about what was happening to it. So when local folk started campaigning against the Department, which they soon would do, there'd be plenty of others only too happy to donate money and other kinds of support from a distance . . .

'I'm hungry. I want to stop.'

John peered into the darkness. There was a big stone ahead, just by the roadside. They sat on it while he fumbled in the sack and made an oatcake-and-venison sandwich with numb fingers. It had stopped sleeting now and the wind had dropped, but it was still black as pitch and very cold. John knew this stone. There was a lochan beyond the brow of the hill behind them. Dark and reedy, down in a hollow between a couple of grassy hummocks, it never got the sun. Bit of an eerie place altogether. In fact, if it hadn't been night-time he might have told Ninian about the water kelpie that was supposed to live there.

'Eat up now. Need to keep moving. Keep warm.'

Ninian took another bite, then hopped down from the boulder and put out the hand that wasn't grasping the remains of the sandwich. Waited for John to take it.

They'd only gone a few paces when John stopped. He cupped an ear in the direction of the lochan. There was nothing but the wind. He moved on again.

Moments later there came a low grunt. John glanced again towards the lochan. Grasped Ninian's hand tighter.

'Just some old staggie with indigestion,' he said. 'Or having a bad dream.'

They walked on. Now there was a hint of movement in the darkness. A big shadowy form keeping pace with them. John quickened his step.

The road dropped down, a bank rising up alongside it, sheltering them from what lay beyond. John started whistling a tune.

The road rose out of the dip, rounded a bend.

'*Oh Jesus!*'

Something huge stood there in front of them, snorting in the darkness.

With what looked like a stupid grin on its big whiskery face.

Hector.

NINE

Strange flowerings of fungus patterned the wall in front of him. Constellations of mildew. John rolled over and looked around. It was broad daylight and he was at the lodge, on a mattress on the floor in one of the empty rooms over the stables. A mattress – *oh God, no* – that ought also to have had a sleeping boy on it.

He threw off the blankets and scrambled to his feet. Clattered downstairs and past the stables, where he could hear Hector moving about inside.

It was a glorious morning. Sky washed clean by last night's rain. Grey stone buildings scrubbed and glistening in the chill sunlight, decrepit though they were. He crossed the weed-ridden stable yard and made his way round to the front of the lodge, where he stood at the porch and gazed down towards the loch. It was looking-glass still, the perfect reflection of the snow-pocked hillside opposite broken only by the dark lozenge of the crannog. Ancient sanctuary from wolves and other enemies more cunning still, it was crowned with three pines and a solitary rowan to keep the witches away.

There was a movement among the sprawl of trees at the

near end of the loch. A small figure making its way down towards the water. Bright red in its jacket, like a beacon for any passing helicopter. John broke into a run and reached the water's edge to find the boy inspecting the barricade of branches and sticks that stretched from bank to bank across the mouth of the burn. It looked not unlike a floating version of his stork's nest log-pile. Except that it wasn't floating but firmly anchored in the mud.

He turned round as John approached, eyes bright.

'I saw him. I saw the beaver! He's got a big tail.' He was hopping up and down. 'He went into his house!' One hand was clutching his crotch. John wondered whether he'd peed himself with excitement.

'Did he now?'

'He did. He did.' He turned, face growing solemn. 'Beavers eat trees.' Pointed to the stand of birches round the end of the loch, punctuated with stumps like a mouthful of broken teeth.

'Aye, they do. Like beavers, do you?'

A nod.

'Did beavers at school, eh?'

'At school.'

Along with wolves and bear. Wild boar and lynx. And all the other species that had been reintroduced. Which were fine, so Ferg had maintained, as long as they stayed behind the wire in the national parks and designated reserves . . . even placid old paddle-arse here, who should have been European but had ended up, through some administrative cock-up, being a dam-building North American instead. And so had already drowned hundreds of acres of good planting and grazing . . .

'Come on now. We'll go and get some breakfast.'

He shook his head. 'I want to see him again.'

'We can come back later maybe.'

'I want to see him now.' The voice starting to rise.

'Ninian, there's people out looking for us. Bad people. We don't want them to find us. And they'll see you here. You must come with me.'

'No.'

He wouldn't meet John's eye now.

'I want to see the beaver. Go away!'

'I can't let you stay out. D'you understand?'

But Ninian had his hands over his ears. Crying and whining. Making funny little movements with his feet. Gripped by something that had nothing to do with bad people or beavers, some kind of blizzard of nameless feelings. John looked on in silence for a moment. Then made a lunge and instantly the boy went hyper, started screaming, a high-pitched, lung-bursting scream. John was thrown off balance by the noise, lost his grip as the boy broke away and dashed off along the bank, storming and raging. John set off after him and heard a sharp slap, almost like a gunshot. Glanced back to see a startled beaver at the edge of the dam, thwacking the water with his tail in warning. No wonder, for this wasn't like any ordinary child's cry. More like an injured animal. Going right through John, ringing round the hillside too as he began to catch up. He was almost within grabbing distance when suddenly the boy jumped off the bank and into the dark peaty water. It was only knee-deep. He started wading out, shaking his head and screaming. John leaped in and splashed after him. The water was bone cold. It was over the boy's waist now but he didn't seem to feel it. He showed no hesitation, no fear. He threw himself forward, started to paddle with his arms. John flung out a desperate hand, grabbed a leg and hauled. The boy's head went underwater, screams turned to

69

gurgles. John heaved again and got one arm round him. Then both. Started to lift him out of the water and for a few shocked moments he went limp and quiet. But as soon as they were back on the bank he came to again, started screaming, wriggling, thrashing about in John's arms. Who was just about to drop him when he vomited. All down John's trousers. But this was the third time they'd fought now and John was getting the hang of it. He regained his grip and held him as tight as possible. Pinioned his arms and watched out for the teeth. Ignored the puke and staggered for the stables.

Hector heard them going upstairs and whinnied. John shouldered open the door and they collapsed together on the mattress. Ninian curled up with his arms over his head, sobbing and panting and shivering, as John wondered how to get the wet clothes off him without collecting a black eye or a broken nose in the process. The boy had still got some fight left in him, even though he didn't know what he was fighting any longer. Or why. John tackled the shoes and socks with care, avoiding the flailing fists, then the trousers and pants, then wrapped the naked bottom half in the blanket. Ninian's hands starting to flap like beached fish now, breath coming in shallow gasps. He let John pull him into his arms and hold him for a while, murmuring softly, before John started teasing one arm out of the sleeve of the jacket. Ninian stiffened, gave a final shuddering sob, a token wriggle of defiance, then went limp. John peeled away the other arm, then the shirt and vest, then rubbed him with the blanket. In this cold, empty room with its creeping rot and peeling wallpaper.

Within a short while Ninian had fallen into a kind of trance. He sat wrapped in the blanket, vacant-eyed, staring at nothing, while John took off his own clothes and gazed down at his long pale nakedness. He rubbed slowly at his temples with chilled fingers, as if it might help him find the answer to the question that had gnawed at him from the moment he'd woken up. Where the hell was his father? And what if something had happened to him? He ignored the rising panic, forced himself to think practically. Either the buses weren't running, or the army had got the area sealed off and he hadn't been allowed in. Of all people, John's dad knew how to take care of himself. The likelihood of Ferg being in some kind of trouble was less than zero. Even if he *had* made it back to the cabin he certainly wouldn't risk coming up here in daylight. So all they could do was stay put for the moment. Not that the thought made him feel much better. Right now he'd have given anything to hear the tuneless whistle, the tread of his dad's boots in the yard . . .

He shivered. Got up and fetched his coat from the corner, the only thing he hadn't put on this morning. Pulled on the dry coat and wet boots over naked flesh, gathered up the puke-spattered clothes and made for the door.

'Are you going to see the horse?' The voice was small and tremulous.

John nodded. 'You stay here, eh? Keep that blanket round you. D'you want the game to play?'

He sniffed and shook his head.

'I'll come and get you when I've a fire going.'

John went downstairs and into the stables, where the wooden stalls had long ago been removed to make way for vehicles. Only the iron hay baskets, a couple of tethering rings and a small cast-iron grate in one wall remained now. Attached to one of the rings, Hector looked round as he came in and blew softly through his nostrils. John walked

71

up and stood close to him. Breathed in the familiar smell, put both arms around his neck.

'Oh Hector, Hector . . . wish you hadn't done that last night. Doesn't change anything does it, mon? Because I still don't know what to do with you, see . . . What if we have to move on again? We can't take you with us. Or set you free to follow us again. Or leave you tied up here to starve.' He shook his head. 'Unless . . . wait a minute . . . I'll be back.'

Round the back of the stables there was an old overgrown drying green. The hedge had run rampant and trees had sprung up tall around it. Just as John had remembered, there was one way in, through a small iron gate. Once in there Hector could forage quite happily for a few days without much danger either of escaping or of being seen by anyone. And if he got desperate, there were a couple of places where the hedge grew thin and he'd probably break through with a few good pushes.

Feeling a little more cheerful, John returned to the stables, unhitched him and led him out to the drying green.

'There mon, you have a good old feed, eh.'

He patted his neck and left, closing the gate behind him.

Then he walked down to the loch-side, where the beaver had at least ensured a plentiful supply of dead birch. He rinsed the puke off the clothes and made a couple of trips with logs and sticks for kindling, then laid a fire in the grate. He went upstairs to get the matches from the sack. Ninian had toppled over on the mattress, sound asleep, his breath clouding faintly on the chill air. He hardly stirred as John lifted him up and carried him downstairs, then went back for the mattress and settled him on it within warming range. The flue was clear and the fire caught easily. After checking outside that no telltale smoke rose from the chimney, John fetched in a couple of branches, propped them against the wall beside the fireplace and draped the wet clothes and blankets over them. Ninian slept on.

Sitting by the fire, naked but for his coat and boots, John gazed through the half-open stables door, imagining how this place would have been in years gone by. The yard echoing to the clop of hooves, the ring of tackity boots on cobbles. Coming and going of stalkers and ghillies and domestic staff. The game larder bursting at the seams. Crackle of pine logs and clink of glasses in the panelled smoking room . . . His grandad, the first of three generations of MacNeils to work on the castle estate, would have been familiar with every last detail. Though John was sure he'd turn in his grave if he could see what it had all come to now.

Ferg's battle to keep Hector, for example, when the Department had first taken over and insisted that the pony should be replaced by a 4x4. Yet six months later, when broken-down Department 4x4s were sitting idle in scores, Ferg was meeting his quota of beasts no problem. No oil-stained hours under the bonnet for him. First time his vehicle packed up he just abandoned it. No leaving carcasses lying out on the hill either, to be picked over by scavengers. And once he and Hector had got the beasts home, there was even the chance for a little surreptitious butchering. The sale of the odd haunch in the village . . .

Though Hector was never going to solve everything. And John could remember Ferg becoming increasingly short-tempered as there were more and more forms to be filled in, more and more delays once they'd been sent off, so that it became harder and harder to get things done. His father had never smiled more than he needed to, but now his face had taken on a look of permanent dismay as the burns became choked, the heather growing rank and deep until even the peregrines and hen-harriers were leaving the hills because there was nothing left for them to prey on. Soon only the scavengers remained, buzzards and hoodie-crows, foxes and feral cats, scuffling over the carcasses of weakling deer that had stayed behind while their more adventurous cousins grew sleek and fat, skulking in the once-forbidden woodlands, thieving from fields and gardens. And Ferg's simple pleas for help – for the hire of a mechanical digger to open up some ditches, for a permit to shoot vermin – simply vanished into the bowels of the Department. Which now lumbered heedlessly on like some great perpetual-motion machine.

TEN

The small blanketed figure stirred again and mumbled in its sleep. John stood up and felt his clothes. Still a little damp, but they'd soon be wearable again. He put more wood on the fire. Being naked made him feel vulnerable. Being *here* made him feel vulnerable. Remote though it was, the lodge stood like a beacon in this empty landscape. The cave up in the crags above. That's where they would've gone last night if he'd been thinking straight. Though it was too late now. The climb was far too exposed in daylight. But maybe they should move up there once it was dark. Ferg would know to look there once he'd tried the lodge.

There was a sudden loud and frantic whinnying. John sprang to his feet and ran out of the stables and round to the drying green, where Hector lay in the long grass, flanks heaving, snorting and rolling his eyes in agony. It only took a moment to realise what had happened, but it was enough to send a chill through him. Below the overgrown vegetation the ground was riddled with rabbit holes. Hector had put his foot down one. Now his right foreleg was bent and crooked and obviously broken.

John crouched down beside him, talking to him, murmuring soothingly, 'There mon, wheesht mon, we'll have you right, good old boy, yes we will.' But as he spoke he knew he was fooling himself. There was only one thing to do for an animal with a broken leg in a place like this. He reached out to stroke him, but Hector tossed his head and drew back his lips. John stood up in torment.

'I should have looked. Oh God, I'm sorry. I'm sorry, mon, I should've looked.'

He felt he might explode with anxiety and guilt. What should he do? He couldn't risk the rifle, not on a still morning like this. The shot would be heard miles away.

Hector had begun to pant. A froth was appearing round his mouth.

John took a deep breath and knelt down once more. 'Mon, mon,' he whispered. He took the gralloching knife from his trouser pocket, his hand trembling so much he could hardly hold it. He fumbled to open it and the blade locked with a click. Hector moaned and blew froth through his nostrils. John kept talking to him, feeling for the big vein in his neck, as his dad had once shown him when they'd come across an injured hind while out without the rifle. 'Good old boy. Won't know a thing.' He found the vein pulsing away beneath his fingers. Laid the blade against it and tensed his arm. And Hector lifted his head. Their eyes met. His large and brown and dulled with pain. John's hot and moist. John shook his head and snapped the knife shut.

He stood up and raced back to the stables and fetched the rifle from upstairs. It was an old one, a good one. A point-two-seven-five Rigby with a Mauser action. Not too heavy to carry, but deadly enough in the right hands. It had originally belonged to the colonel, who had given it to Ferg.

He had passed it on to John when he'd started work and the first time John had used it he'd killed a fine stag, a clean heart shot with its sledgehammer charge of adrenalin that had sent the beast galloping blindly across the heather and out into a lochan, where it had floundered to a halt and sunk down into the dark water. Now the warm smooth wood of the stock fitted snug to the contour of his cheek, the feel of oiled gunmetal was as familiar as his own skin. He slipped a round into the chamber, closed the bolt and put on the safety catch. Then ran downstairs, pausing to glance round the stables door. Ninian peered out from beneath the blanket. Saw the rifle. Interest sparked in his eyes.

'What are you going to do?'

'Shoot a rabbit for our dinner.'

'How do you shoot a rabbit?'

'You point this at it and pull the trigger.'

'Can I come with you?'

'No. Stay here. Keep warm. I'll not be long.'

'Rabbits are good to eat.'

'Aye. Had one before, have you?'

He shook his head and flopped back on the mattress. His eyes went vacant again.

Still wearing only his coat and boots, John dashed back outside and made straight for the bank at the far end of the drying green. He couldn't do this up close, not with Hector looking at him like that. He climbed a short distance up the grassy bank, then lowered himself on to his stomach and wriggled into position behind a small boulder that he could use to support the rifle. Hector lay still now, thirty yards away, his whole body clearly visible between two trees. A downhill shot, but still as easy as anything John had ever taken. His hands were trembling, his eyes felt tight. He

77

rested the barrel of the rifle on the rock and suddenly he heard it. The distant thud-thud, thud-thud. *Oh no, not now, please.* He forced himself to focus, repeated the mantra: don't rush it, get comfortable, legs splayed, safety catch off, steady the breathing, empty the mind, sight the bead just behind the shoulder, take one deep breath and apply pressure to the trigger in a long, controlled squeeze. The rifle bucked in his hands, the noise rattled his eardrums. He let out a long shuddering breath that seemed to go on for ever.

But the helicopter noise was getting louder. He could see it now through the trees, floating up over the shoulder of the hill beyond the loch. He climbed to his feet, then caught a movement down on the drying green. Hector's head, rising unsteadily from the grass, turning from side to side, ears pricked. He'd missed.

'Oh Jesus.'

He hurled himself to the ground, thrust his hand into his pocket for another round, then remembered that he'd only brought the one. He rose again and raced down the bank and around the green. Hector bellowing now and trying to get up. John dashed across the yard. The helicopter almost over the lodge. He raced up the stairs, pocketed more ammunition and raced down again at breakneck speed. Clattered back across the yard and heard the door opening behind him, small footsteps following. No time to turn around. '*Get back inside! For fucksake!*' He kept running. Like the small footsteps behind. Stopped at the entrance to the drying green, steadied the rifle on the rickety gatepost, drew a bead on the broad grey neck. And fired.

The head dropped. John burst through the gateway, crashed on through the long grass. The helicopter noise seemed to fill the universe. Hector was lying quite still with a neat hole in the neck. No life in the large brown eyes now. John turned, urgently looking for cover. And remembered the footsteps behind him. But now the boy was nowhere to be seen. For a moment his mind seemed to seize. He stood helplessly in the open, bare head lowered, rifle in hand. But nothing happened. No hail of fire. No amplified voice telling him to drop his weapon. He looked up again. The helicopter had moved on, scudding down the loch like a dark dragonfly. Then wheeling upwards across the braes and rocky crags towards a high corrie, still deep in shadow.

Emptied of all feeling, John left the drying green and made his way slowly back to the stables again. The fire was still burning, but Ninian's clothes were gone from the drying place. John removed his and started to dress mechanically, pulling on damp pants, trousers, socks. When he got to his shirt he began to shake. Within moments the shaking had spread through his body, hands, legs, nerves, everything, till he felt like an overstrung mandolin. He stood staring at the fire and felt the rage boil up inside him and spill over. Rage and guilt and shame. He wanted to hurl the rifle to the ground but all his training prevented it. Instead he let out a roar and kicked savagely at the branches to send one flying across the floor in a shower of twigs and bark.

'Bastards!' he roared again. 'Fucking bastards!'

His shoulders heaved and he burst into sobs. He stood in the empty stables and wept for Hector. For the folk of Blackriggs. For his home and his half-made fiddle turned to ash. For Davie. For his mum and dad . . .

In time the weeping calmed him. He went upstairs and fished in the sack for something to eat. He took a bite of oatcake but his mouth was too dry and he couldn't swallow. He pocketed a few squares of chocolate for bait and went outside, where he raised the binoculars and focused them on the heights beyond the loch. There was plenty of activity there. At the foot of the corrie a cordon of men seemed to be encircling an area of broken ground, the helicopter hovering above them. Anything on the ground would have frozen, not daring to move, while the men closed in around it. Whatever it was though, it wasn't John, and that was all that mattered for the moment. Meanwhile he had to find Ninian.

John knew this place well enough. He and his dad had spent many nights in the stables when the 4x4 was laid up and bad weather, or plain exhaustion, had ruled out the twelve-mile hike home. They'd brought up the mattresses and blankets for such occasions. But Ninian wasn't in the stables, so John went round to the front of the house and scrambled through a broken ground-floor window. He found himself in a large empty room containing two dead pigeons, a carpeting of mouse turds and a strong smell of damp and decay. Beyond was the hallway and beyond that the staircase, where the ghostly imprints of departed stags' heads discoloured what remained of the wallpaper.

He started to climb and caught the strains of a plaintive hooting that drifted down from some upper floor. Only to be stopped in his tracks by the explosion that rattled the windows and rolled like thunder around the hills. He hurried up to the landing and looked out through the window. A black cloud mushroomed up from the foot of the corrie. He stood and stared for some time as the smoke slowly drifted out of the bowl in the hillside, a dark stain spreading across the clear blue sky. Then another movement as the helicopter detached itself from the ground and sidled away over a distant ridge.

He left the landing and continued upwards. The hooting had stopped but he could tell where it was coming from now. He hurried along a musty-smelling passage, his boots clattering on the bare boards, and climbed the narrow twisting stairs at the end to find himself on a smaller landing, dimly lit by a cobwebby skylight. Two doors led from the landing. The first opened on a small empty boxroom. The other, from behind which now came a long melancholy call, was locked.

John thumped the door with his fist. 'C'mon now, open up.'

'Hoooooooooo . . .'

'Are you stuck in there?'

'. . . oooooooooo.'

'Is there a key?'

'Hoooo.'

There must have been. The door just had a brass handle and the keyhole of an ordinary mortise lock. There was no latch or snib. No other way he could have shut himself in.

'Have you got the key?'

Silence. Then mumbled words.

'Can't hear you. Speak up.'

Feet shuffled towards the door.

'The horse was lying down.'

'Aye.'

'Did you hurt him?'

'Onl– only a little.'

'Why did you hurt him?'

'I had to shoot him.'

'Shoot him dead?'

'Aye. I'm afraid so.'

'Why's he dead?'

'Like I said. I had to shoot him.'

81

'Why did you have to shoot him?'

'Find the key and let me in. I'll explain.'

'Can't.'

'Why? Haven't you got it?'

'No.'

'But you locked the door with it.'

'Yes.'

'So you've lost it.'

'Ye-es.' Beginning to sound tearful.

'Can you not see it? On the floor or something?' If the room was empty like all the others, it must just be lying there plain as daylight.

Sniff. 'No.' Sniff.

John scratched his chin. 'OK. It's OK. Never you mind. I'll just need to give the door a wee push. You stand out the way now.'

He unslung the rifle and propped it against the wall. Stepped back a pace. Then forward, full force, shoulder leading. There was a loud shudder. A crack appeared in the door. John retreated, rubbing his shoulder. Studied the target for a moment. Then lifted his right leg and with all the power he possessed kicked out at the lock with the heel of his boot. The door flew open with a crash.

The boy was standing in front of him. Barefoot. His features split in a grin of amazement and delight.

'You broke the door!' He started hopping up and down. 'You broke the door! You broke the door!'

But it wasn't just the urchin smile that had John's jaw dropping. It was the contents of the room. Strewn about the place in higgledy-piggledy piles and heaps, shadowy in the light from two grimy attic windows and a small hole in the roof, beneath which the floorboards had started to rot. No wonder Ninian had lost the key. There was furniture

82

and carpets and bits of garden equipment. A washing machine. Two glass cases of stuffed birds and small mammals. A long bookcase full of old volumes. A pair of standard lamps. That was what he could see. Not to mention what was buried beneath it all. Including whatever it was that the boy was now retrieving from beneath a table in the corner over there. And returning with it cradled in his arms to solemnly present to John.

A black fiddle case.

John took it and opened it, heart in mouth. Removed an almost brand-new three-quarter-size fiddle. Strings intact, bow clipped into the lid, rosin cake nestling in its compartment. And, wonder of wonders, a carved mouse crawling around the end of the neck where the scroll should have been. Sharp ears, eyes wide, whiskers bristling.

'Look!' He held it out for Ninian to see. 'The mouse.'

But Ninian wasn't interested. He pushed the fiddle back to John.

'Play.'

John looked at him.

'Play.'

'How did you know?'

Ninian smiled again. He must've peeped into the workshop at the cabin when John wasn't looking.

'Play. Play the violin.'

'Here? Now?'

Ninian nodded.

'Aye . . . OK then, why not? I'll play.'

John rosined the bow, then lifted the fiddle to his chin. It was smaller and lighter than he was used to, but as soon as it came to rest on his shoulder he felt as if something had snapped into place inside him.

He flexed his fingers over the neck, gauging the shorter

83

span. Made a couple of practice strokes with the bow. Then started to play. 'Ours Is The Land', the NLA anthem. Not a great tune, not even a very good one, but catchy all the same.

Ninian watched him for a moment, than started to dance. A few hesitant steps. A twirl here. A hop there. Then more and more until he was jigging about as if nothing could ever stop him. And beaming, a smile of innocent childish pleasure that softened his face, put lustre in the brown eyes.

In the damp and gloom of the lumber room John played the mouse-fiddle and Ninian danced.

And soon, despite everything, the music worked its magic. John began to feel that long, deep connection with the stream his life had sprung from. And before long he was smiling too.

ELEVEN

B y the time Ninian allowed him to stop John was tired
out. But he felt calmer, more grounded, back inside his
own skin again. Ready to tackle anything . . .

Ninian hadn't eaten yet today. The dancing had left him
with a sated look. His eyes were glazed and heavy, pale
cheeks flushed. But he still managed to wolf down the
chocolate as soon as John handed it to him.

'We'll go back to the stables. Get something proper to
eat, eh?'

He shook his head.

'Not hungry?'

'I want to stay here.'

John glanced around the room again. He might as well
stay here as anywhere if it was going to keep him happy.
Anything to keep him happy.

'OK. I'll away and get the food.'

Ninian nodded and turned away towards the piles of
lumber.

When John returned, a few minutes later, he could see
nothing but a head poking up above the arm of a chair.
Ninian had unearthed a basket of child's wooden bricks

and cleared himself a small space on the floor. Now, with great care and deliberation, he was laying them out in what seemed to John like a random arrangement of multi-coloured lines and circles. But it must have had some order and meaning for him. John felt almost envious of this strange and secret way of seeing the world . . .

He placed the games console on the floor beside the boy and handed him an oatcake-and-venison sandwich. 'This is all we've left. Get some decent stuff tomorrow.'

Ninian took the sandwich without looking up and started to eat.

'I've brought your jacket too. Here, put it on. It's cold.'

He nodded and took it. John had turned it inside out so that the charcoal-coloured lining was on the outside now. Just in case. Ninian glanced at it and frowned. Then pulled it on and went back to his bricks.

John returned to the stables to collect the remains of their possessions. He was bending over by the fire, back to the door, when there was a sudden clattering of feet. He stood up, heart starting to pound, but before he could turn round darkness fell on him as someone threw something over his head. Someone else grabbed his arms, pulling them behind his back. And something hard pressed against his temple.

'Not a muscle, OK?' came a voice by his ear.

John stood motionless, hardly daring to breathe as his wrists were tied with rough rope. He was manhandled across the room, then pushed to the floor in a corner.

'What you doing here?' The same voice. Coming down at him now as he crouched on the ground.

'My job,' he muttered through the hood. 'Junior stalker. Work for the Department.'

'ID?'

'In my back pocket.'

He started to get up but a boot pushed him back down again. With his arms pulled tightly behind him, his shoulder muscles were already starting to ache.

'We'll see that in a minute. Why the fire?'

'I got wet. Crawling through a burn.'

He felt claustrophobic under the hood. The coarse material was drawn close to his lips and nostrils, constricting his air passages with every breath.

'So what were you doing in the house? Just now?'

'I-I was looking for something to burn. But . . . the place has been stripped.'

If it was the army, surely they'd already know who he was. So why would they be bothering to question him like this? Wouldn't they just have him bundled up and off to Fort George for proper interrogation? Or easier still, disposed of Blackriggs-style? Down in the loch with a bullet in his head and a couple of big stones in his pockets . . .

'You on your own?'

'Aye.'

'Waiting up here till you're dry. Then what?'

The accent sounded local. Which might mean NLA. Maybe even the cell that downed the helicopter. If only he could see.

'Back home again.'

'Where?'

'Strathdon.'

There was a pause.

'What about the horse?'

'He was . . . he was injured. I had to put him down.'

'Injured?'

'He broke a leg. Full of rabbit holes, that old drying green . . .'

Another pause.

'I think we'll see that ID now.'

Before he could raise himself, arms hauled him to his feet and a hand unbuttoned his hip pocket and removed his wallet. Whose contents would reveal nothing. An ancient sprig of white heather, pressed flat, his bank card and a couple of small banknotes, a dog-eared photo of Davie and one of him and Hector up the hill, and the ID card.

Hands pressed him down to the floor again.

'OK.' A pause. 'So where's your rifle?'

'Is it . . . is it not here?'

'No.'

'Must've put it down in the – uh . . .'

A boot caught him in the ribs. Drove the breath out of him.

'We've been watching you.'

The pain spread round his back and down his spine. 'OK,' he gasped. 'It's in the house. Up in the—'

'Search the place. Top to bottom.'

Feet began to move out of the stables.

'No! Wait . . . !'

The feet halted.

'I've . . . I've a young lad with me. Handicapped. He'll throw a fit if you go charging in on him. God's honest. Let me come with you.'

He started struggling to his feet, but the boot pushed him down again.

'Search the house. Carefully.'

The feet departed.

'So who's the lad?'

'My wee cousin.'

'What's he doing here? If he's handicapped?'

88

'It's not physical. I mean . . . he just likes to come out the hill with me . . . sometimes . . . does him good.'

'What's wrong with him?'

'He's . . . kind of slow. And he's scared of strangers. Specially anyone in uniform.'

This provoked no response.

'He'll not like seeing me like this either. Not with this over my head. He'll go mental. I mean, is there any chance . . . ?'

He tensed, half-expecting another blow to the ribs. And instead heard a high-pitched shriek ring across the stable yard.

'Get him in here quick and close the door,' barked the unseen voice. The noise increased and fingers fumbled to release the fastening of his hood. Then he could see. And feel his stomach muscles unclench as he took in the two figures that stood before him, their faces concealed by fine-knit black balaclavas. A further two, similarly disguised, were bundling Ninian through the stables door. A struggling, howling Ninian who had the fiddle clenched firmly in one fist and was striving with all his might to batter his captors with it.

'We couldn't get it off him,' said the shorter of the two apologetically.

'It's OK,' said the balaclava nearest John. 'Let him go.' He turned to John. 'Calm him down.'

As one of his captors turned to close the stables door and the other went to prop John's rifle against the wall, Ninian dropped the fiddle to the floor with a clatter and a dull twang of strings. He closed his eyes, stuffed his knuckles into his mouth and rocked back and forth on his heels, shuddering and sobbing.

'I'll need my hands free,' said John urgently, turning to

present his back. The second man stepped forward and untied his wrists.

John went to Ninian and drew him into a firm embrace. 'There, there. It's OK, it's OK. I'm here.' Still sobbing, Ninian put up a token resistance, then John felt the tension going out of the small body as it slumped against his own. Together they stood in the centre of the empty stables. Bruised fiddle at their feet. The four balaclavas looking uncertainly on. As if there was some elemental quality in Ninian's distress that unsettled even the most hardened of adult hearts.

'I thought you might be army . . .' said John, breaking the silence. Taking in the dark jeans, weatherproofs and walking boots. They could have been poachers, were it not for the weapons. A couple of semi-automatic rifles. Big nasty-looking things with night-sights. And propped against the wall a hand-held mortar. '. . . so I was being careful – what I said, like.'

'Why so?' asked the leading balaclava.

At the sound of his voice Ninian looked up. Saw the masked features and shrieked again. Struggled to break free of John's arms.

'Wheesht, laddie. They'll not hurt you.' John did his best to soothe him. But Ninian continued to wriggle and squirm. Making sounds that alternated between wail and whimper.

John glanced up. 'Any chance you could take them off? The hoods?'

The leader shook his head impatiently.

John remembered the Martian. 'There's a wee electronic games thing up in the attic – with the rest of the stuff. That would maybe do the trick . . .'

The leader turned and nodded to a wiry-looking young

man whose bespectacled eyes gazed intensely through the holes in the balaclava. He seemed about John's age, perhaps a year older.

'Can I sit down again?' John asked.

'Yes.'

Drawing Ninian with him, he returned to the corner, lowered himself to the ground and took a reluctant Ninian on to his lap. Where he buried his face once more in John's chest and made a low groaning noise.

'The army,' resumed the leader. 'You were saying . . .'

John wondered how much to tell them. Now that he was reasonably confident they were NLA, it seemed likely that the more they knew the better.

'The soldiers are after me. I saw the massacre, see. At Blackriggs.'

'Massacre?'

'Aye.'

The eyes narrowed.

'You . . . you don't know about it?'

'No.'

'You're kidding me on . . .'

A firm shake of the head.

John's heart began to pound. Could he be the only person in the world, apart from the soldiers, to know about something so . . . so awful? Surely someone, the NLA of all people, must have heard something by now. He let out a long breath.

'Then I'd best tell you.'

The leader nodded.

'It was like a couple of days ago . . . the army turned up at Blackriggs – down the glen there, on the way to Strathdon.' He gestured vaguely. 'Saturday, I think – though I'm losing track of time. It's Monday now?'

'Tuesday.'

'They landed in the field behind the hotel. I reckon they were looking for whoever shot down that helicopter . . .' He paused, but the masked features gave nothing away. 'It started as a house-to-house. But then there was some kind of argument. With one of the local folk. And the whole thing suddenly fell apart . . . the army lads just went mental. Berserk.' His hands were starting to tremble again. 'There were some of the soldiers . . . who looked kind of foreign . . . darker skins . . . I don't know . . .'

'And you saw this?'

'Aye. I was on my way down with a load of logs. The helicopter landed when I was still in the wood. I watched from the trees with binoculars. The whole thing.' His breathing was coming fast and shallow as three pairs of eyes looked down at him.

At this moment the young man returned with the fertiliser sack into which he'd stuffed everything in sight, including the fiddle bow. John steadied his breathing as the leader upended the sack on the floor and scrutinised the contents. Then picked up the console and earphones and passed them to John.

'Here, we've got the game.' He prised Ninian out of his lap and turned him round to face the wall so that they were sitting back to back. 'You have a wee play now. While I talk with these folk. OK?'

Ninian continued to groan for a few moments. Then bent forward and began to fiddle with the console. Thin music scratched at the silence.

'Maybe you could use the earphones, eh?'

Ninian said nothing, but plugged in the phones and the music stopped.

'Tell me what you saw,' said the leader.

John began to speak but at once his mouth ran dry. His tongue stuck to his palate and he faltered. 'I'm . . . I'm not sure if I can . . .'

'Take your time.'

He steeled himself. After a few moments the words began to flow. And soon he couldn't stop them. For more than half an hour he spoke and when at last he stopped the room was utterly silent. The leader stared down at him with no attempt to conceal his shock. The young man couldn't meet John's eye. The other two simply gazed at him. Even Ninian sensed the charge in the air. He had stopped playing the game and was sitting still and silent, facing the wall.

The leader let out a long breath and shook his head. 'This changes everything.'

John nodded weakly. Dabbed at his eyes. He was drained of all feeling.

'How many . . . um . . .' The leader glanced at Ninian, who'd resumed his game. 'How many fatalities?'

'I didn't really count. Twenty-plus . . . as far as I know, everyone who was there . . . except –' John gestured over his shoulder. 'He's not really who I said he is. Didn't want to let on till I was sure it was OK – knew that you weren't army. I found him there. Afterwards. Hiding.'

'So who is he?'

'He can't tell me.' He screwed a finger at his temple and felt ashamed by the gesture. 'And . . . you've heard nothing about this? Nothing at all?'

'No,' replied the leader. 'But they'd have plans for dealing with something like this. They'd just seal the whole place off.'

'Searching the surrounding area – that's what they said on the news,' John said bitterly. 'Suspects taken in for questioning.'

93

'Roadblocks. Phones down. Local cellnets disabled. That's what they'd do. Easy enough to quarantine the place for a few days while they tidy up.'

'I think they've done that already,' replied John, recalling the digger.

'But you saw the . . . evidence?'

'Oh aye.' His voice felt far away, as if it didn't belong to him. 'Plenty evidence.'

'And you'd know where to find it?'

'If they've not moved it.'

'Foreign-looking, you said? The soldiers?'

'Some of them.'

'So it'll be true then.' The taller of Ninian's two captors spoke for the first time.

'What?'

'Stories we bin gettin'. That some of oor sodger boys'll no gang against their ain folk. They've had tae draft in mercenaries from eastern Europe or some place.'

'There was a Scots boy in charge,' said John.

'There would have been.' The leader spoke again. 'He lost it though. Couldn't control them . . .'

'And you think they saw you?'

'I'm not sure. But I think so. They came to my place anyway. In the wee hours of yesterday morning. We got out in time, me and Ninian. I think they burned the house . . .'

'You and me and Hector,' piped up a voice.

The leader's eyebrows lifted.

'The pony.'

'Hector loved you,' came the voice again. Head still bent over the console, thumbs flipping away. 'So you had to shoot him.' Quite matter-of-fact. As if in the mysterious workings of Ninian's mind, this was the natural order of things.

The leader was now eyeing the small figure with undisguised curiosity.

'Local?' he asked.

'Visiting. Staying with Auntie, weren't you?'

Ninian nodded.

The leader looked at John.

'I don't know her name,' John replied. 'Moved in fairly recently, I think. Lived in one of the new bungalows.'

'Lived?'

John nodded.

'Auntie went shopping,' offered Ninian.

The leader turned to the two older men.

'Check outside. Make sure they haven't left anyone up at the peat hags.' He glanced at John. 'We'd ammunition buried up there. Someone must have tipped them off.' He shook his head. 'This . . . this – Blackriggs . . . this is something else. We'll need to get you somewhere safe. We'll leave the minute it's dark. And we'll have to get this news to the Tod.'

TWELVE

John felt suddenly worn out by telling his story, by the whole business with Hector, by Ninian, by everything that had happened in the last four days. For the first time since he'd watched the soldiers jump from the helicopter at Blackriggs, it felt as if he could safely let down his guard. He would much rather it had been Ferg, but at least these boys were going to take charge now and he wasn't going to have to make any more decisions. And they'd probably be able to make contact with his dad for him.

Beside him, Ninian continued to play with the game. John leaned back against the wall and closed his eyes.

The Tod . . . the fox.

A slight movement of the bracken on a distant hillside. A shadow sliding along the edge of a loch. That was how one of the papers had described him. Some folk said it was Rab Duncan, a former SAS major and local politician, descendant of generations of Highland farmers and one of the authorities' most vociferous opponents, who not so long ago had departed for Canada in order, so he declared, to take care of family interests. Some folk, including the news report John had seen the other night, said it was

Struan Fraser, expatriate billionaire, entrepreneur and financier, relieved by the One Acre Act of ancient family lands he'd restored to Fraser hands for the first time in almost two centuries. And Fraser's wife, visiting from Switzerland, had been tragically killed in the Inverness riots. Some fancied it was Der Fuchs, the notorious former leader of a southern Austrian separatist faction and a fanatical admirer of the works of Sir Walter Scott, who had been persuaded, or maybe hired, by the NLA to run their campaign. Others said it was no single person but a group of disgruntled ex-lairds, businessmen and army officers meeting in Edinburgh or London . . .

Say it *was* Struan Fraser, thought John. Why would a billionaire want to go to ground like a fox and live in hiding? He didn't get it. Because of the land he'd had taken from him? It seemed hard to imagine. To avenge the death of his wife? That was maybe a bit easier to understand. The Inverness riots had shocked everyone in Scotland and beyond. A black, black day for the Highlands, Ferg had said. And it wasn't hard for John to see the truth in that now.

They'd begun as a simple protest, the riots. A protest over the jailing of the Venison Six. Six ordinary folk – though now they'd become heroes – who'd refused to pay the fines handed down to them for taking matters into their own hands and shooting the marauding deer that were ruining their gardens because the Department had let the deer fences fall down. But people's anger and frustration had erupted into violence and the protest had got quickly out of hand. Forty-eight hours later parts of Inverness were still ablaze, the army was on the streets and eleven lives had been lost.

John had been in the Blackriggs store the next day, when

a van driver had come in and started chatting up the lass at the checkout, telling her how he'd been caught up in the rioting. 'Real scary it was,' he said, 'niver seen sae many pissed-off folk in one place in ma life.' Trying to impress her, John guessed. 'Oot for blood they were,' he went on. 'And no jist for jailin' the Six. No way, man. Shoutin' and rantin' aboot everythin'. No enough jobs. Bein' ignored. Whole place run by bastards fae the Department. Bent bastards. Or jist plain fuckin' stupid. Who dinnae unnerstand the Hielans and dinnae care . . . You name it, someone wis bawlin' on aboot it. And the crowd wis startin' tae go mental. Ready tae tear the place apart. You could see the polis wis shittin' bricks. Couldnae handle it at a'. Nae wunner they ended up bringin' in the sodgers . . .'

A packet of sandwiches landed by John's feet.

'Here, something to eat.'

John glanced up to thank the leader but he looked away. Since telling them about what happened at Blackriggs, John had noticed that none of them was able to meet his eye. It was almost as if they were afraid he was contagious.

He opened the packet, passed a sandwich to Ninian and took a bite of one himself. Venison again. It was a miracle, he sometimes thought, that he hadn't sprouted a set of horns.

The stables door crashed open.

'Army! Coming up the hill road. Three trucks.'

The leader was on his feet at once. 'How long?'

'Ten minutes. Fifteen at the most.'

He glanced outside. 'Into the wood, then.' He looked at John. 'Now.'

John was getting to his feet. 'We have to go,' he said to Ninian, trying to keep his voice level. 'Turn off the game. OK?'

Ninian looked up at him and for a moment John thought he was going to protest. But he nodded, removed the earphones and pocketed the console.

John helped him to his feet and stooped to pick up the sack. As they crossed the room his eye fell on the fiddle, still lying where Ninian had dropped it. He hesitated, then reached down and stuffed it in the sack alongside the bow.

'You'd better have this too,' said the leader as John reached the door, handing him his rifle. 'Just in case.'

He slung it over his shoulder and, towing Ninian by the hand, left the stables.

The sky was darkening to the east now and the air was growing chill again. The trucks were approaching the end of the loch, where for the time being they would be able to see only the front of the lodge. But in a few more minutes they would stop and there would be soldiers all over the place.

John and Ninian followed the four men out of the stable yard and round the back, past the drying green. The leader broke into a sprint.

'Time for a bit of a race, eh?' said John.

Ninian's eyes lit up. 'I can win races.'

'Good lad.'

Ninian had no trouble keeping up with him, weighed down as John was by the sack and rifle. Close on the heels of the men, they panted across fifty yards of open brackeny hillside between the drying green and the start of the big wood that ran along the loch-side and sheltered the lodge from the west. Or had once sheltered it before the Muckle Blaw, the great storm, of six years ago, that had cut a vast swathe across the Highlands, splintering every tree from Mallaig to Aberdeen, reducing thousands of hectares of timber to matchwood. Still uncleared by the Department, it was now an open graveyard of bleached silvery corpses.

The leader clambered over a large trunk, naked of its bark, then paused and glanced back as John and Ninian scrambled across the first few yards of brushwood and tangled, shattered limbs. Boots were starting to tramp around the lodge. Voices ringing out across the hillside.

'We won.' John whispered.

'Did we?' Bright eyes.

'Aye. Now, we'll just need to get ourselves further in here. Quietly, eh? Quiet as the wee mouse on the fiddle.'

Ninian nodded. Put his fingers solemnly to his lips and fell in behind as John, following the example of the four men, set off at a creep. Knees bent, heads down, slithering low over obstacles and under fallen trunks. Pausing every now and then to listen. The soldiers were still at the lodge, searching it presumably, though whether it was for him or the rebel boys, John had no idea. He pressed on, feeling the need to bury himself deep in the heart of this dry bony wilderness, to go to ground like the Tod until the danger was past. But it was exhausting work with rifle in one hand, sack in the other, and they were starting to fall behind the men. Five minutes later John paused again. The men had disappeared from view, though he could still hear a faint rustling and crackling not far in front. And now the soldiers sounded closer, as if maybe they were starting to move out along the hillside or the shore of the loch. Up ahead a medium-sized tree had fallen across the upended roots of a much bigger one. It looked from here as if there was a kind of shelter in the hollow where the roots had once been. He moved on and crouched down to peer in. Yes. There was a deep cavity beneath the roots. They could get in there and burrow down out of sight if necessary.

He turned round to urge Ninian on. And froze.

The boy was picking his way through the tangle of brushwood and undergrowth towards the nearby trunk of another fallen tree.

Upon which, tufted ears pricked, tail swishing, eyes ablaze with curiosity and suspicion, stood a large lynx.

THIRTEEN

'Ninian,' John hissed.

The lynx looked up. It seemed thin. The mottled tawny coat was lacklustre and loose-hanging at the ribs. There was matted fur and a large dark mark at the base of its neck, an open wound or sore of some kind. But still no mistaking the power in the muscular hindquarters and forelegs, the large paws planted squarely on the naked tree trunk.

'Ninian!' he hissed again. But the boy paid no attention and kept moving towards it in silent fascination till he was almost within springing distance. Where he held out his hand as if to coax a kitten from a tree.

Eyes unwavering, the lynx slowly lowered itself to a crouch, belly brushing the trunk, and tilted its elfin ears forward. John had never come across a lynx before but he'd heard enough about them since they started escaping. He knew that they were solitary, mainly nocturnal and shy of humans. That the biggest thing they would take under normal circumstances was a sheep or a roe deer. But this one was hurt and hungry and unblinkingly eyeing the advance of what might prove to be either a threat or a meal. Or both.

There was a staccato exchange of voices not far off. The sound of feet running. The black-tufted ears twitched, yellow eyes slid sideways. But only for an instant. John could almost feel the beast's concentration, its consummate control. Every atom of its being focused on the figure before it. Body perfectly poised to spring.

John glanced around. There was enough fallen timber about to screen them from beyond so long as they kept still and quiet. But any sudden movement or sound would betray them to the soldiers at once. Not only them but the NLA unit too, most likely. He sensed anyway that the beast was in far too unpredictable a state for him to risk trying to distract it or drive it away. Despite which, he couldn't stop himself from very slowly lowering the sack to the ground and unshouldering the rifle. Then teasing back the bolt and silently sliding in a round.

Ninian halted. Under the steady gaze of the lynx he began to fish in his jacket pocket. John stood transfixed as the arm went out again, palm upturned, bearing the uneaten venison sandwich.

'Ninian!' He called out in a whisper. 'You can't feed it. It won't –'

The boy turned his head.

Startled by the sudden movement, the lynx arched its back and hissed.

There were voices at the edge of the wood now, only a couple of hundred yards away.

Ninian turned back towards the lynx, stared at it for a short moment, then started to edge away.

The lynx was still arched like a bow, teeth bared, the heavy ruff at its neck bristling.

With damp palms John raised the rifle to his shoulder as slowly and gently as he could. Praying he wouldn't have to fire.

Ninian was frightened now. He was starting to whimper and flap his hands. Stepping backwards through the rustling ground cover.

The lynx took a pace forward along the trunk. Then sank to the crouch again.

Ninian turned to run. Tripped and tumbled down. As the lynx gathered itself to spring.

And John fired.

The report was deafening within the confine of the fallen trees. The tawny body crashed into the brushwood. One paw twitched and fell still. Ears ringing, John kicked the sack down into the shelter of the upended roots and jumped after it, hauling Ninian with him. A burst of semi-automatic fire crackled out and bullets went spitting and thudding into the timber around them.

It was a moment before John realised that they weren't coming from the direction of the lodge or the loch, but from somewhere not far ahead, within the wood, where the nervous rebel unit must have thought they were under attack. And towards which the soldiers' fire was now directed, a hail of bullets that sent John cowering down into the earth with the whimpering boy in his arms. Muttering words of reassurance he didn't feel.

There was a lot of shouting now and running feet. A short burst of return fire from within the wood. Then another fusillade from the soldiers. A deadly storm of metal. Shredding timber, withering dead branches, ripping through the undergrowth. Ninian was now shaking with terror and starting to wail. 'There, there,' John murmured. 'Wheesht now. It's OK, so it is.' He kept muttering and humming tunes and stroking the dark curls. As a high hysterical shrieking erupted from the undergrowth ahead. Almost animal. Worse than the bullets. It went right through John, jarring every nerve, scouring his brain, going on and on. Then, as suddenly as if a switch had been thrown, it stopped and all was quiet. Everyone seemed to be waiting. John with his face pressed to the cold damp earth. Ninian shivering and twitching in his arms.

After a while voices rang out again. Boots started to crunch through brushwood. Soldiers coming in to inspect their handiwork and search for survivors.

John's heart lurched as he remembered the lynx, lying out there for anyone to see.

'Listen,' he whispered, 'we're going to have to play a wee game. Like hide-and-seek, eh? You just bide here a minute. I'll be right back.'

Ninian stirred and sniffed. But stayed put as John released his grasp, sensing the urgency in his voice.

Breathing fast, John crept out of the shelter and tiptoed over to where the tawny corpse had settled down into the brushwood. It was obvious at once that dragging it would make too much noise. He crouched down and put one arm around it, then the other. Lifted it up as gently as possible, surprised at how light it was. It weighed much less than the boy. A couple of stone, he guessed, three at the outside. He crept back to the roots of the tree and rolled the corpse into the hollow, then tumbled in after and flopped down on top of it. It was soft and warm and musky-smelling. Not rank like a fox but woodier, earthier. Ninian stared at it wide-eyed. Then reached out and hesitantly touched the tip of one ear.

'You shot the tiger,' he whispered.

'It's a lynx.'

'But you shot it?'

'Aye.'

'Shot it dead? Like Hector the horse?'

'Aye.'

'Why did you shoot it?'

'Because I thought it was going to hurt you.'

'But it didn't.'

'No, it –'

Footsteps were approaching. John put his finger to the boy's lips. Whispered in his ear, 'You've to keep really still now.'

The tramping boots were close. Down at ground level the crackle of brushwood seemed almost deafening. John could see nothing. All he could do was clasp the boy to him and pray they were well enough concealed in the earthy den with its veil of roots. The footsteps halted; there was a cough and the steady patter of urine on the ground. Hiss of a zip, clearing of a throat. Then a grunt and a loud thud and a shower of earth from the quivering roots. John stifled a gasp as a branch poked him sharply in the back. The tree above him shuddered under the weight of a man who stood there bouncing gently just above their heads.

John held his breath and willed Ninian to hold his. Which he did for a while, then started to wriggle. John's hand crept round to cover his mouth as the man jumped to the ground beyond and moved off.

For another ten minutes they lay still. John alternately cajoling Ninian with the promise of chocolate, threatening him with detection. And Ninian complied. Not so daft that he couldn't sense real danger. Anyway, he was fascinated by the lynx, or what he could see of it beneath John. He kept reaching out and touching it, then pulling his hand away quickly in case it might bite him. With its belly.

Eventually there was the sound of voices moving out of the wood and on to the open ground at the loch-side. John scrambled out from beneath the roots and crept forward to peer through a screen of branches. There was a group of about a dozen soldiers standing around something on the ground. He pulled out the binoculars. The light was going but he could make out four bodies lying on the grass.

Then the soldiers were starting to move off towards the lodge, dragging the rebels with them, four men to a corpse.

John crept back to the edge of the hollow and sat down heavily, resting his head in trembling hands, his mind a fog of shock and anxiety and guilt. Just when he'd thought it was safe to let go . . . And now four men dead because of him, one of them scarcely older than he was. He felt like screaming. How much longer was this going to go on? And what the hell was he to do next? 'Oh Dad, Dad,' he said, 'please come to the cave. I don't think I can take much more of this.'

At the sound of his voice, Ninian glanced up. He seemed to have overcome his fear of the lynx. He was lying on the earth beside it, stroking it, patting it, muttering to it. He held John's eye for a moment, then looked down again.

John took a deep breath, tried to compose himself. They'd better wait a bit in case the soldiers had left someone on guard in here. The light was going fast now. It would be dark soon. Ninian was completely absorbed in his dialogue with the dead beast. Was it only that morning he'd chased him into the loch? Christ, it seemed like a week ago. He ran his hand over his chin, felt the stubble. When did he last shave? The morning after the massacre. Three days ago. Soon he'd be able to measure the days of this vagabond existence by the growth of his beard.

He heard the rumble of departing trucks and stood up

again. The loch was now no more than a dull glint in the twilight. The fallen trees around him a vague chaos of pale shapes.

'It's time to go, laddie.'

Ninian looked up.

'We need to get going.'

A moment's hesitation. 'I want to take the tiger.'

'Take it with us?'

'With us.'

'Oh no, laddie. Can't take the tiger.'

'I want to.'

'We can't. How'm I going to carr –' He stopped, remembering the futility of logic.

'I want to take it. The tiger.' Voice growing querulous.

'Tell you what. You can take a paw. Lucky charm, eh?'

They could do with some of that and no mistake.

'The tiger's paw?'

'Aye.'

Before Ninian could say anything John climbed back down into the hollow, took out his knife and under the boy's curious gaze proceeded to hack off a front paw. It was as big as his fist, with its coarse tawny fur and claws, the hairy soles and rough leathery pads made for silent climbing and snow-walking. He tidied up the loose sinews and threads of fleshy tissue. Rubbed earth on to the bloody end just in case the lad was squeamish and handed it to him. But he wasn't squeamish. Just fascinated. And delighted. He held it in cupped hands and stared and stared, the trace of a smile playing about the soft features. John looked on, feeling pleased with himself. He was getting the hang of this, little by little. He bent forward and slid the blade of the knife into the earth two or three times to clean it. Then closed it and pocketed it.

'Better than the whole tiger, eh?'

Ninian looked up at him.

'You can put it in your pocket.'

He shook his head.

John shouldered the rifle. Grasped the sack. 'Well, come on now.'

Holding the paw before him as if it was a holy relic, Ninian climbed out of the hollow.

They set off in darkness through the broken wood.

FOURTEEN

The darkness lessened as they emerged from the wood on to the open hillside. Above, the clouds were beginning to shift. A handful of stars appeared. Ahead lay the climb for the cave.

They'd gone only a short distance when Ninian stopped and began whining to himself. John squatted down beside him and asked what the matter was.

'My thing,' he answered tearfully.

'What thing?'

He snivelled and wrung his hands. 'My thing.'

'I don't know what you mean.'

'My good thing.' Petulant as well as tearful now.

'You mean the paw?'

Nodded his head.

'You didn't drop it?'

Silence.

'Oh, Ninian. When? When did you drop it?' Pointless question. Because he wouldn't know and even if he did, the heather was so deep there'd not be the slightest chance of finding it. Not even in broad daylight.

Now Ninian was whining insistently and hunching in on himself as if a hostile world was pressing up against him.

'I'll see if I can find it.'

John walked back towards the trees, not even troubling to look at the darkened ground. He knew he'd have to come up with something to replace it. A walking stick maybe. Find him a nice straight one and pray it would distract him. He stopped where they climbed over the remains of the fence at the edge of the wood and peered into the shadowy tangle of timber beyond. He'd have to get in there and rummage about. He glanced down to avoid getting his feet snared in the fallen fence wire and there it was. A small dark shape. Lying on the grass at the foot of a rotten fencepost.

Perhaps it really was a lucky charm. Perhaps the lynx was hovering right there in the darkness beside him, saying, *No hard feelings, John. Did what you had to, eh? So you just let my old paw keep you safe now.*

Perhaps he was going crazy . . .

But he strode almost jauntily back up the hillside.

Ninian stopped whining. Snatched the paw and clasped it to his breast.

'Tell you what we'll do. Make it so you can't lose it again, eh?'

He nodded.

'I'll need the string from your jacket.'

Another nod.

John took out his knife and cut off the toggle from one end of the drawstring in the hem of the jacket. Then pulled out the string.

'Give it here. Just for a minute.'

A reluctant hand reached out.

John took the paw and with the point of the knife drilled

a hole through the soft fleshy matter between two bones. Then threaded the drawstring through the hole, tied the ends together and hung the loop around the boy's neck. The paw dangled at his chest.

'Off we go.'

They started off up the hill again. Ninian followed closely in John's footsteps, panting as he went, each step a battle with the deep heather. There was an old sheep track away to the left – not that there'd been any sheep up here for a few years, but the deer still used it. Shadows drifted across the hillside as the cloud dispersed. Even now, anxious and exhausted as he was, a part of him still thrilled to be out here in this bleak and unforgiving wilderness, especially at night with all his senses on alert . . .

Here was the track now. An indentation in the heather, pocked with deer slots. Ninian was still plodding along behind him, eyes fixed on the paw as it swung at his breast.

'Good lad. Easier going now. We'll be at the cave soon. Take a breather there.'

A light caught John's eye. Brighter than the stars and closer. Moving steadily across the night sky. Moments later the sound reached him, making his heart race. A second light appeared a little way behind the first one. Out hunting in pairs, it seemed. Though not coming this way at the moment. John quickened his pace.

Half an hour later they reached the foot of the crags where, behind a large boulder, the mouth of the cave gaped. John paused on the threshold, recovering his breath as Ninian wandered on ahead, untroubled by the darkness, which swallowed him up at once. John stared after him for a few moments, feeling the sweat start to freeze on his skin, then ducked in, unslung the rifle and slumped down on the granite floor. He had forgotten how big it was, this rocky

112

chamber in the side of the hill. Big and empty and still. Sort of place that could make you want to get down on your knees if you were the praying kind . . .

Beyond, in the dark throat of the cavern, he could hear Ninian scuffling around.

Then the scuffling stopped.

Footsteps followed and he appeared at John's elbow.

'All sticky,' he said, holding out his right hand.

It glistened faintly in the starlight that penetrated the cave mouth.

'Have you cut yourself?'

Ninian shook his head, looking down at his palm in puzzlement. John touched a fingertip to it. Then licked. And stifled a grunt of surprise.

'Is there someone back there?' he whispered.

'Me.'

'Just you? No one else?'

'Me.'

'Sure now?' He felt in the sack for the flashlight. Then reached quietly for the rifle.

Ninian nodded.

'Show me, then. Show me the sticky.'

Ninian squared his shoulders and set off into the darkness again. John followed, shielding the flashlight beam with his hand. It was almost a dozen paces before the ceiling at last started to slant and he had to lower his head. Another few paces to where Ninian hunkered down in a corner. On the uneven rock at his feet were bulky shapes, indistinct in the shadows. John played the beam on them. Backpacks and bedrolls. A camping stove and mess tins. And a small viscous pool of something darker than the surrounding darkness, in which glinted fragments of glass.

Ninian put his finger into the pool.

'Mind the glass now,' said John.

Ninian removed his finger. Licked it and grinned.

'Sweet,' he said.

John nodded. Honey. This must have belonged to the NLA boys.

He opened the first backpack and played the flashlight on its contents. A thick woollen jumper, a water bottle and half a dozen clips of ammunition. He put it aside and picked up the second pack, which was much heavier. He prised open the neck, heart suddenly pounding as he glimpsed the metallic fins of a mortar round. He closed it again at once and, hardly daring to breathe, lowered it to the ground. He turned to the third and last which had in it a pair of wire cutters, an electronic palm reader, a spare pair of socks, a rectangular plastic container that rattled promisingly and, attached to an empty key ring, a miniature photograph frame holding a thumbnail-sized picture of the serious young man with his arm round the shoulder of a plain, dark-haired young woman, who smiled uncertainly at the camera. John looked at it for a long time. Try as he might, his mind wouldn't let him connect the studious face in the picture with the body the soldiers had dragged away from the wood.

He hesitated over the container, but hunger got the better of him. He lifted it out, opened it and winced at the sight of two peppermint tea bags, a tub of yoghurt, a spoon and an individual-sized glass jar of heather honey.

Beside the backpacks, four bedrolls were stacked against the cave wall, and in the shadows beyond them some cartons which turned out to be nothing but the empty packaging from four instant meals. Whatever other provisions there may have been, they must have been carrying them with them.

114

John fetched the water bottle from the first pack. Shook it and sighed.

'Peppermint tea. Warm us up at least, eh?'

He lit the stove. Fetched a mess tin and wiped the remains of the gravy from it with one of the young man's clean socks. Then filled it with water and placed it on the flame.

'Fancy some yoghurt? Can't stand it myself.'

'Strawberry yoghurt?'

John shook his head. 'Just ordinary. But you could put honey in it, maybe? Honey and yoghurt . . .'

Ninian nodded and took the container from John, then busied himself with the honey jar, spoon and yoghurt pot. John dropped both tea bags into the mess tin and waited for the water to boil.

Once the brew was ready he left the stove burning. Its blue flame threw small nervous shadows on the cave wall. He grasped one corner of the mess tin with a sock and tried to sip the scalding liquid without burning his lips on the metal. The tea tasted thin and sharp and was faintly flavoured with tandoori chicken, which a spoonful of honey did little to improve. He reached into the sack for the remains of an oatcake and chewed slowly.

'Is this camping?' asked Ninian, looking up from the yoghurt pot.

John smiled. 'Kind of. Been camping, have you?'

He nodded gravely. 'In the forest. With Dad.' His eyes strayed to the backpacks and bedrolls. 'The people . . . with the black faces. Are they coming back?'

John shook his head.

'I didn't like them.'

'I know you didn't.'

'Are they bad people?'

'Well . . . depends whose side –'

'Did the soldiers have to shoot them?'

'I suppose you could say that . . .'

The answer seemed to satisfy Ninian. He looked down and dipped the spoon into the yoghurt.

What could he possibly be making of all this? John wondered. Trapped in his own weird little world. What sort of chaos was there inside his head? Was it maybe like some mad version of Davie and his colours? Or was there maybe no chaos at all? Was it possible that his world had all the order he needed? Black or white, hot or cold, was or wasn't, liked or didn't like. No complicated emotions, no shades of grey. Perhaps John was the one who lived with the chaos. John and everyone else who inhabited the world of so-called normality, where soldiers could go on the rampage for no obvious reason and murder everyone in a village . . .

At last he could feel the warmth of the tea spreading through his body, easing the tension in his limbs. He stared into the darkness for some time, thinking hard. Might Ferg come tonight? There was no telling. If he knew the soldiers had been up at the lodge, he probably wouldn't risk it. John tried to ignore the sinking feeling, focused on his breath clouding in front of him, mingling with the steam from the mess tin. They couldn't spend the night here anyway; it was too cold. And if they did, they'd have to spend tomorrow here as well, unable to move during daylight. Something was starting to tell him to get off these hills, that sooner or later they'd turn into a trap. The NLA boys had found him easily enough, and it was only luck that the soldiers hadn't too. And then there were – he glanced at the shadowy pile of rebel equipment beside him and shivered – these dead men's things. He didn't want to have to spend the night in here with all that.

'We'll go on tonight,' he said to Ninian. 'It'll be too cold to stay here. We'll get over the hill to Aviemore. My Auntie Morag lives there, my dad's sister. She'll help us. I'll leave my dad a message, and we'll be able to get in touch with him once we're at her place. We'll leave soon. D'you want the game?'

Ninian ignored him. He reached into the sack for an oatcake and started crumbling it into the yoghurt pot.

John picked up one of the pieces of broken glass and swivelled round to face the cave wall. He thought for a moment, then at eye level scratched *John*, followed by a heart with an arrow through it, then *Morag*. His dad would figure that out easily enough. Ferg knew every inch of this cave and would straightaway spot anything new or unusual. All the same, John spat on his finger for safety and rubbed it along the rock floor till the spit gathered a sticky glob of dirt and dust which he worked into the etch marks so they wouldn't appear too fresh.

As he turned back to face the cave again he noticed the palm reader lying where he'd left it on top of the young rebel's pack. He reached across for it and turned it on. A dim glow lit the screen and characters swam up to fill the bookmarked page. His eye drifted across them and he was surprised to find that what he read seemed familiar. He reached for the control with his index finger, scrolled back to the title page and nodded to himself. *Consider the Lilies.* They'd read it at school. The story of an old woman being evicted from her cottage during the Highland Clearances by Patrick Sellar, the Duke of Sutherland's hated factor. It was very poetic, and he hadn't understood all of it, but he'd felt the old woman's sadness and bewilderment right

117

enough. Especially when she was betrayed by the person she'd entrusted with her mortal soul, the minister. Though in the end she'd proved to be a tough old bird who stood her ground and tried not be swayed by the false voices all around her, and did her best to conquer her fears and loneliness . . .

Suddenly the cave filled with an unearthly noise that had him scrambling to his feet and knocking over the stove, which went out, plunging him into darkness. The noise went on as he fumbled for the flashlight, an eerie screeching and wailing. He found the flashlight, turned it on and played the beam away from him, into the centre of the cave, to where Ninian had dragged the sack, taken out the fiddle and was now sitting cross-legged in the darkness. Sawing away at the strings with the untightened bow and singing to himself.

As the beam lit him he glanced up briefly, then laid down the bow and started to finger the strings. Still singing.

Plink. Plunk. Hooeeeohwowow.

For a long moment John stared at him. Comically solemn with the dark curly head bent over the fiddle. Jug-handle ears sticking out. Stubby fingers plucking away like something from some trolls' orchestra.

Then John burst out laughing and laughed till the cavern roof rang.

FIFTEEN

Three times during the night Ninian sat down and refused to go any further. But the frost was tightening its grip on the empty hills and within minutes he began to shiver. Each time John coaxed him to his feet and towed him by the hand until he found his own plodding pace again as they followed the old ways beside whispering burns and into the shadows of looming corries. Past dark ice-rimmed lochans and along starlit ridges. A chill wilderness where nothing moved. Not a deer. Not a hare. Not even a fox.

Shortly before dawn John caught sight of what looked like tilting poles and raised horizontal wheels ahead. In the dim light they reminded him of something he had once been shown in an art book at school. It was a picture of the macabre instruments of torment on which sprawled the corpses of the damned in a medieval vision of hell. But as they came closer he could see they were nothing but the rusting pylons and flywheels of old ski lifts. He walked on and the first faint glimmer of dawn revealed that the hillside was scattered with angled rows of pylons. Between them were the shallow, man-made gullies where once a firm bedding of snow could be relied upon to gather every winter. Now they were grown over with a thick, coarse coat of heather. Old scars healed. All except one, running straight up the hill like a sutured wound. The relic of a funicular railway.

Some distance below, where several lines of pylons converged, sat a low polygonal building. Its roof seemed still to be intact but there were gaping holes in its wooden walls. He waited for Ninian to catch up with him, then pointed down.

'We'll take a rest there.'

Ninian followed his finger but said nothing. He was beyond speech.

They made their way down to the building and ducked inside, breath steaming. It was a big space which had once been a cafeteria but was now stripped of everything except a long counter. John walked around behind the counter and unshouldered first the rifle, then the young rebel's backpack, to which he had strapped two bedrolls, one of them with the fiddle nestling safely in its centre. He unrolled the other, laying out the slim foam mattress and lightweight sleeping bag for Ninian, who needed no second bidding but clambered fully clothed inside the sleeping bag, drew it up to his chin, turned on his side and fell instantly asleep.

John wandered over to a panoramic sweep of paneless windows. Light was seeping into the sky now. A band of mist sketched the wandering passage of the river through the broad valley below. Here and there slim columns of smoke rose from early chimneys.

He stood and gazed out, too tired to think what lay in store for them down there on this still, frosty morning in Strathspey.

High on the hill behind them a lone raven croaked. The sound scoured the silence like a rasp.

Behind the counter Ninian shifted on the mattress.

John had never felt wearier in his life, nor hungrier.

It might be dawn, but he could kill for a fish supper.

STRATH

SIXTEEN

A shallow trench was taking shape at the foot of the tree. It was slow, painstaking work, scraping away the earth with a sharp stick, but it was all John could find. Lucky the frost hadn't taken a grip of the ground. The thick carpet of needles must have helped insulate it. He prodded and pushed and scraped some more, then stood back and wiped his forehead. Picked up the rifle and held it in his hands . . . Just five days ago he'd had a home, and a job of sorts, and his dad and Hector for company. Now he had almost nothing but the clothes he stood up in. He was a fugitive. A fugitive with sore feet and a dull ache of hunger to remind him he was alive. And an eight-year-old with some kind of weird handicap for a companion. The image of an adder came to mind, slithering away into the heather to leave its old skin curling behind it on the bare grey granite . . .

He took the fertiliser sack and split it down the sides, then opened it out lengthwise and wrapped it around the rifle as closely as he could. Wishing he had some oil to give the barrel a last protective coating. He cut three lengths of spare plastic from the ends to use as ties and bound the bundle tightly with them. Then laid it reverently in the trench, levelled the earth over it and finished it off with a sprinkling of pine needles.

'See the squirrel!'

Ninian was pointing and grinning. High in the naked limbs of a larch, a rare red squirrel swayed on the slenderest of branches. Then fired itself, a small russet missile, to a neighbouring branch and hung there in the sunlight, bouncing casually.

'Aye, I see him.' It was a long while since John had last seen one. But if there were red squirrels still to be found anywhere, this was the place. Here in what remained of the Rothiemurchus woods, themselves a relic of the Caledonian pine forest that had once lain like a great green mantle across the Highlands.

He stood for a moment, fixing his bearings. Then scratched a discreet M on the naked trunk of the tree where the deer had scraped away the bark. Just in case he should ever come back again.

'Why are you burying the gun?'

The squirrel had moved on now.

'Because you can't go walking about town with one.' Especially when it was likely to be stiff with soldiers who might be looking for you. 'It's not allowed. And I've nowhere else to leave it.'

'Are we going to the town now?'

'Aye.' How many times had he told him that already? When he was trying to keep him going during the night, dragging him half asleep down the hill this morning.

'Can we buy some more crisps?'

'We'll buy some crisps.'

'I like crisps. Auntie buys me crisps.' A solemn look clouded his face. 'Where is Auntie?'

Taken by surprise, John hesitated. Then lied. 'At her house.'

Ninian nodded. 'At her house.'

That was one thing about him. Everything was true for Ninian the minute he'd seen it or heard it. There was no question that things mightn't always be just how they seemed. It was a bit like being an animal maybe, because nature never lied. Just ask that squirrel. Didn't doubt for one second that the branch he was aiming at was actually there, did he? Like a squirrel, Ninian could only deal in certainties. Which meant that John was going to have to be very careful with the truth from now on.

They set off walking.

'Are we going to see her? I want to see her. And my dad.'

'Look – there's something I need to get straight, Ninian. Auntie's house wa– is at Blackriggs? Where I found you?'

He nodded again.

'One of the new houses? At the end, by the wood?'

He looked blankly.

'Not sure? OK. So . . . Auntie went shopping?'

'Shopping.' Ninian paused. 'With the soldiers.'

'With the soldiers, eh?' John had already wondered, more than once, whether she was the one he saw being dragged up the road towards the store. The one who ended up being questioned by the big corporal. If so, why . . . ?

'Did she tell you she was going shopping?'

He screwed up his face, trying to remember.

'Did she tell you to hide? In the ice house?'

'Yes.'

'And when you went to hide you saw her going? With the soldiers?'

'Ye-es.' Anxiety starting to creep into his voice. John put a calming hand on his shoulder.

'Good lad. Soon be at town. Get ourselves a decent breakfast, eh?'

'Auntie cooks breakfast. Sausages. And toast.'

'Sausages and toast. Grand stuff for wee gannets.'

Ninian grinned. 'Auntie looks after me. While my dad's at the office.'

'Aye, so she does. And d'you know where his office is? Your dad's?'

Another frown.

'Dad comes to see me. With presents.'

'When did you last see him?'

He shrugged, then brightened. 'He's coming again soon. Maybe tomorrow!'

'Aye, maybe. And you don't know his name?'

'Yes I do! Dad! My dad!'

'But Auntie didn– doesn't call him Dad, eh?'

'No! No! No!'

'What does she call him, then?'

'Don't know.'

John shook his head at the strangeness of it. The hopelessness. Mother dead. Father absent. Aunt almost certainly decomposing in a crowded ditch. And not a name among them. Someone was going to have some job unravelling this lot – and it certainly wasn't going to be him . . . Right now he was too exhausted to think clearly about anything except getting to Morag's without being picked up. Then making contact with his dad.

Sunlight fell in broad shafts among the pines. The chill was leaving the air. Somewhere in the distance vehicles rumbled along a road. They were safe enough for the time being, here in the deep wood. But it was only a couple of miles to town.

128

They walked on. Ninian's gaze fixed on John's claw thumb.

'So, you think maybe Dad's coming tomorrow?'

He was on safe enough ground here anyway. One thing he was sure about, Ninian hadn't the faintest sense of the passage of time.

Ninian nodded and smiled.

'That's grand then. Meantime it's me looking after you.'

Now the trees were beginning to thin. There was a farm road up ahead. All potholes and collapsed fencing, with a glimpse of tumbledown buildings in the distance. It felt suddenly too quiet in this big sunlit wood. John began to whistle a tune, Ninian to skip along beside him. 'Brenda Stubbert's Reel'. From Cape Breton, in Nova Scotia, which, old Alec MacNab had pointed out, was Latin for New Scotland. A place where Canadian folk with names like McCrimmon and Beaton still spoke the Gaelic of their immigrant forefathers and wrote fiery, wild-sounding tunes like this one.

He stopped whistling. It was a good tune right enough, the changes from minor to major putting a real good kick in it. But it carried a bad memory that came back now like a sharp jab in the ribs. John had realised some time ago that tunes didn't simply pop into his head at random. There was always a mood or feeling that summoned a particular one from among the scores that hung in some crevice of his mind like a colony of bats clinging to the roof of a cave. But why this particular one? And why now? The last person on earth he wanted to think about at this moment was Kel Foulis. In fact, he'd vowed never to think about him again. Yet here he was, lumbering into John's memory with his cropped ginger hair and pale cruel face, squinting at the corner of sheet music that had worked its way out of the top of John's school bag.

'What's this then?'

'Music.'

'I'm no daft. What kind of music?'

'Fiddle music.'

'Yours, eh?'

John sighed and nodded. Denying things tended to make them worse where Kel was concerned.

'You a fiddler then?'

One of Kel's cronies sniggered.

'I'm . . . learning.'

'Stumpie's learnin' to fiddle.'

The sniggering crony made a rude gesture.

Kel leaned forward, grabbed the sheet and pulled it from John's bag. He studied it, humming tunelessly as he pretended to follow the notes. Then read out the name for the benefit of his followers. 'Brenda . . . Stubbert's . . . Reel.' He looked at John. 'Brenda Stubbert, eh?'

'Sounds psycho to me,' someone said.

'Only psychos play the fiddle,' added someone else.

The others hooted with laughter, pulled weird faces and played air violin.

John stood and waited, as he'd grown used to doing, till they got bored and moved on to torment someone else.

But Kel Foulis hadn't finished yet. And out of the corner of his eye John had spotted Davie watching from the other side of the playground. Wee Davie, who worshipped every faltering stroke of John's bow across the strings. Davie, who now turned pale as Kel Foulis smiled, took a cigarette lighter from his pocket, held up the sheet of music by one corner and set light to it.

SEVENTEEN

Since John had stopped whistling, Ninian was no longer skipping but scuffing his feet in drifts of pine needles as they made their way to the edge of the wood. There they paused. Across the farm road, beyond the tumbledown fence, was an empty field that had run to thistles. John glanced up and down. There was nothing about. They stepped on to the broken metalled surface with an unaccustomed crunch of boots.

Kel Foulis. Like most of the older kids at primary school, John had quickly learned to tell when Kelvin had taken a skelping from his dad, Cameron, the foul-tempered fencing contractor. He'd come slinking into the schoolyard, eyes on the ground like a whipped dog. Then you'd need to make yourself scarce if you happened to have a claw thumb or any other defect he might deem worthy of his attention. Because by break time you could be sure the cowed look would have gone and swaggering Kel Foulis would be cock o' the midden again. Egging on his pals to seek you out wherever you were and lock you in the jannie's cupboard. Or put dog turds in your school bag. Or cram your head down the toilet.

Although Kel was two years his senior, John prayed in bed each night for him to be spared his dad's wrath. Prayed that Cammie Foulis's fence wire wouldn't spring. That his wife wouldn't burn his tea. That all his horses would be winners. But it made no difference, because the more like his father young Kelvin became, the harder and more often Cammie belted him. And the more beltings he was dealt, the more Kel would take it out on the likes of John. Especially John. Who, no matter what he did, always seemed to be in the wrong place at the wrong time. Always seemed to catch Foulis's attention when he was trying his hardest to avoid it. Always ended up frozen by the small, cold weasel eyes that stared from the pale, round face . . . even though he'd learned, after the first few bruisings, that in the face of such overwhelming malevolence there was no shame in meekly performing whatever act of humiliation was required of him. That to show the slightest resistance was to invite the inevitable thumping, and that was plain daft. But the thing that had worried John most was what would happen when Davie started school.

As it had turned out, he needn't have worried. Not at first anyway. For there was something about Davie that put him beyond the reach of physical violence. More than once John had caught Kel eyeing his younger brother with an almost puzzled look, as if he couldn't quite grasp the idea that someone so noisy and energetic and hard to ignore could also be so fragile. In any event, in some animal way Kel had understood that laying a hand on this uncanny wee soul would be taking a step too far, even by his standards.

With his slim, nervous build, mousey hair and piercing blue eyes, Davie MacNeil had bounced into primary school on his first day with all the enthusiasm of someone who knew that he was setting out on the biggest adventure of his life. That here he was going to learn important and exciting things about the world. No matter that his shirt hung out and his hair stuck up on end, no matter that his school bag was full of useful, interesting, dusty and even sticky things that had lain under his bed for six months, no matter that he sang or talked or whistled all the time, the teachers took to him at once because he was so quick and eager to learn and to make friends. And when they came to see the other side of Davie, as they soon did, when they saw him struggle to do things that were beyond him, the frustration reducing him to black despair, they were as kind to him as they could be.

Which was where he had been the very opposite of Ninian, thought John. Bursting with curiosity and intelligence, at least Davie had always been able to explain when things were wrong . . .

Up or down, you knew what you were getting with Davie. When he was bright, people wanted to be around him. When he wasn't, they tended to leave him respectfully alone. And no matter what kind of mood he was in, he was never nasty or devious but always seemed to think about other folk before himself. Though his popularity proved to have one drawback. It made it impossible for Kel Foulis to overlook him. So he bided his time, knowing with his bully's cunning that although he couldn't touch the wee lad physically, other opportunities for amusement would come along in due course.

Kel didn't have long to wait. One day, so John learned, Davie's class was told to design a calendar for the month. Like all the other children, Davie set out the days and dates, put a fancy border round the list, added the name of the month and began to colour the whole thing in. But after a while he got up from his place and went to the shelf where

133

the box of coloured felt-tipped pens was kept. He rummaged through it for some time, then stood back with a downcast look.

'What's the matter, Davie?' asked the teacher, a young woman called Miss Stewart.

'There's no yellow.'

'Can you not use another colour?'

Davie looked at her in bewilderment and shook his head.

'No?' echoed Miss Stewart.

'That's not how they are,' Davie replied.

'How do you mean?' asked Miss Stewart.

'Wednesdays.'

'What about Wednesdays, Davie?'

'Wednesdays are yellow,' said Davie.

'Yellow?'

'Aye.'

'Always?'

He nodded.

'And Tuesdays?'

'Pale blue.'

'Always pale blue?'

'They just are.'

Some of the children started to giggle.

'I see.' Miss Stewart sounded interested now. 'They're never anything different?'

Davie shook his head.

'And . . . um, do you have colours for anything else?'

Davie nodded again, hesitant now that he was the centre of attention.

'Can you tell us?'

'Well . . . aye. Letters and numbers.'

'Letters and numbers? Can you give me an example maybe? What's the letter . . . say, D, for Davie?'

'Green.'

There was more giggling.

'And the number five?'

'Purple.' No hesitation.

'And they're always the same? D's always green and five's always purple?'

Davie nodded.

'And what about whole words? Names maybe? Would you have a colour for my name perhaps . . . Stewart?'

Davie thought for a moment.

'Red . . . and white.'

Now the whole class was whispering and tittering.

'Children, children,' said Miss Stewart, her eyes bright, 'this is very interesting. Very interesting indeed. I think it's possible that Davie has something called synaesthesia. It's when one sense, like our sense of colour, is set off by another, like our sense of language. And d'you know what? I think it must be a nice thing to have. Isn't that so, Davie?'

Davie shrugged, as if it wasn't something he'd ever given any thought to.

'Did you know that's what it was, Davie?'

He shook his head. 'I just thought . . . everyone did . . . see the colours.'

There was more giggling.

'Well,' Miss Stewart smiled, 'I don't think everyone does. I think it's not all that common. But maybe some of us do. We'll see, shall we? Does anyone else here have colours for things?'

A forest of hands shot up . . .

Word went round the school in no time. By lunch break the news had reached the ears of Kel Foulis and his gang.

They came up to Davie in the playground and stood around him in a circle. John saw what was going on and moved closer. If he intervened now, things could turn nasty at once. It was better just to be on hand.

Davie looked up at the bigger boys uncertainly.

'What colour's my name, then?' asked Kel.

Davie's gaze dropped to his feet.

'What colour's Kel Foulis?' Kel repeated.

'Deep red and dark brown,' he replied softly.

'Blood and keech,' muttered one of the cronies.

Too right, thought John, as the others sniggered and poked each other in the ribs. Although he knew fine that it wasn't really how this thing of Davie's worked.

'See lots of colours then, do you?' Kel continued.

Davie hung his head.

'Lots of lovely pretty colours, eh? Like a wee fairy? Cos that's what you are. Just a wee fairy.'

'Gay boy!' said one of the others.

Davie looked at them in confusion.

John prepared to step in. But Kel Foulis just glared at Davie and said, 'On your bike, gay boy!' Then turned away. The gang followed him.

That evening Davie was subdued. After tea John went up to their room. Davie was on his bed, reading a book.

'What's up?' asked John.

Davie put down the book and frowned.

'Gay's when two laddies go together, isn't it?'

'Aye. Or lassies.'

'Is that bad?'

John shook his head. 'Just how it is. For some folk.'

Davie looked at him. 'Do gay folk love each other?'

'Aye. Guess they do.'

'So are we gay? You and me?'

136

John shook his head and laughed.

'Then it wasn't true. What he called me.'

'No. Course not.'

'I hate things that aren't true,' said Davie. He went back to his book.

And that, John remembered thinking, was his brother through and through. It wasn't being called gay that had bothered him. It was that it wasn't true.

EIGHTEEN

Kel Foulis pursued Davie relentlessly after that. He was always careful to avoid physical contact, but he never missed the chance for a taunt or jibe. Which was how they had found themselves in Alec MacNab's garden that day, under a cloud that turned out, for John at any rate, to have a silver lining.

For a time Davie seemed to share in its blessing too. From the start he went with John to his weekly fiddle lesson. It was partly, John knew, because he didn't want to have to walk home from school on his own, though he would never have admitted it. But it was also because he liked going into the kitchen to help Bella with her baking, or sometimes simply sitting in the old puddock's music room and looking on admiringly as John struggled to hold the awkward instrument properly and draw the bow smoothly across the strings so that it didn't sound as if he was treading on cats. After a few weeks Alec declared that he was pleased with John's progress and, to John's amazement and delight, produced a three-quarter-size fiddle. They began smuggling it back and forth from the lessons in an old game-bag so as not to attract attention.

Now that there was a fiddle at home, Davie pestered John to play all the time. But pleased and flattered though John was, he found it hard to ignore the voice that told him Davie was just humouring him. For he knew that if Davie had taken the trouble he could have been a far better player himself. Perhaps, John thought now, it was because Davie had known that he wasn't going to be around for very long. Whatever it was, it didn't stop him seeming to take as much pleasure in the fiddling as John did. John would never forget the day Alec had first taken them into his workshop or the look of fascination on Davie's face as the old man showed them the marvels awaiting them there in his Aladdin's cave. Like the pair of callipers he'd made for measuring the thickness of the wood. Used the metal heel of his boot, a piece of an old steel ruler, a welding rod and the top of a tube of eye ointment. Cost him a shilling, he said. Accurate as anything you'd pay three hundred quid for. And the bending iron for shaping the ribs, for giving the fiddle its figure. A masterpiece of improvisation, with its curvy length of old copper piping, a soldering iron stuck up one end. Every fiddle was a unique and living thing, Alec explained. Every piece of wood imprinted with its own distinctive grain, so no two instruments could ever sound exactly the same. And as if that wasn't enough, there was the intricacy of it all, the inner workings, like the bass bar that helped to amplify the lower frequencies. The sound post that conducted the vibrations between the belly and the back. And the strangely shaped and delicate tools needed to work such acoustic miracles.

A bit like rigging a ship in a bottle, Davie had declared with authority. John was sure he'd never seen a ship in a bottle, let alone tried to rig one. He wondered, yet again, how on earth Davie came up with things like that. He could remember the conviction in Davie's face as he'd said it. He could also remember that it had been a fine spring day, daffodils nodding in the sunshine on the grassy bank behind the MacNabs' house. Yet something had left him feeling uneasy.

Then a couple of weeks later had come the incident with the sheet music in the playground. After that, Kel and his gang had started calling John 'Brenda', after the name of the tune. This had seemed to disturb Davie much more than it should have done, John thought.

'They shouldn't be calling you a lassie's name,' Davie said repeatedly, his voice close to despair.

'It doesn't hurt me,' said John.

'But they shouldn't,' Davie went on.

The mood persisted and as spring passed into summer he seemed to withdraw into himself. His eyes shone less often with admiration when John picked up the fiddle. He grew quieter at school and spent more and more time at home in their bedroom.

'Why don't you take him to the Linn pool?' John's mother suggested one Saturday morning after breakfast. 'He needs cheering up. I'll make you a nice piece to take with you.'

'Aye,' said Ferg from behind his paper. 'He needs out. Fresh air. Get some colour in him.'

They took their bicycles. It was a hot day, sunlight dancing through the dust from the track that ran alongside the river. The trees like carvings in the still air. A mile upstream from the village the river dropped over a waterfall and rushed through a deep rocky ravine and out into a wide pool with a shingle spit down one side. The Linn pool. Hot as it was now, there had been heavy rain the previous week and the water still ran deep and peaty and cold. Overhung by trees, a narrow humpbacked bridge arched the mouth of the ravine, its stonework mossy with age. Already there was a gathering of boys there, some of them in swimming gear. The bolder ones were jumping off the parapet into the water. It was a good height, enough to be frightening, maybe twenty feet. The less daring ones sat on the shingle to watch and shout comments.

John spotted Kel Foulis and his cronies among the crowd on the bridge. He stopped the bike.

'C'mon, we'll go somewhere else.'

Davie shook his head.

'You sure now?' John glanced at the bridge.

Davie nodded. 'There's this stuff you get in rivers. Pyrites. Fool's gold. I want to find some.'

The look in his eye said this was not negotiable. Could he have known what was going to happen? John had since wondered.

They parked their bikes and went down to the spit. John sat on the warm shingle and watched the jumpers showing off. Davie removed his shoes and began to paddle through the shallows in his shorts, peering into the dark amber water, reaching in every so often to pick something up and examine it. Soon he had a little pile of sharp-faced stones which revealed glinting flecks of gold when he turned them in the sunlight. He seemed absorbed and happy for the first time in weeks.

John lay back on the shingle and closed his eyes. He listened to the soft chuckle of the river. The heat of the sun warmed his body.

There was a sudden crescendo of cheers and catcalls. He sat up, realising he had fallen asleep. He looked around. Davie was not on the shingle. All around him, eyes were on

141

the small figure that now strode up the track towards the bridge.

'C'mon, ye wee poof.' It was Kel who now commanded the attention of the crowd on the bridge.

The figure peeled off its shirt as it walked and flung it down.

'Let's see ye jump, then.'

John scrambled to his feet.

'Stop him,' he bellowed. 'He can't swim . . . he'll drown. Stop him, someone!'

For a moment all activity on the bridge ceased. It seemed to John as if everyone turned to Kel. But Kel did nothing. Just watched as Davie came on up the track.

John broke into a run. He raced up the bank to the track. On to the track and up the hill towards the bridge. Past Davie's shirt, lying there in the dust.

'Davie! *Stop! Davie!*'

'You too, Brenda,' someone shouted from the bridge. There was more cheering and laughter.

They wouldn't let him jump, surely. Someone would stop him. Someone *must* stop him.

But Davie was on the bridge, pale and skinny in nothing but his shorts. He seemed half the size of the boys around him, who were now making way for him. John ran faster, not wanting to believe what he was seeing. Some of the boys were looking at Davie nervously now. But as he came towards the parapet Kel stepped briefly forward and said something to him, then moved out of the way and watched as Davie hauled himself up on to the mossy stonework, swayed there for a moment, then leaped.

There was a split second of silence. John froze. Then a splash and a loud cheer. John turned and raced back down towards the pool.

The cheer died away.

By the time John reached the shingle there was a deep silence.

Pausing only to kick off his shoes, John flung himself into the cold water and struck out for the bridge. His heart was in his throat as he dived and he couldn't hold his breath. He came up spluttering. He gulped in air and dived again. Despite the sunlight, the peaty water was murky and the deeper he went the less he could see.

Five times he went down, holding his breath till he thought his lungs would burst, surfacing just long enough to take in a searing gulp of air, then diving again. He was about to go down for a sixth time when hands grasped him and began towing him back to the bank. He tried to fight them off but he no longer had the strength. Then he was being hauled out of the water to collapse on the shingle.

He lay there sobbing, exhausted, oblivious of what was going on around him, until at last the world shrank away and with it all his pain and bewilderment and confusion.

NINETEEN

They buried him in a corner of the little kirkyard that looked out at the hills. Almost everyone in the village turned out. They stood with heads bowed in the shadow of the bent old larch that sheltered the gravestones with its gnarled branches. It was an overcast day. John watched the small coffin being lowered into the freshly dug grave and thought how lonely Davie was going to be down there in the cold earth all by himself. He couldn't bear to look.

As they were driving back to the village afterwards they passed Kel and his cronies, waiting on their bikes at the corner of the wood. For an instant Kel's and John's eyes met through the funeral-car window. Then Kel looked down and turned away.

Later, in the small hours, with the empty bed gaping beside him, John heard his mother's sobbing through the bedroom wall, and his father's gruff voice trying to comfort her. It felt to him as if the house itself was groaning with sorrow.

A tragic accident, horseplay that had gone wrong, concluded the sheriff at the Fatal Accident Inquiry in a featureless modern courtroom in Aberdeen. Davie, the

144

pathologist had explained, had been suffering from a rare, undiagnosed heart condition which had caused him to have a fatal heart attack as he went down into the cold water. And since, the sheriff had continued, despite the taunting he had jumped of his own free will, there was no case for anyone to answer, even had any individuals been named. Which of course they hadn't, since Kel Foulis and his gang had closed ranks and the police had got nothing out of them.

At the time John hadn't understood about Davie's heart. How could you not know about something like that? he kept asking himself in the days after the inquiry. He was still half expecting the bedroom door to open at any minute and Davie to come bursting in and hurl his school bag on the floor . . . The thought gnawed at him until he could no longer keep it to himself and one evening at tea he asked his mum and dad.

'Questions'll no bring him back,' Ferg had replied. His look telling John that the subject was closed.

And so it was. Davie's name was never mentioned from that moment on. Not in Ferg's presence anyway.

Now, seven years later, it struck John that maybe the pathologist had been right in a way. Maybe Davie had had a heart condition, though not of the sort that were usually identified by post mortems . . .

Other things changed too that summer. For the rest of the holidays, whenever John's and Kel's paths crossed Kel avoided his eye. Then, in the autumn, Kel moved on to secondary school and found himself other prey.

John's twelfth birthday came in September and that Christmas holidays he started going out on the hill with Ferg to learn the stalking. Christmas Day, the first without Davie, was so awful that John could remember almost nothing about it. But he kept himself going by tending his Davie shrine and throwing himself into the fiddling. The music, more than anything else, seemed to help him cope with the empty feeling inside. He moved up to secondary school just before his thirteenth birthday. Now his playing was starting to settle in, with good strong bowing and clean fingering, the start of some fine ornaments and grace notes. And soon along with the music came the making, as he started to feel an urge to get his hands on the tools and the oil and the fresh-cut wood, the clamps and moulds. He was fifteen when he started to pester old Alec, who eventually relented, dug out some offcuts and agreed to give up some of his secrets. And as the first carcass began to take shape on the bench in front of him, John felt almost as if it was himself he was remaking. A stronger, firmer, truer version of the original. Then one evening, just before he turned seventeen, Ferg announced at tea that he'd heard that Graham Thompson, the plumber, could mebbe use another fiddle in his band. And though the thought of playing in public made his knees go weak, John's heart jumped at the note of approval in his dad's voice.

Sometimes, though, the loss of Davie would still hit him out of nowhere like hail from a clear blue sky. It was almost like a physical blow and he'd have to sit down and breathe slowly and wait for the pain to pass.

Keeping himself busy with Ferg was one way to prevent this happening too often. He was enjoying being out on the hill with his father more and more, each day bringing with it a new sense of adventure and discovery. He loved the easy way Ferg handled the rifle and spyglass, almost as if they were extensions of his body. He loved the smell of blood and heather and gun oil that clung to the leather spyglass case, the canvas rifle sleeve and the game-bag, bulging with their dinnertime pieces and the thermos. And he loved the way his dad was so sure of the ground, could tell just where they were from a single boulder or bend in the sheep track, even when the mist was down and swirling densely in front of their noses. Ferg's knowledge of everything around them – birds, animals, plants, even stones – seemed to John to be without limit, and gruff as he could sometimes be he was never impatient with John's questions. Most of all though, John loved the occasional approving glances he received when he had done something particularly well. He would never forget the day he had shot his first stag, and the look of pride on Ferg's face as he observed the age-old ritual, dipping his fingers in the warm crimson blood and smearing it across his son's forehead. But despite all this, John couldn't help noticing how now there was a raw, brittle place inside his father, which he kept closed off, and how he was liable to snap if he felt people were getting too close to it.

Eileen, John's mother, meanwhile, had always tended to fuss over the boys. Now there was just him she fussed over him twice as much. Sometimes he liked it. Sometimes it made him feel claustrophobic. But he loved her and longed to make it better for her when he saw that she had been crying, which it seemed she often had. Though as time passed he became less sure whether her tears were for Davie or for the gulf that even he could see was widening between her and Ferg. But it still shook him deeply when at last she announced that she was going. And although he had got over the initial shock and sadness of her absence, had begun to get used to the new routine of weekly phone calls and the regular train journey to Newcastle, even now, eighteen months later, there were times – like the present – when he simply longed for her to be there, to hear her voice, see her smile, feel the warmth of her hug.

By now John had left school and was working full-time with Ferg. He had made his second fiddle. As well as playing from time to time in Graham Thompson's band, he had started his own with a group of musicians his own age. Kel Foulis, meanwhile, had turned into an unshaven slack-bellied lout with no job who had already been sacked twice. The first time by his father for taking a swing at him with a fencing hammer, the second for pilfering from the village store where he was briefly employed as a shelf-stacker. Now he dossed in some stinking bothy up behind the castle and spent his days loitering down in Ballater with a gang of other unemployables.

The old puddock's prophecy seemed to have come true. And while the fiddling was giving John a new sureness of spirit, the hard physical work with his father was putting solid muscle on his calves and thighs, his arms and shoulders. Girls, he had noticed with relief, were starting to take an interest in him – and he in them. He'd had several encounters, though so far he'd met no one who interested him enough to want to spend much time with.

Looking back, the shivering tongue-tied lad that Bella MacNab had found crouching behind her garden hedge with his wee brother now seemed like someone else entirely. And until four days ago John would have told anyone who had asked him that he was happy with his life . . .

TWENTY

In a former caravan site on the very edge of Aviemore was an encampment of makeshift dwellings, rusting mobile homes and abandoned vehicles. From among the tin roofs and tarpaulins, cooking smoke rose into the morning sunlight. At first glance John wondered whether it might be travelling folk. But a closer look suggested something more permanent.

Beyond, the road crossed the river and railway line before joining the N1, the main north road from Perth to Inverness. In the distance John glimpsed the fluorescent striped barrier of an army checkpoint. It would have to be the caravan site.

He stopped and glanced about. Then helped Ninian over the fence and climbed after him.

'Can you get into town this way?'

A couple of crop-headed boys were kicking a football about on a vacant patch of grass. The larger of the two gave John a sullen glance, then nodded and pointed across the site to a hedge on the far side.

John and Ninian threaded their way between the shacks and shelters and vehicles. Some people stared curiously as

they passed. Others seemed indifferent. Ninian was looking around with interest.

'Poor people live here,' he announced.

John nodded. There was hardly a town in the Highlands
these days that hadn't sprouted something like this at its
fringes.

'I'm not poor. My dad's rich.'

'Is he now?'

'Yes. He buys me presents. Maybe he's going to bring
one tomorrow! Are you poor?'

John smiled. He must certainly look it. In his three-days
stubble and filthy clothes and backpack. The lad tooling
along behind him in his inside-out jacket. A pair of tinkers,
that's what they must look like.

'Aye, I guess I am. Now, anyway.'

A mangy yellow dog trotted up and sniffed at Ninian's
leg. Ninian smiled and made to pat it but it growled
and bared its teeth. His face crumpled. He edged away and
reached for John's hand.

'Let's get out of here.' John quickened his pace.

There was a small gate in the hedge. It opened on to a
litter-strewn path which crossed the river by a footbridge,
then passed beneath the railway to run along the backs of
the shops and houses that fronted the main street. Last time
John had been over with his dad to visit Morag, eighteen
months ago maybe, there were still some tourists about, the
place seemed to have some life in it. Now, through a gap
between the buildings, he glimpsed the dark bulk of an
army truck trundling slowly down the main street. As it
passed, a boarded-up shop and shabby house fronts were
revealed, the roofs of the old leisure complex visible
beyond, derelict hotels rising up like the remains of some
giant stone circle. John could feel the emptiness around

him, even in the unkempt yards at the backs of the buildings. The presence of soldiers made his spine prickle. It was all he could do not to break into a run.

Shortly the path met a lane, which passed under the railway line once more and ran into a cul-de-sac, where a development of half a dozen bungalows was sheltered by a small birch wood. John made for the second-to-last bungalow. A wrought-iron gate opened on a short gravel path flanked by tidy borders. This was one place at least that hadn't run to seed yet. John swung the gate open and crunched up the path, pausing at the front door, with its frosted glass and carriage lamps, to take off the backpack. Then he rang the bell and waited. No one came. He rang again, thumb hard down on the button. There was a raised voice from somewhere inside. Hurried footsteps approaching. The door opened.

'Yes?'

It was a young woman in a bathrobe and towel turbaned around damp hair. Skin at her throat still pink from the shower. Bare legs steaming in the cold air.

'Eh . . .' He was momentarily tongue-tied. 'Is . . . er . . . is Morag here?'

She shook her head and raised a hand to stop the turban coming undone, which caused the bathrobe to fall open at her breast. She drew it sharply across with her other hand in a gesture of annoyance.

'When will she be back?'

'About three weeks.'

'Oh.'

'Can I help?' The suspicion was plain in her voice. She was weighing up the backpack, the bedrolls, the scruffy appearance.

'Aye, well . . . I'm not sure . . . I'm her nephew. John.

John MacNeil. And this is my – my wee cousin. I was hoping that we could – maybe – stop by for a while. We've been walking, see . . . ran out of fuel.' He spread his hands sheepishly, attempted a smile.

To his surprise he was rewarded by what seemed like a glimmer of recognition. She frowned, looking at him hard. Then shook her head slowly.

'John McNeil . . . you'll not remember me. I'm . . . My mum's an old friend of Morag's, Hazel Grieve. I'm Lila. You played the fiddle, didn't you?'

John nodded.

'I spent a summer holiday with Morag when I was, oh . . .' She shrugged. 'Here, you'd better come in.'

'Thanks,' said John. 'Thanks very much.'

She nodded. 'Morag's away visiting. I'm house-sitting.' She opened the door wider and stepped aside.

For a moment John was reminded of the old MacNabs' house. The watery light in the hallway, the possessions, the sense of order. But of course it was more modern, by about a hundred years. And it was spacious and airy. He could see through the open doorway into the sitting room, where picture windows offered a fine view though the birch trees to a small loch.

She gestured. 'You can take a seat in there. While I get some clothes on. I'll not be long.'

'The pack . . . What will I . . . ?'

'It's OK where it is just now.'

John led Ninian into the sitting room. Lowered himself into a large leather settee and let out a long sigh to feel the weight off his aching legs at last. Ninian sat down beside him, mimicking the sigh, then leaned his head back against the leather and closed his eyes.

John gazed out of the windows, past the trees and the

little loch, to the distant Cairngorms, looming huge and prehistoric in the clear morning light. It seemed hard to believe that that's where they'd been last night. Two insignificant, exhausted specks, stumbling in the darkness through all that ancient wilderness.

Already Ninian's breathing was settling into the slow rhythm of sleep. John glanced down at the dark curls, the gently fluttering eyelids, and felt a sympathetic wave of drowsiness sweep over him. An irresistible urge to let his own eyes close. Just for a minute . . .

'Must've been a long walk.'

He opened them again with a start.

She was standing in the doorway wearing jeans and a fleece, and a look of faint amusement. She was in her early twenties, he guessed. Slim built with short dark hair, pale complexion and grey-green eyes. The nose short and straight, the features clean, almost boyish. Could have been Irish, though she sounded as if she was from the west.

'Sorry . . . long walk, aye.' He nodded, gathering his thoughts. 'We're on our way down to Perth.' The lie came readily. 'Ran out of fuel a couple of hours ago. Thought we'd get a bus . . .'

'Not today you won't.' She shook her head. Then caught John's quizzical look. 'Have you not heard the news then?'

'No.'

'The NLA hit an army convoy on the N1 this morning. Just north of Drumochter. So no one'll be going anywhere right now. Not south. Not Perth way anyway.'

'Oh.'

'Aye. It'll be a day or two before anything gets moving again.' She looked down at him directly, her eye running

153

over the stubbled chin and crumpled clothes and filthy boots. 'Do you want to stay?'

'That would be . . . well, aye, if you don't –'

She nodded, her face relaxing into a smile. 'It's fine by me. But you'll have to fend for yourselves. I've to be at work in twenty minutes.' She turned and pointed. 'The kitchen's through here, bathroom there, guest room there. Twin beds, so you'll be fine.'

'That's very kind . . .' John began, but she went on, 'I'll be back mid-afternoon.' She turned to go, then stopped. 'You didn't tell me his name.'

'Ninian.'

'Ninian.' She nodded to herself.

At the repetition of his name Ninian stirred. Opened his eyes. Then tugged at John's hand and started to whine.

'I was . . . er . . . wondering . . .' John spoke hurriedly, not wanting to detain her. 'Could we make some breakfast? It's a while since we've eaten.'

'Help yourself. It's all there.' With a wave at the kitchen. 'Afraid there's no milk though.'

'I'll go to the shops.'

'There's a spare key on the hook.' She pointed towards the back door, then disappeared back into her bedroom.

John and Ninian made for the kitchen. There was a small wall-mounted television over the breakfast bar. Ninian pulled up a stool, found the remote control and turned it on. Squeaky voices and comic music filled the room as John foraged through cupboards and fridge, disappointment growing. It wasn't only milk that was missing. There was no bacon or sausages or eggs. Nor any decent bread. Just a lot of dried fruit. And yoghurt, again. A tub of spreadable butter. Half a jar of jam. A dense brown loaf that looked like a brick of peat. Carton of orange juice. No

154

wonder the lassie was so skinny. And here, thank God, at the back of a cupboard, a pack of mini-cereals.

'D'you want Frosties?'

Ninian nodded without taking his eyes from the screen.

'There's no milk. D'you want them dry?'

His gaze slid sideways for a moment. 'Juice. And Frosties.'

John shrugged. He placed a bowl of cereal and a glass of juice on the breakfast bar and turned away to find the kettle. Ninian tipped the juice over the Frosties, plunged in the spoon and began to eat noisily.

'See you later.' Her voice rang out as the front door opened, then closed.

John couldn't see a kettle anywhere. But there was an object a little smaller than a microwave that seemed to be some kind of automatic beverage dispenser, offering a choice of tea or coffee. The sort of thing you'd order from a gadget magazine. He shook his head, made himself a slice of peat-toast and waited for the dispenser to deliver a muddy-looking cup of tea. He wished he had the nerve to go to the shops now and buy the ingredients for a good fry-up. But far more than that, he wished Morag was here. Being in this comfortable modern house with its tidy wee kitchen and deep settees and picture windows, all so normal, made him long more than ever for someone to take into his confidence, someone to pour out his story to, some-one who'd know what to do about Ninian, someone to help him, for Christ's sake . . .

There was a portable phone on its charger at the end of the breakfast bar. Without thinking he lifted it from the cradle, pulse quickening as he heard the dial tone. He began to dial his home number, then stopped. What was he doing . . . ? There *was* no home, and anyway, if the

155

authorities had the slightest interest in him they'd be monitoring calls to his number, whether it still worked or not. What about his mum though? He felt a sudden irresistible longing to hear her voice. He dialled the Newcastle number, but before it could ring a recorded voice cut in: 'We regret that at this time only local calls are possible. We apologise to customers for any inconvenience.'

John snorted and slammed the phone back on its cradle. He looked across at Ninian, whose head was beginning to droop over the soggy, orange-stained mess in the bottom of his bowl. His heart sank further. How much more of this . . . this responsibility could he take?

'Time for sleep, eh?' He went to lift him off the stool and to his surprise Ninian offered no resistance, but put his arms around John's neck and let his head flop forward. There was something almost comforting about the musty unwashed smell of Ninian's hair, the softness of his cheek against John's stubble. He was tempted for a moment to hang on to him. But he carried him through to the guest room and laid him on the bed, took off his shoes, pulled the cover up.

'You've done well, laddie,' he said.

The boy gave a little murmur and drifted into sleep.

Back in the kitchen, John finished his breakfast. But now, with a soft mattress and oblivion at last in sight, he felt suddenly too wired for sleep. He flicked vainly through the TV channels, knowing he'd find nothing but Channel One, the government twenty-four-hour news service. He caught the end of the weather and then a story about the anti-government rioters who had set up a no-go area in Inverness's Springfield housing estate, denying entry to the authorities by means of barricades manned by stone-throwing youths. 'A present-day Falls Road,' said the reporter, referring to the Northern Irish troubles of the previous century. Tagged on to the end of this story was a report on the worrying influx of what the journalist called 'migrants' to the neighbouring Bught Park. What he really meant, thought John, was that the place had become a refugee camp. A home to the steady stream of folk from all over the Highlands whose livelihoods had in one way or another been destroyed by the troubles. Though a city council spokesman seemed more concerned about the damage the fast-spreading camp might do to the park's sports ground than the welfare of the 'migrants'. John yawned, true, deep weariness at last beginning to take hold. Now the programme returned to the studio where an army spokesman, a clean-featured major, blandly presented an update on the conflict itself. John's eyes were starting to droop. He reached out to switch off the TV, then stiffened. '. . . Donside hamlet of Blackriggs . . . known NLA stronghold . . . fierce resistance by heavily armed units . . . undisclosed number of terrorists killed . . .' He was instantly wide awake, heart thumping, rage beginning to boil as the images flooded back yet again and he wondered savagely what kind of world it was where being a middle-aged salesman with a cheap briefcase made you a heavily armed terrorist. And resisting fiercely meant standing in helpless terror outside your apartment as two swarthy soldiers held you still, while a third took an industrial nail gun and prepared to put a nine-inch bolt through your forehead, pinning you to your own front door. The major droned on with his prepared statement, his features settling into a scowl of palpable indignation as he came to the details of the latest outrage, the large explosive device that had been remotely detonated that morning on the N1 just north of Drumochter Pass, narrowly missing a column of

157

Inverness-bound troops and prompting renewed security measures of the utmost rigour in Badenoch and Strathspey district.

Which meant right here, noted John.

The major's face faded from the screen. As suddenly as it had boiled up, John's rage evaporated in a fog of exhaustion. He switched off the TV and went through to the bedroom, where he lay down fully clothed on the second bed and closed his eyes.

TWENTY-ONE

It was well into the afternoon when he was woken by laughter. He glanced across to see that Ninian's bed was empty.

He got up and followed the sound into the living room, where Lila and Ninian were sitting on the floor surrounded by sheets of paper. It seemed to be a drawing competition. Half the sheets bore simple but clearly recognisable sketches of people and animals. A man with a fishing rod, a dog with a bone, an old woman with a shopping basket. They were caricatures, features exaggerated, humorous poses. She could draw all right. But the rest were covered with childish scribblings. A rampage of careless lines and blobs, uncoordinated squiggles and zigzags, paper-tearing strokes and jabs.

Lila looked up at John and smiled.

'Show John your hamster,' she said to Ninian.

Who maintained a frown of ferocious concentration as he added a final flourish to his masterpiece. Then sat back and brandished a sheet in whose centre a dense black dot was surrounded by several uneven, vaguely concentric circles.

'Hamish,' he announced. 'My hamster.'

'That's great,' said John.

'Really good!' added Lila with a wink at John. She gestured to the settee. 'Like a cup of tea?'

'Sorry – I . . . er . . . never got to the shops.'

'No bother. Afraid I was in a bit of a hurry earlier on. Juice, Ninian?'

Busy with further embellishments to his hamster, Ninian paid no attention.

Lila got up from the floor. John watched her as she went through to the kitchen. Listened to the running of the tap, the opening of cupboard doors. And wondered whether he was dreaming, whether he was going to wake up at any minute and find himself back in the cave.

'Ninian's been telling me about the tiger,' she called.

'Oh aye.'

'How you shot it.'

'Aye.'

'What was it? Really?'

'A lynx. There's a few about.'

'Aye, I've heard.' There was a clink of crockery. 'Are they dangerous?'

'Not really.'

'He likes that old paw, does he?'

'Aye.'

Sound of a teapot being filled. 'Getting a bit manky, I'd say . . .'

'I hadn't noticed.'

'Ready for the bin.'

'I doubt you'd get it off him.'

She reappeared with a tray of tea and biscuits. Put them on a low table and sat down opposite John in an easy chair.

'Biscuit, Ninian?'

This time he nodded, without looking up. Reached out a hand and demolished a biscuit in two mouthfuls.

'Would you show me the paw?' she asked.

He scowled and shook his head. Crossed his arms at his chest.

She looked at John, eyes flickering over the claw thumb. That sooner or later snagged everyone's glance. That had shaped so much of his life, insignificant though it was . . .

She smiled. 'I haven't been down Perth way for a while.'

'My nan's there. His nan's sister.'

'That'll be nice.' She poured the tea, tapping the pot with her finger. 'Proper stuff for a change. Can't stand the dishwater from that thing.' Passed John a cup. 'So . . . d'you still live over Strathdon way?'

'Aye. Used to be at the stalking. Till a few months back.'

'And now?'

He shrugged. 'I get by.'

'Like the rest of us.' She smiled again. Then glanced at Ninian. 'Well, you can stay as long as you want here. It'll be good to have some company. What does he like to eat? I'll get some stuff later.'

John racked his brain. 'Crisps mainly. But don't you bother . . .'

'Hmm. You like chicken nuggets, Ninian?'

He nodded.

'Spaghetti?'

Another nod.

'Listen, I do the bar at the Spey View. Only pub left here now.' She laughed shortly. 'It's my job. If you feel like coming up this evening I'll get you your tea there.'

'Well . . .'

'We've live music on tonight. The Deuchary Ceilidh Band. From down Dunkeld way. They're old, but they're

161

great.' She tucked her feet under her in the chair and pulled a wry face. 'We all have to do something to stay cheerful, eh?'

'Cheerful. Aye.' He sipped from his cup.

The sleep had left him feeling thick in the head, like old damp tweed. Though running through it like a strand of wire was the anxiety. What did she really make of the two of them? What had Ninian said to her? She'd already figured out more than she was letting on, he was sure of it. Did he dare leave the house and spend the evening in a public place? And just what the hell was he going to do with Morag not here to help him?

Lila reached down to hand Ninian another biscuit.

John cleared his throat. 'I was . . . er . . . watching the news. The bomb. At Drumochter.'

'What did they say?'

'That it just missed a column of troops. They'd be meaning vehicles, eh?'

She nodded. 'Aye. They would.' Then hesitated. 'And it didn't miss them either. Got the leading two. Blew them clean off the road. I've heard there were a good few soldiers dead.'

She registered John's look of surprise. 'It's not that far, Drumochter. News travels fast.'

'So . . . d'you think they'll be tightening up round here? Cracking down?'

'Definitely.'

'Right here? In the town, like?'

'It's possible.' She shrugged, then glanced at her watch. 'Look . . . I've to go and see someone before I get back to work. Need to get going.' She rose and pulled on her jacket. 'You'll come up to the Spey View for your tea, then? Sixish, say?'

'Well . . . OK, if I can keep him awake,' he replied, keeping his options open. 'It was an early start this morning.'

She smiled. 'See you if we see you, then?'

'Aye.'

TWENTY-TWO

'You can't wear it outside your coat, laddie. We're going to a pub!'

Morag's utility room was well equipped and Ninian's jeans were now clean. His shirt and sweater too. His hair was glossy and brushed, face and fingernails scrubbed. Scents of soap, shampoo and washing powder wafted from him. The only discordant note in all this fragrance being the subtle but persistent pong of the decomposing paw, which dangled prominently on the outside of his jacket, dripping bathwater.

'No, no! I'm not wanting to take it from you. Just get it inside your sweater. So folk don't have to see it.'

In the bathroom, Ninian had submitted himself to John's ministrations without a murmur. Now he was whining and flapping his hands. Eyes averted, head turned away as John fumbled with the zip of his jacket, struggled to tuck the paw down the neck of his sweater. Where it would nestle damply against his chest.

As soon as he got the chance John would have to try and scrape the flesh off it. Otherwise the bloody thing'd start crawling about on its own.

164

'It's my good paw.' Ninian was mumbling crossly now. 'Keep it on my string.'

'I know fine it's your good paw. I'll not take it away. Your lucky paw.'

'Lucky.' He brightened. 'My lucky paw!'

'Aye. So it is.' The ghostly presence of the lynx flitted through John's mind, a shadow on the darkened hillside . . .

They left the house and set off up the close. John was clean too. Clothes washed. Body scrubbed to the utmost crevices. Hair brushed. Stubble that could almost pass for the designer variety. He'd definitely keep it, maybe even let the beard grow. And not just for the camouflage. He hadn't given his appearance much thought recently, but in Morag's bathroom he'd found himself in unfamiliar territory, surrounded by cosmetics and toiletries, drying underwear draped over a radiator, nightdress hanging on the back of the door. His senses had seemed to go on to some new kind of alert as he inspected himself in the mirror.

Early though it was, it was quiet outside. Another unaccustomedly cold clear night, swarming with stars. The close was deserted, everyone indoors. Wood and peat smoke sharp on the air. He wondered for a moment whether there might even be a curfew. But then the pub would be shut and Lila would be back. Was he crazy to be running this risk? Maybe. But after the mad, heart-stopping intensity of the last few days he longed for normality, for company, for noises and faces and voices in which he could lose himself for the evening, not to mention the prospect of a few hours' respite from Ninian. And anyway, anyone looking for him would be after a clean-shaven youth on his own, not a partially bearded traveller with a young lad in tow.

He would use the time this evening to suss Lila out, he told himself, figure out whether he could trust her. Then, if

165

he thought she was up for it, he'd enlist her help to start getting things sorted. If not . . . well, he'd deal with that tomorrow.

A few minutes later lights beckoned and muted sounds drifted towards them from the rear of the Spey View, a large and decrepit Victorian fishing hotel. At once John began to feel anxious again. The door of the public bar swung open and a gale of laughter spilt into the night. He reached down and took Ninian's hand.

'Will they have crisps?'

'Aye, they will. And a TV. Lila said. There's a room upstairs.'

Warm and bright and smoky, the small public bar was already crowded. There was a babble of voices, international shinty on the TV. Lila spotted them and stepped out from behind the bar, shouldered her way through the throng.

''Fraid it's a bit busy in here.' She greeted them with a smile. 'Come on through to the lounge. It's where the band'll be.' She led the way. 'I'll bring some food. Chicken for you, Ninian. And fish OK for you, John?'

For a moment all the noise and bustle threatened to overwhelm him. He felt like one of those cartoon knights who'd taken a dunt on the head and stood immobilised with his armour cracking around him like crazy paving.

Lila misread his hesitation. 'Or maybe you'd rather chicken?'

'Oh . . . aye . . . no, I mean – fish . . . grand.'

The lounge was a bigger, more formal room, though it had seen some action in its day, the upholstery worn, the fake panelling all scuffed and chipped. There was a small stage at one end, a bar down one side. The tables were already starting to fill, a home-printed flier on each: *The*

Deuchary Ceilidh Band. By popular demand, Silver Jubilee
Tour. Still going strong after Twenty-Five Years, Scotland's
Top Toe-tappers . . .

Ninian tugged John down at an empty table. He seemed
excited by all the activity. He wriggled on the stool, looked
up at the vacant stage, peered around at the people, examined the flier upside down and fiddled with the beer mats.
John went to the bar and ordered an Irn-Bru and a pint,
watching the head settle, thick and creamy. The sudden
longing like an ache in his throat.

There were a couple of lassies moving among the tables
with plates of food and drinks. Lila's helpers. But when it
came to John's and Ninian's turn, it was Lila herself who
brought along the tray with a breezy smile.

'That's you then!' She set down the plates of chicken and
fish, along with two bowls of ice cream. 'Enjoy your meal
now. I'll take him upstairs later. If he gets bored. OK,
Ninian? Watch some cartoons?'

Ninian nodded and began solemnly attending to the
chicken. Which demanded to be helped on its way with
slugs of Irn-Bru, one per nugget.

John watched him for a moment, noticing the intense,
almost obsessive concentration that seemed so fierce and
yet so fragile. It made him want to throw up a wall against
anything that might spoil Ninian's pleasure . . .

He turned his attention to his own food. The fish was
breadcrumbed not battered, and in place of the vinegar
bottle there were sachets of tartare sauce. But it was tasty
all the same, with the chips and peas. First hot meal he'd
had since before . . . well, finding Ninian. The pint was a
beauty too. Sliding down the gullet, smooth as honey. He'd
manage another of those, no bother. He was beginning to
feel warm and content. The broken wood and the cave at

last starting to belong to someone else, the long cold walk through the empty hills.

Ninian had already finished his ice cream. Now he was wolfishly eyeing John's, spoon wavering in his right hand, ready to pounce.

'Go on then, wee gannet.'

The spoon plunged in and delivered a big dollop to the open mouth, where it sat for all to see, melting in pale rivulets on the tongue as mischief and delight flickered in the brown eyes. He was a good-looking lad, right enough, thought John, with the dark curls and fine strong features. Something in the face that said he wasn't stupid either. In fact, just to see him you'd never know . . . Though Lila had twigged OK. That business with the pictures. The hamster. She might not be letting on, but she knew.

There was a commotion at the door at the far end of the room. People struggling in with instrument cases. Old guys with thinning hair and jowls. Huffing and puffing. Pulling faces as they lugged their stuff between the tables. They stepped up on to the stage and started organising themselves. A look in their eyes saying they'd done this a thousand times before. Familiar banter rippling back and forth. Nodding to people in the audience.

'Is this the band?' asked Ninian.

'Aye, it's the band.'

'What will they do?'

'They'll play. Good music. You'll like it.'

'Will I?'

'You will.'

He looked up at John almost shyly. 'Are you in the band?'

'Och no, laddie! Not me.'

'Why not?'

168

'I'm not nearly good enough.'

'Oh.'

A party of four was squeezing noisily around the next table, drinks in hand. Three men and an ample middle-aged woman, who wheezed as she tried to make space for herself at the small table. Now she was looking at John and Ninian. Brothers, she'd be thinking. She caught John's eye, gave him a friendly smile.

He returned it and she leaned over.

'We've been really looking forward to this, y'know,' she said. 'They've banned it where we stay. Up Dingwall way. Can you believe it? Banned live music in the pubs. Said it was threatening public order!' She gave a wheezing laugh and shook her head.

'Is that right?' said John.

'Aye.'

'That's bad.'

'Can you believe it . . . ?' She smiled resignedly. Then shrugged and turned back to her companions, who were discussing a rumour, or maybe it was a news report – having missed the start of the conversation John couldn't be sure – that the bombing at Drumochter had thrown up fresh clues to the Tod's identity. Whichever it was, they sounded almost overexcited, John thought, as if they'd felt some kind of reverberation from the explosion themselves. As if they might at any moment burst into rage or panic.

The Deuchary Ceilidh Band comprised two fiddles, accordion, banjo, bass and drums. Now that the musicians were all lined up, restlessly fingering their instruments, there was an infectious kind of energy about them. They looked suddenly years younger.

There was a chorus of whoops and wolf whistles as the

older of the two fiddlers stepped forward to the mic. He was short, with a high forehead, a fringe of thinning silver hair and a relaxed, easy energy that let the audience know at once that they were in good hands. His eyes twinkled as he introduced the band as 'the best ceilidh outfit this side of the grave'. Then launched into what promised to be a protracted tale involving a virgin and a ripe pair of socks. Already the strained, pinched faces in the audience were giving way to smiles. There were sudden explosions of laughter, not all at appropriate moments. John sensed that these folk had an almost manic determination to be entertained.

Maybe Ninian sensed it too. He was becoming fidgety, rattling his spoon against the inside of the ice-cream bowl, rocking on his stool. John hushed him and he stopped for a minute. Then started again. John noticed that the woman on the neighbouring table was looking their way again. Studying Ninian, it seemed, not so much in disapproval as curiosity. Something perhaps even bordering on recognition. She looked up and caught John's eye. Smiled again. Then leaned forward to speak. At which moment the fiddler delivered his punchline to howls of laughter and loud applause, which were still ringing as the band cracked into the first set of reels, and the woman returned her attention to the stage.

John watched in growing appreciation. The boys could play. No doubt about it. They might be mostly in their sixties, but there was still a crispness there, a bite, with the grace notes and nifty paradiddles, the mouth-watering chord progressions and sudden ripples of syncopation. Enough to set John's bum clenching with pleasure. And this was just the warm-up set. Later, when they really got going, some of the tables would be moved away for dancing.

Ninian had fallen under their spell too, tapping his foot, nodding his head. Intently watching the bows fly across the strings, the fingers dancing up and down the keys. The reels were followed by a set of marches. Then more patter from the fiddler before they glided into an achingly tender rendering of 'Niel Gow's Lament for the Death of His Second Wife', the tune Alec MacNab had been playing the first time John and Davie went into his house, as John now knew. A tune penned in sorrow two and a half centuries ago by one of Scotland's most venerated composers.

But now Ninian was starting to grow restless again. Perhaps it was the change in the pace of the music. John forced himself to his feet. 'We'll go and find Lila, will we?' Ninian nodded. Apologising as they went, John squeezed between the tables and led Ninian out of the lounge. At the end of the passage he stuck his head through the door of the public bar and caught Lila's eye. She finished serving and came out to join them.

'Ready for some cartoons, Ninian?'

'Can I have crisps?' he asked.

Her eyes flickered towards John. Who nodded.

'Sure you can.' She took his hand and he trotted happily after her towards the stairs.

John stood in the passage for a moment watching them go. Thinking that right now he wouldn't mind a bit of looking after himself . . .

He began to feel the music dragging him back, but the beer was straining in his bladder and he had to make a detour via the men's. Back in the lounge he saw that his and Ninian's places had been taken. He made his way to the bar and ordered another pint, then scanned the crowded room and spotted a single empty seat, right by the corner of the stage. The band was playing an old ballad now, the bespectacled banjo player singing in a husky, wavering tenor. John was handing over his money as Lila appeared through a door at the back.

She nodded to him. 'That's him settled upstairs. Happy as Larry.'

'Thanks.'

She smiled. 'No bother.' Then glanced at the audience. 'Good crowd, eh? I wasn't sure – with the bombing . . .'

'Aye. I was wondering myself on the way here. Whether there might even be a curfew.'

'Nah. Nothing like that. Just a bit more of the usual hassle . . .'

John fingered his pint. 'Come in here, do they?'

She shrugged. 'Haven't done for a while . . .' She looked across at the band. 'It's getting busy now. Think I'll stay through here. Good excuse to hear the music, eh?'

'They're fine players, right enough.'

She picked up a glass. Held it to the light. Squinted.

'He's a good kid, that Ninian.'

John nodded. 'I'd best get back to my seat.'

'Aye. On you go.'

He ran the gauntlet of the crowded tables without spilling his pint and took his seat by the stage, almost at the feet of the fiddler, who was now working his repertoire of banjo jokes.

'How do you tell when a banjo player's in the wrong key?' He paused, gave a little trill on the fiddle. 'You look to see if his fingers are moving.' He glanced across the stage. 'Isn't that right, Jack?'

Instrument cradled in his lap like a bed-warming pan, Jack groaned theatrically and rolled his eyes behind the spectacles. The audience tittered.

'This banjo player leaves his banjo in the back of his car

while he goes for a pint. When he comes out of the pub, he finds his back window smashed –' another little trill on the fiddle – 'and now there's two banjos lying there.'

Jack nodded wearily, affected a smile of patient martyrdom, removed his glasses and started polishing them. The audience laughed and clapped. The second fiddler took advantage of the applause to slip off the stage and start making for the door.

He hadn't got far before the first fiddler raised an accusing finger. 'The baby of the band,' he called out, shaking his head. 'That's Marvin. Only fifty-five. And he can't even hold a half-pint.' There were cheers and whistles. Marvin turned at the door with a broad grin and a rude gesture. 'On you go, son,' continued the first fiddler. 'You'll feel better in a minute . . .' He waited for the laughter to subside. 'Now – anyone know the difference between a trampoline and a banjo? I'll tell you. You take off your boot –'

The double doors swung loudly open at the back of the room. The fiddler paused, expression hardening, as all eyes slowly turned to where two armed soldiers were now framed by the doorway.

One of them stood expressionlessly. The other cleared his throat.

'See your IDs, please.'

There was a collective groan of exasperation as people started to fumble in pockets and purses.

'Have some music while you work,' muttered the first fiddler, turning away from the mic, then glanced at the box player who counted them in for a set of jigs.

But John's heart and mind were thundering way ahead of the beat. He shifted on his stool, hand going automatically for the wallet in his hip pocket. Pulled it out and opened it. To an eruption of chill sweat as he registered that the ID card was missing. The NLA unit at the lodge. They never gave it back. Well, that was him fucked now. Good and proper.

And there was another shock on its way. An even nastier one. As he glanced nervously at the soldiers making their way between the tables, the one who didn't speak reminded him of someone. He felt the blood drain from his face as he took in the sallow complexion, the curved nose and luxuriant dark moustache, and realised it was the one from Blackriggs who had shot Gordon and his father, the hotel-keeper.

The panic was in him like a spate now. Roaring in his chest and head. Mouth empty of saliva. Skin running hot and cold at the same time. He glanced wildly around. No one to help. And no way out without being spotted the minute he stood up. At his shoulder, the band were working their way mechanically through the jigs. No joy in their playing now. John's eyes came to rest on the second fiddler's empty stool. The fiddle lying there. His disordered brain locked on to it and seized solid, unable to grasp at any more thought as the detail flooded his vision, the high gleam of the varnish, the powdering of rosin on the fingerboard, one tuning peg a slightly different colour from the others. And quite suddenly, from somewhere just below the ceiling it seemed, he was watching himself step up on to the stage. To looks of blank amazement from the other members of the band. As he picked up the fiddle, sat down on the stool and joined in.

The tune was an old one. 'Jamie Rae'. He knew it well, thank Christ. Slipped right into autopilot, fingers moving of their own accord as his brain raced off again, kicked into life by the sudden activity. He registered the look of intrigue on the faces nearest the stage. And Lila staring at him from behind the bar, though he couldn't make out her expression. But he did see her reaching below the counter and a moment later the house lights dimmed a few degrees. Enough to shadow the faces in the audience and make the soldier from Blackriggs squint with annoyance at the ID card he was inspecting. While on the stage around John, the musicians' astonishment had now given way to a kind of bemused appreciation as they realised that he could at least play. The soldiers were moving gradually forward through the tables. John fiddling like a man possessed, praying that the set would last until after they'd finished and gone. And now the fiddler was mouthing something at the box player. Who nodded, letting slip a sly smile for John as the tune changed, holding his eye. And for all the panic in his head John couldn't ignore the sudden thrill of collusion as the name of the new tune came to him. 'Wee Tod'. He briefly returned the knowing look. An exchange that was lost on the soldiers as they continued to move through the audience, doing their best to ignore the scowls and whispered asides that greeted them at each table. They were almost at the very front when, to John's dismay, the box player nodded them out and the set ended with a chord. The soldiers paused and looked up, as if they'd grown used to their musical accompaniment and were momentarily confused by its absence. But whether he'd caught John's lock-jawed expression, or he'd planned to play on anyway, the box player glanced briefly at the soldiers, winked to John and counted them in for a second set. Now the final ID cards were being scrutinised almost at John's feet. For the first sixteen bars of the new tune he hardly dared breathe but kept his head lowered and concentrated on the movement of his bow. Only when at last the soldiers moved

175

off in the direction of the bar did he look up and catch the urgent stares of the other musicians, to realise that he'd been playing a completely different tune from the rest of them. He smiled sheepishly and corrected himself. Across the room he could see that the soldiers were talking to Lila. Oh God, were they going to make her take them upstairs? But she seemed to be responding evenly, almost light-heartedly, as if they were nothing more than a couple of tricky customers who needed a bit of humouring. And shortly they headed for the exit. Where now the dimly lit silhouette of a third uniformed figure waited for them. It caught John's gaze and held it like a magnet. Big and burly. Swaggeringly confident of its own physical presence. Some-how John kept playing. Doing his best to hide behind his fiddle and ignore the galloping of his heart that had noth-ing to do with the music. But all too soon the set came to an end, and as the applause started John glanced anxiously at the doorway. To see that he was still there, in conversa-tion with the other two soldiers. A moment later they all turned to leave, stepping out of the shadow of the dimmed house lights and into the brightness of the passage beyond. John's heart threatening to burst from his chest as the young corporal's face was revealed.

The square head with its ginger stubble.

The fleshy mouth and pale skin and small, cold weasel eyes.

Kel Foulis.

TWENTY-THREE

The house lights had come up again. The room was full of noise. People were chattering with relief, getting up from their tables, moving around. The musicians were leaning over to pat John on the back, shake his hand. But whether to congratulate him on his playing or his lucky escape, he wouldn't have known. He sat there, stunned and still. Unable to hear anything but the blood pounding in his ears as he stared down the passage after the retreating figure of Kel Foulis.

The fiddle was starting to rattle in his hands. He stood up, forced himself to focus and his eye fell on Lila, smiling at one customer as she pulled a pint for another.

Ninian. That's what he needed to do. Get upstairs and check whether the lad was all right. He glanced around, uncertain where to put the fiddle. Then felt it taken from his hands as Marvin, who had been watching the whole episode from the back of the room, stepped forward with a grin and said something that John couldn't hear. John nodded distractedly, mumbled an apology. Then stepped off the stage and began to shoulder his way through the crowd.

He was almost at the door when someone blocked his path. The woman from the neighbouring table. She smiled at him with blatant admiration. 'That was right good, the playing. Does your wee brother play too?' He shook his head. 'He's bonnie-looking, so he is. Reminds me of some-one.' She gave an asthmatic laugh. 'Can't think who though. On the telly maybe. Oh well . . .' She smiled again, turned and disappeared into the throng.

Now John felt desperate to get out of the crowd, away from all the attention. There were people in the passage too, making their way to and from the toilets. Someone lurched into him and he lost his balance. Put out his left hand to steady himself and realised with a shock that he'd had it thrust deep in his trouser pocket. Like he used to when he was at school, to hide his deformity from view . . .

At the end of the passage he climbed the stairs and found himself on a small landing with three doors leading off it. From behind one came sounds. He opened it as the roar of a speeding motorbike climaxed in a monstrous crash, followed by tinkling and clattering, then a cackle of demented laughter. Ninian was reclining on a beanbag, opposite a large TV. His jacket and sweater discarded on the floor. It was the publican's sitting room, John guessed. A small, cluttered, low-ceilinged room with a fake log fire and a shabby red velour settee. A coffee table strewn with old magazines and crumpled crisp packets, empty cups and glasses. Half a dozen framed fishing cartoons hanging askew on the walls. The mantelpiece almost completely hidden by postcards. And in one corner, its door leaning open, a glass-fronted cabinet crammed with cheap orna-ments and mementoes.

To which, it would appear, Ninian had been helping himself. Arranged on the beanbag beside him was a family

178

of three small carved wooden bears. Father, mother and infant. Lined up, watching the cartoon with him.

John closed the door behind him and slumped down on the settee. Sat in silence for a moment, feeling his pulse start to slow again.

'How's it going, laddie?' He reached out to tousle the dark curls.

Ninian gave a half-smile, half-grimace and pushed his hand away.

It was warm in here. And safe from the world downstairs. And oddly comforting to be back with the lad, who hadn't the faintest idea what was going on all around him.

'Can I see the bears?'

He shook his head.

'Oh, go on. Please.'

'They're mine.' Ninian put out a hand to cover them. 'My bears.' But he had turned to look at John directly. And there was a playful glint in his eye.

'Just one, then. The dad. Just for me.'

He giggled. Pushed the outspread fingers deeper into the beanbag. Burying his treasures securely beneath them. 'No, no!'

'Not the dad one?'

'Not him.'

'The little one, then. Tell you what – call him Ninian, eh?'

His mouth opened in amazement. 'Ninian?'

'Aye. Why not?

He burst into delighted laughter. Eyes shining with glee. 'Ninian the bear!'

'Ninian the bear. Can I see him? Please?'

He held John's gaze for a moment. Then bent forward

and peered theatrically beneath his palm. Withdrew the smallest bear and handed it to John.

'You can have him. Ninian the bear!'

'Thank you.'

For Ninian's benefit, John inspected the little carving as if it was a rare treasure. He was surprised by what he saw. It wasn't the typical modern representation of a bear. Not at all. For one thing it was on all fours. For another, cub though it might be, there was nothing cute or cosy about it. This young bear was full-snouted, heavy-haunched and shaggy. There was something almost heraldic about it, as if it had wandered out from some coat of arms on its way to root for grubs in the forest.

John held it in his hand, thinking what a daft name Ninian was for a bear, and was struck by another more intriguing thought.

He lowered himself from the settee to the floor by the beanbag. 'Will you show me the other two? The mum and dad? No, no . . . I don't want them, like. You just hold them and show them to me . . . Aye, that's it. Grand!' He was careful not to engage Ninian's gaze too directly. 'Now, if this one's called Ninian, this little one, can you tell me what the mum's called?'

Ninian stopped smiling. Uncertainty in the dark eyes.

John pointed at the two bears in turn with his finger. 'What's Ninian's mum called?'

Ninian looked John straight in the eye. Unguarded and quite serious now. 'Yvonne,' he said. Then closed his fist around the wooden carving. Placed his arm behind his back. Out of sight. 'Yvonne's gone to heaven. Yvonne the bear.'

John nodded slowly. 'Aye, so she has. She's happy there,

eh?' He smiled. 'Good lad. So what about the dad? What's his name? The dad bear?'

This time the response was unhesitating. 'Dad!'

'Just Dad, eh?' Trying to keep the disappointment from his voice. 'No other name? Like Yvonne?'

Ninian frowned, evidently bewildered. Then shuffled round in the beanbag and fixed his attention on the screen again.

John turned the carving over in his fingers. Tiny letters were stamped on the sole of one foot. *Souvenir of Bern.* Wherever that was. He placed it back on the beanbag at Ninian's side. Looked at the small shoulders, shoulder blades visible beneath the checked shirt, the dark head slightly cocked in concentration. Who was he, this lost boy with no identity? Who asked John for nothing but needed everything he had to give and more. Who seemed to trust him more completely even than Davie had done . . . And what was the unknown world he carried inside him? For surely everyone had some kind of skeleton that held up their lives, didn't they? Some kind of framework of memories and feelings, people and places and things? But perhaps Ninian didn't, or if he did perhaps he couldn't see it. Which was why he needed so much help . . .

'Oh, laddie,' said John under his breath, 'what the hell am I going to do with you?'

As he sat back on the settee the door opened and Lila came in. She walked across and stood in front of the fire. Glanced at Ninian, sunk into the beanbag, and smiled.

'You all OK up here?'

Ninian ignored her.

'Fine, thanks.'

She looked across to John. 'That was good – the fiddling.' There was no acknowledgement of the drama.

Just a look of appreciation. 'I didn't know you still played . . .'

John felt himself blushing. 'Aye, well . . .' he mumbled. 'Haven't for a while. Just . . . felt like it tonight . . .'

'Then you should feel like it more often. The band were impressed. They told me.'

'Oh . . .'

'Anyway. They're back on again now. For the dancing. D'you want to come down? Or take him home? Or maybe wait till later . . . ?' She nodded to herself. 'Aye, why don't you wait and come back with me? That might be better.'

John nodded, happy for someone else to be making the decisions.

The strains of music drifted up the stairs and briefly mingled with the sounds of the TV as she left the room.

But John had lost his appetite for tunes. For this evening at any rate.

He leaned back in the settee and closed his eyes, feeling the dull rhythmic thumping of feet vibrating through the weary old timbers around him.

TWENTY-FOUR

'C'mon, sleepyhead . . .'

John clawed for consciousness at the feel of a hand on his shoulder. He was thick-headed, dry-mouthed. The little room was stuffy and airless. The TV flickered and muttered to itself in the corner. At his feet, Ninian was slumped across the beanbag.

Lila switched off the TV. The sudden silence seemed to sharpen John's senses, forced him to wake up.

'It's time to go.' She was squatting at the beanbag now, stroking the head of the sleeping figure. Which opened one eye, then closed it crossly. Groaned and drew in its knees.

'Come on, Ninian. We'll get you home to your nice bed.'

The dark head burrowed into the cushioning with muffled grunts.

Lila looked up and caught John's eye. He slid off the settee and joined her. Grasped the recumbent figure beneath the arms and gently lifted. 'Come on, Ninian. We can't stay here all night.'

Ninian's eyes were open now. He was scowling but not resisting, a dead weight in John's arms. Then he saw the bears which had tumbled off the beanbag and were scattered on the floor.

'My bears! I want to take my bears.' His voice was instantly edged with the familiar whine, as if it had been laid against a grindstone.

'But they're not yours to take.'

He was starting to wriggle now. An arm reaching down.

'Yes, they're mine! My bears. My three bears.'

John heeded the warning signs. Set him on his feet. And at once he stooped to gather up the bears, clasped them to his chest.

John glanced apologetically at Lila.

'Do you have bears like that, Ninian?' she asked. 'At home?'

He stared at her, momentarily uncertain. Then said, 'My Bern bears.'

'Bern bears?' She glanced at John, who echoed her look of surprise.

'It's where they're from,' he said. 'Says so. On them. He must have some too. Where is it, d'you know? Bern?'

'Switzerland.' She looked pensive for a moment. 'Och well. You'd better take them. I'll square it with the boss later.' She helped Ninian on with his jacket. Pulled the sleeve up over his fist, still bulging with bears. 'First that manky old tiger's paw. Now the three bears. Quite a wee collection, eh?'

Ninian clung to his new trophies.

Outside it had begun to snow gently. Small soft flakes drifted down through the pool of yellow light outside the back door. Lila turned it out as she left. For a moment the darkness was total yet alive with the flutter and brush of flakes on eyelashes, nose, cheeks.

'I love this.'

As John's eyes adjusted he could see her outline. Standing still on the doorstep, face upturned.

'The Christmases we never had.'

'Why's that?'

'We lived in England when I was a kid. Basingstoke.' She shook her head in disgust. 'Never snowed there. Not that it snows much anywhere these days, I guess. But you know what I mean . . .'

'Can we make a snowman?' Ninian was tugging at John's hand.

'Tomorrow maybe. If it lies.'

'I want to make one now.' The grindstone starting to turn again.

'But it's late . . .'

Lila caught John's eye. Then squatted down in the road in front of Ninian. And he watched, intrigued, as with elaborate gestures she tried to roll a tiny snowball from the thin film that covered the tarmac. Then stood up, dusting her hands and shaking her head.

'Not enough snow, you see.' She pulled a face. 'Tell you what though – we'll make one in the garden at home.'

John was impressed. Whether or not she'd figured out about Ninian's condition, she'd got the measure of him all right.

'Why Basingstoke?' he asked as they set off down the lane. He noticed that Ninian had now swapped his hand for Lila's.

'My dad. When I was a kid he worked as a project manager with a big software group down there.'

It was strangely quiet out here. The darkness close. The snow muffling their footsteps. Like being wrapped in velvet.

'When did you come back?'

185

'When I was fourteen. Dad quit the full-time job to move back and take over his dad's croft. And do some part-time teleworking for his old firm.'

'Where?'

'Up in Wester Ross. Gairloch way.'

'Some change for you. A teenager, like.'

'Hawthorns Basingstoke to Gairloch High.' She laughed in the darkness. 'Some change, aye.'

The small footsteps had fallen behind. John turned round to see that Ninian had stopped in the gateway of a house some yards back, where he had found something interesting on the ground.

'C'mon now, Ninian. We need to get home.'

Ninian paid no attention. He squatted in the snow-filled shadows by the gatepost.

John had begun to walk back towards him when he heard a vehicle turn into the street. Moments later headlights raked the darkness around him, thick now with falling flakes. Then there was a muffled rush of feet behind him and he felt Lila's hand at his shoulder. She was tugging him urgently into the gateway where Ninian crouched by the hedge. Then leaning back against the gatepost and drawing him into a deep embrace. The cold tip of her nose against his cheek. Her body, bulky in its coat, pressed close against his. Stunned, John could do nothing but meekly submit as her hand came snaking round the back of his head and refused to let him go. Her breath warm and moist on his face. Her scent rising up his nostrils on the sharp, cold air. Then there was a hot whisper in his ear. 'Army!' And his heart pounded as he nodded slowly against her snow-dampened hair. Buried himself in the embrace. While Ninian still crouched, hopefully unseen, in the darkness

186

behind their legs. Absorbed in whatever it was he'd found under the hedge.

John heard the vehicle slowing. As it drew level a spotlight bathed them in harsh white light that threw the dark filament of Lila's hair into relief, beaded with melting snow. For a moment he feared the vehicle might be going to stop. There was a scuffling and muttering at their feet now. John turned his face away from the road and whispered into the darkness, 'Shh now, laddie! Stay where you are!'

The scuffling paused.

The vehicle had slowed to walking pace.

Lila drew his head round. Raised her mouth. Lips crushing his. Full and warm.

The nearside window rolled down.

'Wahey!' crowed a voice. 'Gie her one fer me, pal!'

Guffaws of laughter as the spotlight slid away and the vehicle accelerated off down the street.

Lila waited till it turned the corner at the end. Then pulled away and stepped out into the road, blinking and brushing the snow from her hair.

'That kept them happy!'

Still half blinded by the spotlight, John could hear the indignation in her voice. The amusement too. The blood was throbbing in his cheeks.

'Thanks,' he said. It came out as a croak.

'My pleasure,' said Lila. And laughed.

There was a rustling behind them as Ninian emerged from the hedge. Scowling like some pygmy scalp-hunter, with the limp sac of a deflated plastic football clutched in one hand.

John reached out.

'Home now.'

But the scowl deepened and he shook his head.

'C'mon now. It's cold here. And dark.'

'No.' He turned away, facing the hedge again. Folding his arms across his chest. Starting to rock from side to side. Whining to himself.

Suddenly John had had enough of this evening. He wanted just to grab the lad and sling him over his shoulder, ignore the screams and run all the way home if necessary.

But before he could do it Lila was there. Squatting down in the shadows and talking to Ninian softly. Soothing, coaxing, cajoling. Taking one hand in hers, then the other. And in no time at all he'd stopped whining and was stepping out into the road with her, biddable as a lamb.

John joined them as they passed under a street lamp. Lila turned towards him in the snow-speckled spill of light and mouthed something, then winked. Seeing from his blank look that he hadn't got it, she mouthed again, *'Jealous!'*

'Oh.' John nodded, feeling the blood rush to his scalp again. He moved round behind Ninian and fell into step the other side of her.

'How did . . . I mean . . . what did you say to him?'

'Just now?'

'Aye.'

'Told him I'd show him where a real bear used to live.'

'Can you?'

She smiled. 'Of course.'

Five minutes later they reached the bungalow. The security light came on as they walked up the path. There was a good couple of inches of snow lying now and still it was coming down. Getting thicker, if anything, till there seemed to be more flakes than darkness.

Ninian had been silent on the way back, head low, eyes

on the ground. But now there was something determined in the way he peered around.

'Is this the garden?' he asked, scuffing his toes in the snow.

'Aye.' John knew what was coming next.

'Are we going to make the snowman?'

'In the dark and the cold . . . ?'

The small jaw started to set.

'OK.' John turned to Lila. 'You go on in . . .'

He crouched down to start rolling up a big snowball. And wondered, yet again, what the hell he'd got himself into here. Making a snowman in a blizzard in the middle of the night for a daft boy. Who was standing by in the glare of the security light, watching proceedings with the unforgiving eye of a chief inspector of snowmen. The flakes settling on his head and shoulders so that he was starting to look like a small one himself. John trundled the ball a few yards across what he took to be the lawn. The snow was moist and it gathered layers like a Swiss roll as it went. Soon it was big enough to make into a body. He brushed the snow out of his eyes. Shook the drips from his hair. Pulled his collar close and started work on a smaller roll for the head. Ninian had stopped watching him now and was bent over at the flower bed by the front door, heaving at something which broke suddenly loose so that he staggered backwards. He recovered himself and marched through the tumbling flakes towards John, proudly holding a half-brick from the edging of the flower bed.

'For his nose!'

Oh laddie, you haven't a clue, have you . . . ?

'Grand,' said John. 'But maybe better for a foot, eh?'

Ninian looked momentarily crestfallen.

'Get me another. Then he'll have two.' They could be put back again in the morning.

'Two feet for the snowman!' He smiled and trotted back to the flower bed, leaving a flurry of footprints in the snow behind him.

Time to get the job finished and back indoors, thought John. He shaped up a round head and placed it on top of the body. Snow was going down the back of his neck, fingers starting to get cold. Ninian had no gloves either. Here he came now with the other half-brick. Set them both beneath the body. Two red feet. Like a . . . a puffin. Well, hardly. But would the chief inspector be happy with it? That was the question.

He stood back. Snowflakes the size of large coins now, drifting steadily down in their countless trillions.

'So . . . how's that?'

But suddenly Ninian seemed to have lost interest. Clutching his fingers. A pained look on his face as if he might be about to cry.

'Come on. We need to get inside. Get warm.'

Ninian trotted to the front door, flapping his arms like a wounded bird as he went. Opened it himself and headed down the hall, trailing snow behind him, straight for the living room, where Lila was setting a pot of tea and mugs on the table. He stopped in the middle of the floor and started to howl.

John paused at the front door long enough to knock the worst of the snow off his boots, then hurried after him.

By the time he got to the living room the howling had already begun to take on that wild, unhinged, animal quality. Somewhere between a bellow and an ear-splitting shriek. Lila was trying to persuade Ninian to let her warm his hands in hers. But he wasn't having any of it. Pushing her away, hiding his head, waving his fingers in agony as the blood forced its way back into them. Red and raw like small uncooked sausages.

His distress disturbed her, John could see. She looked up at him. He nodded and went towards Ninian. Reached out and pulled him into a bear hug.

'C'mon, we'll have a wee cuddle, eh?'

The howling increased and he began to struggle, but not as hard as John knew he could. Standing in the middle of the room, John held him tight. Then lifted him and carried him over to the settee where they sank back together. John pulled his coat around them and Ninian offered no resistance when he reached down for the fingers and closed his own large hands over them.

'There. Make those fingers better.'

The dark head nodded and sniffed. The shoulders twitched. He grizzled quietly against John's chest.

Lila busied herself fetching biscuits and milk. Then she looked over and smiled. 'Cup?'

John nodded.

'Would you like a dram with it? I think Morag keeps a bottle somewhere.'

'I . . . I don't really . . .'

'Just a wee one. To warm you up?'

'OK then. Aye.' He shifted the boy on his lap till they were both comfortable.

It took her a minute to find the bottle, hidden away in a cupboard. She poured a shot into a tumbler and placed it on a small side table at the arm of the settee, along with a cup of tea and a couple of biscuits. Then she poured herself a small dram, took her own tea and sat in the chair opposite.

She raised her glass. '*Slainte!*'

191

'*Slainte!*' He took a cautious sip of the whisky and felt the spirit instantly warming his belly.

Lila sat back in her chair and gave him a long smile. Her face was full of curiosity.

'So, John MacNeil,' she said, 'what's the *craic* then?'

TWENTY-FIVE

John took another sip of whisky. Holding on to the glass helped disguise the tremor in his hands as he wondered what to say.

Now she had her feet tucked up under her again and her head tilted slightly to one side. Waiting for him to answer.

Almost before he was aware of it, he'd started to talk. But not about Blackriggs, or Ninian. Not about their flight across the hills or Kel Foulis. Not any of these, but about Davie. How he looked, walked, sounded. The things he liked, the things he hated, the things he did that were plain annoying. His amazing ear for a tune. The weird business with the colours. How he had worshipped his big brother. Laughed at his bad jokes. Loved his fiddling. Called him Captain Hook to make him smile about his thumb. Tried to cheer John up when Kel Foulis and his cronies had been at him. But could plummet so quickly into the depths of his own despair. And was really just too fine a wee soul for this rough old world . . .

John set down the tumbler and clasped both arms round the dozing boy on his lap as he continued to tell her everything he could remember about Davie's short life. Opposite,

Lila sat perfectly still until he came to the events at the bridge, when she leaned slightly forward and cupped her chin in one hand. And finally it came out, the thing he'd never dared voice to anyone but himself, not to his folks nor the police nor the kindly sheriff at the Fatal Accident Inquiry. Could he have done anything to prevent it?

Lila let his question hang unanswered. Then got up without a word and left the room. She returned shortly with a pack of tissues, which she handed to him. At that moment the electricity died and they were plunged into darkness.

'Shit!' she exclaimed softly. 'Here, you stay put. I know my way around.'

John pulled out a tissue and dabbed at his eyes. He heard a match strike in the kitchen and she returned carrying a candle in a saucer. She placed it on the table between them and sat down again.

'I've never told that to anyone,' he said at last when he could find his voice again. 'Don't know why I told you now.'

She looked at him for a long while. 'I expect you needed to.' She opened the whisky bottle. 'We've all got things we need to say. When the right moment comes.' She leaned across and poured another shot into his glass. Then she smiled warmly. 'And you know what, I think you already answered your own question.'

'Which one?'

'The one about whether you could have stopped it happening . . .'

'How's that?'

'When you said that you thought he actually wanted to go. I don't think you'd've been able to do anything. Not that made any difference.'

194

'Hmm.' He felt utterly drained now. But strangely clear-headed. As if a breath of wind had begun to stir a seven-year-old fog.

She smiled again. 'He was right about the fiddling anyway. And you kept it up.'

'Aye.' He took another sip of whisky, then moved the now sleeping Ninian off his lap and on to the settee beside him, covering him with his coat. 'But I've still not written a tune for him . . .'

'I'm sure you will. D'you still have one?'

'A fiddle?'

She nodded, fishing in her bag for tobacco and papers. 'Want one?'

'Hmm, well . . . aye. Go on then.'

She rolled two cigarettes. Lit them both with the candle and passed one to John.

He took a drag and felt instantly light-headed. He waited for the feeling to pass, then began to speak again. Now he told her what had happened, from the moment five days ago when the helicopter had landed at Blackriggs, to the moment a few hours ago that he had recognised Foulis in the pub. He told her everything he could remember. Everything except for one thing – the whole business about Ninian. He couldn't really understand why he held back, when part of him longed so much to let it all out. Trust was certainly nothing to do with it now, not after the way she'd handled the army patrol in the street. But when it came to it, something just stopped him telling the truth. He made up a story instead about having been asked to look after his wee cousin for a few days – the wrong few days as it turned out, he added for good measure.

Now Lila looked at him for a long time in shocked

silence. For a moment John even wondered whether she believed him.

Then she said softly, 'They tortured my father, you know. Picked him up at the Inverness riots. He'd organised a bus-load of protesters from Gairloch. To support the Venison Six. That's all.' There was a note of quiet bitterness in her voice now. 'They took him to Fort George. Accused him of cyberterrorism. Because of the teleworking, I suppose. But all he'd done was post the bus times on the local net. They beat him so badly he couldn't walk for a month.' She paused as if the memory of it had momentarily robbed her of her voice. 'Of course he was angry about what was going on. Everyone was. So he went on a demo to have his say. It's a free country – or so we thought. But he was no terrorist, my dad – cyber or any other kind . . . And for that we had to watch him crawling about the place on his hands and knees for a month. Stubborn old sod that he is . . .' She gave a short laugh, but John could see her eyes moistening. 'I guess we all have our reasons to hate them, eh?'

'Aye.'

She ran her hand across her face. 'But that's my story. What about you? What are you going to do now?'

John let go a long sigh. 'I'm not sure. My dad'll be going spare. I've got to find a way of getting hold of him. But I don't know how to any longer, not without them knowing. I mean . . . I reckon they'll be watching the house, what's left of it. Monitoring phone calls. Keeping an eye on the buses and so on. Checking up on his friends – and mine. It really scares me if I think about it, Lila. These folk – the ones I saw at Blackriggs – they're total animals . . .' His hands were starting to tremble. He tried to push the images from his mind. 'So . . . I guess I just need to lie up somewhere for a while – figure out how to make contact with my dad.' He caught her eye and shook his head. 'Don't worry – I'm not asking to stay here, put you in any danger or anything.'

She smiled. 'You can stay here as long as you like. And you'll be safe.'

'Well . . . thanks. But I wouldn't . . .'

She pointed at the sleeping figure on the settee. 'What about him?'

John shrugged. 'Stuck with him, I guess. For the moment.' Which was true.

'Then you should definitely stay here. But listen – what about the NLA? Couldn't they help you?'

'Mmm,' John said slowly. 'I'd been thinking about that – that perhaps I need to get back in touch with them. See, you'll mebbe think this is daft – but I've this kind of idea that I need to be able to speak out about what happened. At Blackriggs. It's been going through my head ever since. Kept me going across the hill. I was the only person there, see – the only person that knows the truth . . .'

She nodded approvingly.

'Those poor bastards at the lodge,' he went on, 'the rebel lads, they said that their high-heidyins, the boys in charge, would find somewhere safe for me.'

'You mean like some kind of witness protection . . . ?'

'Aye, I suppose so.' He sighed. 'Though when they offered it they didn't know that it was me was going to get them all killed an hour later.'

'But . . . it sounds like you had an impossible choice to make . . .'

He nodded uncomfortably. 'I guess so.'

'So do you know how to get in touch with them? The NLA?' She looked at him intently.

He gave a weary shrug. 'Haven't a clue.'

She said quietly, 'I do.'

Somehow this came as no surprise. He'd been right to trust the instinct that he'd find sanctuary at Morag's place . . .

'I wonder . . .' Lila glanced down at her watch. 'Christ no! One thirty already.' Shook her head. 'It's way too late now. But first thing tomorrow.' She paused. 'Not exactly a high-heidyin himself. But he'll know how to make contact.'

Ninian sighed and turned in his sleep. One arm and half a leg flopped over the edge of the settee.

She glanced at John. 'Should we get him to his bed?'

'Aye.' John stood up.

'Can you manage?'

He nodded. Bent down and gathered up the sleeping figure, carried him through to the bedroom and laid him on the bed. Took off the coat and shoes. Started on the trousers, but there was a wriggle and a muffled groan of protest. So he left the trousers on and drew the covers up. Stood there for a moment looking down at the soft features relaxing into sleep again.

'Sleep well, laddie,' he whispered. 'We'll see what's what, the morn.' He left the room, putting out the light.

TWENTY-SIX

In the sitting room Lila had rolled and lit another cigarette. As John sat down again she took a deep drag. Held the smoke in for a long, pensive moment, then exhaled.

'Can I ask you something, John?' Now there was a slight hesitance in her voice.

'Ask away.' He drained the remains of the whisky but held on to the tumbler. Sensing what was coming.

'Do you . . . know what fragile X syndrome is?'

He shook his head.

'Well . . . it's what Ninian's got. I'm almost certain of it. And if I'm right, then – I'm not quite sure how to put this –' she took a nervous drag on the cigarette – 'then either you're not his cousin or his folks aren't looking after him the way they should.'

She looked at him and waited. Her eyes large in the candlelight.

'How d'you mean?' he said sharply.

'I mean that he's handicapped. Quite seriously, I think. See . . . before I came here I started training to teach special-needs kids. We learned all the different conditions.

Fragile X was one of them. And it wasn't just theory. We did placements in schools. I saw it for myself.'

'Oh aye?'

'Aye . . . and though everyone knows about Down's syndrome, hardly anyone knows about fragile X. Yet there's maybe half as many kids with that as with Down's. It's genetic. A kind of mutation of one of the X chromosomes – you can see it on a microscope, the X looks as if one of its legs is about to fall off. Fragile X, see . . . ?' The confidence had returned to her voice now. She went on. 'Anyway, plenty of kids have it . . . though it's more obvious with the boys than the girls. It makes them hyperactive. Impulsive. And compulsive. Short attention span – all that kind of thing. Folk often put it down to bad behaviour at first. Which can be really hard for the parents until they know the score. They just think they're not doing their job properly.'

John said nothing. Listening to Lila talk like this made him realise that very soon everyone was going to want to get their hands on Ninian. Either because of what he was or because of who he was – or rather wasn't. Probably both. It made him want to run back to the bedroom and check that Ninian was still there. He couldn't possibly give him up after all they'd been through together. Not yet anyway . . .

'Are you OK, John?' There was sympathy in her voice. But there was something in her look that said she was going to see through what she'd started.

'Aye.' He could feel himself colouring. 'Go on.' Hating her for what she was about to do, struggling to accept the inevitability of it.

She stubbed out the cigarette in a neat, deliberate gesture.

'But I guess the most obvious thing is that they don't really like people . . . I mean, they get easily upset by other folk. They don't like to be looked in the eye. Prone to tantrums.' She paused. 'It's not the same as autism, but some of what they do is similar. Like watching the same TV programme over and over. Obsessively arranging things. And the physical stuff, the signs of anxiety . . . hand-flapping or head-shaking.'

Her knowledge was making John jealous. Her self-assurance. As if in some way it already granted her a superior claim to Ninian.

'But the main thing is the mental handicap,' she went on. 'They just can't figure things out – or handle abstract ideas. The world's black and white to them, exactly how they see it. There's no shades of grey. And they can't follow a line of thought, not like you and me. Like, if today's Tuesday, tomorrow must be Wednesday. Or, it's raining outside so I'll get wet if I don't wear a coat. They can't sequence things in their mind, see. They can't share what's in it either. You saw the picture of the hamster. He can probably see one quite clearly in his head, but he hasn't the faintest idea how to get it across . . .' She paused. 'But the hardest thing of all is that they can't ever tell you how they feel. Poor wee souls.'

John thought of the tantrums. The pain and distress so obvious, yet so impossible for Ninian to express.

'Go on,' he said.

'So . . . it's really hard for them to function on their own in the world, these kids,' she continued. 'Almost impossible, in fact. And what happens is they become incredibly dependent on the folk who care for them. I've seen it and it's really touching. The kids love them. And I mean *really* love them. I'm talking about their folks, of course. Unless it's a very, very unusual situation.' She paused, looking at him directly. 'And what I think, John, is that no fragile X kid I've ever heard of would have a cousin who didn't know about it. And even if they did, no responsible parents would ever let him look after them . . .' She let out a long breath, then added, 'Don't get me wrong, John. I think you're coping brilliantly. But you're not used to it. And I don't think he's your cousin.'

Now she sat back in her chair with an uncertain smile.

'You've no proof,' said John, more aggressively than he meant to.

'You're right,' she replied, struggling to maintain the smile. 'I don't. Not that you're not his cousin, anyway. Because Ninian'll never be able to tell me the truth about that.' She reached for her glass. 'But whether he's fragile X or not? Well . . . there's plenty of clues. Like long faces and sticking-out ears, for a start. OK, his face isn't so long. But the jug-handle lugs. Hard to ignore, no?' She gave a nervous laugh. 'Then there's the muscles round the mouth. They can be a bit slack. And the skin. Very, very soft. Almost like velvet.' This time John couldn't help nodding. The weight of evidence starting at last to bear down on him. 'Sometimes they've this funny wee crease that runs down the sole of the foot, between the big and second toe. And there's one more very common thing – with a weird name. Macroorchidism. That's big balls to you and me . . .'

She looked at him. The whisky had brought a flush to her cheeks.

John nodded again, remembering now what had snagged at him that first evening at the cabin, when he'd seen Ninian naked in the bath.

'I'm not his cousin,' he said.

'What are you then?'

202

'Nothing. No relation.'

'So, who . . . why – I mean . . . who is he?'

John shrugged. 'I don't know.'

Her eyes widened.

'Go on! You're kidding me.'

He shook his head. 'I found him. In Blackriggs. Hiding.'

Lila whistled softly. 'My God! And he can't tell you who he is . . . ?'

'No.'

'And you'd never seen him before? Knew nothing about him? Not even that there was anything wrong with him?'

'No.' For a moment John was back in the ice house. Seeing the small wild figure, hunkered down in the gloom.

'I couldn't leave him.'

She nodded slowly. '*How* long ago was this?'

'Less than a week.' It felt like ten years.

'On the run with a fragile X kid . . .' Her eyes filled with sympathy. 'John, John . . . no wonder you're knackered!'

Much later the electricity came back on, triggering the outside security lamp as it did so. For a short while the dark void of the window swam with the ghostly silhouettes of birches. It had stopped snowing.

Lila stretched and turned her head from side to side. John felt jarred. As if the sudden intrusion of light had wrenched them from the safe, comfortable half-world of whisky and candlelight and back to the here and now of unanswerable questions and impossible decisions.

'Right now I'm not sure what we should do,' said Lila, rising to her feet. 'Though there's one thing I'm sure of: I wouldn't trust the authorities with him for two seconds. Not if his aunt had even the slightest connection with the NLA.' She started gathering up the cups and glasses with abrupt, angry movements. 'Police. Army. Civil authorities. They'd use him somehow, I know they would. I'd never trust them. Not a single one of them. Bastards!'

The sudden outburst took John by surprise. Shocked him into activity. He heaved himself out of the settee. Everything about him was tired now, and on top of it all he felt woozy from the whisky. It seemed as if they'd been blethering all night. He picked up the teapot and milk. Followed her unsteadily through to the kitchen.

She looked round at the sink. 'We'll talk to my friend. Tomorrow. See if he's got any ideas.'

It was cramped in the small kitchen. John was suddenly aware of how close he was standing to her. The memory of the kiss came back and he felt the blood flowing into his cheeks. As she reached up to put the glasses away in a cupboard his eye was drawn to the outline of her uplifted breasts.

'You don't need to do this for us,' he said.

'I know I don't.' She turned and looked at him. 'But I want to.'

She closed the cupboard door.

'I want to do my bit for the cause. And for you.' She nodded. 'And for Ninian. Whoever he is.'

TWENTY-SEVEN

How was John to explain to Ninian that he had to stay indoors this morning? That he couldn't go out and build another snowman because there were soldiers or policemen who might come looking for him?

He couldn't, of course. And John knew it well enough by now. But that didn't stop him wishing with all his might that he could. It was only eleven o'clock and already he was done in. Lila had gone out early and come back with provisions, then gone off again. Ninian had eaten a hearty breakfast, then refused point blank to watch TV or play with the games console. Out of sheer perversity, John suspected. So they'd spent the morning playing every game he could think of. Built dens with the furniture and blankets. Made stepping stones with the magazines. Put up a castle of old books. Eaten half a packet of biscuits. Gone to sea on the settee cushions. The place looked like a bomb had hit it. And the moment he let his attention wander, Ninian started whining. Bored and frustrated, John could feel his temper being stretched to the limit.

To make matters worse it was a beautiful day. Clear skies, bright sunshine, birch trees casting slim blue shadows on crisp snow. John couldn't remember when he'd last seen a picture-postcard scene like this. Though there was something deceptive about it, something in the air that set his stalker's instincts on alert. He could taste it on his tongue, metallic. A hint of violence building. Meteorological violence – of the kind that was only too frequent these days.

Ninian didn't care. Sitting with his back to John now. Nose pressed against the big glass sliding doors in the living room, ignoring him. In a silent fury. He'd been there for the last ten minutes, winding himself up for a tantrum. Like the weather maybe.

Well, he could stay there for the moment, John thought, taking advantage of the respite to make himself a cup of coffee. Though he guessed he'd have to drink it quickly. The television over the breakfast bar was on, the sound turned down. Brightly dressed, hyperactive young presenters were encouraging a group of overexcited kids to fling yellow gloop at one another. He turned away, waiting for the dispenser to do its business, and watched the small figure through the kitchen door. Knowing that Ninian could see his reflection in the window, that the minute he strayed out of view the tantrum would begin. Fragile X. He'd been right last night. Even the naming of Ninian's condition, the saying-out-loud of it, seemed to have taken something away from him. Now he was no longer a lone figure in the wilderness but someone who belonged to an identifiable tribe, or clan even. Now he would always be fragile X, in the same way that John would always be a MacNeil . . . Not that any of this did anything to make him more normal. Even his name, Lila had said last night – Ninian, it was a saint's name, kind of other-worldly, wasn't it? Ninnyish even . . .

Thump, thump, thump. There was nothing other-

206

worldly about him now. He'd started to bang his head rhythmically against the window. Gurning to himself.

'Careful of the glass,' John called out.

The gurning rose to a whine. John started to catch mumbled words.

'I hate you, I hate you.'

Leaving his coffee, he went over and squatted down behind him. Not too close.

'C'mon now. There's a good programme on TV. See if you like it, eh?'

'Nooo.' Shook his head. 'I hate you. Hate you.'

'Go on. Of course you don't.'

'I do. Hate you. Hate you.'

He'd begun to flap his arms. And before John could get out of the way, he clambered to his feet and pushed past, stamping hard on one of John's hands as he went.

'Ow!' cried John angrily. 'That was sore.'

'I hate you. I hate you,' mumbled Ninian, burying his head under the remaining cushion on the settee. Bum in the air like an ostrich.

'Well, I hate you too,' John retorted.

The bum gave a wriggle. The cushion lifted and the head peered round. With a smile of sly delight.

'I hate you! I hate you!'

'And I hate you too,' echoed John.

Ninian stood up and came towards him. Almost laughing now. 'I hate you! I hate you!'

John advanced. 'I hate you too,' he growled.

And before he knew what was happening, Ninian had clasped his arms around his waist and was hugging him. Tight as he could. Still muttering, 'I hate you. I hate you.' Dark curly head pressed close against John's stomach.

John felt something softening inside him. Put his arms around the boy's shoulders and returned the hug.

They stood still together for a moment.

'Can I get my coffee now?' asked John.

'Noooo,' he mumbled into John's jumper. 'I hate you.' But offered no resistance as John started to steer him gently towards the kitchen, then halted as his eye was caught by the ticker strip that had appeared at the foot of the television screen. And the words that were now scrolling across it:

Breaking news. NLA arms shipment intercepted. Copenhagen-registered trawler Marie Claire *held off Cromarty coast. More soon . . .*

There was something about this that sounded familiar. He flicked over to the news channel, where the presenter was in mid-report. '. . . and this latest blow to the rebels comes just hours after the NLA leader, the shadowy figure previously known only as the Tod, was positively identified as billionaire financier Struan Fraser. The identification came last night . . .'

The door opened noisily and Lila came in, the urgency in her look shattering his thoughts like a hammer blow.

'Get your things. Quick. We've got to go. Right now!'

John gaped.

'What . . . ? How . . . ?'

'Just get your things. I'll explain once we're away.'

Her hands were shaking. Face drawn and bloodless. This was obviously no joke. John shook himself from his stupor. Dashed into the bedroom and gathered up their few bits and pieces. Stuffed them in the backpack. Then out into the hallway, where Lila was now helping Ninian on with his jacket and boots. Muttering softly to him about bears and snowmen.

She glanced up at John and nodded.

'I've borrowed a car. You'll have to get down in the back. I'll find something to put over you.'

Lila opened the front door. Glanced out. 'Right. You need to get straight in and down on the floor.' She looked at Ninian. 'We're going to play hide-and-seek. In the car. You and John can hide. I'll drive. OK?'

He smiled uncertainly.

John took his hand.

'Go,' ordered Lila.

They hurried down the path. There was an ancient Volvo estate sitting in the roadway, engine running. John heaved the pack into the rear, then scrambled across the back seat. Crouched down, then reached over and pulled Ninian in after him.

'Good lad! See if we can keep them from seeing us, eh?'

Ninian nodded. But the anxiety was plain in his face.

'Now. We'll both get down here. Like a pair of wee mice. Lila's going to put a cover on us. Keep us cosy!'

Which a moment later she did. An old tartan travelling rug. Followed by what felt like several empty cardboard boxes. Ninian protested, even though they didn't weigh anything.

'Makes it look like we're not here, see.'

That seemed to amuse him. He chuckled as Lila climbed into the driver's seat.

'You OK back there?'

'OK,' grunted John.

The car pulled off. Rear end sliding on the frozen snow as it swept round the turning circle at the end of the close.

'There's a search on,' said Lila without turning her head. John had to strain to catch what she was saying. 'Foulis and his mates. They're at the pub. They've been there about half an hour.' He pictured her face set. Hands clenched tight on the steering wheel. 'Ransacking it. And they're stopping folk in the street. Getting ready to do a house-to-house by the looks of it.'

'What are they after?' He had to ask twice so she could hear through the covering of rug and boxes.

'Not sure. I didn't stop to ask. I came back here as fast as I could.' She changed gear. 'But they'll have had a tip-off. Or maybe someone'll have blethered last night. It could be weapons. Could be you. Could even be something to do with the Deuchary boys. They're not unknown to play the rebel song . . .' She changed gear again. 'We can't take any chances though.'

'Where are we going?'

'My friend's place.'

'Is that safe?'

'If we can get there . . .'

John squeezed Ninian's hand and whispered, 'Another adventure, eh?'

Ninian shook his head and mumbled something inaudible above the engine noise.

The car slowed at a junction, then pulled forward again, turning sharp right as it did so. The hiss of packed snow gave way to the rumble of wheels on wet tarmac. They must be heading up towards the main intersection with the N1, John reckoned.

But they'd only gone a couple of hundred yards when Lila started to slow down again.

'Oh shit!'

'What?' John asked. 'What is it?'

For a moment there was no reply.

'Checkpoint. Stay down.'

In the gloom under the blanket John reached out and

put a finger to Ninian's lips. 'We've to be extra quiet now,' he whispered. 'Still as we can.'

The car continued to move slowly forward. But at any moment now it would stop. Then there'd be voices. Heads peering through the window. Asking what's that behind the front seats. There, that bulge under the rug . . .

Instead of which there was a squeal of wheels and a sudden jolt. The car juddered to a halt and stalled. John and Ninian thrown against the front seats with the force of it. Lila's loud exclamation of surprise and anger. As something large and heavy and noisy burst out in front of them. Slewing sideways in the slush. Accelerating away up the road with a roar of engine and stink of exhaust. Followed shortly by shouts. A splintering crash and a grinding of metal. Then a burst of automatic weapon fire. A screaming of brakes.

And a shocked '*Jesus Christ!*' from Lila.

A moment's silence. Then feet clattering. A lot more shouting. More firing. Staccato bursts, sharp and deadly. And panic-stricken muttering as Lila fumbled with the ignition.

'Come on! *Come on – please!*'

Something thwanged off the roof of the car and whined away. A searing smell of metal sharpened the air. John could stand it no longer. He shrugged off the blanket and boxes and clambered up. As the engine turned at last. Lila let out the clutch. And the car rocketed backwards. Shuddering wildly from side to side as they reversed at high speed for the safety of the turning from which they'd just emerged. John's head swinging front to rear, front to rear. As he tried to grasp what was happening ahead and at the same time keep a look out behind. While Ninian, who had now scrambled up on to the back seat beside him, bounced up and down. Squeaking with excitement.

They were coming up to the turning now. Lila slowing

down. Right hand hard over. Rear wheels swinging off the slushy tarmac and back on to packed snow. Then starting to slide. Unaccustomed to reverse, she over-corrected. The vehicle spun sickeningly. Performed two complete revolutions. Before coming to rest with a bump, one rear wheel slipping into the shallow ditch at the roadside. The nose still sticking out into the main road. From where John could now clearly see the fight that raged round the checkpoint, two hundred yards distant.

There was a crackle of fire from assault rifles. A frantic bellowing of commands. A tinny clang and whine as another stray round ricocheted off the car.

'Out!' he shouted. Wrenching open the door. And hauling Ninian with him. To land in a heap in the snowy road. Where Lila joined them a second later. Face pale, eyes wide. Fragments of bark scattering down around them as a high-velocity round embedded itself in the trunk of a nearby tree.

John crawled forward on his stomach and halted behind the shelter of the front wheel. He reached into his coat pocket and brought out the small binoculars. Peered round the wheel and focused. Muddy skid marks on the tarmac showed where the truck had come roaring out of the woodland track and swung in front of them a hundred yards from the turning. A further hundred yards ahead stood the checkpoint, consisting of an armoured glass booth, not much bigger than an old-style phone box, a lightweight metal barrier and two jeeps, one on either side of the road. John pictured the accelerating truck smashing aside the barrier before the soldiers manning it could even register their surprise. Fifty yards beyond, it must have braked hard and come to a halt. The tarpaulin rear covering would have been flung up, the tailgate dropped and a handful of black-clad, black-masked figures would have leaped out and dashed for the cover of the trees. While the remaining pair, lying flat in the bed of the truck, opened fire on the soldiers with a light machine gun. One of them, wounded by the soldiers' return fire, had now crawled half into the shadow of the truck's interior and lay curled in the foetal position. His comrade continued to fire intermittent bursts, ensuring that there was no possibility of movement at what remained of the roadblock. Where the twisted metal barrier now lay skewed across the road and the glass of the empty booth had shattered and turned opaque. Beside it, one soldier had fallen by his squat, bullet-riddled jeep, whose hood had sprung up, an angry cloud of steam issuing from its drab olive jaws. His comrade was partly visible through the open passenger door. Hunched down below the dashboard, speaking into something. One arm dangling at his side. Across the road, sheltered by their vehicle, two young soldiers were crouched back-to-back, weapons levelled in opposite directions.

For a short while everything fell quiet. One of the young soldiers edged to the corner of his jeep and glanced at the other vehicle. Hoping, John guessed, for confirmation that help had been summoned. But he was disappointed. For the wounded man had now slumped forward across the dashboard of the jeep. The watcher's comrade, meanwhile, was looking at the sky. Head tilted, ears straining. John's heart racing as the implication of reinforcements dawned on him. He and Ninian and Lila would be scooped up and taken off for interrogation. As witnesses. Or accomplices. Didn't matter much which. Because in the hands of the authorities they'd be fucked either way. He eased himself away from the wheel and started to crawl backwards. What chance did he have of getting into the driver's seat unseen? Driving the car out of the ditch without getting shot at? Hiding it in the woods? Hiding *them* in the woods? Pulling off some kind of miraculous stunt to get them out of this mess?

There was a sudden sharp burst of fire from the trees on their side of the road. Followed moments later by an explosion and the smell of burning fuel. Greasy black smoke drifted up above the treetops. John stopped crawling and flattened himself on the ground. Peered under the car. He couldn't see the booth or the burning jeep with the wounded soldier in it. But he could see the other one, across the road, with the two young men now huddled up against it in terror. And at that moment, from out of the trees beyond, something came sailing slowly through the cold blue air towards them. Trailing a thin arc of smoke behind it. It landed a few feet away from the jeep and exploded in a small shower of sparks. It made no more noise than a firework. Yet at once both soldiers toppled sideways. A strangely doll-like movement, almost as if they were play-acting. In the brief silence that followed, John half expected them to climb to their feet again and dust themselves down. But one lay perfectly still. After a short while the other started to squirm and moan.

From the trees came a bellowed command. One by one, eight black-clad figures emerged on to the road, four from each side. The first pair glanced perfunctorily at the two jeeps and the three prostrate figures in the road, then sprinted for the truck. The others followed, the final two pausing briefly by the wounded soldier to deliver a volley of kicks to his unprotected head and torso. Which elicited muted sounds of agony. Moments later they were eclipsed by the first clatter of a distant helicopter. John felt his bowels loosening. He scrambled to his feet and ran round the car as the truck started up and took off at high speed, skidding left on to the N1 and disappearing to the south.

'Get in,' he said to them both. 'You drive!'

Lila climbed in and turned the ignition. John glanced around under the trees for dead bracken, fallen branches, anything to put under the wheel that had sunk into the ditch. Then remembered the Volvo's heavy rubber floor mats. He hauled one out from beneath Lila's feet. Pressed it firmly into the snow in front of the sunken wheel.

'Manual or auto?' he shouted.

'Manual.'

'Put her in second. Keep your revs steady. Go when I say.'

He slithered round the tail end of the car. Kicked out a decent purchase for his feet in the snow. Put his shoulder to the bodywork and shouted 'Go!'

The engine whined angrily. She was revving way too hard. There was a smell of burning clutch. The wheel spinning furiously, digging itself into the snow. 'Lower your revs,' John bellowed. Then braced his feet and gave a muscle-cracking heave. Snow flew everywhere. The engine note dropped as the wheel bit on rubber. The car lurched away from him and he sprawled full length across the mat.

He picked himself up and scrambled into the passenger seat. 'Let's go.'

Lila nodded. Then pulled out on to the main road and headed up towards the N1.

As they passed the remains of the checkpoint John glanced at the two young soldiers lying still on the tarmac in the muddy slush. One was dead. His throat and part of his chest torn away. A look of intense surprise on his blackened, blood-spattered features. The other had crawled up the road a few yards, a long smear of blood behind him. He tried to lift his head as they passed. He didn't look a day older than John.

215

TWENTY-EIGHT

The helicopter hovered above the remains of the check-point. John craned his neck to keep it in view through the rear window as they swung south down the N1. His gaze held fast by the bulging dragonfly eyes and bulbous nose. The slender muzzles of the machine guns sprouting from its cheeks. He held his breath, waiting for it to come to life again. To start sidling forward. But after a while it settled slowly out of sight behind the trees.

'It's landing.'

Lila nodded. Kept her eyes on the road. Gripping the wheel as if the effort was the only thing holding her together.

Ninian sat very still and quiet on the back seat. He looked as if he might start to whimper at any moment.

'Is it far?' asked John.

'Just up there.' She nodded to the right, to the thickly wooded hillside that stood parallel to the road.

Things stamped and bellowed uncontrollably in John's mind.

'Know what it was all about?' There was a tremor in his voice which he could do nothing about. 'Back there . . . ?'

She shook her head.

'Nothing to do with the search? Just coincidence?'

'Expect so.' She sounded close to tears. 'Keeping the army on their toes.'

'On their toes, eh?'

Lila made no reply. Just gripped the wheel and stared straight ahead.

John gazed off at the snow-covered Cairngorms, pristine in the early afternoon sunlight.

Half an hour later they were in deep shadow. The car was hidden among the trees a few hundred yards back. John could feel the cold gathering as they walked down the track into the thickly wooded hollow where the cottage squatted. He shivered as he took in the unfenced, snow-covered garden at the front. The old tumbledown stone kennels at the back. And set slightly apart, the rough wooden shed crammed to bursting with tools, logs, fuel cans, sacks of peat and a partially dismembered motorcycle. There was no sound except the whisper of a burn somewhere among the dark, crowding trees. Between them, Ninian had begun to drag his feet and mutter mutinously. John didn't blame him. He knew places like this. He'd never understood why folk should choose to live where there was no light. And no view. Where rain and frost and mist could drain down and settle all around.

'He's not here.' Lila's voice was flat and lifeless.

'The bike . . .'

John pointed to the pieces of machinery in the shed.

She shook her head. 'The quad bike.'

A thin column of smoke rose almost reluctantly from the cottage's single chimney.

'Fire's going.'

'Doesn't mean anything. He'll have it banked down with peats.'

'What do we do?'

'Go in and wait, I guess. Hope no one comes looking.' She saw his quizzical glance. 'It'll be open. It always is.'

The cottage was a simple two-up, two-down. Kitchen and front room on the ground floor, two small bedrooms upstairs and a freezing cold bathroom tacked on at the back, no doubt. Though it was warm enough in the kitchen, with the dull glow from the black iron grate. And the comforting treacly smell of the peat smoke that curled up the chimney. Familiar too, in a way, with all the bachelor clutter. Outdoor clothes, uncleared dishes, cans of beer and an old music system. One easy chair. And a small pine table, half covered with papers and magazines. *Natural Regeneration and the Caledonian Pine Forest. Conifer Infestation in Oregon and Washington. Annual Report of the Timber Society of Tasmania.*

Lila was wandering around the room. Picking things up and putting them down again. She seemed listless and anxious.

'Would he mind if we made a cup?'

She came to. Forced a smile. 'Aye. I mean, no . . . I'll do it.' She moved across to the sink and started to fill the kettle. An old metal one designed for a flame or a ring.

John stepped out to check on Ninian, who had declined to come inside and was now building a snowman. Which struck John as being not quite right, somehow, helping oneself to the virgin snow in a stranger's garden. But it was too late now. He'd begun and there was nothing to do except lend a hand while the kettle boiled. He seemed to have recovered himself anyway. Frowning with concentration as he gathered up a big roll of snow. Chortling as he slipped

218

and landed on his bum. John looked on, envying him his capacity to forget. Or was it his inability to remember . . . ?

Lila came to the front door. 'Tea's ready.'

Ninian paid no attention. Planted a fist-sized snowball on top of the boulder-sized torso. And grinned. 'His head.'

'Looks grand.' John smiled. 'I'm going in. D'you want to stay out here?'

Ninian nodded. 'He needs legs. And ears.'

'OK. Come in when he's finished, eh?'

Back in the kitchen, Lila had taken her coat off. Her pale face was flushed with the warmth of the little room. She seemed less agitated now, though still distracted. They sat on plain chairs at the table and sipped their tea in silence.

John glanced round the room, looking for clues to the owner's identity.

'Who is he?' he asked. As Lila put down her cup and started to roll a cigarette. 'D'you want one?' He shook his head. She reached in her pocket for a lighter. Drew deeply and exhaled.

'His name's Billy. Billy Lowrie. Used to work for the Department.'

John waited for her to go on. But she didn't.

'What did he do? For the Department?'

'He had a job with the forestry division. Field research into natural propagation or something like that. But he got fed up with them. Or they got fed up with him.' She shrugged. 'Now he gets by. Like the rest of us . . .'

'And has connections . . .'

She shot him an anxious glance. 'He'll not thank me for letting on.'

'It's OK.'

'It'd be better if you leave me to do the talking.'

John nodded. 'How d'you know him?'

'From Argyll.'

'Argyll?'

'School placements. My training.'

'Well . . . he's tucked away nicely here, right enough.'

Lila continued smoking in silence, restlessly fingering the cigarette.

John gazed into the fire. Then looked up again. 'Did you hear the news? About the Tod? That it's definitely Fraser?'

She nodded.

'I saw it on the TV,' said John. 'Just before you arrived. Any idea what he's like? Fraser?'

She shrugged again. 'Very rich. Very clever. Very . . . charismatic. And totally ruthless, I should think. You'll have read all the same stuff as me.'

John nodded. You had to have been living in a hole in the ground not to have heard Fraser's life story. 'Raised in the Black Isle. School in Inverness. Five years in the army before he went to work in the City. Then the business deals. The homes in Florida and Switzerland. The big estate here – before it was taken off him by the One Acre Act . . .'

'And his wife killed in the riots,' Lila went on. 'Poor soul. So he raises a civil action against the government for her death. And the authorities retaliate by investigating his Scottish business interests for fraud.' She laughed shortly. 'That was the thing that really got him, so they say. Not the estate. Not his wife. But the threat to his business empire . . .'

'But to go to earth like . . . like a tod? If it really is him. When you've everything he has? It doesn't really make sense to me . . .'

'It's just in his make-up, I guess,' said Lila. 'All or nothing. He's totally committed to the cause, by all accounts – whether he's actually the Tod or not. My dad said he gave a huge amount of money to the official protest campaign, right from the start. Then it seems he got more involved still when a bunch of hardliners pushed off with some of the campaign funds . . .'

'Which was when things started getting out of hand . . . the bombings and shootings.'

'Aye.' She shook her head. 'Random violence. I think there were some real hard cases mixed up with it all. And maybe he just couldn't bear to see something he was associated with being so badly mishandled. Plus the other stuff, of course. The personal stuff.' She tossed her cigarette end on to the fire. 'I guess he had plenty of reasons to want to take charge . . .'

John nodded thoughtfully. 'Or maybe he's just a rich boy who likes to play soldiers.'

'Maybe.'

She fell silent and her gaze drifted to the window.

John looked back to the steady glow of the peats. Feeling the warmth on his face. Soothing him. Drawing him gradually away to another place, where the coal flickered ruddily in the open grate of old Alec MacNab's front room. Where Bella would sometimes bring them tea when they came in from the shed on a cold afternoon. And maybe persuade them to take out their fiddles for a tune before John had to get home. And all at once, curling into his head like the smoke from the peat before him, came a handful of notes, a slight movement in that place where, every once in a while, all the notes of all the melodies he had ever known were pulled and tugged, like plankton in some ocean current, until they came together in a new formation. And the first breath of a new tune drifted through his mind. But before he could grasp it firmly he heard something else. Muted by the trees. The throaty burble of a quad bike.

Lila stood up and ran a hand nervously through her hair as the bike halted outside, grumbled to itself, then fell silent. A moment later there was a man's voice, raised in surprise. Followed by a shriek from Ninian. Who burst into the kitchen, made straight for the chair, threw his arms around John's waist and buried his head in his lap.

Billy Lowrie stepped over the threshold and halted at the sight of his unexpected visitors. The first thing John noticed was that he was a good deal older than Lila, probably in his early thirties. He was sandy in colouring, bearded, short and muscular, with very pale blue eyes. There was something in the way he held himself, a kind of controlled aggression, that made John want to get up from the chair and meet him face to face. But he couldn't, pinioned by the sobbing Ninian, whose head was still buried in his lap. So he sat where he was, feeling uncomfortable and exposed.

But Billy ignored him.

'Hello, Lila,' he said.

'Hello, Billy.'

'Long time no see, eh?'

She nodded.

'Aye, well . . .' He tipped his head towards John. 'Who's your friend?'

'John's Morag's nephew, Billy – you mind Morag, it's her house I'm sitting . . . we just met yesterday. He came to the house, looking for Morag . . . and – and now he needs a bit of help, and I thought maybe you could . . .' She hovered awkwardly, then gestured at the teapot. 'Would you like a cup? We made some while we were waiting.'

'Haven't forgotten your way around, then?'

Lila blushed.

'Aye, I'll take a cup.' He nodded at Ninian. 'Who's the wean?'

'He's –' Lila began.

'Ninian –' said John.

They looked at one another.

'We . . . er . . . don't really know,' said Lila.

Billy frowned.

'That's kind of why we're here . . .' She turned to the stove and picked up the kettle.

Billy glanced at Ninian again and scratched his beard. His pale blue eyes flitted around the room, as if making sure everything was still in place.

Ninian had stopped sobbing. But he still clasped John around the waist as if his life depended on it.

'It'll be the bike that gave him a fright,' John volunteered. Suspecting this might not entirely be the truth. 'He's . . . um . . .'

'Handicapped,' offered Lila from the sink.

Billy nodded. John said nothing.

Lila handed Billy his mug of tea. Then leaned back against the sink and folded her arms tightly across her chest.

Billy lowered himself into the easy chair and took a slow, deliberate sip of tea. Then looked at John in silent scrutiny.

'So . . .' he said, 'and what kind of help would you be after, then?'

Lila glanced at John, then started to explain. But Billy interrupted. 'Can the boy no speak for himself?'

'Aye, I can speak,' replied John as levelly as could. 'I was at Blackriggs. When they did the killing . . .' Billy's features remained impassive, from which John guessed that he must already have heard about it.

As he told his story Ninian started to become restless. He shifted his head from side to side and eventually turned it enough to peer at Billy out of the corner of one eye. Instantly a little grunt escaped from him and he buried his face in John's lap again.

'Does he ken what we're talking about?' Billy interrupted.

'No,' John replied.

Lila leaned across and said softly to Ninian, 'D'you want to come outside with me and finish the snowman?'

Ninian shook his head. 'Stay here,' he mumbled.

She glanced around the room and her eye fell on a cardboard box standing in a corner. It was full of small fir cones. 'Can I . . . ?'

'Help yourself,' said Billy.

She took them to John and put them down on the side of the chair furthest from Billy. 'Something to play with,' she said to Ninian. 'If you get bored. We have to talk, see.'

John continued. He noticed that unlike Lila, unlike even the rebel boys at the lodge, Billy was not letting himself get involved in this story. He was listening with a look that seemed dispassionate and calculating. Even when it came to the incident at the checkpoint, John found it hard to tell whether he'd heard about it or not. He waited, relieved to be finished, while Billy looked steadily at him. Then shrugged.

'So what d'you want me to do about it?'

Ninian was now eyeing the box. He slid out of John's lap, crouched on the floor and upended it. Fir cones rolled in all directions. Billy winced.

'Look, Billy,' said Lila, 'there's no way we can trust the authorities with him. Especially not if there's the slightest chance he has any connection with . . . with your folk –'

'How d'you mean, my folk?' asked Billy quietly.

'Och, come on! Who d'you think I mean?'

He looked at her steadily. 'It's no a game y'know, Lila.'

'I know that, Billy,' she replied, her colour rising again. 'But we thought that maybe the NLA might help find out who he is . . . where he belongs.'

'Why should they do that?'

Lila looked over at Ninian who was now happily arranging fir cones on the floor. It was a complicated pattern, vaguely helix-like. The family of wooden bears stood guard at the centre of it.

'Because someone has to. He needs special care. Someone's got to take responsibility for him. Your folk – they're an organisation, aren't they?' She glanced at John. 'But John here, he's just one guy on his own. He's no experience of looking after someone like this.'

Billy's gaze slid across to the fire. 'And where d'you come into this, Lila?'

'She's just helping us,' John cut in. Lila glanced sharply at him but he ignored her. 'I'd never met her before yesterday. She didn't ask any questions.' He let the challenge to Billy rise on his voice. 'Just took us in, like. And she's nothing to do with—'

'I am now though,' Lila said. 'Since what happened on the way here . . .'

'OK.' Billy leaned forward. 'So what exactly is it you want, eh?'

Lila glanced at John. 'Somewhere to keep our heads down, I guess. For a while. A way for John to make contact with his dad. Get the car back to my friend. And find someone to take care of Ninian properly.'

'I see. And what's in it for my folk, as you call them?' There was a hard glint in his eye now. 'Why'd they want the hassle, eh?'

He's playing with us, thought John. This was not a good

225

place to come. He'd known it as soon as he walked down the brae into the gloom of this hollow. And so had Ninian, now he came to think of it . . .

But Lila was ready. 'Because John's a witness to this . . . this atrocity, Billy,' she said. 'The only witness. To what's got to be the worst thing that's happened in this fight so far.' There was anger in her voice now and outrage. 'You know what they did to my dad, Billy. Well, what they did to these folk at Blackriggs was something far worse. Can you imagine the terror they must've felt? Watching their neighbours being cold-bloodedly butchered. Shot in the head. Or raped. Or having their throats slit like animals. And knowing there was nowhere to go. Knowing their turn was coming. How can anyone have the right to do that to another human being, Billy? Surely there's nothing can justify it. And the folk who do it should never be allowed to get away with it. No matter who they are. Government. NLA. Whoever.' Billy was looking at her intently. And no wonder, thought John with a jolt. Flushed in the face, her breathing coming fast, her grey-green eyes wide, she looked passionate and beautiful. 'So if your folk'll take care of Ninian,' she went on, 'then John will promise to testify wherever he has to. Speak the truth about what he saw. In any court, anywhere. When all this is over.'

Billy continued to stare at her for a long time. Then turned to John. 'Is that right?' he said.

'Aye. Aye, it is.' Though as he spoke he pictured the scene at the checkpoint, and the words rang suddenly hollow.

Billy looked over at the figure on the floor. Which had started to hum to itself now. As the bears plodded one after another through the fir-cone pattern, rippling out in eccentric waves towards the door.

'Hey!' he said. 'Bear boy! Ninian!'

Lila looked urgently at him, shaking her head. But it was too late. Absorbed in what he was doing, Ninian turned round instinctively at the sound of his name to see Billy looking at him. His face crumpled at once. He let out a long wail, scrambled from the floor and rushed headlong from the room, scattering fir cones and bears in his wake.

Lila dashed after him.

Billy sat watching as John leaped up from the chair and followed her.

'Kids never did like me,' he said with an unapologetic shrug.

TWENTY-NINE

Five minutes later John and Lila met up in front of the cottage. It had begun to snow again. Billy stood in the doorway watching the flakes drift down.

'Can't find him.' Lila's glance slid anxiously from John to Billy and back again.

John shook his head. 'Me neither.'

'Tried the shed?' asked Billy.

Lila glared. 'I can't *find* him. That means I've looked. Everywhere. He's vanished. Run off into the trees.'

Falling snow deepened the gloom of the hollow. The trees seemed to crowd in closer.

'Ninian! Ninian! Nin-i-an!' Their voices were muffled. Echo-less.

At Lila's request Billy headed grudgingly uphill and was swallowed at once by the trees behind the cottage. Lila set off along the track that continued beyond the hollow. John dropped down among the pines below, threading his way between the close-standing trunks, clambering over brush-wood, straining for a glimpse of movement in the murk ahead. He recalled the first morning together, when they'd hidden up by the old shepherd's cottage in the overgrown plantation. The first moment that he'd thought he'd lost Ninian. Only a week past. When he still had Hector. Christ, how he missed him. The softness of his muzzle, sweet grassy smell of his breath, solid reassurance of his slow muscled bulk . . .

'Nin-i-an! Where are you?'

But his voice was lost at once. Deadened by snowflakes and pine needles and rough absorbent bark.

Where would he have gone? John asked himself. And knew at once the pointlessness of the question. Knew that the only thing certain would be the unpredictability of his choice. Though even choice was too strong a word for Ninian.

The snow was growing heavier. It was only mid-afternoon but the light seemed to be fading. John tripped on something unseen. Steadied himself. Calmed his breathing. This wood was enormous and silent. The lad could be anywhere. Something shifted in the gloom ahead. A fall of snow from a branch. A figure picking its way stealthily through the trees. Too large for Ninian. A deer perhaps, or a man, or even men . . . and for a moment it seemed to John that the whole wood had come alive with the flitting shadows of warriors, a silent army of clansmen, wrapped in animal skins against the cold, weapons muffled with rags. As if the present troubles had created a disturbance in the pattern of time, a fissure through which shades were summoned from the past . . . John shook his head and tried to ignore the feeling of rising panic. He stumbled on, moving ever further downhill. Calling, pausing, looking. Calling, pausing, looking. As the snow drifted ceaselessly through the trees, furring branches, clinging to trunks, piling up on the undergrowth. He started to picture Ninian having fallen and knocked himself senseless, or perhaps simply having lain down exhausted at the foot of a tree. One more snowy contour in the forest floor, indistinguishable from all the rest. 'Ni-ni-an!' he called. Not wanting to admit that it was hopeless. That he could pass within a few feet of a supine snow-covered body without noticing. That it would take them days to quarter this wood to any real effect . . .

He had no idea of how long he'd been going, only a vague sense that he must be near the foot of the hill, when he caught the sound of voices. His heart jumped as he imagined it was Billy and Lila coming down to tell him that all was well, they'd found Ninian.

He stopped, orientating himself towards the sound. It came from below him. The voices were not those of adults. High-pitched, childlike, they rose and fell as if in a chant or singing game. He moved on downhill towards a faint lessening of the gloom ahead. Little by little the slope levelled, the wood thinned, the snow-filled sky expanded. Ahead, following the margin of the trees, a tumbledown stone dyke turned ninety degrees to enclose the corner of a field. A sheltered place where huts and tents had sprung up. Wreathed in the smoke of fires lit to ward off the cold. At the very edge of the wood, trees had been roughly felled for fuel and dragged out to the field, smashing down what remained of the dyke as they passed. There in the broken ground, among the stumps and scattered stones, was a circle of children and youths. Almost ghostly in the steadily falling snow.

For a moment John wondered whether they were playing a game. But before he could catch the words that rang out he sensed the hostility of the group towards the single small figure that stood at the centre of the circle.

'Big lugs.'

'Weirdo.'

'Numpty boy.'

Speckled with snow, the figure was sobbing. Shoulders heaving as it rocked back and forth. Contorting its body as if trying to disappear into itself.

'Gonnae stand there greetin' a' day?'

'Dinnae wanna fight?'

A stick sailed through the air and struck the figure on the shoulder.

It gave an anguished wail but didn't move.

'Wee piece o' shite.'

Laughter rippled round the circle.

'Feart tae fight.'

Voices picked up the refrain.

'Piece o' shite. Feart tae fight.'

Hands smacking thighs in time.

The figure lowered its head and squirmed. Covered its ears with its hands. As one of the larger youths stepped forward from the circle.

John strode out from the trees. Heart on fire with schoolyard memories. He opened his mouth and bellowed:

'LEAVE HIM ALONE!'

His rage filled the space between the trees, the snow-filled air, spilled out into the field, summoning curious faces to tent flaps and the entrances of huts.

The youth stopped and watched in silence as John broke into a run, lumbering towards him across the rough ground. The circle dissolved, its members melting away. The youth took a step back. A feebly thrown fir cone caught John on the side of the head. He let out another roar and they turned like starlings.

Ninian remained where he was, unaware that his tormentors had fled. He flapped his hands. Made small

231

gasping sounds. As the snowflakes settled on his bare head and shoulders.

'It's all right, laddie. I'm here, I'm here. It's all right.'

John scooped him up and gathered him into his arms. Feeling his own warm tears mingling with the cold melting snow on Ninian's hair as he stood there in the empty corner of the wood. Oblivious to the eyes that looked on from the encampment. Ninian sobbing and shuddering against his chest.

A long time later John set him down and together they turned back into the trees. It was hard going, climbing through the snowy wood to Billy's cottage, but Ninian stumped along uncomplainingly in John's footsteps. After a while he struggled up level and put out his hand.

John took it and gave it a squeeze. 'You're a good lad.'

Ninian looked up at him and said solemnly, 'Lila told me a secret.'

'Oh aye?'

He nodded. 'Where a bear lives. She's going to show me.'

'Is she now?' John replied. 'Won't that be grand!'

The sky had cleared now. Through a break in the trees John could see west, away down Strathspey and on over the crowded white peaks beyond to where a low bank of pewter cloud lay motionless but menacing on the far horizon.

It held his eye and for a moment he had the same feeling of something brewing that he'd had back in Morag's house – was it only that morning? God, it felt like a week ago.

He turned away and Ninian trotted after him.

THIRTY

Two hours later the sky was brilliant with stars. John steered the quad bike along the track beyond the cottage. Concentrated on getting the hang of the unfamiliar four-wheeled vehicle. It was squat and muscular and seemed to exert a firm grip on even the softest snow, with its rough balloon tyres. A kind of mechanical Hector, though a good deal more responsive. Hector had only had two speeds to speak of, thrawn old bugger. Slow and stop . . .

Lila and Ninian were bunched up together on the bike behind him. The elongated seat was padded and heated. Ninian had his gloved hands thrust deep into John's coat pockets. Behind him, Lila held heated passenger grips. The air-temperature reading on the instrument panel was minus twelve and falling. The snow hissed and crackled beneath them. John could hardly remember the last time there'd been a frost, let alone one that had dropped into double figures.

At the edge of the wood he slowed down, extinguished the headlamp and halted in the shelter of the trees with the engine idling. Allowing his eyes to adjust to the starlight, scanning the open, snow-covered hillside ahead. He shivered. Despite Billy's confident assertion that they'd nothing to worry about, he felt suddenly vulnerable and exposed. As if the soldiers were possessed of some huge all-seeing eye that would spot them the minute they moved out from the shelter of the trees.

'Everyone OK?' he asked over his shoulder.

Lila nodded.

'You ready, Ninian?'

Ninian grinned and extracted a gloved paw in an attempt at a thumbs-up.

'Here we go then.'

He moved off slowly. Feeling his way with the headlamp off. Following the track out towards the line of the hill road. The faintest of bike-shaped shadows keeping pace on the snow beside them.

By the time they reached the bothy an hour and a half later, John's cheeks felt raw and scoured by the bitter air. His jaw set in a frozen rictus. Sandwiched between the two adults, jolted this way and that, Ninian had been nodding uncomplainingly in and out of sleep. Now, as John lifted him to the ground, he started to whine and flap with his gloved hands. Lila climbed down stiffly with the look of someone who feared she would never get warm again.

The bothy stood on a patch of level ground in the bend of a burn. A foul-weather haven for the wind-farm construction workers and maintenance men who had frequented the Monadhliath hills until that night six years ago when the Muckle Blaw had swept indiscriminately across the Highlands, flattening forests of trees and wind turbines alike.

It was not a wooden and corrugated-iron hut of the kind

234

John knew so well, but a small prefabricated shed made from some lightweight modern building material. Inside, despite the dusty sense of abandonment, it seemed draught-free and dry. It was equipped with two pairs of metal-framed bunks, a wood stove and a stainless-steel sink. The sink had a waste pipe but no taps, the nearby burn providing all the water necessary. Any other comforts there might have been, a table or chairs, had long gone.

John returned to the bike and retrieved two carrier bags from the pannier. He hadn't yet had a chance to ask Lila what she'd said while he'd been towelling Ninian down in the cottage's cramped bathroom. But whatever it was, Billy seemed to have changed his tune by the time they'd come back into the living room. Promising to make contact with the NLA high-heidyins, with a special request to try to trace Ferg MacNeil. Loaning them the bike to get across the hill to the safe house on Loch Ness-side. Even putting together a load of provisions for them. In one bag there was a packet of sausages, a sliced loaf, a couple of cans of Irn-Bru and a quarter-full bottle of whisky. In the other, an armful of small logs.

Lila had her arms around a shivering Ninian. Who offered no resistance as she rubbed and hugged him warm.

'Bloody freezing.' The breath clouded thickly before her face.

'I'll get the stove lit,' said John.

It was modern and it drew well. The fire took quickly and soon it was roaring. John went outside to fetch the backpack. He breathed in, savouring the resiny scent of pine logs on the sharp air. Then walked on past the bike, boots squeaking in the snow. When he was a fair distance off he stopped and stood for some minutes under the glittering vault of the sky. Letting the utter stillness and silence lap around him. The knife-pure air in his nostrils. The pale silhouettes of the snowy hills rolling away in all directions.

Back in the bothy, Lila and Ninian had shed some of their layers of clothing and were squatting together in front of the open stove. In their gloved hands they each held what looked like a short length of fence wire. On which, skewered lengthwise, blackening sausages sizzled and dripped in the flames.

Ninian turned at John's approach and looked up.

'We're cooking.' He smiled. 'I like cooking.'

John dragged a mattress off one of the bunks so they could sit in a row in front of the fire. Once the sausages were done they wrapped them in bread and munched them, licking the grease off their fingers and passing round the cans of Irn-Bru. Making sure Ninian got the last swig. After which he burped and giggled.

'I want to see where the bear lives,' he said to Lila.

'The bear?' Lila looked momentarily puzzled. 'Oh aye. The bear! Bruno the bear.'

'Bruno?'

'Bruno.'

Ninian's solemn nod said that it was important to know names.

'Well . . . we can't see him right now. But I can tell you about him. Bruno used to live in a park near here. He had lots of friends in the park.' She stared into the fire, as if she could see them there among the flames. 'Big lumbering bison. Cunning grey wolves. Pretty wee arctic foxes with white coats and black noses and sharp teeth. Big hairy old wild boar. Shaggy bulls with great horns. And lots of smaller beasties, like pine martens and red squirrels. Badgers and otters. Polecats and stoats and weasels. Bruno was happy there with a cave to sleep in and his own playground to play in. He even had an old tree stump to climb if he felt like it. Or scratch his back on. Or sharpen his claws.'

Ninian's head was turned. One side of his face in shadow, the other lit with the flicker of firelight. As he gazed at Lila wide-eyed.

'People liked coming to see Bruno and his friends,' she went on. 'It helped them imagine what it was like here thousands of years ago. When there were no parks and all the animals lived free in the woods and hills and glens . . .'

Bit like today, John was tempted to add. But he merely caught her eye and smiled. The planes of her features shadowed and softened by the firelight. The grey-green eyes faintly dreamy with the story-telling. He thought of the way she'd looked at Billy's when her passion had been roused. He wanted to reach out and touch her face with his fingertips.

'But one day,' she went on, 'poor Bruno got a terrible toothache. His face swelled up and he started to growl at everyone. So they gave him something to make him go to sleep and took him to the dentist. But it wasn't strong enough. And while they were looking in his mouth to see what was wrong, he woke up feeling very cross. He sat up and bashed the dentist and the dentist fell over. And before anyone could do anything, Bruno was out the door and away down the road.'

Ninian wriggled with delight.

Really? signalled John with raised eyebrows.

Well . . . kind of. Lila gave a sideways nod. And grinned.

He envied her the way she could tell a tale like this. It made his stories sound clumsy and amateurish. And he envied the way Ninian looked at her . . .

'So Bruno ran away. And for a long time no one could find him. They looked everywhere. Up the hill. In the woods. Down by the river – bears love to go fishing, you see. Even round town, in case he'd started visiting folk's rubbish bins . . .' She paused for effect. 'And d'you know where he showed up eventually?' Turned to Ninian, who looked as if his eyes were about to pop out of his head, and smiled. 'In the wood just beyond Morag's house! Where you and John built the snowman. He'd found a big hole under a fallen tree. Someone's wee dog got the fright of its life when it went sniffing about the hole and there was a growl and a great big paw came out. Its owner got a fright too. She told the park people. And they came and tried to get Bruno out, but he just curled up in the hole and wouldn't budge. Nothing they could do was any good. They couldn't get at him to give him a jab and send him to sleep again. And he wouldn't poke his head out to eat anything they left for him. In the end they were about to go and get a crane to come and move the tree, when someone remembered that he liked pizza –'

Ninian giggled and clapped his hands.

'– yes, pizza! So they phoned the pizza shop and said we want your biggest, tastiest pizza. And we want you to deliver it to a Mr Bear who lives under the big fallen tree in the wood. And the pizza came –'

'What kind of pizza?'

'The best. With hot sausage and olives and peppers and anchovies – even a fried egg on top. Everything . . .'

Ninian was starting to rock back and forwards. His face lit with a smile of pure glee.

'So they left the pizza outside the hole. And watched. And waited. And they knew the good pizza smell would be drifting into the hole. And tickling Bruno's nostrils. And making his tummy rumble. And sure enough, at long last, out came a shiny black nose. Sniffing the pizza. And then a pair of beady black eyes. And then a shaggy brown head. And a great big body. And there was Bruno, sitting by the tree eating his pizza. And so—'

'Bern bears eat pizza,' said Ninian matter-of-factly. Looking at Lila.

'Your wee bears? The wooden ones?'

'No, no. Real bears.'

'Like Bruno? Real bears?'

'No. Bern bears. My dad threw them some pizza. They ate it.'

'You've been to Bern, have you?' asked Lila. 'Been to the bear pit?'

He nodded. Serious now. 'Lots of times.'

'Lots of times? On your holidays?'

Now he shook his head. 'No. At the weekend.'

Lila glanced sharply at John.

'So . . . do you live in Switzerland, Ninian?' she asked. 'Is that it?'

He nodded again. 'By the big lake. My house. And my dad.' He yawned. 'I'm sleepy now. Finish the story. I want to go to bed.'

THIRTY-ONE

As Lila settled Ninian in one of the bunks John went down to the burn for water to put with the whisky. He could hear it whispering beneath the snow, but it took a moment to find a place where it ran clear. He bent down and plunged an empty Irn-Bru can into the icy water, gasping as it closed over his fingers. The can filled with a gurgle. Tomorrow, if everything turned out as Billy had said it would, they would hand Ninian over to folk who would know what to do with him, how to look after him properly, how to find out where he really belonged . . . John stood up again and glanced westwards, to where the rim of the sky had grown dark and heavy and lost its glitter. The thought of tomorrow filled him with dread.

Back inside, Lila had Ninian cocooned in one of the sleeping bags. She was telling him another story. His eyelids were drooping as he struggled to stay awake till the end. As John entered, they flickered open once. Then closed and stayed closed.

John carefully measured whisky and icy water into the remaining can.

'That old paw's really mingin' now,' said Lila, sitting

down beside him. 'It's about ready to fall to bits. But he'll not let go of it.'

John nodded and replaced the cap on the bottle. 'We'll have to see if we can get it off him, the morn.'

He passed her the can and watched as she tilted back her head to sip the diluted whisky. The pale skin at her throat sheened by the firelight. The little grimace of satisfaction as the spirit bit.

She handed it back to John.

'Switzerland, eh?' he said, taking a sip. He was starting to get a taste for whisky.

She nodded.

'It would explain the accent. But not much else . . .'

'Not to us maybe. But it's another piece of the jigsaw, I guess. For them that'll do the finding out . . .'

She reached in her coat pocket for tobacco. Rolled two cigarettes, lit them and passed him one.

'That's the last of it.' She grinned. 'Will we survive?'

John shrugged. 'I don't really anyway.'

She raised a sceptical eyebrow. Blew a stream of smoke. 'You know, I thought we'd lost him this afternoon.'

'So did I.'

'He doesn't seem any the worse for it though. That's one thing about these kids, they can bounce right back as if nothing ever happened. Sometimes . . .' She smiled wryly. 'If you're lucky . . .'

'He did today.' John drew on his cigarette. 'He knows a lot of things, that laddie . . .'

'How d'you mean?'

'I mean . . . things we don't necessarily know.'

'Like what?'

'Like places. People. As if he kind of sees through things. You saw how he reacted to Billy . . .'

A shadow crossed her face.

'Sorry. I didn't mean it like that . . .'

'No, no. Not Billy – he can be difficult, I know. It's OK. But these kids . . . see, I think it's easy to end up believing that because they're different they've some sort of powers.'

'Powers?'

'Well . . . like you said. That they're specially gifted. Like . . . holy fools.' She gesticulated with the cigarette. 'But I don't think that really helps them – or us either.'

Layers of smoke hung like ghostly strata between them.

'So . . . d'you think they see things differently from us?'

She nodded. 'I'm sure they do. Because they can't work things through like we can. And that makes them innocent, I guess, in a way . . . but they're also chaotic wee souls. And I know they'd be in big trouble if we weren't there to help them.'

John frowned. 'Seems to me Ninian's like . . . missing some of the filters normal folk have.'

She nodded again.

'So surely accepting that is part of being able to help him . . .'

'Yes.' She gazed thoughtfully into the flames. 'It's just that when I was doing my placements I came across a few ignorant folk who really did believe kids like these had special powers. And the trouble is – if you think that, it doesn't take much to start thinking they're also protected in some weird way. Kind of untouchable. Which is just total nonsense when it comes to fragile X kids. Look at Ninian – he's as vulnerable as anyone you'll ever meet.'

You never met Davie, John thought.

'He is, aye . . .' he replied, flicking his cigarette butt into the stove and waiting for her to go on.

But she didn't. Instead she pulled up her knees and laid

her head on them. Looked at him sideways and smiled. 'Sorry, I can be a bit of a pain when I get going on things . . .'

John shook his head. 'It's interesting. You know a lot about it. A lot more than me, anyway.'

She said nothing but stayed as she was. Head on one side. Looking at him, still smiling.

'You warm enough?' he asked after a little while.

She nodded.

'We'll close up the stove then.' John put in a couple more logs and shut the door with its small smoke-stained panel of glass. At once the cheerful flicker died to a dull glow. Shadows swooped in from the corners of the room. A thick, warm darkness that smelled of heated iron and pine logs and burnt sausages.

John leaned back on the mattress. 'I didn't mean to speak badly of Billy. He's been right good to us.'

'He has that.'

'And I've you to thank for it.' He paused. 'What was it you said to him?'

She thought, then shrugged. 'Nothing really. He just . . . suddenly got interested in Ninian . . . in his story.'

'He'd a funny way of showing it.'

She gave a wry smile.

'How long . . . I mean, you've known him a while . . .'

She didn't answer for a moment.

'Aye, well . . . I should've said – maybe . . .'

'No matter. He's –'

'It was just a fling really. Didn't last long.' She sat up now. 'Long enough to land me up here though . . .'

John waited, not knowing what to say. A log flared in the stove, making the shadows jump and dance around them.

243

'He was the environmental manager on a big felling operation over Oban way,' she went on. 'When I was on a placement. They transferred him up here to Rothie-murchus. The Caledonian pine projects. And I followed him. Packed in the teaching and ended up behind the bar at the Spey View.' She gave a self-deprecating smile. 'What a loser . . .'

'How old were you?'

'Twenty-one.'

'And now?'

'Twenty-three.' She looked at him. 'And you?'

'Eighteen.'

'I thought you were older. Must be the beard.'

John felt himself blush. 'So what went wrong?'

'Well . . . see, Billy's grandad was a miner. His dad never had a job his whole life. Thought all lairds should be strung up. So Billy learned his politics young enough. And the trees . . . well, the trees were always his thing from when he was a lad. So it was all mapped out for him, really. Study the forestry. Then go on to work for the Department. And he was committed, right enough . . .' She looked down, her face in shadow. 'But he'd not been here for long when, well – he started to see things differently. See what a mess it had all become. Got friendly with some local folk. And so . . . it was like he just swapped one way of thinking – one set of ideals – for another.'

She gazed at the ruddy glow beyond the glass of the stove door. Reached for the can and took a sip of whisky.

'He started going off. I wouldn't see him for days. And I guess the idea of what he was doing started to sink in. Sabotaging things. Blowing them up.' She looked down and said quietly, 'Maybe even folk too . . .' She shook her head. 'That wasn't for me. No way.'

John took the can from her and drank.

They sat in silence for a while.

'So what about this, then?' asked John. 'You and me and Ninian. On the run, in the hills . . .'

She looked at him.

'You didn't need to come.'

'Oh yes I did. After what you told me about Blackriggs. Ninian or no Ninian. Helping you, helping him . . . like I said last night, it feels like I'm doing my bit.'

'Even though we might get caught . . .'

She shrugged and smiled. 'Aye.'

The stove light put a distant look in her eyes.

He looked at her for a long moment.

'I think you're daft,' he said.

THIRTY-TWO

J ohn wasn't sure whether it was the cold or the lessening of the darkness that first woke him. But he was immediately aware of both as he opened his eyes. Along with the hardness of floor under his hip.

He scrambled up, rubbing a stiff neck. Cursing himself for sleeping longer than he'd meant to. He shivered and pulled his coat close around his body. The stove had gone out. First light faintly staining the grimy window. Lila heard his movement in her sleep and shifted on the mattress. Ninian was motionless, a dim form on one of the bunks.

He went to the door and stood looking out. The air was full of small soft flakes. The finest coating of powder on the frozen doorstep. It could only just have come on. But they'd need to get going all the same. Before they ended up stuck here with no food or heat.

When he turned back Lila was up and rummaging through their possessions. She glanced at him and smiled, her face puffy and creased from sleep.

'I know I kept back some of those sausages for breakfast.' There was a puzzled note in her voice.

Ninian was also awake. He was sitting on the bunk, facing the wall. Head bent. Doing something.

John pointed.

'Ninian,' said Lila, 'know anything about three sausages?'

Ninian shook his head. Back still turned.

'You sure?'

He nodded harder. Then pulled his jacket over his head so he was completely hooded by it. And hunched his shoulders.

Lila struggled to contain her laughter.

'What you up to, Ninian?'

No reply.

'Are you eating those sausages?'

She went towards him and he turned round slowly. Lifted the jacket just enough to peer out. A sheepish grin on his face. Mouth corked with a whole sausage.

'What are you *like*, laddie?' Lila laughed out loud.

The grin spread delightedly.

John looked on, his feelings running riot in the snowy dawn.

There was no laughter an hour later. The wind had picked up now, moaning itself into a gale. Whirling numberless flakes across the frozen landscape from a slate-coloured sky. The road had vanished and John had only the fluorescent snow poles that alternated left and right by which to navigate. His eyelids were starting to gum together, the whiskers in his nostrils stiffening in the freezing, snow-laden air. Again he thought of Hector. Solid, reliable Hector. Plodding unfalteringly homewards, head down through the rain or sleet or snow. Shielding John from the wind with his bulk . . .

There was a sudden flurry of thumps on his shoulders and head. Ninian's arm shot forward, the mittened paw waggling furiously. There, materialising out of the gloom ahead, was a tall slim pillar raising its arms into the heart of the blizzard. And there another. And another. Until they were surrounded by snow-shrouded turbines, some standing, others lying where they had toppled to the ground, uprooted by the Muckle Blaw.

And there, through the driving murk, was a hut. The door was half off its hinges and the inside was full of wind-blown snow. But they stopped and dismounted all the same, swinging arms and stamping feet in its shelter. Only glad to be off the bike and momentarily out of the worst of the blizzard. Whose howl now seemed to be underscored by an eerie humming, as the wind thrummed through the axle housings of the locked and long-defunct turbine blades.

Lila stood looking up with wonder. The gale was encrusting the creaking columns with driven snow. Whipping up weird sculptures around their feet. 'Like angels,' she said, shaking her head.

Crucifixes more like, thought John with a shiver. Ninian didn't like it here either. He had turned to face the wall of the hut. Rocking backwards and forwards with his hands over his ears, eyes on the ground.

John put an arm around his shoulders. Steered him back to the bike.

'You OK to carry on?' he shouted to Lila.

She shrugged. *Do I have a choice?*

They were about to move off again when there was an anguished wail from Ninian. John turned to see that he had taken off a mitten and was clawing at his jacket.

'My paw! My lucky paw!' Tears welling at his eyes. A bubble of snot at his nose. 'My tiger's paw!'

John's heart sank. It must have disintegrated at last. Come off its string. He put out a tentative hand towards Ninian's chest. Ninian looked up, eyes momentarily full of hope, as if John would find it where he had failed. But of course there was nothing there. No malodorous lump beneath the layers of clothing. No lucky talisman to keep them safe any longer. Ninian started to wail in earnest now. Lila leaned forward, encircling him with her arms. Talking to him with hushed voice, trying to soothe him. But Ninian wouldn't have any of it. He shook his head from side to side, pushed her away.

'I'm sorry, laddie,' said John firmly. 'We can't stay here. Have to get down the other side first. Then we'll see what we can do about your paw.'

Which only made Ninian wail louder. But at least he didn't try to get off the bike. So John set off again before he could change his mind. Ninian sat behind him, howling into the blizzard, thumping his fists in slowly diminishing fury against John's back as they threaded their way between the ghostly shapes of the ruined turbine forest.

THIRTY-THREE

When they finally came to it, the gate was half buried in snow and they almost missed it. The air had grown still now and a dense white mist had settled over the hill. John stopped the bike, turned to Lila and pointed. Lila looked dazed with cold and exhaustion but managed a twitch of the mouth that almost passed for a smile. Between them Ninian seemed frozen to the seat, his head lolling in what John hoped wasn't a hypothermic stupor. But he sensed the absence of the bike's movement and looked up groggily, eyes unfocused.

'Nearly there now,' said John. 'You've done well, so you have.'

Ninian didn't reply.

It was all John could do to stop himself slumping forward over the handlebars. He forced himself to start the bike again and move on.

A breath of wind stirred and the mist shifted. There below, just as Billy had described them, were the three standing stones on a snowy knoll, now looking like a coven of white-bonneted witches. And there in the gloom beyond was the small farmhouse, with the steading at its shoulder and the dark mass of a wood beyond.

Tam Nicol. He's the community shepherd. Say Billy sent you. I'll get word to him. He'll see you right.

As they entered the yard John felt the knot tightening in his stomach. The burble of the bike seemed deafening after the emptiness of the hillside. Though even here the sound was muffled by the deep snow that blanketed the ground and clung to the roofs of the dilapidated buildings. There was evidence of recent traffic. A tractor, by the looks of it. And footprints going in at the back door. Tam Nicol would have been out feeding the beasts.

As John and Lila dismounted it began to snow again. Ninian sat there snivelling, refusing to budge. John lifted him bodily from the bike and carried him to the back door, where he lowered his head and flapped his hands, started whining about the paw again. Lila drew him to her, put an arm around his shoulders, as John knocked on the door.

There was no reply.

He knocked again. When still no reply came he pushed at it and stepped into a dingy back porch. Lila followed with Ninian. Ahead, along a short passage, light spilled from the kitchen. They entered to find a weather-beaten middle-aged man in overalls and checked work-shirt sitting at a cluttered table, nursing a mug of tea between thick-fingered hands. A greasy deerstalker at his elbow. He looked at them without change of expression.

'Tam Nicol?'

'Aye.'

'Billy Lowrie sent us.'

'Oh aye.'

The voice was as flat as the eyes.

Ninian whined, the sound muffled by Lila's coat. She stroked his head lightly. Smiled at Nicol. 'Billy said you'd –'

Her eyes widened as the door at the far end of the room was flung open. Nicol hurled himself sideways out of the chair, knocking the mug flying. A burly figure in a winter camouflage suit and hood burst in. Dropped to one knee, weapon raised. For a moment John thought he must be aiming at whoever it was who was simultaneously coming in through the other door, behind them. He threw out an arm to push Lila down out of harm's way. Then froze at the press of cold steel against his skin. And the bark of a voice whose familiarity would have raised the hairs on his neck were they not already standing.

John moved forward to the wall as told. Placed his gloved hands wide. Spread his legs. Unable fully to grasp what was happening. He stared blankly at the puddles of melting snow he was making on the floor. His mind filled with one thought only, that maybe their luck really had disappeared with the paw. He flinched as the frisking hand slid into his trouser pocket to remove the clasp knife. And tossed it on to the kitchen table with a clatter. He heard Lila's sharp intake of breath as she too was frisked.

The gun was removed from his neck. John turned his head to see Nicol climbing to his feet from the floor beyond the table. The hooded man stood over him. John's pulse lurched as he took in the sallow complexion, curved nose and thick dark moustache. The one from Blackriggs again. He prodded Nicol towards the door with his weapon. The shepherd's overalls had come undone at one side as he fell. Revealing thermal underwear now stained with spilt tea. He was crushing the rim of the deerstalker in one fist.

'Turn around. Now.'

John turned slowly. His eye lingering on the grey-and-white mottling of the camouflage suit, the corporal's stripes on the shoulder. Until he could no longer resist the urge to look up. To the bullet head and cropped ginger hair and fleshy features of Kel Foulis.

He felt his solar plexus contract. Wrestled for breath. As he tried to take stock of something that seemed almost too strange to believe. Foulis was looking him up and down without a glimmer of recognition. And slowly, as in a dream, it came to John that Kel Foulis had no reason to know who he was. No reason to associate the name of the fugitive witness from Blackriggs – if he even knew it, and even if he did it was a common enough name – with events that had taken place more than seven years ago, when they had both still been children, in a village in another glen. No reason, even then, to recognise the dishevelled and bearded figure that stood before him now, unless he had been aware of who he was looking for, which it appeared he was not.

'OK. Stay right there.'

John glanced instinctively at his left hand. As if to make sure that the thumb had not somehow made itself visible through the glove. But Foulis had now turned his attention to Ninian. He studied him intently as he hooked up a chair with his foot and straddled it. Weapon grasped in one hand. Camouflage suit straining across corpulent thighs. He was a lot bigger than he used to be, thought John. And probably a lot stronger too . . .

'Turn him around,' he said to Lila.

Lila's hands trembled as she gently disengaged Ninian. 'Turn round and say hello to the man,' she said unsteadily.

Ninian looked first at John. Then at Foulis. And instantly covered his eyes with hands. Shook himself free of Lila's grasp and dived under the table. Where he began to howl.

253

'Leave him!' said Foulis as Lila made to step forward. Though John could see that even he found something disconcerting in Ninian's unremitting wail.

'Takin' him tae see his dad, eh?' His eyes flickered from John to Lila and back again.

Lila's hands continued to tremble.

John looked at him blankly.

Foulis's stare hardened. 'I said – are you takin' him tae see his dad?'

'His dad . . . ?'

'You deaf?'

'But . . . we don't know who his dad is.'

Foulis snorted derisively.

'Then what you doin' wi' him?'

'Looking after him. While we try to find out who he is.' John struggled to keep his voice level. A part of him threatening at any moment to become the petrified ten-year-old once more.

Ninian's wail was rising to a hysterical pitch as he cowered beneath the table. In the grip of God only knew what terrifying feelings Foulis was stirring up for him. The sound made John angry. Not just with Foulis but with himself. For letting them all down. For allowing them to be led into this trap. Which Billy Lowrie had had a hand in, he knew with sudden certainty. For not listening to his instincts in that gloomy hollow in the woods. For the present crawling fear that he could barely contain . . .

Foulis raised a hand to his head. 'That bluidy screechin'. You . . .' He turned to Lila. 'Shut him up.'

Lila hesitated.

'Go on. Get in there. Do whatever. Just get him quiet.'

Lila dropped to her hands and knees and crawled under the table.

'So. John MacNeil. That you, eh?'

John's palms erupted in sweat. He nodded.

Foulis scowled. 'I knew a John MacNeil once. Right wee bastard, he was.' He paused. 'And you – you were at Blackriggs, eh? Seein' things you shouldn't've . . .'

Any minute now Foulis was going to march him outside. Make him kneel down in the snowy yard. Or put him up against the wall . . .

'. . . but we'll worry about that later.' Foulis sniffed. 'And here you're tellin' me you don't know who wonder boy is, huh? C'mon. Do I look daft or somethin'?'

'I don't,' John replied. 'Honest, I don't.'

Foulis thrust his head forward. 'Then you're in deep shite. You and Mary Poppins there.' He stared unblinkingly. Until John was certain he must recognise him. 'Unless I start gettin' some answers.'

A single shot sounded outside. Muffled. And yet very close. It felt as if the kitchen would burst with silence.

Ninian started to wail again. Lila's edgy murmur spilled out from beneath the table.

'Look,' said John with all the control he could muster, 'I found him at Blackriggs. Hiding. After you'd gone. I'd no idea who he was then and I still don't now . . . I think he used to live in Switzerland . . . I know he's handicapped. I also know he'll not be able to take much more of this. I mean . . . at this rate he'll be no good to you at all. Whoever he is.'

The door opened again and the moustachioed man returned. Stamping snow off his boots. Blowing on his fingers as he lowered his hood. To reveal a perfectly shaven head.

The conviction that John was lying was still plainly imprinted on Foulis's face.

255

'So you're no tellin' . . .' He sighed. 'Ah well. Suit
yoursel' then. We'll just have tae see what Mary Poppins
has tae say. C'mon then. Out you come.'

He nodded to the moustachioed man. Who reached
under the table for Lila's arm. But she elbowed him off and
scrambled out unaided. Then turned back for Ninian.

Foulis shook his head. 'Leave him there.'

Lila's eyes flashed. 'No, I will not. John's right. If you
frighten him any more he'll get ill. And let me tell you something: you don't want a sick fragile X kid on your hands,
believe me.'

She bent down again. But this time Ninian edged away
from her, whining and mumbling, until he was crouching
in the furthest corner. Facing the wall with his hands over
his head. Rocking backwards and forwards. She backed
out without him, fury in her face now.

'*See!* It's maybe too late already . . .'

Foulis shrugged. 'Billy Lowrie was none too chuffed wi'
you, y'know. For dumpin' him.'

Two spots flared up on Lila's pale cheeks.

'But then you turned up wi' this wee gem,' he paused,
wagging a finger at Ninian, 'and I'll bet he was ready tae
forgive you anythin'. Must've thought all his Christmases
had come at once. So . . . the kiddie's dad. Maybe we can
persuade you tae tell us, eh?'

He nodded to the moustachioed man, who turned to the
kitchen range and lifted back the circular cover of the larger
of the two hobs. He leaned forward and spat on it. The gob
of spit sizzled and disappeared almost immediately.

Lila stiffened as the moustachioed man reached out for
her wrist. She gave a little cry as he pulled her towards him.

Foulis waved his weapon casually in John's direction
and wagged a warning finger. Then turned to Lila.

256

'Where is he, then?'

Lila shook her head.

'Don't know?'

'I don't . . .'

The moustachioed man forced Lila's arm out over the plate. Where she instinctively bunched her fist. And closed her eyes.

Say something, John wanted to scream at her, scarcely able to believe what he was seeing. *Say anything. Whatever comes into your head.*

The sinews were tautening at her neck as the man started to push downwards. Casually pressing the curled fingers closer to the surface of the hot plate.

Now she opened her eyes. And for a long defiant moment held the moustachioed man's gaze, her face contorted with the effort of resisting. Then her shoulders slumped. 'OK,' she said, her voice trembling. 'I know who his father is.'

Foulis nodded and the moustachioed man released the pressure on her arm.

'So?'

She glanced across the room but was unable to meet John's eye. 'It's . . . it's Struan Fraser. The Tod.'

John gaped in disbelief.

'Now we're gettin' somewhere,' said Foulis with a self-satisfied smile.

THIRTY-FOUR

For a short moment John felt almost weightless with relief. If what she had said was true, and if someone in authority had known Fraser's identity all along, then it was Ninian they'd been after all the time, not him. Ninian they'd come to Blackriggs for . . . But if it was true, when did Lila realise? Just now? Or did she already know? And if she knew, why hadn't she said anything . . . ?

Lila was breathing heavily. Standing by the cooker shaking her head. As if to deny the horror of what was going on here in this dingy farm kitchen.

'But I haven't the faintest idea *where* he is.' She shot John an imploring glance. 'It's the God's honest truth.' She looked back at Foulis. 'And neither does John.'

Foulis nodded to the moustachioed man. Who tightened his grip on Lila's wrist and started to push down again.

Beneath the table Ninian screamed.

John began to speak. Quietly. Desperately.

'You can't do this – hurt her, I mean – I don't know what he'll do . . . he's not like normal kids, see . . . his . . . medication – we don't have it . . .' Lila nodded fiercely. John steeled himself to hold Foulis's eye, still expecting to be

258

recognised at any moment. 'He could have a fit – a really bad one . . . might damage him permanently – kill him even – is that what you want?'

'Surely he's no use to you dead,' added Lila.

Foulis had begun to frown. Slowly he raised his hand and the moustachioed man once again ceased his downward pressure. Foulis's gaze shifted to the figure under the table. Now sobbing and mumbling to itself.

Lila went on, 'If you want to use him—'

'Shut up,' said Foulis.

But Lila continued, 'If you want to use him to flush out his – the Tod . . . get him to negotiate or whatever – God knows what you want to do . . . you've got to get him somewhere he can be looked after properly . . . given the right medicines, like John says . . . taken care of by people who know how—'

'I said shut *the fuck up*!'

For a moment the room was almost still. All four adults remained motionless. Only Ninian continued to move and even he was silent now. Then Foulis turned and grunted to the moustachioed man, 'Let her go.'

The man gave Lila's wrist a petulant little downward push so that a gasp of fear escaped her and she twisted to break free of his grasp. At which he grinned and released her wrist so abruptly that she staggered across the room and into the table with a crash and a clatter as things cascaded to the floor. She stood there swaying. Struggling to collect herself.

'We'll take 'em outside,' said Foulis. 'Let someone else decide what to do wi' 'em.' There was disappointment in his voice, but also a note of relief, thought John.

Lila crawled back under the table, muttering soothingly, coaxing Ninian out.

Large snowflakes drifted past the kitchen window.

'He'll need something to eat,' said Lila faintly as they emerged and stood up together. Ninian wouldn't look at Foulis, but clung to her hand and hung his head. 'It helps calm him down. Biscuits. Bread. Anything . . .'

Foulis rolled his eyes but nodded to his comrade. Who rummaged through the kitchen cupboards and came up with the remains of a packet of oatcakes.

Foulis leading, the other man bringing up the rear, they made their way outside. John breathed deeply, sensing a slight freshening of the wind. Enough to bring a trace of moisture to the flakes that whirled down. Halfway across the yard he noticed something lying in the snow by the corner of the steading. A discarded deerstalker. Lila also saw it and their eyes met for an instant. A few paces further on she stumbled. John put out a hand to help her and felt her press something into his gloved palm. His knife. As she recovered herself she caught his eye again and this time held it steadily. With the same beseeching look she'd given him in the kitchen. The moustachioed man told her to keep moving. As they entered the steading he turned to pull the doors to and John slipped the knife into his coat pocket.

Inside the building, concealed behind hay bales, stood a pair of squat military vehicles like large jeeps. In the cab of one, two uniformed figures sat waiting. Foulis approached and spoke through the cab window with the figure at the wheel, then stood listening for some time, nodding as he did so. Finally he turned round and beckoned the party to the rear of the other vehicle, where he opened the door on a wire-caged interior.

'You two,' he nodded at Lila and John, 'in there. I'll take the kid up front with me. Where I can keep an eye on him.'

Lila shook her head. Started to speak. But John intervened.

'You'll have to take her too. He'll not sit there with you, not on his own. You'll not be able to drive.'

Although, in truth, since the last screaming fit Ninian had become silent and withdrawn. His eyes dull and inward looking. As if he had gone somewhere from which he might not wish to return.

'Have we any cuffs?' Foulis asked.

Lila's eyes widened in outrage. 'You can't . . .'

'Not him,' Foulis glared at her. 'You.' He turned to his comrade. 'Cuff her tae the passenger door. And you – in the back there. Now.'

'Wait . . .' John held up his hand. 'Can I . . . suggest something?'

Foulis looked at him suspiciously. But nodded all the same.

'There's a toy – a game . . . in the backpack. That we had with us on the bike. It might help keep him quiet.'

Foulis glanced at Ninian. Then gestured to his comrade, who disappeared for a minute and returned with the backpack. John offered to take it but Foulis shook his head. The moustachioed man peered at the bedroll with the mouse-fiddle in it. Then, without unstrapping it from the outside of the pack, raised muscular arms, upended the pack as if it was a paper bag and shook it till their few possessions tumbled out on the muddy ground. Foulis poked them around with his foot, then bent and picked up the games console. He switched it on, squinted at the screen, nodded and passed it to Lila.

'Get that repacked and in the back,' he ordered John. 'And you wi' it.'

John did as he was ordered and climbed into the cage.

By craning his neck he could see through the wire-mesh partition into the front, where Ninian and Lila were now taking their places. The moustachioed man handcuffed Lila's left wrist to the interior handle of the door. He then returned to the back and climbed into the cage with John. Foulis locked them both in, peering at John for a moment as he did so with a faintly puzzled look that set John's heart pounding like a trip hammer.

Turning to face the front again, John saw Lila place an oatcake and the games console in Ninian's lap, then lay her free right arm protectively around his shoulders and pull him close to her. As Foulis lowered his bulk into the driver's seat Ninian shrank and gave a little moan. Pressing his face to Lila's coat as if he could disappear into it.

They left the farm with the second jeep following. Engines labouring as the heavy vehicles forged through deep snow. They'd be going to Fort George most likely, thought John, just east of Inverness. Built to garrison Hanoverian troops after the Battle of Culloden in 1746. Back in business again nearly three centuries later for the same essential purpose. Repression of troublesome Highlanders. It would take a while to get there in this weather though, even if there did seem to be the beginnings of a thaw.

Weapon across his knees, the moustachioed man sat opposite, staring at John impassively. John gazed past him out of the small rear window, doing his best to avoid eye contact. He draped one arm over the backpack, fingers nervously tracing the seams in the waterproof fabric. Trying not to remember the stories he'd heard about the interrogation centre at Fort George, or the Lubyanka as it was popularly known, after the infamous KGB prison in Soviet Moscow. Trying not to think of Lila's father, or the others who were known to have fared even less well there. Trying, above all, not to speculate on what might have happened to Tam Nicol. His fingers worked their way under the flap of the backpack, burrowing inside the end of the bedroll until they closed on the neck of the fiddle. They felt out the familiar contours of the mouse's head, a fingertip coming to rest on the point of one of its ears. And pressing till it hurt. A reminder that he was at least still alive.

Ten minutes after leaving the farm the second jeep began to sound its horn and flash its lights. Both vehicles slowed to a halt. Foulis left the cab with a curse and walked back. Conferred with the second driver for a few moments, then returned.

'Always playin' up,' he grunted through the partition. 'Cheap eastern European shite. Bit like you, eh, Ivan?'

John's guard shrugged and smiled humourlessly. Then felt in his pocket and pulled out a small plastic dispenser of breath fresheners. He tapped it briskly three times over the open palm of his hand. Placed the sweets in his mouth methodically, one after the other, and began to suck noisily.

'We'll push on. They'll follow,' said Foulis over his shoulder. He accelerated away, wheels spinning on the snowy road.

John continued to stare through the jeep's rear window. It was hard to make out anything much in the dull white landscape through which they were passing. Did Ivan have a family, he wondered? An olive-skinned wife he would make love to when he returned eventually to wherever he came from? Dark-eyed children to hold on his knee and tell of his adventures in a far-off country called Scotland? In a far-off hamlet called Blackriggs . . .

The road dipped down and started to follow the shoreline of Loch Ness. Across fields and through trees John caught glimpses of gunmetal water. Foulis seemed to be pushing the pace, paying too little attention to the treacherous surface. Every so often the vehicle lurched, the tail swinging unsteadily.

John began to catch a persistent whine. At first he thought it must be the engine straining. But after a little it changed pitch and tone. Began to fall and rise. And settled into a high protracted hooting that had him back in the gloom of the ice house in an instant. The sound chilled him, even though this time he knew what it was. An anxiety so intense it teetered on the edge of reason.

Foulis was unsettled by it too.

He grunted something John couldn't hear.

Lila responded with a soothing murmur.

But Ninian kept up the hooting.

Foulis raised his voice. 'I said, shut him up.'

'Wheesht now, Ninian,' John heard Lila say. 'You've to be quiet.'

But the hooting continued.

Suddenly Foulis thumped the steering wheel with his fist. Let out a bellow like an angry bull.

'You *STOP* makin' that racket, you hear . . .'

The sound was shockingly loud in the small, confined space. Next instant there was a blur of movement in the cab. A curse from Foulis. Sounds of a scuffle. A shriek from Ninian. Then a bone-jarring jolt, a chaos of movement and noise. And John was momentarily upside down, apparently suspended in mid-air. Before being hurled against the wire mesh of the cage where he bounced several times and came to rest. The breath driven out of him. Consciousness with it.

THIRTY-FIVE

John shivered and opened his eyes. He sensed that an unknown amount of time had passed. All movement had ceased. He was lying in the cage alone and the floor was not where it should have been.

He sat up slowly and examined himself. He was bruised and shaken and there was a pain in the side of his head. The vehicle had come to rest on its side, tilted at an angle against the raised verge of the road. The rear door had fallen open. All was ominously silent.

Head throbbing, he started to climb out of the vehicle and was halted by a shriek. High and childish. An elemental scream of fear. He scrambled down, slithered out into the snowy road and looked back the way they had come. A hundred yards distant a small figure was running for its life. Pursued by a burly figure in a winter camouflage suit.

Without thinking, John began to run. Boots skittering on the slippery road, arms flailing as he struggled for balance, breath coming hard and sharp in his chest. He couldn't tell yet whether it was Foulis or Ivan. Nor did it matter. All that mattered was that no harm should come to Ninian. Who was now darting off the road and vanishing between trees. Followed by his pursuer, who reached the place moments later. Slipped and stumbled as he turned. Glanced back down the road as he recovered himself. Eyes briefly meeting John's. Then disappeared among the trees.

John ran on. Breathlessly reached the track they had taken, winding down through a small wood. Turned on to it without breaking his stride, when something moved out from the trees and slammed into him, heavy and solid, knocking him to the ground.

He struggled to get up but a muscular body pressed down on him. Sturdy fingers closed around his neck. Mint-scented breath filled his nostrils. And he fell back to the ground again, thrashing and gasping. He tried to drive his knee up but it was blocked by something firm and unyielding. He clawed with his fingers but could get no purchase on anything. The grip tightened at his throat and he felt himself beginning to go limp. His strength ebbing away. His eyes were closed and a crushing tightness was beginning to take hold of his chest when he heard Ninian cry out again. The sound was distant and distorted, but it summoned some deep reflex. Sent his hand burrowing into his coat pocket for the knife. He pulled it out and tried to prise it open one-handedly against his thigh. But it clattered from his fingers and he scrabbled at his side until he could feel it once more. The blood was roaring in his ears as he wedged it beneath him. His lungs felt as if they were ready to explode. His fingernail found the notch in the blade. He pulled. The blade sprang open and he slipped his fingers down to take the bone handle in his palm. He grasped it firmly. Raised his arm as far as he could and drove forward with all the force he possessed. Meeting little resistance as the blade penetrated clothes, flesh, whatever lay beyond. At once the pressure on John's throat eased as Ivan stiffened,

266

gave a grunt of surprise. Then his mouth opened wide. As John, unable to see where the blade had entered, sliced upwards. A long gralloching stroke that had his shoulder muscles screaming. Until steel grated against bone. And as Ivan swayed above him, roaring in rage and agony now, John instinctively withdrew the blade and drove it in again, this time twisting as he went. The roar stopped abruptly. The hands went slack around his neck. He saw the glazed look that had come over Ivan's face as he toppled sideways. Felt his own breath return in shuddering gasps. Felt the warm slick blood that coated his hands and wrists and forearms.

For some time he could do no more than lie on the ground, gulping for air like a man saved from drowning. As the burning pain in his throat and chest slowly subsided to a dull throb. The roaring in his ears receded.

Eventually he hauled himself to his knees, then clambered to his feet and stood with the knife hanging limp from his hand. Unable properly to comprehend what had happened. Feeling fogged and dazed and utterly removed from the body that sprawled on the ground before him.

He forced himself to breathe deeply. As his mind began to clear, his first thought was that Ninian mustn't see the blood. He bent to wipe clean the blade of the knife. Then grabbed handfuls of snow and began to scrub feverishly at his exposed skin. But there was nothing he could do to disguise the droplets that had reddened the snow all around.

He sensed a presence behind him. Turned slowly to find Ninian standing there on the track between the trees, looking silently on. He seemed calm, if deathly pale. It was hard to imagine that this was the child who a few moments ago had been running for his life.

Ninian looked down curiously at Ivan's corpse and the crimson stain that was now spreading out from beneath it.

'He's bleeding.'

John nodded uncertainly.

'He was chasing me. I was frightened.'

'I know you were.'

'Did you kill him?'

'Well . . .'

'Like Hector? And the tiger . . . ?'

'Aye. But . . .'

'You're good at killing.'

John's stomach lurched. He swallowed back bile. Shook his head so fiercely that Ninian looked crestfallen.

'Oh Ninian . . .' he muttered half apologetically. And stood for a moment staring vacantly at the corpse. Breathing heavily. As he passed the knife from one hand to the other.

'The jeep crashed,' Ninian said. 'I got out and ran away.'

John looked up, dragging himself from his trance. 'So you did.' He closed the knife. Then bent and started to go through Ivan's pockets. 'And Lila . . . what about Lila? Is she all right?'

Ninian hesitated. 'She wanted me to stay . . . there . . . but – but . . .' His lower lip began to tremble.

John forced a smile. 'It's OK. It is, really. You did fine. So . . . she spoke to you?'

He brightened. 'Yes. What are you looking for?'

'Keys.'

'They're in his trousers. I saw them. When he put the things on Lila.'

John lifted the tunic and pulled out a chain attached to the belt beneath it. He fumbled with unsteady fingers to unclip a ring of keys.

'Good lad!' He took Ninian's hand. 'Now we need to get her out. Before the other jeep gets here.'

The snow on the road was starting to turn slushy. They headed back for the vehicle as fast as they could.

'What about the other man?' John panted. 'The one who was driving?'

'I climbed over him.'

'Is he hurt, then?

Ninian nodded.

Twenty yards short of the vehicle, Ivan's semi-automatic was lying in the road where he must have flung it down as he set off after Ninian. John stopped and picked it up. It felt cold and alien and brutal after the familiar simplicity of his stalking rifle. He stood hefting the weapon uncertainly in his hands. There was no sign of activity from the jeep.

'Are you going to kill the other man too?'

'*No!*'

Ninian flinched.

'Sorry. No, I'm not. But I'm going to go and see how he is. So I want you to wait here till I call out that it's OK for you to come. This is very, very important. You understand me now? You've to wait till I call.'

Ninian nodded solemnly.

John walked slowly forward, holding the rifle at the ready. The way the vehicle had come to rest, with its underside exposed and its offside wheels protruding uselessly into the air, made him think of a cast sheep. That might at any moment start wriggling in a vain attempt to rise . . . But now he could see the figure slumped on the ground near the front. Foulis had his back resting against the edge of the running board, his head fallen forward on his chest. The ground around him was littered with glass.

269

He was breathing heavily and one leg was bent awkwardly. The trouser was torn and through the rent in the fabric was a white glimpse of bone.

John levelled the rifle at him and advanced step by step. His hands felt clammy on the steel. He gripped it tight to stop them trembling.

Foulis lifted his head. On his chalk-pale face the eyebrows were an almost clownlike smear of ginger. A bruise welled on the bridge of his nose. He focused on John, took in the levelled weapon. His eyes widened with fear.

'Lila,' John called out, his gaze fixed on Foulis, 'you there?'

After a long moment there came a muffled cry from inside the cab.

'OK,' John called again. 'Everything's OK. I've the keys. I'll have you out in a minute.' His voice felt high in his aching throat. His breathing was fast and shallow.

A sound was coming from Foulis. Sweat beaded his forehead. Shock now mingling with the fear on his face. He ran his tongue over dry lips.

'You . . .' he mouthed, 'you . . . you . . .'

John was momentarily at a loss. Then he realised where Foulis's gaze was directed. He glanced down to see that his glove had come off and the claw thumb was plain to see. Pink and naked in its deformity.

Foulis nodded and grimaced.

John gave him a long look. 'Aye, Kel. It's me, John Mac-Neil.'

Foulis returned the look and for an instant something moved in his pain-clouded eyes. Some reminder of the past that brought an almost wistful softening to the thick dull features. John's heart tripped expectantly.

Then Foulis's look hardened again.

'Christ al-fuckin'-mighty,' he said hoarsely. 'After all these years.'

'All these years,' repeated John emptily. He couldn't think of anything else. Now that this moment had finally arrived.

Foulis shifted on the ground. Winced. Straightened his back. 'So . . . what you gonnae do, eh? Now you've got me? Gonnae shoot me? Huh! You've no got it in you! You dinnae hae the guts . . .'

John thought of all the times he'd imagined a moment such as this over the last seven years. Imagined his hands round Kel Foulis's neck. Kel's nose splitting apart and fountaining blood. Kel toppling back unconscious to the ground. Kel looking up in dazed and abject defeat . . . Yet now that the moment had come he felt none of that rage. Just cold contempt.

'. . . and I'll tell you why,' Foulis continued. 'Because you always were a wee shite, that's why. And what's changed now, eh? Eh . . . ? So you can just put that down . . .'

John listened to the hectoring tone that had once turned his blood to water. Not so potent now though, was it? With Kel Foulis lying there, pale and dazed, like some hamstrung animal. He even allowed himself a fleeting moment of pity. Picturing the rise and fall of Cammie Foulis's arm. One end of a leather belt wrapped around the bunched fist . . .

He brushed the thought away and raised the muzzle of the rifle an inch. Noting how the fear returned at once to Foulis's eyes.

'See this?' He took one hand from the weapon and pointed to his sleeve.

Foulis's gaze shifted to the dark bloodstains.

'This is Ivan's.'

'So . . .' Foulis struggled to maintain his bravado. 'You've learned somethin' after all, then . . .'

'Oh aye.' John nodded slowly. 'I've learned plenty.'

He stroked the safety catch with his thumb.

'But what about you, Kel? What've you learned?'

Foulis licked his lips.

'Nothing to say, eh?'

Foulis stared silently.

'Nothing to say about Davie?'

Foulis's shoulders slumped.

'Nothing to say about the daft lad you've scared half witless? Nothing to say about all those poor bastards at Blackriggs?'

Foulis's eyes slid away.

'I'll tell you why you've nothing to say.' John snorted in disgust. 'Because you've learned nothing. That's why. You've never learned fuckall. You sad sonofabitch . . .'

He raised the rifle to his shoulder. Sighted it on a point between Kel Foulis's eyes. Felt the trigger under his forefinger. Breathed in and for a long moment held his breath.

Then lowered the rifle again.

He turned and walked away.

LOCH

THIRTY-SIX

The snow had turned to sleet and the wind was rising. Rivulets of water were starting to trickle out of the drifts. The first dark streaks of tarmac beginning to appear in the empty road.

'You OK to walk?' John shouldered the backpack, which he had retrieved from the cage.

Lila nodded. She was leaning heavily against the wing of the jeep, massaging her hip with one hand. The gash above her ear had stopped bleeding and John had cleaned the worst of the blood from her face. Ninian had joined them, scrambling around the back of the vehicle to avoid having to confront Foulis. Once again he seemed intrigued rather than alarmed by the blood. He studied Lila's face for a moment, then took her hand and laid his head against her side. Lila nodded towards the other side of the vehicle and raised an eyebrow.

'Injured,' said John. 'Not going anywhere. But there's the others, the other vehicle. Could be along any minute.'

He eyed Ivan's rifle, lying where he'd set it down on the roadside.

275

Lila let go and stepped unsteadily into the road, Ninian following.

'Where to?'

'Anywhere.' He picked up the rifle and held it for a moment, looking at it. Then heaved it into the undergrowth. 'Away from here. C'mon.'

For the first half-mile they had no choice but to keep to the road. A steep bank fell away to one side. Dense forestry climbed the hill to the other. Despite the veil of sleet, John seemed to see their surroundings with unnatural intensity. The dull sheen of the loch. The bedraggled look of a buzzard flapping off the dyke at their approach. The mole behind Lila's ear where blood had matted her hair.

'How long have you known?' It burst from him in a sudden explosion of anger.

She looked up. Confused and shocked.

'Wh–what? Known what?'

'About Ninian.'

What little colour there was drained from her face.

'Since yesterday.'

'Christ, Lila!' He was almost shouting. 'Why didn't you say anything?'

Tears began to well. 'I . . . I wasn't sure at first. And I didn't want to . . . give you any more to worry about.'

He snorted. 'That was thoughtful . . .'

'Oh, John . . . I mean – you'd heard the news. But I guess you hadn't seen the pictures. They're so alike . . . he's the spitting image of his dad. Or if you *have* seen the pictures, you didn't put two and two together. And things were difficult enough as they were yesterday . . .'

'Well, they're a bloody sight more difficult now. Thanks to you.'

She hung her head. 'I know.'

'But how . . . what . . . I mean – what *right* had you to keep it from me? Christ! It's him, a human being, we're talking about. Not some lost dog . . .'

Ninian had begun to hover around them as they walked. Glancing at them anxiously.

'Like I said . . .'

'So what made you sure?'

'I . . . I . . .' Her voice was almost inaudible now. 'I talked to Billy.'

'You *what*?'

'I talked it through with Billy. While you were still out finding Ninian. He'd seen the pictures too. Spotted the likeness straight away.'

'So that's why he changed his tune. Came over all co-operative. Jesus! Foulis was right. Billy must've thought all his Christmases had come at once.' John stopped and rounded on Lila. 'Look at the state of us! You. Me. The laddie. Is this what you wanted. Is it? Holy *shite*!'

Tears were rolling freely down her cheeks now. 'I'm sorry, John. So, so sorry. I-I thought it would help us . . .'

'Well, how wrong you were . . .' He smacked his fist into his open palm. 'And last night. At the bothy. All that stuff about your ideals, doing your bit . . . I mean, what was that all about, Lila? If you were keeping this from me?'

She turned away, shaking her head.

'So why didn't you say anything then? You'd already talked to Billy. You were convinced.'

'Because . . . oh John, I'm such a fucking idiot, I know . . . because Billy persuaded me to keep quiet.'

'He . . . persuaded . . . you . . . to . . . keep . . . quiet.' John shook his head in disbelief. 'And just how did he manage to do that?'

277

'Said it was better that as few people knew as possible. Especially you. Till we were safe.'

'And you fell for that – that shite!'

She nodded wretchedly. 'I-I didn't know what he was up to.'

John clasped both hands to his head.

'Goddammit, Lila! I . . . I just . . . don't know what to believe any longer. Or who.'

She dabbed at her eyes. 'I don't blame you . . .' she said softly. Then turned away to Ninian, who had begun to whine and rock from side to side.

'It's OK, darlin'.' She bent down and drew him to her. 'It's OK. We're all fine really. Here, let Lila give you a hug.'

Ninian made a brief show of resisting. Then let his head drop forward on to her shoulder.

John strode back and forth, glancing up and down the road until at last they straightened up again and set off. Ninian clasping Lila's hand.

In due course the ground began to level and a set of gateposts appeared. John turned into a potholed private driveway.

'See if we can find something with wheels,' he said.

The drive ran down towards the loch. Shortly it bent round the edge of a small wood, taking them out of sight of the road at last.

'What about the other one?' Lila asked hesitantly. 'Moustache. I never asked . . .'

'He . . .'

'John killed him.' The childish voice rang with pride and admiration. 'He was chasing me. John fought him. On the ground. There was blood . . .' He paused, looking uncertainly into the two older faces. Not understanding what he saw there.

'Did you?'

John looked past her. Nodded.

He sensed her stiffen and draw slightly away from him.

'Jesus,' she said softly.

'C'mon,' he said. 'We need to keep moving.'

John. Ninian called him John. He'd never called him anything before . . .

As they came closer to the shore the driveway forked one way towards a large house, distantly visible through trees, the other in the direction of a stable block. John made for the stables, where they passed through a stone archway into a courtyard. The place was deserted, but parked in an open bay was a battered pick-up. He walked up to the driver's door and looked through the window. There were no keys in the ignition. He opened the door and found the hood release catch. Lila and Ninian stood by as he reached down into the engine compartment and fiddled with wires for some moments. Then stood back shaking his head.

'Battery's flat . . .'

Lila pointed to closed double doors on the opposite side of the yard. The doors were unlocked and they stepped into the gloom of a vacant garage. John stood in the doorway, defeated by the emptiness of the place. But Lila walked on towards the grimy window at the far end. She peered through it for a moment, then turned.

'I think there's a boathouse.'

'So . . . ?'

'We should get across the loch if we can. It's NLA territory the other side. They're in control there.'

John looked at her uncertainly. Then nodded. 'OK.'

Behind the stable block a track ran across a paddock to the trees that fringed the loch. Beyond them, at the water's edge, was a wooden shed. Beside it a jetty.

The boathouse door was padlocked, but the place had not been well maintained. Where the paintwork had weathered and flaked away the timber looked rotten. John searched for something to use as a crowbar. Finding nothing he settled for a large stone and struck the padlock repeatedly as hard as he could. The woodwork around it began to disintegrate. Eventually one of the fixings gave way and the padlock fell free. The door swung open on a dock. In it rocked an inflatable with an ancient outboard motor. Hanging on the wall were four faded orange life preservers.

'Are we going in the boat?' Ninian's face lit up.

'If there's fuel in it,' John replied.

He clambered in and unscrewed the cap on the tank. Although he could see nothing, there was a strong smell and he could hear the faint swashing of liquid when he tapped the side.

'My dad has a boat,' said Ninian as John helped him in. 'On the lake.'

Lila took down three life preservers and stepped in after him.

'It's got two of those.' He pointed at the outboard as Lila helped him on with the orange vest. 'He takes me in it.'

'Does he now?' said Lila.

He nodded.

John waited till they were settled, then firmly grasped the toggle on the starter cord and tugged it.

Nothing happened.

He tugged again. And again. And again. The smell of fuel growing stronger. He forced himself to pause. Counted to fifty. Then pulled firmly and steadily and at last the outboard fired. He nosed the craft forward until Lila could reach out and slide back the bar across the doors. He nudged them aside with the bows and headed out into the open water.

Once they were well clear of the boathouse he glanced over his shoulder. There was no sign of life on the shore. Nothing moved at the house, the stables or, as far as he could tell, on the road beyond.

Out on the loch the water was rougher than it had appeared from the shore. John opened the throttle and the lightweight craft went bouncing across the waves in a cloud of icy spray. Ninian and Lila huddled in the bows, bulky in orange as they clung to the thwarts and each other. John sat upright in the stern, one hand clamped to the tiller, jaw set to the wind. Despite the driving sleet and bitter cold, the looming hills ahead, the dark unmeasured depths below, he felt a strange exhilaration . . .

'What happened,' he shouted to Lila, 'in the jeep back there?'

'How d'you mean?'

'When it crashed . . .'

She nodded and pointed at Ninian.

'He hit him.'

'Who?'

'Ninian . . . hit Foulis.'

'Did he?'

'With the game thing. On the nose.'

'No!'

'Aye. Smack on the bridge. Made him shout. And let go of the steering wheel.' She grinned. 'Must've hurt like . . .'

'Whoa.' John began to chuckle. 'He's some boy!' He could feel the laughter catching him deep in the belly. Soon he was lifting his head to the wind and roaring and shaking as the tears poured down his cheeks. In the bows Lila's smile widened until she too had her head thrown back, one hand to her side. Ninian's delighted giggle added a treble note to the windblown chorus of laughter.

John wiped his eyes and set a diagonal course for the gaunt tower of Urquhart Castle. It faded in and out of view like an apparition as the wind sent violent squalls of sleet down the loch. Beyond the ruin there was a bay. Some distance back from the shore, the village of Drumnadrochit. Whose houses were becoming visible through the sleet, a few minutes later, when the outboard spluttered to silence and the inflatable drifted to a halt. Two hundred yards from land they wallowed aimlessly in the waves. John reached for the oars and dropped one with a clatter, feeling suddenly weak and light-headed as images of Ivan poured without warning into his mind and his stomach heaved. He picked up the oar again with a hand that had begun to tremble. Closed his eyes, shook his head as a spasm of nausea gripped him. Then another. Bile flooded into his mouth and he leaned over the side, vomiting into the waves.

Lila was hunched up in the bows, both arms around Ninian. The first signs of a dark bruise spreading down the side of her face. She watched him anxiously.

John scooped up water, rinsed and spat, splashed his face. Gripped the oars to steady trembling hands and started to row. Battling against the wind and waves.

Between the shore and the village there was a low-lying area of bog and scrubby woodland through which a river rushed towards the loch. Against the gathering spate, it was all John could do to propel the inflatable a few strokes upstream into the shelter of the nearest trees. He struggled on to the bank and helped Lila and Ninian out in turn. Ninian said nothing. Hardly opened his eyes, but stood shuddering with cold.

'We'll have to get him warm,' said Lila.

John nodded and reached out to lift him up. But Ninian pushed him away.

'Take my hand then. The walking'll warm you up.'

Ninian didn't respond. But he didn't resist when John reached out and clasped one gloved hand.

They set off through the trees, heading in the direction of the village. Soon they reached a snowy clearing where an unmetalled road led away from a couple of low modern buildings. Storage sheds, perhaps, or light industrial units. John paused as he saw movement on the hillside beyond the village, now distantly visible above the treetops. He reached into his coat pocket for the binoculars. Raised them, steadied his hand and focused. Stood there for several moments. Then lowered them again.

'Soldiers,' he said. 'Soldiers on the road. A convoy. Heading for Inverness.' He fumbled with binoculars. 'I . . . I thought you said the rebel boys were in control . . . this side.'

'They are.'

'So what's the convoy doing?'

Lila shrugged. 'It's the main road from Fort William to Inverness.'

'And . . . ?'

She tilted her chin at the hills, rising steeply from the loch-side. 'That's where they are, the NLA. Glen Affric and beyond. The wild—'

'I know what's there,' John snapped. 'So . . . we'll need to find a way to get on.' He was mumbling to himself. Thinking aloud. 'Try to find a vehicle maybe. Aye . . .'

'I think we need to get warm and dry first,' said Lila quietly. 'All of us.'

For a moment John had difficulty focusing.

'We need to get warm, John. Please.'

'Aye. OK. Get warm . . .'

He glanced up the track towards the village. But Lila

shook her head. 'Not there. I don't think we can risk it.' She cast an eye at the buildings. 'What about one of those?'

The sheds were almost identical, with roll-down fronts to allow vehicles in. Both were locked. But around the sides glass-paned doors opened on to small offices, neither of which looked as if they'd been occupied for some time. John returned to the nearest. Picked a stone from the ground, wrapped it in his woolly hat and smashed the glass. He reached inside and released the catch.

From the office a short corridor led past a small kitchen and toilet to another door, which opened into the main area of the shed. It was about the size of a tennis court and empty but for two wooden pallets, their loads shrouded in polythene. In one corner was a large pile of discarded cardboard boxes and a small industrial incinerator, only a little bigger than a household stove. The hammering of sleet on the metal roof reverberated through the empty space.

Lila eyed the incinerator.

John hesitated. But she frowned and nodded urgently at the dazed and shivering Ninian. Whose cheeks had started to take on a bluish tinge.

'Chance it with the smoke, eh?'

'In this weather . . .' She nodded again.

John retrieved his matches from the backpack. Once the incinerator was roaring he left Lila to settle Ninian by the warmth and went out in search of wood. When he returned Ninian was staring into the flames, munching on the remains of the oatcakes from Nicol's kitchen. He coughed, a deep hacking sound and a spray of crumbs.

Lila was bent down behind the pallets. She straightened up.

'See what I've found.'

She squatted down at Ninian's side. Held out her hand.

'Look.'

On her palm stood a plastic Loch Ness monster with three humps, wearing a tartan Jimmy bunnet and a mane of ginger hair.

Ninian ignored her. Continued to stare into the flames.

She placed it on the ground beside him.

'There's box-loads of them over there. Want to come and see?'

After a moment Ninian scrambled to his feet and silently followed her to the pallets. John joined them as they peeled back the polythene and prised out a box. He carried it back to the fire and opened it. Ninian tipped it up, scattering hundreds of identical monsters over the floor. He stared at them, head to one side. Then knelt down and set to work arranging them. He coughed again.

'I was wondering,' said Lila, 'maybe one of us should go up the village. Get some medicine if we can. Food. See the lie of the land . . .'

John frowned.

'I doubt anyone'll be looking for us here yet. Even if they've found Foulis. And there'll not be many folk about in this weather anyway.' She looked at him. 'D'you want me to go? You stay, look after Ninian . . .'

'No . . . I mean – aye . . . you go.'

She made for the door.

'I'll be as quick as I can.'

John sat down on the ground and held out his hands to the flames. He knew he should join in the game. Help organise the army of monsters as they went marching, in formations known only to Ninian, across the floor. But he couldn't. He felt too crazy. Too strung out. He'd have given anything to be Ninian right now. Who could soak up any amount of horror and uncertainty because he couldn't carry it with him from one moment to the next. Who had hardly even any idea of who he was. Or where he'd been. Or where he was going. And who had certainly never killed a man. Never felt cold steel driving through muscle and soft tissue and organs until it grated on bone . . .

Drowning in his thoughts, it was a while before John realised that Ninian had stopped playing and had climbed to his feet. He was standing a few paces away, surrounded by monsters, eyeing him intently.

'Are you OK?' John tried a smile but the muscles in his jaw wouldn't work. His bruised neck and throat had begun to ache.

Ninian coughed but said nothing. Kept looking at him and walked over, trampling monsters as he went. He stopped an arm's length away.

'You look funny,' he said.

John hesitated. Then nodded.

'Why do you look like that?'

John stared numbly at the pale face with its runny nose. Its fringe of dark curls and solemn brown eyes.

At length he said, 'I did something I wish I hadn't. Maybe I'd no choice . . . but that doesn't make it any better.'

Was that really the truth? he wondered as soon as he'd said it. Had he really had no choice? Could he not have somehow just . . . immobilised him? He thought of the crushing weight of the heavy body, the mint-scented breath, the hands at his throat, and shuddered – he could still feel them there . . .

Ninian continued to look at him. Then stepped forward and put his arms around John's neck. John sank forward. Breathed in the damp child smell. Felt the lump rise in his throat.

'We'll see you right,' he muttered. 'So we will.'

THIRTY-SEVEN

At the sound of footsteps in the empty warehouse John struggled to leave the murk of the dream-forest through which he was having to lead them on their perilous journey. They were children together, Lila and Ninian. His children. And he had to take them to safety. But the tall pine trees were really wind turbines which concealed the flitting ghosts of ancient clansmen, who leaped forward brandishing oars to bar his path. Only to melt away in flurries of snow as he stepped towards them.

He had fallen asleep on the two bedrolls, laid one on top of the other in front of the incinerator. Beside him, Ninian had drifted off in an upholstered swivel chair from the office, a plastic monster in each hand. Snuffling and wheezing in his sleep.

He opened his eyes and took in the unfamiliar surroundings. The reality of their predicament starting to drive the fog from his mind. Lila was clutching a carrier bag. Rain dripping from her hair. Her face. Her clothes.

'How d'you get on?' he asked.

'OK.' She set down the bag. Shook her damp hair. Took off her coat and walked over to the incinerator, rubbing raw hands. The rain had washed a thin trickle of blood down her neck from the scalp wound. There was a look of exhausted defiance on her face. John longed to put his arms around her.

'. . . and I got cough syrup. For adults.'

'Oh . . .' He focused again. 'All they had, eh?'

'Lucky there was a shop at all. You should've seen the place.' She squatted down and stared into the flames. 'It was half deserted. Abandoned. Looked like there hadn't been a tourist there in years. The houses all boarded up.'

'Soldiers?'

She shook her head. 'Seems there's been more trouble at the squatter camp in Inverness. Rioting. Folk taking pot-shots at the army. That's where the convoy was heading. Extra troops from the Fort William garrison.'

John glanced at the army of Loch Ness monsters marching across the floor. 'So what are we going to do?'

'Try and make contact with the NLA again.'

John shook his head. 'It's far too dangerous.'

Lila raised an eyebrow. 'I thought you wanted to. I thought you wanted to find a vehicle. Head up into the wild country . . .'

'I wasn't thinking straight. We don't even know who we can trust any longer. Let alone how to make contact with them.'

Lila looked at him. 'Which means you still trust me . . . even after everything? Billy . . . and Foulis?'

'Aye, Lila. I do.'

'Oh, John . . . I-I . . .' She looked down at her hands, then said solemnly, 'Thank you.' She paused. 'But . . . but I think you're forgetting something.'

'What's that?'

She glanced at the sleeping figure in the chair. 'His

father. I mean . . . now we know who he is, surely we have to try and get him to his dad?'

'His father,' repeated John slowly. 'So we're really certain, are we? I mean absolutely one hundred per cent . . . ?'

'You've only to see the photos, John. It's as plain as the nose on your face. Not to mention Switzerland and everything. And Foulis knew just who he was looking for, didn't he?'

'He did that.' John sighed. 'Poor wee soul.'

'Brave wee soul.' Lila nodded at the sleeping figure. 'So now we should get him back to where he really belongs.'

Again John shook his head. 'I still think it's too dangerous. Fraser's right in the thick of it. Things won't be going well for him, not now that they know who he is. And that boat they intercepted, with the weapons . . .' He looked at Lila. 'Can we not just, well . . . go to ground, I suppose? Like Fraser. For a while. Till things calm down.'

'With a fragile X kid on our hands?'

'Isn't that why Fraser sent him to Blackriggs in the first place? To the aunt or whoever she was? To hide him away. Keep him out of harm . . . even though it didn't work out. So is it not best for everyone if we take care of him for now – till this is over?'

'But, John! For all we know, Fraser thinks he's dead. Everyone's heard about Blackriggs now. It's been on the news – you saw it yourself. And the authorities won't have been putting it about that Ninian's still alive, that's for sure. They'll be doing anything they can to undermine Fraser's morale. I mean – for God's sake, he's already lost his wife . . .'

'Then we'll have to find some way of letting him know he's OK.'

'Handing him over. That's the only way. Honestly.'

John gave her a stubborn look. 'I just don't think we should put him in any more danger. I really don't. Anyway, Fraser's got his hands full fighting his fight. He'll not thank anyone for showing up in the middle of it with an eight-year-old fragile X kid. Even if he is his son. Even if we knew how to find him . . .'

Now Lila gave an exasperated shake of the head. 'I don't get this, John. I don't get where you're coming from all of a sudden . . . I mean – you simply want to run out on all this now? Head for the hills? Lie low?'

'Aye, Lila. That's what I want to do.'

'What about *your* dad? Don't you want to get in touch with him?'

'Of course I do. But we told Billy about him – everything about him. So he could get someone to make contact with him. Remember?' He held Lila's eye until she looked away. 'Which means that even if they weren't before, the authorities will be right on my dad's tail now, for sure. Watching his every move. If they haven't already picked him up. There's nothing I can do about it.'

Lila was silent for a while, then she asked quietly, 'What about me?'

'I'd like you to come with me.'

'Do I have a say?'

'Of course you do . . .'

'So what if I don't want to?'

'Why wouldn't you? I'd look after you . . .'

'Because . . .' She was trying to keep her voice level. 'Because I just might feel it was more important to try to find Fraser, or at least get word to him that Ninian's OK. I'd go anywhere to find him now, just for the satisfaction of blowing Billy Lowrie's cover . . . And anyway – what about Blackriggs? What about speaking up? Fraser needs to know the truth. The whole world needs to know the truth . . .'

John shook his head. 'I've changed my mind.'

'You've . . . changed . . . your . . . mind.' She stared at him. 'D'you mind my asking why?'

'Because I'm sick and tired of it all.'

'Oh. I see. Sick of what precisely?'

John's voice rose. 'Don't make me spell it out, Lila.'

'You mean yesterday – at the checkpoint?'

'I said, don't push it. Please . . .'

'But hang on a minute here. Shooting up an army road-block's not quite the same thing as wiping out a whole village of civil –'

John shook his head fiercely.

She looked at him. Mouth open. Understanding slowly dawning. 'You mean the foreign boy . . . moustache . . .' She started to colour. 'Oh my God, John . . . I mean, well . . . that was surely self-def –'

She caught his look and fell silent.

At length she said, 'OK, I'm sorry . . . I understand . . . I think.' She tried to smile. 'But that doesn't alter the fact that we still need to get Ninian to his father.'

'No, Lila. It's just too dangerous.'

'But . . . try to put yourself in Fraser's shoes, John. He needs his son, desperately I should think. He's probably more vulnerable than he's ever been. Now his name's out. Him getting Ninian back right now could be critical to the whole thing . . .'

'So . . . ?'

'So Fraser needs whatever help he can get. Because he's fighting for a principle . . . something good and decent. For folk to be able to live as they choose. As individuals. To do the best with their lives. Without being trodden all over by the Department.'

John's eye fell on the mouse-fiddle, lying naked and ruptured on the concrete floor where he had taken it from the bedroll. A crack running across its belly where even the foam mattress had failed to shield it from the impact of the crashing jeep.

'There's no such thing as a decent principle,' he said, 'when innocent folk are getting killed by it. You said so yourself. At Billy's.'

'No, I did not. I said the exact opposite. I said there's no ideal that justifies killing innocent folk.'

'OK. And where does that leave Struan Fraser?'

'On the right side, as far as I'm concerned. Whatever his faults. Trying to undo a wrong. Trying to hand something back to the folk it belongs to – and I don't just mean the lairds . . .'

'Aye. Who it belongs to – which is just where the whole mess began,' interrupted John, remembering something Ferg had said the day after the downing of the helicopter. 'How can you own something that's been here since before we could walk upright and'll be here long after we're gone?' He shook his head. 'It doesn't belong to us, the land. We belong to it, if anything. And the real point is who *cares* for it. See, if folk had understood that, we'd never've got ourselves into all this in the first place –'

'Whatever . . .' Her eyes flashed. 'Anyway, he's also trying to get rid of a bunch of rotten folk who don't deserve to stay in power. And for my part I'll do whatever I can to help him. To let my dad know he didn't take a beating in the Lubyanka for nothing. To show that two-faced sonofabitch Billy Lowrie that he can't go round betraying folk. To teach animals like Foulis that they can't get away with their killing . . . And I guess I'd hoped – after all you've been through – that you'd feel the same.' She paused, chewing her lip. 'But I can see now that I was wrong.'

Ninian coughed in his sleep and shifted in the chair.

John said nothing.

Lila shook her head wearily. 'I just don't know how you can even think of keeping him from his dad, John.'

'I want to do the best for him.'

'You're not even qualified . . .'

'He's no worse off than when I found him . . .'

'He needs proper care, for Chrissakes, John! Not running round the countryside dodging soldiers. Sleeping in empty warehouses. Cold and hungry and frightened all the time. And Fraser needs him just as much as he needs Fraser.' She looked at him. 'D'you really want to end up working for the Department again?'

'What d'*you* think?'

'Then it's time you wised up. Because right now I think you're being selfish. Selfish and naive and . . . and gutless.'

'I'm sorry you think that, Lila,' said John coldly.

She looked at him for a moment in silence. Her face seemed paler than ever.

'But that's only half of what I *really* think,' she said. 'D'you want to hear the rest?'

'You're going to tell me anyway.'

'OK. I think you just don't want to give him up. I think . . . you've let him become like . . . some kind of . . . substitute for Davie.'

John felt the anger rising.

'You keep Davie *out* of this!'

Lila flinched, but held his gaze. 'But I think it's true, John. And I also think it's high time you let go of the both of them.'

'Then you think wrong!' John glared back at her. 'Now, I'm going outside.' He stood up. 'You – you can do whatever the fuck you want.'

He started towards the exit, footsteps ringing angrily in the empty space. He was almost at the door when Ninian gave a loud groan. Slithered off the chair and landed in a drowsy heap on the floor, where a coughing fit took hold of him.

John ignored him and stormed out, slamming the door behind him. Took a dozen furious paces and halted. He picked a stone from the ground and hurled it with all his strength in the direction of the loch. Then another. And another. Resisting the image of Ninian with his shoulders racked with coughing . . . At length he stopped hurling stones and stood, head bowed in the rain. Then turned back to the shed and quietly opened the door again. He stood there uncertainly, anger still bristling in his veins.

Lila had got Ninian sitting up on the floor and now she was crouched by the shopping bag, rummaging for the bottle of cough mixture. She had heard him come back in but she didn't look his way. She poured a full adult measure into the calibrated cap and walked back to Ninian.

'There now.' She held it out and Ninian slurped up the mixture. Spluttered. Let his head flop forward against her chest. 'I don't feel well,' he muttered.

'I know.' Pouring another capful. 'This'll help.'

'Is that not . . . ?' ventured John.

Lila gave a firm shake of the head. 'It won't kill him. And we could all do with some decent rest.'

Obediently Ninian slurped again. Then looked up at her. 'I want to see my dad.'

She nodded. 'It's OK, darlin'. You're going to.' And raised her eyes to look steadily at John. 'Isn't that right?'

John felt the anger flare again, then die.

He sighed and nodded. 'Aye,' he said. 'So you are, laddie.'

'There. See? Now just you get close to the fire. John'll get some more wood. And we'll all have a bite to eat.'

She turned to the shopping bag and started to busy herself with the provisions.

John hovered by the door.

'Could you . . . er . . . did you see the smoke?'

'It's pissing down out there. Could hardly see the end of my nose.'

'Oh . . . aye. OK.'

She was right. The world outside seemed to be turning dirty grey and dissolving. All John could hear was water, everywhere. Already much of the snow had gone. He scoured the damp ground for anything that might burn. Trying to let the cold air and concentration restore his equilibrium. Through the trees he could see the loch, flecked with whitecaps now. A boat was making its way through the choppy water, heading towards Inverness. A small motorised fishing boat that must have come up the Caledonian Canal, through the locks – if they were still working. John stood and watched it for a moment as, through all the turmoil in his mind, something unexpected began to fall into place.

Clutching an armful of damp wood to his chest, he made his way briskly back to the buildings.

THIRTY-EIGHT

Lila and Ninian were sharing a meat pie, munching together in the gloomy deserted warehouse with its boxfuls of obsolete monsters. She looked up briefly as he came in, shadows playing across her face in the flickering light from the incinerator. He could feel the traces of their argument spiking the air like faint echoes of some seismic disturbance.

He put the wood down by the incinerator, shook the rain from his hair, then sat down beside them. Lila reached into the shopping bag and held out a pie. He took a bite, not sure whether he was hungry or not. He badly wanted to share the thought that had just occurred to him. But from the drooping of Ninian's eyelids he guessed that the medicine was taking effect and that he was about to drop off at any moment. He put the pie down and waited.

Between mouthfuls Lila was telling Ninian a story about how the Loch Ness monster was really an old boggart. A kind of mischievous spirit, who had taken on the prehistoric form of a plesiosaur and sunk to the bottom of the loch where, over the centuries, he'd forgotten his boggart ways. Ninian was struggling to keep listening. His head began to loll. A minute or two later it fell forward and he slumped like a doll. With his snot-caked nose and crumbs around his mouth, a half-eaten piece of pie clenched in his fist.

Together John and Lila undressed him and got him into one of the sleeping bags. Moments later he was motionless on the mattress, a nimbus of dark hair spilling out of the top of the bag. Was it only the night before last that John had slept in a bed himself, at Morag's? It felt like a month.

Rain continued to hammer down on the roof as they settled again on the floor in front of the incinerator. Lila sat cross-legged, elbows askew, rolling cigarettes in her lap with tobacco she'd bought at the shop. She lit both and passed one to John.

'I'll quit when all this is over,' she said with a wry grin.

'Me too.' John took a drag and coughed. Then leaned forward.

'I remembered something when I was out there just now. Something that I think might be important.' He turned round and reached for Ninian's trousers. Pulled them to him and felt the patch pocket on the leg. Then opened the flap and took out the postcard with the statue of the Little Mermaid on the rocks in Copenhagen harbour. He turned it over, thankful that he'd remembered to remove it when he'd washed the clothes at Morag's. It was hard enough to decipher as it was.

'Listen to this.' He read slowly: *How is my boy? I hope you are well. I will be arriving on 25th November. I will bring you a present. Looking forward to seeing you. Marie Rose sends her good wishes and so do I. Uncle Peter.*

Lila looked at him expectantly.

'What's the name of the boat they intercepted?' he

asked. 'The arms shipment from Denmark. Did you ever hear the name?'

She frowned. Then shook her head.

'I'm pretty sure it was Marie something . . .' said John.

'Wait a minute . . . Marie . . . Claire?'

'Aye.' John nodded. 'That was it. And what's the date today?'

'Sixteenth . . . no, seventeenth.'

'So the twenty-fifth's just over a week away.'

She nodded.

He passed her the card. 'You know what I think this is, Lila? I think it's a message for Fraser about another arms shipment. Copenhagen, Denmark. *Marie Claire, Marie Rose* – sister ships.'

'On a postcard?' She squinted at it with a doubtful look.

'Aye. I thought about that too. But you know what? Nothing electronic's safe these days. They can get into anything. So maybe mail's the safest of the lot.'

'Hmmm. Maybe . . . so they would have mailed the card to Ninian . . . the aunt would have read the message and got in touch with Fraser somehow?'

'Something like that, I guess.'

'So then why does Ninian still have it?'

'Because . . . the aunt would have known that the soldiers would search her house when they came. She maybe thought it would be safer for Ninian to have it on him when she hid him in the ice house.'

'Maybe. And who's Uncle Peter?'

'I don't know. Probably just a code name for the supplier. But whoever it is, if they're channelling messages via Ninian, this one won't have got through.'

'So we need to get it to him – is that it?'

'Aye. You see . . . maybe the last message was intercepted, which is how they stopped the boat. But if this one has only got as far as Ninian, then there could be a chance that the information's still safe. And it could be critical to Fraser . . .'

Lila nodded appreciatively. The tension of the argument had left her and the firelight softened her features. She smiled.

John felt himself blush, partly at the compliment, partly because her earlier taunt had hurt him and it continued to rankle. But he made himself return the smile and for a moment it seemed to float there in the space between them.

'I'm – I'm sorry . . . about just now, Lila,' he said. 'Really sorry. I was a bit . . . crazy, I guess.'

She reached out and touched his arm. 'Don't think about it, John.' Her face grew serious. 'You're a good guy. Truly you are. And you had . . . every reason to be crazy. I'm sorry too. There are things I shouldn't've said.'

John blushed for the second time. 'It's OK. You were probably right. And of course we've got to find Fraser.' He tapped the postcard. 'Specially now.'

She nodded. 'We were lucky Foulis didn't search Ninian.'

'Aye, we were.'

They sat smoking in silence. Their eyes met and for a moment they held one another's gaze. John felt a tremor enter the air.

'You know something?' she said. 'I've actually never met anyone less gutless in my whole life. I mean . . . when I think of what you . . . did . . . back there . . . the way you've taken care of us . . .'

She was sitting forward again but looking at him differently now. In a new way. With something like respect. His heart missed a beat as he realised that what she had been referring to was Ivan. It made him feel shocked and giddy, but at the same time very much alive. It was a feeling unlike any he had ever had before.

'I only did what anyone would've,' he mumbled.

She made no reply but looked steadily back at him. Her pale face framed by the boyish dark hair. The silence deepening. As he waited for the moment to pass. But this time it didn't. The tremor returned. John's heart starting to pound. Then Lila was leaning towards him, eyes half closed. Offering him her mouth. Her lips soft and full. And suddenly he was drowning in the taste and scent and feel, the warmth and tenderness of her. As they toppled down on the remaining mattress together. Two shadows breathing and moving as one in the dim glow of the flames.

Later, as he was on the verge of sleep, a sequence of notes drifted into John's mind. They were vaguely familiar, although in his semi-conscious state he struggled to remember why. It came to him that it was the beginning of the new tune he'd first heard in his head at Billy Lowrie's cottage. But before he could begin to memorise them, sleep overtook him.

THIRTY-NINE

It was past nine in the morning when Lila gently woke him. John groaned and pulled himself back on to the mattress. Some time during the night he had rolled on to the floor. Now he was stiff all over and his throat ached.

'Your breakfast, sir.' It was half a meat pie and a swig of Irn-Bru. She crouched beside him, smiling.

He rubbed at his neck.

'Are you OK?'

'Sore.'

'Let me see.' She leaned forward and pulled open the neck of his shirt. Her fingers felt cool on his flesh. He thought of the previous night.

'Boy, that's some bruising.' She sounded concerned. 'Are you sure you're OK? You can swallow all right?'

He nodded. 'It's just bruises. Don't think . . . he . . . did any real damage. Anyway, what about you? You OK?'

'Aye, I'm fine.'

'How's the head?'

She touched the place behind her left ear where she had been bleeding. 'Healing up OK. I'll live.' She smiled again.

301

There *was* something different in the way she was looking at him. He hadn't imagined it last night. Whatever it
was, it seemed to make her softer, more feminine. While
leaving him feeling somehow . . . older. Wiser even. More
in control. He smiled back at her. Then glanced around
the empty warehouse. And felt instantly anxious at the
thought of what lay ahead of them.

Curled up on the other mattress, Ninian didn't want to
wake up. He looked pale and doped and out of sorts,
though the cough seemed to have gone.

'So how are we going to find Fraser?' John asked
through a mouthful of pie.

'Try to contact the NLA again, I guess.' Lila had already
begun to gather together their few possessions.

'D'you . . . ?'

'Know anyone else?' She laughed unevenly. 'I think we
should try the squatter camp. It's full of poor folk from
the glens. And the farms, what's left of them. Who can't
make a living any more since the fighting began.'

'So how do they survive at the camps, then?'

'Handouts, I think. Anyway, it's supposedly ideal
recruiting ground for the NLA – that's what someone was
saying in the bar the other night. Folk're already at rock
bottom when they arrive. They hate the government
anyway. And by the time they've been at the camp for a
week or two they'll sign up for anything.'

John shook his head sadly at the thought.

'If there's trouble there now, I'm sure the NLA'll be
behind it,' she said. 'At the camp and in the housing estate
beside it. It shouldn't be too hard to make contact with
someone.' She looked at him. 'What d'you reckon?'

'Springfield Estate?' said John.

She nodded.

'I heard about it on the news a few days back.'

'So did I. They've put up barricades, the folk there – to keep the army out. I should think that's where that convoy you saw was headed . . .' She turned to Ninian, who was still toying with his portion of meat pie.

'We've some walking to do today,' she said. 'Can you do some walking, Ninian?'

'I want to go in the boat,' he replied. Without looking up.

'We can't go in the boat,' said John. 'It's run out of fuel.'

'I want to.'

'Can't always do what we want to,' said Lila gently but firmly.

To John's surprise he simply looked at her. Then shrugged.

'Where will we walk to?' he asked.

'Inverness. It's not far.'

'I don't want to go to Inverness.'

'Inverness's OK.'

'My mum was in Inverness.'

John and Lila exchanged glances.

'My mum's dead.'

'Would you like to see your dad?' asked John.

Ninian shook his head.

'No?'

'No!' He turned away and started to gurn to himself.

John began to fill the backpack. For a moment he eyed the cracked fiddle, still lying there like a small silent corpse on the concrete floor of the shed. Should he feed it to the incinerator? An offering to whatever god might guide them safely to Fraser? But the thought of the notes that might one day stream from it, when all this was over and he had the time and the tools to fix it up again, was enough to make him reach for the bedrolls. He strapped the sausage-shaped bundle to the top of the backpack once more.

They left the shed and walked up the road to the village. It was still raining. Here and there patches of dirty snow mottled the sodden grey landscape. The hilltops were hidden in cloud. Swollen burns tumbled headlong through dripping woods towards the loch.

Ninian stamped along a little way behind them, muttering and whining. He wouldn't look John in the eye and thrust his hand away.

Lila stopped. Waiting for him to catch up.

'Maybe he knows something's up.'

'Maybe he does.'

The village had an eerie sense of desertion. Half the houses boarded up. The single shop not open yet. Nothing stirring but a ginger cat, which slunk into an alley at their approach. They climbed the short hill out of the village. Past the closed and empty visitor centre, with its once garish but now faded renderings of the Loch Ness monster. Like an abandoned fairground float, thought John, sad and tawdry. Though Ninian, pausing to look up in wonder, clearly thought otherwise. He said nothing, just stood and stared, while John looked at the display board in the vacant window with its poster for the Deuchary Ceilidh Band's silver-jubilee tour. Across which large letters stencilled in red ink spelled out the word CANCELLED. Beneath, someone had scrawled, 'YOU MEAN BANNED' in equally large black letters. Followed by three angry exclamation marks.

Once out of the village they walked down the side of the main road in silence. Keeping their eyes open for paths that might lead up into the relative safety of the woods above them.

'I've been trying to figure something out,' said John. 'Foulis knew who Ninian was. And he knew that you knew and I didn't – because that's what Lowrie would have told him. So why did he go through that charade – asking us where Fraser was? You didn't say anything to Billy about that, did you?'

Lila stared down at the loch and eventually replied, 'Maybe Billy didn't trust us. Maybe Foulis and Billy didn't trust one another. Maybe Foulis just wanted an excuse to . . .' She gave a shudder. 'Who knows?'

John nodded. 'Doesn't make any difference . . .'

'No. It's past.' She moved closer to him and felt for his hand.

Ninian was plodding ahead now, brandishing a stick he'd found at the roadside.

'Will he . . . ? Is it curable?' John asked. 'The things they can do these days . . .'

Lila shook rain from her eyes. 'You mean gene therapy? Yes, I guess so. If it ever becomes legal again . . . if they ever get all the lawsuits and ethical wrangling sorted out. Otherwise . . . no, it's not curable. But he could still grow up to lead a more or less independent life. With the right care and support. From people who love him.'

'Aye, well. I hope they're there for him when he needs them.'

'Starting with his dad . . .' she added.

The sound of an approaching vehicle reached them. John glanced to left and right but the hillside was steep here and there was nowhere to leave the road. All they could do was plod on, heads down against the rain, and hope they looked too dispirited to be of interest to anyone.

Moments later a dilapidated van appeared, coughing black exhaust. It slowed as it drew level with them. The driver leaned across and rolled down the window. Looked them up and down. He wore filthy overalls, smears of oil on his unshaven jowls as if he'd just slid out from beneath a vehicle.

'Inverness?'

John nodded.

'You'll be for Bught . . .' It was more a statement than a question.

'Bught?'

'Bught Park. The camp.'

'Oh. Aye, well . . .'

Lila stepped forward. 'Are there . . . many checkpoints – on the road? The laddie, see.' Pointing to Ninian. 'He's handicapped. Terrified of soldiers.'

The driver craned his neck for a glance at Ninian, who was busy poking his stick down a drain. 'Just the one. On the outskirts of town. I can let you out before it.' He let slip a knowing smile. 'Take a nice wee walk down the riverside, eh? About twenty minutes to the camp.'

She nodded gratefully.

'Hop in then.'

They squeezed up beside him on the bench seat, first Lila, then Ninian, then John. The cab smelt powerfully of onions and overheated engine oil. The van rattled and swayed. Something in the back clanked loudly.

'Where you from?' the driver asked.

'Up Glen Affric way,' answered John vaguely.

'Must've been walkin' a while.'

'Aye.'

'Hard times, eh?' His tone was sympathetic, though not without a trace of condescension.

'Something like that,' muttered John.

The driver nodded. Then reached for the radio. A familiar country-and-western tune faded in, competing with the engine noise. John put his arm along the back of the seat. Felt Lila's head press back gently against it. He stared ahead at the dull glisten of the empty road, listening to the twangy guitars and adenoidal voices, the driver's tunelessly whistled accompaniment. Trying to ignore the anxiety building in the pit of his stomach . . .

A sudden tension entered the cab, jolting him from his reverie. The music had stopped. A voice was speaking.

'. . . successful raid on what is believed to be NLA headquarters. In the early hours of this morning government forces stormed a remote farmhouse in the Tain area. Communications equipment was destroyed and a large cache of weapons uncovered. Seven people have been taken to Fort George for questioning. There are unconfirmed reports that the newly identified NLA leader, Struan Fraser, was among them . . .'

Curtains of rain continued to swing down the loch. At the roadside stood the shell of a recently burnt-out cottage, the charred remains of the roof timbers pointing accusingly towards the sky.

The driver had stopped whistling.

'That us all knackered, then,' he said cheerfully.

Lila and John stole sidelong glances.

Ninian sat between them, head lolling again, oblivious.

FORTY

In recent times, as the weather had become more and more unpredictable, the level of the River Ness in spate had risen steadily year on year. Now the high-water marker on the opposite bank was almost completely submerged. Only the crowns of the neighbouring bushes were visible above the oily surface of the water, which was dark brown with silt and moving faster than John could run.

John had an unwilling Ninian's hand tightly clasped in his own as they followed the narrow elevated path downstream towards the sandstone and granite buildings of Inverness, just visible through the trees. But it was the torrent, eddying and swirling, that held John's eye. What was down there in the tumbling murky depths? he wondered. Rushing unseen towards the sea? He thought of Lila's story. If ever an old plesiosaur wanted to make a run for it, now would be the moment. He pictured the blunt rounded head rising out of the muddy floodwater. Swaying on the end of its long leathery neck. Turning to look at him as it sailed by and winking. Saying, that's me away now, John. Had enough of all this. And if you've any sense, you'll be after me . . .

With each step closer to the camp, John felt more uneasy. Making contact with the NLA again, meeting Fraser, saying goodbye to Ninian, let alone what the steadily rising river might do . . . now he just wanted it all to be over as soon as possible.

The path took a sharp turn around a large earthworks, the start of the flood defences that the van driver had mentioned. Following the news bulletin, he'd become talkative for the last few miles of the journey, eager to impress with his knowledge of camp history. In recent years, he explained, Bught Park had begun to flood regularly, year after year, until eventually the damp had got into the Springfield housing estate on its edge and it had had to be condemned. This provided the perfect solution to the authorities' dilemma when the first wave of poor folk began to appear from the country. But it took no time for the vacant and dilapidated houses on the estate to fill up, so that further arrivals were left with no choice but to spill out into the park. Which was when the flood defences were thrown up – not that anyone had ever had much faith in them . . . But they'd be fine there, he'd concluded, glancing at Lila. Find plenty of their own folk, playmates for the laddie, get a shower and a hot meal . . .

John glanced through thinning trees to the vast encampment of makeshift shelters that sprawled across what must once have been open green playing fields. Now it was a sea of mud, the whole scene blurred by rain and the smoke from cooking fires.

In the centre of the camp a large, circular two-storey building rose above the hovels. Once an indoor sports complex, the steady stream of humanity flowing back and forth suggested that it was now doing service as the soup kitchen. It was the only thing of any permanence in the whole landscape, apart from the fringe of low-rent housing blocks whose silhouettes were distantly visible through the rain.

Closer at hand, on a ten-yard corridor of grass between the encampment and the flood defence, a football match was in progress. A raucous crowd of boys and dogs splashing in and out of the small ponds that had begun to appear at the foot of the embankment.

But Ninian was more interested in the dwellings.

'Funny houses,' he said.

John nodded

'I don't like them.' He sniffed. 'I'm hungry.'

'We'll find you something to eat soon, darlin',' said Lila.

On top of everything else, this reek of poverty and wretchedness made John feel uncomfortable and ashamed. It was no way for folk to live. Like rats in the mud.

'Can you take the pack?' he asked.

Lila nodded.

'See that place, then?' He pointed to the sports complex. 'We'll meet there in an hour. I'll find out what I can.' He unshouldered the pack. Turned to Ninian. 'You go with Lila, OK? Get something to eat. And you see and look after her, now.'

Ninian nodded solemnly and reached for Lila's hand.

Lila gave a small, tense smile and touched John's cheek with her fingertips. 'Take care.'

John turned away and was soon swallowed up in a maze of alleys. He wound his way between sagging tents of polythene sheeting. Weird castaways' huts spliced together from wooden pallets and branches and old gates. More elaborate constructions of timber and un-cemented breeze blocks and metal sheeting. Ancient vehicles without wheels. Even an old henhouse lashed to a rusty trailer. Every fifty yards or so there was a floodlight on a pole and, at less obvious intervals, standpipes and battery charge points. The authorities had taken what steps they could to delay the inevitable unrest for as long as possible.

John could feel his spirits being dragged down still further by the endless patter of the rain. The squalor and damp of the ramshackle dwellings. The glimpses into their gloomy interiors. Although wherever he turned there were people making their way briskly through the mud, huddled under capes made of sacking, refuse-bin liners, old blankets, whatever came to hand. Faces pinched and grey, but each with a particular look of expectancy. And as he began to catch muttered drifts of conversation, John realised that it was rumour that was giving these downtrodden folk their air of purpose. *The Tod has definitely been caught . . . the rebels are going to surrender . . . the flood defences won't hold . . . the army's getting ready to move in . . .* A sense of impending catastrophe was everywhere and it seemed to charge the camp with frantic energy.

For all the rodent bustle, one or two camp-dwellers still seemed happy enough to stop and answer John's questions. From which he soon learned that Lila had been right, and that the man he wanted was Jocky Ramage. Otherwise known as the Damage. A right wee heidbanger, who not so long ago had been lording it over a cell block in Glasgow's Barlinnie jail – and might very soon be back there if all or any of the rumours proved true. But in the meantime he was serving as NLA recruiting sergeant and self-appointed camp quartermaster. Purveyor of exotic provisions and supplies and . . . well – services, you might say . . . of all kinds – if you had the readies . . . though it was still a bit of a mystery how he got here . . . or what his connection was exactly with the rebel boys . . . there were some things you just couldn't fathom . . . anyway, he seemed to have a line to rebel command . . . some folk even said he was being paid for each new recruit he signed up to the cause . . . John would find him in the big trailer across the park, eighth lighting pole along . . . but here, hadn't someone seen him going out just now? . . . better leave it an hour or so, he was never away for long . . . specially not with what was brewing now . . .

John turned back for the sports complex, his mind spinning with the chaos around him, the river so close to bursting its banks, the army preparing to smash down the barricades and force its way into the housing estate, the possibility that Fraser had been captured . . . He was aware, for the first time since leaving Blackriggs, of a sense of utter powerlessness. He understood the look in the camp-dwellers' eyes. It felt as if his fate and Ninian's and Lila's all hung in the balance. As if they were just so much living flotsam being whirled downstream on the flood of changing fortunes.

FORTY-ONE

It was mid-afternoon when John left Lila and Ninian for the second time. They had found themselves a corner of the main sports hall, which had been transformed into a vast open dormitory, the floor a sea of camp beds and mattresses, sleeping bags, piles of possessions. Everywhere people were clustered around radios, waiting for news. But so far there had still been no official confirmation of Fraser's capture. Nor any denial, for that matter. The rain was still coming down steadily. The noise and crush of people made John's head ache. He walked in the direction of the river. This was the long way round to Ramage's trailer, but he needed to get clear of the fetid rat runs. Breathe in fresh air, raw and damp though it was. He heard the muted roar well before he reached the embankment. The ponds at its foot had grown larger. Trickles of water starting to leak from its surface. Then he noticed something else. Some way downstream, beyond the limit of the camp, the housing estate folk had raised barricades on the road that passed between the edge of the houses and the river. At this distance they looked not unlike a handful of untidy hovels from the camp that had been lifted up and dropped

313

there. But it wasn't the barricades that caught John's eye, it was the pair of military vehicles that were moving slowly up the road towards them. And the huge heavy moving machine that lumbered along behind.

He walked on a little faster.

The alley turned a corner and broadened out into a kind of clearing. Three sides were formed by the now familiar assortment of shacks. The fourth by a large and dilapidated mobile home, outside which a number of people were milling.

As John approached, the door of the trailer opened. The rumble of music spilled out, along with a thick waft of alcohol and tobacco. A man emerged and another from the crowd immediately climbed the steps to take his place. The door closed again. Someone else detached himself from the group and sidled towards John. He was bristle-headed, with the build of a bouncer and a bouncer's appraising eye.

John took a deep breath. Discussing it all with Lila – what he was going to say, how he was going to play it – was one thing. Being here was quite another.

'Aye, aye,' said the bouncer.

John nodded in reply.

'Lookin' for someone?'

'Aye. Mr Ramage.'

The bouncer inflated his chest.

'And who's wantin' him?'

'John MacNeil. Though it'll not mean anything to him.'

'So whit's it ye want?'

'That's for Mr Ramage, if you don't mind.'

The bouncer scowled.

'I do mind. You tell me first, sonny.'

'I'm sorry, I can't.'

'Too bad, then.' The bouncer shrugged. Turned to go.

'It's to do with Struan Fraser,' said John, 'the Tod.'

'Whit to dae wi' him?'

'Something he needs to know.'

'Oh aye?'

'Aye. And I think Mr Ramage might be pleased to be the one who tells him . . .'

The bouncer cleared his throat. 'Mebbe ah didnae mak masel' clear, sonny. Naebody sees Ramage till ah hear their business first.'

John looked at him steadily and tried to ignore the thumping in his chest. 'All right then. You can tell him I know where Struan Fraser's son is.'

'Whit . . . ?' The bouncer looked confused. 'Howdya mean?'

John took a chance.

'You heard about Blackriggs? The killing?'

He nodded suspiciously.

'You know Fraser's lad was there?'

A cautious, non-committal shrug.

'Well, he was. And he's still alive. And it's possible Fraser doesn't know it.'

'Naw, naw.' The bouncer shook his head dismissively. 'Bin' readin' too many fairy tales, son.'

'I'm being serious.'

'Noo ye're just wastin' ma—'

'No, I'm not. And you can tell Mr Ramage I've proof.'

Mistrust still clouded the man's eyes.

'OK. I'll say it again. I know where Struan Fraser's son is. It'll cost you nothing to tell Mr Ramage that.'

The bouncer gave him a grudging look. 'Wait here,' he muttered and turned for the trailer.

John stood obediently in the rain, ignoring the curious stares of the other hangers-on. Trying not to listen to the nagging voice that told him he was already out of his depth. Shortly the door opened and a young man made a hurried exit with the bouncer hard on his heels.

'OK you,' called the bouncer from the cramped porch at the top of the steps. John climbed the steps and halted as he ran some kind of electronic detector over him, then swiftly and expertly frisked him and finally held out his hand.

'The blade.'

John reached into his trouser pocket. It felt different to the touch now. As if it had been somehow changed by the bloody work it had done. He'd been tempted several times in the last twenty-four hours to throw it away. But each time for some reason he'd been unable to. Even now he didn't really want to give it up.

'I'll have it back when I go, please.'

The bouncer grunted and opened the door into the trailer. Where the air was so thick with cigarette smoke and the smell of stale beer that John caught his breath as he stepped inside. A long settee lined one wall. Beyond it an opening led to a sleeping compartment in which someone was moving around. On a low table opposite the settee was a quantity of drink and a large television. The flickering screen frozen on what appeared to be a scene from an action movie. In the far corner, in a deep leather chair, sat a small, wiry-looking man with a thin, almost gaunt, face, pocked cheeks and heavily lidded eyes. At whose side the bouncer now stationed himself, leaving John to hover awkwardly in the doorway. The seated man was about Ferg's age, in his mid-fifties, John guessed. He had short-cropped grey hair, heavily tattooed forearms and a tight-fitting black T-shirt which showed off a slim but well-muscled torso. He tapped nicotine-stained fingers in time with the subterranean grumble of tuneless background music that seemed to come from the sleeping quarters. And for some time studied John in silence. John's heart beat faster. His throat felt dry.

'Whit's aw this aboot Fraser's lad, then?' He had a deep smoker's rasp.

'I've some information about him,' John replied as steadily as he could.

'So . . .' Ramage raised one practised eyebrow.

'It's for Mr Fraser himself. I can't pass it to anyone else.'

Ramage reached for a cigarette which the bouncer dutifully lit for him.

'Then ye've a problem, son.' He exhaled slowly.

John steeled himself. 'Because Struan Fraser's been caught?' he countered.

'Because . . .' Ramage closed his eyes wearily. 'Ah'm no runnin' fuckin' errands for some bumfluff schoolkid ah've never met before in ma life.'

John tried to ignore the insult. 'So the Tod hasn't been caught?' he persisted. 'See, if he has I'll just go now. I don't want to waste your time. Or mine.' He paused. 'Or maybe you don't know . . .'

'I decide who stays or goes.'

'OK. But I don't think we're getting anywhere . . .'

'That so? Convince me, then. Who are you? Why're you here?'

John's palms felt clammy. He glanced at the settee. No invitation was forthcoming.

'My name's John MacNeil,' he said. 'I used to work for the Department. At the deerstalking. And I was at Blackriggs when the soldiers came . . .'

Ramage sat and smoked continuously, his gaunt face giving nothing away, as John told him the story, or at least

317

as much of it as he thought Ramage needed to know. When he had at last finished, Ramage leaned back in his chair, lit a new cigarette from the stub of the last one and nodded slowly.

'Why should I believe you? Wan good reason, eh?'

It seemed quieter in the trailer now. As if insects had stopped humming. John realised the music had been turned off while he'd been talking. He wondered if Ramage had ever killed a man. And how he would react to learn that the 'schoolkid' who stood in front of him now had. Perverse though it seemed, the thought gave him strength.

'Well . . .' he replied, 'you could start by asking the army about two soldiers in a crashed jeep. On south Loch Ness-side. One dead, a foreign boy. The other injured, name of Corporal Kel Foulis.'

'Ah see.' Ramage blew a smoke ring. 'And . . . ?'

'And there's a boy Billy Lowrie. At Aviemore. Government informer.'

The smoke ring was spreading out. Thinning as it drifted to the ceiling. 'But the sodgers are sodgers. And the boy Lowrie's a snitch. So I cannae ask them.' He stared at John. 'Can I?'

'I guess not,' John replied.

'The kiddie. Who says ye've got him?'

John reached into his pocket and pulled out the smallest of the three bears. He handed it across.

'It won't mean anything to you. But get it to Mr Fraser. Or let him know about it. If you can . . .' He paused but again the challenge went unacknowledged.

Ramage held the bear in the palm of his hand. Then shrugged. 'Could've picked it up at Blackriggs.'

John nodded. 'But I didn't.'

Ramage studied him. 'Whit's in this for you?'

318

'Nothing.'

Ramage coughed. The disbelief plain in his look.

'I just want the lad back to his dad, where he belongs,' John continued. 'In safe hands. Folk who can look after him . . .'

Ramage shook his head. 'Where I come fae, naeb'dy does somethin' for nothin'.'

John searched the hollowed, unexpressive face and wondered what kind of world they did come from, this wiry wee hard case with his bristle-headed sidekick? And what did either of them know or care about the Highlands? Like the camp folk said, it was hard to see what connection they could have with the rebel cause. Though maybe a fight like this made for strange bedfellows . . .

Ramage continued to look back at him. Opened his mouth to speak. When a woman's voice called out from the sleeping compartment. Lazy. Knowing. Amused almost.

'Hey, Jocky . . .'

He glanced over his shoulder with a grunt of annoyance. 'No now, doll.'

'No, listen, Jocky . . .' Insistent now. 'You should get this to Fraser. You should.'

Ramage rolled his eyes. 'Why's that?'

'Cos it's the truth.'

'Whit truth?'

'Whit he's tellin' you. The boy there. Believe me.'

'You been listenin' in on us?'

There was a soft giggle.

Ramage shook his head. 'Anither wan o' your feelin's, eh?'

A pause. 'You know me.'

'Aye,' muttered Ramage.

The bouncer nodded in obvious reverence.

John seized his chance. 'You've nothing to lose . . . surely . . . at least tell him what I've told you.'

In Ramage's hesitant glance John read something else. He was nervous of Fraser . . .

The music began to grumble again.

Ramage took out another cigarette. Waved the bouncer away irritably and lit it himself. Then smoked most of it in silence, inhaling deeply, holding in each lungful as if it would help him weigh up John's request.

'How soon . . .' he asked at length '. . . could we . . . hae him here?'

'How soon can you can get Mr Fraser here?' John replied.

'Jee-zus.' Ramage exhaled with a grimace, as if something had fouled the taste of the smoke. 'Ye've picked yer moment tae come askin' fer Fraser, haven't ye? Sodgers aw set tae come in wan end. River the other.'

John shrugged. 'I'm sorry, Mr Ramage, but it has to be Struan Fraser himself. No one else. If he's still free, that is.'

'I heard ye. So he's here in the camp? The laddie?'

John said nothing.

Ramage snorted. 'Dinnae worry. We've nae time tae piss aboot tryin' tae find him.'

'So you'll make contact with him?'

Ramage nodded grudgingly. 'I'll dae whit I can.'

'I'm not sure what that means . . .'

He rolled his eyes in exasperation. 'It means I cannae work fuckin' miracles – awright? Get word up the line. That's aw I can dae . . .'

'OK then. And thank you very much.' John turned to leave. 'You'll find me—'

'Here,' said Ramage abruptly. 'I niver said ye could go.'

John glanced around the trailer. 'You don't want me hanging around here, do you?'

'Dinnae want ye wanderin' aff either.'

'I'll only go back to the sports centre. You'd find me soon—'

'Ye're gaun naewhere, sonny.' He gestured at the settee. 'Wait there.' And disappeared into the sleeping quarters, pulling across a sliding partition behind him. While the bouncer moved over and propped himself in the doorway.

John sat down and waited in silence. He felt relieved. Surprised. And more than a little proud of himself. Things could have turned out so differently with someone like Ramage. But now he could be almost certain that Fraser had not been caught. And he had got what he'd come for without having to give away anything about the *Marie Rose*, which he and Lila had agreed he should use only as a last resort. He wished Lila could have been there to see it. Wished Ferg could've been too, come to that.

He glanced at the bouncer, who had produced a girlie magazine from his pocket and was leafing slowly through the pages with a look of bored resignation. On the table opposite John, the screen continued to flicker. He gazed idly at the frozen image, trying to work out was going on. It dimmed suddenly. Brightened and dimmed again. Several times. As if some other electronic device was causing interference. Or draining a shared power supply. Ramage must have some kind of communications equipment in there . . . The warm, stale air and the soft murmur of voices from behind the partition were starting to have a soporific effect on him. He thought drowsily of Lila and Ninian back there in the sports centre and wished he was with them. Did Ninian really sense that something was up? Whatever Lila might have said, he was sure that in its own way nature had been even-handed with Ninian, sharpening some of his faculties to make up for the others that were defective or missing. Maybe he even knew he was going to see his father. Like a dog that knew its owner was coming home. Or that there was an earthquake on the way . . .

When John woke up it was almost dark outside. The bouncer was asleep at the other end of the settee. Mouth wide open. Snoring.

He sat for a while in the half-darkness, the sleep slowly leaving him. He didn't want to be here any longer, separated from Lila and Ninian with the minutes ticking by.

Along with the bottles on the table were some paper plates. He found a pencil and scribbled *I'm at the sports centre*. Then propped the plate against the television.

He tiptoed towards the bouncer. Paused for a moment, eyeing the pocket where he knew his knife was.

The bouncer sighed and turned his head.

John moved gingerly past him. Silently opened the door and stepped out into the dusk.

FORTY-TWO

The camp was deep in shadow. Rain continued to fall, though not heavily enough to extinguish the fires that had sprung up at the barricades among the houses on the estate. John glanced past them and on towards the river. Where the bulky outline of the heavy moving machine was just visible in the half darkness, waiting like some huge and patient predator. It would not, he needed no telling, be put to use where it was needed most – on the flood defences, in place of the solitary truck that stood there now, surrounded by a small group of camp-dwellers. An apathetic audience for the handful of council men who were half-heartedly ferrying sandbags up the embankment, as if they were tempted just to leave the water to do its work. Wash away all the unsightly human debris thrown up by this conflict.

He moved on, joining the camp-dwellers who surged in increasing numbers towards the sports centre, their huts and tents abandoned for the relative safety of the circular concrete building with its second storey and flat roof. Some faces were haggard with tension, others dull with resignation. Everywhere there was a babel of voices, an edge of hysteria. John wondered if Lila and Ninian were safe there.

323

The lobby was now almost impassable. In the dining area folk had staked their claim to tables, chairs, corners of tables, the floor below tables. John threaded his way among them but saw no sign of Lila and Ninian. The main hall was no less crowded, every inch of floor space now taken. He worked his way slowly along the aisles and eventually spotted them in the far corner. They were sitting side by side on a mattress. Heads bent close together over what looked like a borrowed picture book, from which Lila was reading, her arm around Ninian's shoulder. Both faintly smiling and both unaware that they were being watched.

John's heart turned a cartwheel, his thoughts rushing back again to the previous night, in the warehouse. But he couldn't afford to do anything that might reveal his trump card to Ramage's folk should they happen to be following him. He forced himself to move on.

He returned to the dining area and took his place in the queue. His stomach began to rumble. He bought a pie and a polystyrene cup of coffee. Then made his way out into the lobby. He was looking for somewhere to sit down when he caught the faint strains of music.

Clutching the coffee and pie he set off in pursuit. The sound led him out of the lobby and down a corridor to a smallish room at the end, designed for table tennis or meetings. There were forty or fifty folk sitting on the floor. The overhead lights were off and someone had produced a couple of paraffin lamps, which softly illuminated the semicircle of musicians who'd arranged themselves on chairs amid a clutter of battered instrument cases.

Two fiddles. A guitar. A bodhrán. Low whistle. Concertina. The players were all ages. A fiddler lassie who couldn't have been more than eleven or twelve. An old fellow with a polished skull and bushy white sideburns on the low whistle. Seventy if he was a day. They were working through some simple jigs, feeling their way with each other, finding the natural groove. And the audience was with them. Swaying and tapping their feet where they sat. The only smiling faces John had seen in the whole place.

He found a space on the floor. The jigs ended and the musicians nodded and smiled to one another. Pleased with what they'd shared. They fingered their instruments, wondering what to play next. Then the concertina player was off with a fine old reel that brought a smile as John remembered the title: 'The Spey in Spate'. One by one the others joined in. And as the sound filled out and the tempo settled and the tune started to drive along and the audience and musicians stamped their feet together, John felt the rush of adrenalin he knew so well. The inability to sit still or concentrate any longer. The overwhelming urge to join in, to become part of the music. He peered at the clutter around the musicians, spotted a spare fiddle, half out of its case. He got up, apologising to his neighbours, made his way round the wall and bent down by the instrument. The guitarist was first to catch his eye. He smiled and nodded OK. John picked up the fiddle and pulled up a chair.

More and more folk were coming in all the time now. The audience must have already doubled since John had been here. And the concertina player kept the tunes coming. John was starting to hit his stride when he saw them standing against the back wall. They must only just have arrived. Lila's eyes widened with surprise as she caught sight of him. Then she smiled and it felt to John as if all the tension in him gave way for a moment. She bent and whispered to Ninian. Who looked up and grinned. Then immediately looked down again at his feet.

When the music came to an end John laid the fiddle

across his knees. But this time he heard the applause only as a distant rush of sound. Because now he was aware of something else. The notes he'd been hearing these past days on the fringes of his consciousness were starting to materialise. Hanging for a moment like dust motes in his mind before gradually arranging themselves into something more coherent. The first four bars of a jig. And of their own accord his fingers were feeling them out on the strings. Then the fiddle was back under his chin. The bow started to move in his hand and he was playing them out loud. Hesitantly at first, then more confidently. He repeated the phrase, extending it to eight bars. Played it again. And as he reached the end, the notes for the second eight came tumbling almost complete into his head. Now the other musicians started to join in. It was a simple tune. Light-hearted and infectious. And by the time they'd played it through twice, everyone had got it. They gave it one more turn before the older fiddler led them into another tune, and another and another. Finally he glanced at John and nodded as they returned to the new tune to finish the set. John's heart bursting with the thrill of playing his own composition. As he watched Lila smiling and clapping and swaying against the wall. And Ninian who had now stepped out and begun to dance, to the amusement and delight of those nearby who had moved aside to make room for him. He was leaping and skipping and twirling in an ecstatic trance. As if, for a brief moment, the music had freed him from all the unknowable burden of being Ninian.

At last they came to an end and the room erupted with claps and whistles. Ninian stopped spinning and stood at rest, shoulders heaving, dark eyes shining, beaming from ear to ear. Sensing that the applause was as much for him as for the musicians.

The guitarist leaned across.

'Good tune that. Has it a name?'

'Well . . . aye, it has a name.'

'What is it?'

'"Davie MacNeil's Jig".' It came straight out.

The guitarist thought, then shook his head.

'Don't know it.' He looked at John. 'One o' yours?'

'Aye.'

'Davie MacNeil, eh?'

'Aye.'

He nodded appreciatively. 'Good tune. Good tune.'

John looked down, turning the fiddle in his hands. Awkward at the compliment. Then heard a commotion. He looked up to see the bouncer scowling purposefully as he picked his way across the crowded floor.

FORTY-THREE

John followed the bouncer out into the night. The rain had stopped and a cold wind had got up. It blew ragged clouds across a three-quarter moon. Filled the camp with the flap and rattle of tents and other loosely built structures. The spotlights were off now. John caught the moonlit glint of running water at the foot of the embankment. The glow of fires at the barricades, where now he glimpsed activity. Rebel supporters on the move, flitting furtively between the buildings. Lit here and there by the sweep of an army-vehicle headlight or a searchlight perhaps. The low rumble of engines carried towards him on the wind.

At the trailer Ramage greeted him with a cold stare. A vein pulsed at his temple.

'By Christ, son, you picked yer moment tae go runnin' aff.' He drew on his cigarette with a hand that trembled slightly. 'Any other time and ye'd get a bluidy good seein' to . . .' He blew a long thin stream of smoke. 'Now you pin back yer lugs and you listen. Cos I'm only goin' tae say this the wance. In exactly –' he glanced at his watch – 'forty-seven minutes, Fraser's comin' intae they hooses.' He gestured vaguely towards the estate. 'Exactly ten minutes

328

later he's leavin'. Wi' or wi'oot the wean. And it's up tae us tae make sure it's wi'.' He fixed John with a look that was intended to be menacing, but this time failed to conceal his disquiet. 'You've nae fuckin' idea what ye've stirred up here, son. Jesus, I'd rather stick ma dick in a wasp byke . . .' He shook his head. 'So, we now hae exactly forty-six minutes tae fetch the kiddie and get him ower tae the hooses. And pray that in the meantime the bastard river disnae get us. And the sodgers dinnae start the charge o' the fuckin' Light Brigade.' A look crossed his face. 'Ye've got him, right?'

'Oh aye,' said John. 'He's in the sports hall. I can fetch him right now. But I need a guarantee.'

'A *whaat*?'

'A guarantee that it's Fraser who'll be there. I can't hand him over to anyone else. I said so at the start . . .'

'See here ya wee . . .' Ramage clenched his fists and the tattooed forearms bulged. John wondered whether he was going to hit him. 'Dinnae you start on aboot guarantees the noo. We've nae time. Look – Fraser's heard yer story. He knows aw aboot the wee toy. Seems he's ready tae take you on trust – though wi' aw whit's gaun oan the noo, I think he needs his fuckin' heid seein' tae. Know whit I mean? Any road, it's his choice. And ma bollocks on the block. So you jist fetch the kiddie. And let's get this ower wi', eh?'

John looked at the gaunt face and the unspoken plea in the cold, hard eyes. He guessed that Ramage would have struck himself some kind of deal over Ninian's return. But right now it seemed to be fear of Fraser's authority that was driving him. Along with mounting panic at the prospect of what the river might do. Or the army. Or both . . .

'Come on then,' John said. For his part feeling strangely calm now that the waiting was over. Here at this moment

329

of crisis, it was Ramage that was out of his depth, it seemed, not John.

They left the trailer and hurried between the ramshackle dwellings. An air of abandonment seemed to have settled over the darkened camp.

'So whit like is he, the kiddie?' asked Ramage breathlessly.

'How d'you mean?'

'Is he . . . like . . . totally daft?'

'No.'

'He can walk and talk, eh?'

'Aye, he can.'

Ramage fell silent for a while.

'Fraser's wan brave bastard. I'll say that fer 'im.'

John nodded.

Now the entire population of the camp seemed to have taken refuge at the sports centre, thronging the lobby and crowding the stairs to the first floor. With Ramage and the bouncer following, John elbowed his way through to the main hall and the agreed rendezvous point with Lila. He prayed they would have had the sense to return there since seeing him leave the music session. But the hall was now so crowded it was impossible to see more than a few feet in any direction. They began to pick their way across the floor when the lights suddenly went out. There was an eerie moment of stillness before alarm crackled through the darkness like a charge of static electricity. A collective groan went up around the entire building, followed by curses, sighs and cries. Flashlights came on, one of them belonging to the bouncer, who passed it to John as he continued to pick his way through the bodies towards the far corner, heart tripping as the wall became visible. Where Lila and Ninian should have been there was a young family sitting in a row. Four dazed faces caught in the beam of the flashlight. To one side of them, where the backpack had been propped, a pile of belongings. To the other, an old woman stretched out on the floor. Hands behind her head, gazing resignedly into the darkness.

John scanned the length of the wall, then turned, shaking his head.

'They'll be here somewhere,' he said with more confidence than he felt.

'They'd better be,' replied Ramage grimly.

Back in the lobby doorway John halted. He rose up on the balls of his feet and played the flashlight across the shadowed faces of the seething mass before him. Towards the rear of the crowd the beam fell on the no-longer-illuminated sign for the women's toilets. Then glanced off something that glinted. The frame of a backpack, swaying above the surrounding heads. Lila's head came into view, although John couldn't yet see whether she had Ninian with her. He waved and shouted her name and eventually she looked up, the relief plain on her face.

They fought their way outside and paused on the steps. A deeper darkness had settled now. The moon had gone in and the power to the sports centre, the housing estate, the whole area had now been deliberately cut. Only across the river in the town centre could the sodium glow of street lights be seen. Here there was nothing but the occasional glimmer of a lamp in the camp and the distant flicker of fires at the barricades.

John started to help Lila off with the backpack. Ramage looked at him sharply.

'Ye're no' takin' that. Could hae onythin' in it.'

'Aye, like a broken kid's fiddle.' John glanced back to

the lobby. 'I'm not leaving it there, that's final.' He turned to the bouncer. 'You got my knife?'

'In the trailer.'

Ramage was eyeing Ninian uncertainly.

'We're takin' ye tae see yer daddie,' he said.

Ninian shook his head and shuffled and wouldn't look at him.

'Ninian . . .' Lila crouched down and took his hands. 'We're going to see your dad now.'

He muttered something that John couldn't hear.

Ramage couldn't conceal his impatience. 'Fer Chrissake!' he mouthed at John.

'We have to, darlin',' said Lila to Ninian. 'He's your dad.'

But now Ninian pulled away from her. He crossed his arms at his chest and began to shuffle his feet in jerky little circles. There was a lump gathering in John's throat. The strange fractured movements made him think of some delicate machine whose antennae were trying to turn in every direction at once, in danger of being overwhelmed by the mass of competing signals they were receiving.

Ninian muttered again and this time Lila bent close.

'Tell me what it is,' she said.

He shuffled some more, then spoke too softly for John to hear.

Now Lila smiled and nodded. 'Sure you can do some more dancing, darlin'. When we've seen your dad.'

Ninian looked up at her. 'Will John play? When we've seen my dad?' He turned to John. 'Play the band?'

'Aye.' John swallowed. 'I'll play for you.'

Ninian nodded solemnly and took Lila's hand.

'Fuck me,' muttered Ramage, shaking his head.

They set off once more through the camp. The muted

roar of the river was now constant. Although the moon had gone in, John could see a ripple of movement along the crest of the embankment. The rain might have stopped but the waters were still rising as the saturated hills continued to drain themselves into the deep trench of Loch Ness.

As they hurried among the darkened dwellings the wind plucked at their coats, cold and raw. It carried with it another sound that John couldn't at once identify, a faint drumming. As they drew nearer to the edge of the camp the sound intensified. John could tell that it wasn't mechanical, that there was something human in its menace as it swelled, reached a crescendo, then died away again. It was followed by the shouts and jeers of a large crowd. After a few moments' silence it began again. This time his mind filled with the image of batons and shields, and the grotesquely padded, helmeted figures behind them, whose battle call was now accompanied by the slow, deep pulse of heavy engines.

They paused at the limit of the camp, where trees had once lined the road that separated the houses from the park. But they had long since been hacked down for fuel and now only their stumps remained. Here it was still dark and silent. All the activity seemed to be to the right, along the river bank, and some distance ahead, on the townward edge of the estate. Ramage led them hurriedly across the road and into one of the smaller streets that ran into the heart of the estate. Unlit housing blocks rose up around them like the walls of a canyon. Ninian began to whine and drag his feet.

Closer now and louder, the call and answer of alternate drumming and jeering continued, while yet another sound made John's heart trip. The clatter of a helicopter. He looked up to see a single disembodied searchlight sweeping the estate from the darkness of the sky above, probing the dark spaces between the buildings.

They emerged from the canyon into an unlit street of uniformly shabby two-storey houses. All were daubed with anti-government slogans and most had boarded-up windows. There were a couple of rusting cars with no wheels and a profusion of litter. The only suggestion of life was the occasional dim light that escaped through chinks in a window-board. There was also a filthy pick-up truck in the barely discernible livery of Inverness City Council, parked outside the house on the first corner. In the back of it John could see the tips of traffic cones and a couple of shovels sunk into a pile of earth or gravel.

Ramage walked towards the truck, then turned up the path to the house, which was boarded like its neighbours. He gave a series of raps on the door and nodded at John to unshoulder the backpack. At close quarters John could see what a state of disrepair the place was in. Slates were missing and a section of guttering dangled uselessly from the eaves. The front of the building was stained and discoloured with damp, and slabs of rendering had fallen from the walls.

'C'moan, c'moan!'

Ramage urgently repeated the sequence of knocks.

The door started to open and at that moment there came a violent explosion of sound as, several streets away, battle was finally joined at the barricades and voices were raised in a wave of fury. Along with cheers and the pounding of charging feet. The thud of projectiles. Sudden sharp detonations. The roar of engines and wail of sirens. A clank and rattle and grind as heavy moving machines ploughed into waiting obstacles on the far edge of the run-down housing estate.

Ramage glanced sharply at John and stepped aside. 'Here's as far as we go, son.'

'Aye, well,' John said. 'Thanks.'

Ramage shrugged. Then he and the bouncer hurried away down the darkened street.

'What about my knife?' John called after them.

But the two men turned a corner and were gone.

FORTY-FOUR

The door of the house was held open by a bearded man in council overalls and a woollen hat pulled low on his forehead. They stepped past him into a narrow, empty hallway. The sounds of battle faded as he closed the door behind them and gestured to John to set down the backpack. Then ushered them upstairs to a first-floor room and followed them in. Lit only by a portable lamp, it looked as if it had been used as a dosshouse or shooting gallery. The floor was strewn with litter, the only furniture an old stained settee and a grime-encrusted table. Most of the plaster had flaked away from the walls and a mouldering smell hung heavily on the air.

John waited for the door to open again and Fraser to come in. But it didn't and the four of them stood there in silence for what seemed like a long time. Then John realised that the man was looking intently at Ninian. His eyes glistening in the lamplight. Eventually he pulled off the hat and crouched down to Ninian's level.

'Hello, Nin.'

Ninian stood looking at him uncertainly.

Despite the clothing and beard, despite the features

deeply creased with exhaustion and strain, there was no doubting the physical resemblance. He had the same stocky build as Ninian. The same dark hair and slightly sallow complexion. The same handsome face and intelligent brown eyes.

He stayed crouching and opened his arms.

'It's me, Dad. I'm going to look after you now.'

Ninian stared at the ground.

'I've got presents for you.'

Ninian looked up and shuffled his feet as Fraser, still crouching, slowly put out a hand. After a moment he took it and allowed himself to be drawn gently into an embrace. His father's overalled shoulders heaved with silent sobs.

John felt Lila's hand steal into his.

Eventually Fraser stood up and blinked. He looked at John and Lila in turn, his eyes still brimming. He began to speak, then stopped, apparently lost for words.

He cleared his throat. 'This means . . . more to me than . . . anything I can say.' There was still a tremor in his voice. He glanced down at Ninian, who stood beside him, looking at his feet again. 'I . . . I thought I'd lost him, you know.'

John nodded. This was neither the brisk, khaki-clad rebel commander he'd pictured, nor the suave business tycoon. This was just an ordinary-looking middle-aged man, worn out and overcome with emotion.

Fraser held out his hand. 'John . . . John MacNeil?'

'Aye.' John felt the warmth in the handshake and looked into Fraser's face. It was open and filled with gratitude.

'And . . . ?'

'Lila. Lila Grieve,' said John.

'Lila.'

She smiled as Fraser earnestly took her hand. It was

hard to imagine this same man taking decisions that had resulted in people's deaths.

'I don't know yet how I'm going to thank you both for this. But believe me, I will. We'll meet up again, when this is all over, I promise.' He turned back to John. 'So . . . John . . . you found him – at Blackriggs . . . and managed to get him all the way here to Inverness . . . to me . . . without being caught?'

'Well, not quite . . .'

Fraser nodded. 'Yes, of course. Ramage has told me some of the story. Extraordinary. Quite extraordinary. And I want to hear the whole thing from you when we've more time. But now, well – we can't stay long, it's not safe here.' He gestured outside. 'I'd hoped to be away before all this began, you see. Though things don't always go the way you want.'

'How *are* you go . . .' John began. Then stopped, worried that he might be overstepping the mark.

But Fraser nodded. 'To get away?'

'Aye.'

'You saw the cart outside? We've been using it for months to move things around. Weapons, explosives and so on – there's a false section of flatbed, beneath the gravel – in the base of the cart. And there's a council depot at the far side of the estate. We can get in and out the back way without going anywhere near the main roads. From there . . . well, we have other arrangements.'

'But you're surely not going to . . .' John glanced in horror at Ninian '. . . not beneath the gravel . . . ?'

Fraser smiled for the first time and John noticed the deep lines at his eyes. 'No, no. He'll sit up front with me. The council worker bringing his lad back after a ride. If we see anyone, that is. Which at this time of day we won't, not

338

with what's going on out there. The depot's only three blocks away. But we need to be off before the trouble catches up with us.'

Ninian had begun to shuffle his feet and whine. 'I don't like it here,' he mumbled.

'It's OK, Nin. We'll be away soon.' Fraser felt in his overall pocket and produced a tube of sweets. Ninian poured himself a fistful and began to munch.

'You'll have discovered that trick . . .' Fraser gave a wry smile.

The memory of their first few days together – at the cabin, the lodge, the cave – tugged at John. Even though they seemed as if they belonged to another lifetime.

'Now,' Fraser continued, 'before we go I've a question for you, John.'

John looked at him.

'How would you feel if I were to tell you that it would strengthen my hand with the government immeasurably to say that I had a witness prepared to testify about the killings at Blackriggs?'

The question caught him off guard. It also made him angry. Had they not done quite enough for Fraser already? They'd risked their lives to get Ninian here. And now Fraser was going to take him away. Probably for ever.

'I . . . I don't rightly know,' he said, feeling the colour rush to his cheeks. 'I think . . . there's questions *I'd* want answered first.' He looked hard at Fraser. 'That's mebbe not what you were wanting to hear, Mr Fraser.'

But Fraser shook his head. 'No, it's fine. It's a truthful answer to a difficult question. Of course you need time to think about it. And to have your own questions answered. I understand that. So, now . . .' He pulled a scrap of paper from a pocket. 'Here's an address in Inverness. You're

339

going to need to lie low for a while. Get there as soon as you can. It's quite safe. My folk are expecting you. They'll take care of you. And they're in contact with me . . .'

He paused as a sound reached them. A dull clanking and grinding, as if the surface of the road was being torn up.

'OK. We're going to have to be out of here in a couple of minutes. So what I want you to do is give us half an hour. You'll be all right here. Then make your way straight to this address. I'm afraid I can't arrange for you to be taken there; it's too dangerous. But mingle with the crowd and don't do anything to draw attention to yourselves, and you should be fine. Now, is there anything I can do for you before we go?'

Well, that was something, thought John. 'Aye – aye, there is,' he replied.

'Go on.'

'I really need to let my dad know I'm OK. I haven't seen him since the day before . . . Blackriggs. He was going over to see friends in Aberdeen. Ferg MacNeil. I've no idea where he is now. He could even have been picked up by the authorities . . .'

'All right.' Fraser nodded. 'Ferg MacNeil. We'll see what we can do. And Lila?'

She was looking urgently at John. *'The postcard!'* she mouthed.

'Oh God, aye, what am I thinking of?' He took it from his pocket. Suddenly he couldn't wait for this all to be over. 'I think this was meant for you.' He passed it to Fraser, who squinted at it in the lamplight. Then stood up straight and struck his palm with his fist so forcefully that Ninian flinched.

'This changes everything,' he exclaimed. In the few seconds it had taken him to read the message, all the tiredness seemed to have left his face. 'This is the next best thing you could have brought me after my son.' Something commanding had been restored to his physical presence, an air of natural authority. One thing Ninian would never have, thought John.

For a moment he wondered whether Fraser might be going to embrace him. But he just smiled broadly and said again, 'This changes *everything*!'

The machine was drawing nearer. Ninian had put his hands over his ears and hunched his shoulders.

Please go now, thought John. I don't think I can stand this much longer.

'Right,' said Fraser decisively. 'Assuming all goes well, you'll hear from me in a couple of days' time.' He reached down and ruffled the dark curls. 'Are you going to say goodbye to John and Lila, Nin?'

Ninian shook his head. Fraser smiled apologetically. 'Not his strong point, I'm afraid. Guess I'll just have to do it for him.' He shook them each again firmly by the hand, looking them in the eye as he did. 'You risked your lives for him – and for me. I'll never be able to repay you fully for that.'

He took Ninian's hand and they turned towards the door.

A lump rose in John's throat.

'Goodbye, Ninian,' he said, hoping he might look round.

But he didn't.

Lila said nothing. Tears were rolling down her cheeks. She raised her hand in a half-wave at Ninian's retreating back as he followed his father on to the landing.

The door closed behind them.

FORTY-FIVE

They stood together in the empty room, lost for words, drained of feeling, uncertain what to do next. Lila wiped her eyes and John put his arm around her shoulders. Above the noise of the approaching machine they could hear Fraser's and Ninian's footsteps reaching the foot of the stairs, the front door opening, then closing . . .

Then all other sound was drowned out as the machine turned into the street. Its nightmarish grinding, rattling and clanking made it impossible to do anything but remain standing there with their hands over their ears. The noise went on for what felt like an endless time, then suddenly stopped. There was a short eerie silence. Followed by the sound of rushing water. Then an ear-splitting crash and an impact that seemed to shake the building to its foundations. Lila cried out in fright as the lamp tumbled from the table and smashed, plunging them into darkness. John felt for her hand and clutched it as shockwaves continued to reverberate through the building, accompanied by the clatter and thud of falling timber and masonry. Until at long last the movement and noise ceased and all that was left, once more, was the sound of rushing water.

It was some time before John stirred himself. He felt for the door, opened it and stepped gingerly on to the landing.

'What can you see?' Lila called from behind him. 'Be careful,' she added.

As his eyes adjusted to the darkness he caught his breath. What had once been the hallway was now filled by the scarred steel bucket of the heavy moving machine, as if frozen in the act of trying to scoop the occupants out of the house. Directly below John's feet, where moonlight now spilled on to a welter of splintered wood and crumbling plaster, the top few steps of the staircase rested on the roof of the machine's cab. Beyond was a gaping hole where the front door had been. A torrent of moonlit water raced through the ground floor of the house.

The landing gave a sudden ominous creak and he took a hasty step back towards the doorway. He beckoned to Lila and she tiptoed forward.

'Oh my God,' she said under her breath. 'D'you think they got away?'

John had no answer to that. He was thinking of what he'd once read in a Department safety leaflet. Six inches of floodwater will knock a person off their feet. Two feet will float a car . . . And this, he reckoned, was at least waist deep. He could scarcely imagine the force of water required to sweep something the size of this huge machine through the front wall of a house. Even a house in such a shoddy state as this.

'D'you think there's someone in there?' asked Lila, pointing at the roof of the cab.

John leaned forward and called out, 'Hello . . . anyone there?'

There was no reply.

343

'Maybe I'd better take a look.' He glanced around. 'Here, hang on to the door frame and take my hand.'

Holding tight to Lila, he stepped gingerly on to the landing. His heart jumped as it creaked again, shifting under his weight. Then seemed to settle. He put a foot on the top stair. No movement. Another. It felt solid enough, wedged on to the cab roof. He let go of Lila's hand and stepped down, then knelt on the roof and leaned over till he could see in the cab window.

'Empty,' he called back. 'Must have managed to get out. Or jumped clear.'

'Hope he could swim,' said Lila.

The distant noise of fighting had died away now. In its place was the sound of sirens. And the relentless rush of water through the ground floor of the house. It had already risen in the short time since John had first stepped on to the landing. It looked as if it must be chest deep now.

'Don't think we'll be going anywhere tonight,' he said, climbing back on to the landing.

'So what are we going to do?'

John shrugged. 'Sit it out, I guess. Till the water goes down. Maybe try and get some sleep. It's late enough. And there's nothing else to do.'

Lila shook her head. 'Pity the backpack's down there.'

'Halfway to Norway by now, I should think.'

So he wouldn't be repairing the mouse-fiddle after all, he thought sadly. Spared from the flames, it had finally been offered to the waves.

'How are we going to stay warm?' Lila shivered.

They stepped across the landing and into the only other upstairs room. It had an ancient double mattress on the floor and, crumpled in a corner, a couple of blankets. A third was pinned up at the window for a curtain. Lila pulled

344

it down and a little more light entered the room. Wrinkling her nose she picked up the two blankets from the floor, shook them out and spread one over the mattress.

'Beggars can't be choosers.'

Fully clothed they lay down on the mattress, pulled the other two blankets over them and huddled close.

For some time they lay in silence, listening to the rush of water and each other's breathing.

'He wasn't so bad after all, was he?' said Lila.

Her breath was hot on John's face.

'Who?'

'The Tod. Mr Tod. The wily fox.'

'Not . . . really what I expected.'

'How not?'

'More . . . ordinary.'

She was quiet for a moment. Then she nestled closer to him.

'Know what? We're all ordinary. No matter which side we're on. Or what we're doing about it. You. Me. Fraser. Billy. Foulis. That poor soldier laddie at the checkpoint. Even Ivan.' She sighed. 'The only one who isn't is Ninian.'

Neither of them spoke for a while.

Then John said quietly, 'I hope to God they made it.'

'So do I,' she whispered. 'So do I.'

Some time in the middle of the night John woke up, stiff and cold. Lila had stolen the blankets and was sleeping deeply, a dim grey mound rising and falling gently beside him. He got up and went to the landing and looked down. The water had dropped back a little now but it was still flowing fast. Too fast to risk wading. Through the hole where the front door had been he could see into the street. It seemed quiet. Moonlight silvered the surface of the flood.

The marooned buildings rose up like a grey concrete archipelago.

He went back to the bedroom and lay down again. Would anything that had happened this evening really make any difference? he wondered. If Fraser and Ninian had failed to get away, then the answer was almost certainly no. For John, the whole of the last week would have been a terrifying exercise in dashing around to no great purpose, with more probably still to come. At least that's how it seemed right now. But if they'd made it out ahead of the flood, would Fraser find strength from having Ninian at his side again? Would the *Marie Rose* and her cargo of arms somehow help reverse the NLA's fortunes? And would he, John, have played his part in great events? Or would he just have been some random piece of flotsam who happened to have been whirled into Fraser's path at an opportune moment . . . ? He was getting too tired to think clearly now. But he was still too wired for sleep. Beside him, Lila sighed and rolled over. He wished he had a fiddle so he could play himself to sleep. Somewhere in his weary mind he could vaguely hear notes, the first scratchings of another tune. But without an instrument he had no key to unlock them. And in the end he resorted to the old ones, the ones he knew. He might as well count quavers as sheep.

He lay drifting in and out of sleep, listening to Lila's soft breathing, until first light began at last to creep into the eastern sky. Then he got up again, climbed down over the cab and dropped into the water. The chill made him gasp. But it was only shin-deep now and the current had lost much of its force. He squeezed past the machine and waded out into the street.

Some way off, flashlights were winking. A small group

of people clustered around what might have been a vehicle or a boat, he couldn't tell at this distance.

He stood looking for a while, then went back inside and woke Lila. She groaned and pulled the blankets round her.

'Come on,' he said gently. 'We can leave now. The water's down.'

She rubbed her eyes. 'Ohhh . . . what time is it?'

'Don't know. But it's getting light.'

'OK.' She nodded sleepily and sat up. Then sniffed and wrinkled her nose. 'Ach. These blankets are mingin'.'

She scrambled up and shook herself.

Together they climbed over the roof of the empty cab and dropped down into the water. They passed through the ragged archway in the wall and made their way out into the street.

It was almost daylight now and the floodwater glinted dully as it lapped at the ankles of the buildings. Walls, lamp posts, vehicles, all were festooned with branches, litter, garments, polythene sheeting, shreds of canvas and anything else from the camp that floated. In the end the river had done what the army had failed to do. It had washed the camp from the face of the earth. The resulting scene looked like the aftermath of some chaotic watery carnival. John wondered how the camp-dwellers had fared in the sports hall, whether they had all managed to get on to the upper storey, or even the roof . . .

The party of rescuers was working its way down the street. They wore orange survival suits and waders and towed an inflatable. A gaggle of curious children splashed along at a distance behind.

John and Lila waded towards them.

'You OK?' called out one of the rescuers as they approached.

347

'Aye, we're fine,' John replied, 'but I was wondering . . . have you seen any council maintenance trucks round here. Flatbed?'

The first rescuer shook his head.

'Lost one have you?' said another.

'Aye. I . . . er . . . had it parked outside my place last night.'

'You work out of the depot?' A third tipped his head towards the edge of the estate.

'Um . . . aye. Did you come round that way?'

The man nodded.

'But nothing in the street?'

'Not that we've seen. Though wi' the force o' that water it could be miles away by now.' The rescuer shook his head.

'Aye. Suppose it could. Well . . . thanks anyway.'

John turned away and felt for Lila's hand.

In the gathering light they waded on down the street.

GLEN

FORTY-SIX

John had forgotten how peaceful the little kirkyard could be. It was a couple of years since he'd last been there. Hardly anything had changed. The grass was still neatly tended and clumps of daffodils grew among the graves. The old bent larch wore a shimmer of green and in the clear spring light the hills seemed close and gentle.

He sat down in the sunshine and closed his eyes. The place might not have changed, he thought, but he certainly had. His mind drifted back to another afternoon, just a few months ago, when pale winter sunlight had cast a dull sheen across the vast expanse of floodwater that still, a day and a half after the river had burst its banks, engulfed the low-lying parts of Inverness. It was as if, after so much conflict, the Highlands had finally resolved to purge themselves with a grand emptying of Loch Ness into the sea.

They'd seen it, he and Lila, from the cab of an anonymous delivery van as they were driven north over the whaleback Kessock Bridge to an undisclosed location in the far north of the country. Although he could make an informed guess, John would never know exactly where they had spent those next two weeks. The last hour of the journey in, and the first hour of the journey out, had been deliberately undertaken in darkness.

They had awoken the following morning to find themselves in a comfortable whitewashed farmhouse at the head of a long, low treeless glen. Money had been spent on the place. Apart from the house itself, which had luxurious bedrooms and bathrooms and a large sitting room with a panoramic view of the surrounding hills, there were stone outbuildings containing more bedrooms and reception rooms. It was more like a hotel than a private house, though a hotel with no guests apart from John and Lila. A hotel with a staff of two, a discreet middle-aged foreign couple who introduced themselves as Stefan and Maria, and who appeared to have been told to do everything they could to make their guests comfortable, but to answer no questions.

John and Lila spent the first day in a daze, too exhausted to concentrate on anything but still too pent up to be able to settle. There was so much uncertainty. Had Fraser and Ninian got away? The fact that John and Lila were here didn't necessarily signify that they had, for hadn't Fraser said that he had already primed his folk to take care of them before he had come to meet them at the housing estate? Then there was Ferg. If Fraser hadn't got away, the message would never have got through to his folk to try to contact Ferg and he would still be in the dark. But even if all was well with Fraser, and Ferg had been contacted, what was happening now, and how long would they have to remain here? It was still a week until the twenty-fifth of November, when the arms shipment was due to arrive . . .

John felt in limbo, unable to decide what to do or where to put himself.

'How long are we going to be here?' he had asked Stefan after breakfast.

'My instructions are to look after you for as long as need be,' came the polite reply.

'So is Mr Fraser all right then?'

Stefan inclined his head. 'I do not know Mr Fraser. Would you care to go walking? Or perhaps fishing? We have some excellent trout in the hill loch. Or maybe you would rather stay indoors. We have a pool table. And many fine movies.'

So they lounged in the house, ate, talked distractedly, dozed, played pool, tried to watch movies, aware all the time of the luxury of their surroundings, but unable fully to appreciate it. From time to time they checked Channel One, the government news channel. It made no mention of Fraser. But that, they concluded, meant nothing because even if he had been captured, or his drowned body had been discovered, the authorities could well have had their own reasons for keeping the news to themselves.

They went to bed early and that night John's nightmares started. He woke himself in the small hours with a shout of terror. He sat up in the darkness trembling, with the image of Ivan still clear before his eyes, the smell of mint-scented breath in his nostrils. Lila fumbled for the light switch, then put her arms around him, hugging him tight and murmuring soothing words in his ear. But the image remained, as if burned on his retina, so vivid that despite Lila's gentle touch he could not be sure for a long time what was dream and what was reality. Eventually her tenderness coaxed him into the present, but Ivan lingered on in his mind and it seemed as if hours had passed before he finally fell asleep again.

*

Next day they slept late and, despite the interrupted night, woke feeling less exhausted. They walked to the loch in the morning, letting the exercise and fresh air restore their energy. Then, in the early afternoon, came the first real evidence that Fraser and Ninian had got away. A muddy Land Rover drew up to the house and to John's utter astonishment out climbed Ferg MacNeil. John couldn't remember when, if ever, he and his father had last embraced. But now they flung themselves into one another's arms and Lila stood by watching as they clung together at the front door, laughing and slapping each other on the back. When Ferg at last drew away he dabbed at his eyes with his sleeve.

John introduced Lila and they went indoors and settled in the big sitting room. As if she had known of his arrival in advance, Maria appeared immediately with food and a bottle of beer for Ferg, who was hungry after his journey and accepted them gratefully.

'So . . .' he said, taking a swig from the bottle, 'are you just going to sit there? Or are you going to tell me what's been going on?'

'Maybe you should tell us first,' said John. Despite their joyful reunion, he felt suddenly awkward at the thought of sharing so much intensity with his father.

But Ferg was insistent. 'Ach, I've nothing much to tell, son. And anyway, I can't talk with my mouth full.'

So John began. Ferg sat thoughtfully eating as he listened. When he had finished the sandwiches he settled back into the settee, stretched out his legs and put his hands behind his head. His eyes never left John's face for a second. It was as if he was drinking in a sight he had thought he might never see again.

John told him as much of the story as he could bring himself to. As he spoke he watched his father's face and noted the horror and anger, the sympathy, indignation and outrage that swept across the usually impassive features. Even when Davie had died John had not seen his father in tears. But now, as he came to recount the events at the lodge and Hector's death, Ferg's eyes swam again and this time he reached into his pocket for a handkerchief.

Lila sat quietly throughout, as if she realised that this was something John needed to be able to do on his own, without interruption. But as he reached the jeep crash, and skated over the details without mentioning Ivan, she looked at him with a depth of understanding in her grey-green eyes that he had not seen before.

It was almost dark by the time he finished. Maria had cleared away Ferg's lunch and brought in a tray with tea and cakes. Lila got up to pour the tea. She passed Ferg a cup. He took it, looking at John and nodding pensively.

'Aye, aye, son,' he said after a while, 'you're not the laddie I left when I went to Aberdeen three weeks ago. That's for sure.' He took a sip of tea. 'What you've been through, eh? Who'd have thought it . . .' Now there was a mixture of pride and regret in his voice. 'You've changed, so you have. Something's different about you. Can't quite put my finger on it . . .'

'Putting on weight, I should think,' said Lila, handing round the cakes.

'Speak for yourself,' said John.

One day he would be able to tell his father about Ivan. About how his old life had stopped there in the snow at the roadside by Loch Ness as his breath was being squeezed out of him. But he wasn't ready yet . . .

'What about you?' he said.

'Time for Ferg's tale, eh?' His father smiled and set down the teacup. 'It'll not take long.'

He had gone to Aberdeen as planned on the Friday, he explained, and returned on the Sunday night. But the bus had stopped at Strathdon as someone had got on and warned the driver that the road ahead was blocked by the army. Ferg's stalker's instinct had told him to stay where he was, so he'd spent the night in the pub, listening to the rumours. Next day he'd borrowed binoculars and walked out to a place in the hills where he knew he could safely look down on the cabin. Seeing the burnt-out ruin he'd waited in an agony of suspense till that night, then set off on a wide detour out to the lodge, and finally on up to the cave, where he'd found John's message. There was still army activity in the Cairngorms and it had taken him the next two days to get to Aviemore, only to find Morag's house empty and the whole place swarming with soldiers. At that point he'd reluctantly concluded that if he ended up getting caught it would only make matters worse and that the only sensible thing would be to make himself scarce for a few days. 'I knew you'd be looking after yourself fine, son, wherever you were,' he said. Then added with a wry smile, 'At least, that's what I kept telling myself.' So, he went on, he'd made it down to Glasgow without being picked up and lain low in a friend's flat there for a couple of days until finally, last night, there'd been a knock on the door and a complete stranger had invited himself in and spent an hour persuading Ferg to accompany him to where, he claimed, John was being looked after in safety.

In his usual gruff way Ferg made light of it all, but John could see that the worry had taken its toll on him. He looked thinner in the face and there were dark bags under his eyes.

But now he seemed to be starting to relax. That evening, after they'd eaten, he opened the well-stocked drinks cabinet in the sitting room and chose a fifteen-year-old malt whisky. John and Lila stuck to beer. Two or three drams later, in a quiet moment when Lila was out of the room, Ferg put a hand on John's arm, leaned forward and winked. 'That's a braw lassie you've got yourself there, son,' he said. It was true. John felt butterflies at the thought. He hadn't really had much time to consider it yet. But Ferg was right, she was braw. More than that, she was someone who had started to find a place in his heart. And that was an altogether new feeling . . .

But Ferg wasn't finished. In a confiding tone John had not heard before, he said, 'You know . . . not knowing where you were . . . having nothing but my neb,' he tapped the side of his nose, 'to tell me that you were OK . . . well, it made me think about a few things.' He paused and looked down at his hands. 'Your wee brother for a start.' John tried not to show his surprise. This was the first time Ferg had mentioned Davie in nearly seven years. 'See, I don't think I'd ever really accepted that he was gone – not till I thought I might be about to lose you. It was something, I'll tell you. And now . . . well, I know fine what I've got and what I haven't got any longer. And I'm right glad I do, son.' He smiled and gave John a look of such affection that it made his eyes prickle.

A few moments later Lila came back into the room.

'Sorry, am I interrupt—'

'No, no, lassie,' said Ferg, smiling. 'We were just blethering on about how long we might be staying here. Eh, son?'

'Something like that,' said John.

'So what's the verdict, then?' she asked.

'Haven't a scoobie, darlin',' said Ferg with a broad grin.

'But I'll tell you what – this is the best hotel I've ever been in. So we might as well make the most of it.'

They all laughed.

But the cheerful mood that stayed with them for the rest of the evening did nothing to prevent John's nightmare returning in the small hours of the morning. This time he awoke quivering and sweating and convinced that he was soaked in blood, and despite all Lila's comforting he was still awake when dawn broke.

FORTY-SEVEN

The next day Stefan had come into the dining room while they were finishing breakfast and asked John if he would care to follow him. Beneath the back stairs a low door opened on to steps that led down into a cellar. Here, a set of shelves on the far wall slid back to reveal a small room, little bigger than a cupboard. Its walls were covered with racks of communications equipment and there was room for one stool, which faced a screen set into the racking, with a miniature camera mounted above it. Stefan directed John to the stool, glanced at his watch and turned on the screen, then left John to himself. The screen flickered briefly then cleared to reveal Fraser's face. For a moment John thought it might be a recording. But Fraser opened his mouth and said:

'Good morning, John. Are you comfortable there?' His beard had been trimmed and he also looked fresher, more rested.

'Aye, we're fine, thank you,' John replied.

'Good. I have a lot to talk to you about, John, and also to thank you for. But I'm afraid it can't be now. I'm told this link won't be secure for very long, so I'll have to come straight to the point. I've had further confirmation that our Danish friends will be arriving as planned. This puts me back on a slightly more level playing field with the government, as far as the use of force is concerned. Do you follow me, John?'

John nodded. Suddenly his mouth felt dry, his heart had begun to thump.

'So. My previous request. Have you been able to give it some more thought?'

Over the last few days John had turned it over in his mind a hundred times and rehearsed a dozen different answers. But now that he heard Fraser voice the question he felt tired and confused and angry, and uncertain about the future, and what he wanted more than anything else was to be left alone.

'Well, aye,' he said.

'And . . . ?' Fraser's look was expectant.

'Look . . . I'll be straight with you, Mr Fraser. I'm grateful for your hospitality here, truly I am . . . but I feel like I've done enough for you already – we've done enough, Lila and me.' Suddenly the anger was surging inside him and he was close to tears. 'See, I don't think you've any idea what it was like . . . with Blackriggs, with Ninian, with Billy Lowrie and the soldiers, the camp, Ramage . . . Jesus Christ, Mr Fraser, I killed a man – killed him with a knife –' tears had begun pouring down his cheeks – 'and now I've to live with that for the rest of my life . . . let alone the things I saw at Blackriggs – and all because of you and the government and something that was nothing to do with me . . . till – till I ended up there – at Blackriggs – at the wrong moment, just minding my own business. Don't you see that, Mr Fraser? I've had it with arguing and fighting and folk

getting killed, whoever's side they're on. I've just had it . . .
I'm sorry –'

His voice trailed off, choked with tears.

Fraser looked on solemnly from the screen. When at last
he spoke, his voice was full of sympathy.

'No, John, it's me that should be sorry. You've had a terrible, terrible time, I know. And I forget how . . . young you
are. And what a lot I'm asking of you. And you're quite
within your rights to say no, tell me to back off –'

But John ignored him. 'See, even if I wanted to help
you,' he went on tearfully, 'I don't know that I could.
Because . . . it was – it was . . . what they did at Blackriggs
– I hope I'll never see the like of it again in my life . . . But
then – then I saw some of your boys do something terrible
too. And I thought, they're both just as bad as each other.
So how could I be a witness for either side?' The anger was
thickening his voice now. 'Can you tell me that, Mr Fraser?
Can you?'

'I know, John.' Fraser nodded gently. 'I know. I heard
about what happened at Aviemore and I truly regret what
you saw. I regret it deeply and I can't defend it. I still have
a job coming to terms with this myself sometimes – the fact
that we all have it, this dark side, and it finds its way out
at times like these . . .' He paused. 'But what I do believe
is that the *worse* wrong has been done by the other side, by
the government. You worked for the Department, you and
your father, John. You saw it close up. The neglect, the mis-
management, the . . . cynical disregard for this fine,
beautiful land of ours . . .'

'Oh aye.' John brushed away tears. 'I saw that all right.
Me and my dad saw plenty of that. But . . . but – that didn't
mean we had to pick up our guns and go out killing folk,
did it?' His voice was rising. 'I mean – how could it come

to that? Fighting and killing like this? How, Mr Fraser, *how . . . ?*'

Fraser shook his head sadly. 'It's a long story. A long, wretched story. But the fact is that it did. And what I want now is to end it just as soon as I can – today, this minute, if I could. So just hear me out on this . . . if you can?' He looked at John pleadingly and John felt suddenly spent. He nodded in resignation. 'You see,' Fraser continued, 'I believe there are two things that will help bring a stop to all this. The first is for the government to know we can carry on meeting their force with our own – *if we have to*. That's down to our Danish friends. And John, you must believe me when I say that we've always tried to achieve what we wanted by peaceful means first. Force has only ever been the means of last resort.' He cleared his throat and went on. 'And the second is for them to know they'll be shamed by the full story of Blackriggs when it comes out – which, believe me, it will, because we'll make sure it does.' He paused and now John felt as if Fraser was look-ing right into the back of his head. 'But the story will only be credible if it's backed by the sworn testimony of an inde-pendent eyewitness. Which is where you become the key, John, because quite apart from the fact that you *are* the only witness, you're also young, you have no political axe to grind, you have great personal integrity – I've seen it, and I know people are going to believe you. And your story, your account of what happened there, is the one thing ordinary people won't stomach. The one thing that'll really turn public opinion against the powers that be and either bring them to the negotiating table or bring them down.'

It was becoming airless and stuffy in the little room. John felt light-headed.

'What if I just say no?' he replied.

Fraser nodded. 'That's your prerogative. Of course it is. And I can see that you want to put all this behind you now, John. Be free to get on with your own life – I don't blame you; I would too.' Now he was speaking very softly, almost as if he might be talking to Ninian. 'But the thing is, John, it may seem hard to understand, but I don't think you really have a choice. And you haven't since the day you turned up at Blackriggs. The die was cast then. In the same way that it meant you brought Ninian to me, now it means you'll be a witness to what happened there.'

John stared blankly at Fraser. He wanted to scream.

'You see,' Fraser went on, 'sometimes life throws things at you that you just have to do, John. You've already done one of them. Done it magnificently too. You've taken care of my son for me. And handled some tough, tough things along the way – things that most people wouldn't have to deal with in a lifetime. And now there's one more thing for you to do.'

John felt as if the walls were closing in on him.

'Why?' It came out as a croak.

'Oh John, do I have to spell it out for you? Because you're a player now. In a very big game, as it happens. Not by choice, I know. But that's how it is. We don't choose everything that happens to us. And if you want to live your life to the full from now on, if you want to engage with the world and make your mark, if you want to find your true purpose, John, you can't just sit on the fence like a dithering youngster. Your real life starts here, John. Your grown-up life. And you need to grasp it with both hands.'

He paused.

'You know . . . you said it was nothing to do with you, that it was just your bad luck to turn up at Blackriggs when you did. But you're wrong there, John. And I was wrong just now when I said that that was where the die was cast. Because it was actually cast the day you were born. You belong here, John, here in the Highlands. And it's your birthright to be able to go on living here, happily and peacefully and prosperously. But if it means fighting for that right, then that's what you have to do. To preserve your dignity as a man in the face of a wrong that's been done to you and everyone around you. And if you can do what I ask, John,' he went on, 'then I think we've a decent chance of the Highlands finally becoming a place where people can live and work as equals. Not owned by the lairds, the old way. Not trampled over by the Department, the so-called modern way. But in some new, fairer way where everyone has a proper stake in – all of this . . .' He raised outspread hands and looked at John in silence for a long time. Then he asked softly:

'What do you say?'

John could feel his resistance being worn away by the passion in Fraser's face and voice. For a moment it transported him into the future and he glimpsed himself making a living, raising a family, playing music, all in this place he loved from the depths of his soul. As the image faded he felt the anger and tension leave with it. He sat for a long moment in silence, then said, 'Aye. I'll do it.'

Fraser let out a long breath. 'You'll never regret this, John, I promise you,' he said. 'Whatever happens, you can be proud of this decision till the day you die.' Then he smiled. 'Now there's one immediate practicality . . . and I'm afraid it may not be easy for you.' He paused. 'I'm going to have to ask you to make a statement to a lawyer. And that, I'm afraid, means going over what you saw at Blackriggs in every detail, remembering everything you possibly can. It won't be very pleasant, John . . . although I think you might also find it helpful. Would you be willing to do that?'

John nodded. 'I would, aye.' He felt exhausted.

'Good, then I'll get someone over there as soon as possible.' The relief and gratitude in Fraser's face were plain to see. 'And now I must go.' He smiled. 'But before I do I have something to show you.'

He glanced down, then held up a piece of paper that filled the small screen. It was mainly blank, but in the centre was a dense black dot surrounded by several uneven, vaguely concentric circles.

John felt his throat tightening.

Fraser lowered it so that John could see his face again. 'It's for you. He says it's the tiger.'

John nodded, unable to find his words.

'Maybe you'll tell me about it one day?' said Fraser.

'Aye,' said John. 'Aye, I will.'

Two days later a lawyer had arrived at the house. In his jeans and sweatshirt he didn't look like a lawyer, but he seemed friendly and professional as he explained to John what he was going to do. There was a study on the ground floor of the house, across the hallway from the sitting room. It was small and comfortable, a book-lined den. Here he set up his camera and microphone and little by little, over the next two days, guided John through the events at Blackriggs, gently and patiently but always firmly, making sure no detail was left out. It was hard going and at times John broke into a sweat and wanted to run out of the room as he found himself reliving all the terrible feelings he'd experienced there in the wood. The horror and fear and revulsion at what he'd seen. The shame and guilt at having seen it, let alone survived it. By the end of the second day he felt utterly drained, but also strangely lightened, as if a great load had been lifted from him.

Although they had talked only about Blackriggs itself, and not about any of the things that had happened after, John's nightmare seemed less intense that night. Lying in bed next morning, he found himself imagining a day when he might even be able to talk about Ivan in the same way he had talked about Blackriggs to the lawyer. The more he thought about it, the more clear he was becoming that, from one perspective at least, he had done no wrong. He had only to think of those hands around his neck to know that he had simply obeyed the first law of nature: kill or be killed. He didn't think anyone could ever blame him or call him to account for that. But he also knew that this was a rational way of thinking, and it wasn't his rational mind that woke him in terror in the middle of the night . . . Anyway, there was something else, something more complicated, or maybe more simple, that continued to gnaw at him. Whatever the circumstances, the fact remained that he had taken away someone's life. And somewhere, in some distant foreign country, there was, perhaps, a family just like John's waiting for a husband, a father, a brother, a son who would never come home . . .

The twenty-fifth of November, *Marie Rose* day, as they had now christened it, came and went. So did the day after. Still they heard no word. By now they'd been there for over a week. Most mornings the lingering sensations of the nightmare had left him by the time they'd finished breakfast and John could enjoy the time doing nothing, being with Lila, feasting on the food Maria prepared, luxuriating in everything the house had to offer. Lila was enjoying it too, he could tell from the ready smile and brightness in her eyes, the warmth and affection she showed him in their moments alone together. Though he could see that Ferg was growing restless and anxious to know what was going on. But apart from Channel One there was no news, and with no phones their isolation was complete.

Then, on the afternoon of the twenty-seventh, Stefan came into the big sitting room, where the three of them were playing poker for matchsticks. He cleared his throat discreetly.

'I think,' he said, 'you might care to turn on the television.'

Ferg looked up in surprise. 'Channel One?'

For the first time since they'd been there, John noticed a faint smile hovering around Stefan's lips.

'Channel One,' he said with a nod.

FORTY-EIGHT

John glanced across the small, sunlit kirkyard. Lila was waiting in the car with the window wound down. She saw him look up. She smiled and gave a little wave. Somewhere nearby, lambs bleated.

He took the fiddle out of its case, sunlight dancing off its varnished surface. He held it admiringly – as he still did, every time. A gift from Fraser. The best money could buy. Would he ever make one as fine as this himself? He doubted it. But it was something to aim for, all the same. You only had to touch it with the bow and it sang.

Ferg had come down to Edinburgh with him to buy it. To help him choose, they'd agreed. Not that Ferg knew the first thing about fiddles. But it was a good pretext for them to spend time together. There had seemed to be so much to do in the weeks since leaving the farmhouse . . . or maybe it was that those few strange days in limbo had been so intense that they'd both needed to pull back, find their own space again. In any event, they'd spent the day companionably in Edinburgh. And on the way home, perhaps helped by the rhythm of the train, they'd slipped easily into conversation about everything that had happened, not just since Blackriggs, but since John's childhood, all the important things they'd never really discussed before. They'd talked about Davie and John's mum, about Ninian and Lila, about Ferg himself and his plans for the future.

They'd talked about John too. What he was going to do now – now that everything had changed. How only a few months ago he had imagined his life on the hill stretching ahead of him as far as he could see. But how now, suddenly, it felt as if the world had thrown open its doors to him. There would be a job for him, Fraser had said, on any one of a whole number of schemes he was setting up across the Highlands. There was the possibility of making something out of the playing and fiddle-making. There was also the chance of going back to study again . . .

In truth, the thought of the future made him feel nervous and uncertain. He knew that he had seen and done things most people of his age – most people he knew – couldn't even begin to imagine. Things that would mark him for life and probably set him apart for ever. They were present, like a faint shadow, trailing all thoughts of what lay ahead of him. And he knew he would have to find the way to live with them.

For the immediate present, it was easier not to think at all. He was quite content helping Ferg rebuild the cabin, which Fraser had persuaded someone to sell to him for a knockdown price as the hated Department was being wound down. It was soothing, the hard physical work. It allowed his thoughts and feelings time to settle. The nightmares were becoming less frequent, although there were still times when they left him feeling shaken and dazed the next morning. But he still hadn't spoken to Ferg of Ivan.

And now . . . summer lay ahead. There was the cabin to finish. Later on, he and Lila were going to Switzerland to see Ninian. And then there was the Blackriggs memorial. The stonemason had been commissioned and the date for the unveiling was set for early September. That would be a good time to make decisions, John thought.

He could feel the sun warming his back.

He looked down at the granite gravestone in front of him, glistening with tiny specks of mica in the clear spring light.

Davie MacNeil, it said simply. *A short but extraordinary life. Rest well.* And the dates.

John rosined the bow, tucked the fiddle under his chin and began to play.

AFTERWORD

A note on the One Acre Act

The Land Reform Act, commonly known as the One Acre Act, was the legislation by which the newly independent Scottish Parliament brought about wholesale land reform. It superseded the Land Reform (Scotland) Act of 2003.

Simply put, it meant that any privately owned land in excess of one acre (the reasonable garden plot of a free-standing house) was subject to compulsory acquisition by the government of Scotland, which would henceforth own it on behalf of the people of Scotland.

Former owners, and any new tenants who chose to, could then rent land on terms, and with rights and responsibilities, set down in the Act. The Act also provided for an initial rent-free period of five years for former owners, to stand in lieu of compensation for the compulsory acquisition. Thereafter, normal market rents would apply.

Furthermore, the Act established the Department of Land, to oversee the implementation of its terms, supervise transfers of ownership, collect rents and manage those parcels of land for which no rental applications were made.

In the Highlands, the effects of this legislation were, as

371

intended, to drive away many of the large private land-owners, who, thus deprived of their assets and the possibility of passing them on through inheritance, chose not to sit out the rent-free period but took the nominal cash compensation sum (ten per cent of market value at the time of the legislation) and went elsewhere.

Following the Blackriggs massacre and the end of the Troubles in the Highlands, the Act was repealed and the Department of Land was dismantled.

ACKNOWLEDGEMENTS

A book is seldom the work of just one person. This book is no exception. There are four people without whom *The Witness* would not have seen the light of day, and I owe them my special thanks: Henry Irvine and his mother, Pru Irvine, for inspiration with the character of Ninian, and their patience and generosity in answering my endless questions; my agent and friend Jenny Brown, who kept faith when I came close to losing mine; and my wife, Sarah, whose insights, lovingly given, have made this a better book than I could ever have written on my own.

Many other people have helped me in different ways with the book and I thank them all: Allan Massie, Brian McCabe and James Robertson for their support and advice as fellow writers; Pete Clark and the late Duncan Mac-Donald for their love of the fiddle and fiddling; Andrew Gordon and Allan Macpherson-Fletcher for their wisdom in matters of the land; Andrew Ogilvy-Wedderburn for his knowledge of all things military; Annie Blaber, and Allan and Marjorie Macpherson-Fletcher, for providing the peace and solitude I needed to complete the book; Anna-Wendy Stevenson, Angus R. Grant and Luke Plumb for their fine musicianship and friendship; Alex Findlay of the Birnam Tap for his unfailing hospitality; my daughter, Anna, for her eagle eye and perceptiveness beyond her years, and my son, Jake, for his enthusiasm and belief; Harriet Wilson at Macmillan, for recognising that this story could flourish in a different form from the one in which she originally read it; and, finally, the Scottish Arts Council, for the award of a writer's bursary.

JJ, May 2006

A selected list of titles available from
Young Picador

The prices shown below are correct at the time of going to press. However, Macmillan Publishers reserves the right to show new retail prices on covers, which may differ from those previously advertised.

Julia Bell

DIRTY WORK   978-0-330-41521-7   £9.99

Julie Bertagna

ZENITH   978-0-230-01534-0   £9.99

Lian Hearn

THE HARSH CRY OF THE HERON   978-0-330-44961-8   £6.99

Suzanne Phillips

MISS AMERICA   978-0-330-44870-3   £9.99

All Pan Macmillan titles can be ordered from our website, www.panmacmillan.com, or from your local bookshop and are also available by post from:

Bookpost, PO Box 29, Douglas, Isle of Man IM99 1BQ
Credit cards accepted. For details:
Telephone: 01624 677237
Fax: 01624 670923
Email: bookshop@enterprise.net
www.bookpost.co.uk

Free postage and packing in the United Kingdom